WHITE KING RISING

A NOVEL BY

LEE KESSLER

White King Rising
Copyright © 2008 by Lee Kessler
Published by Brunnen Publishing

Printed in the United States of America

ISBN-13: 978-0-615-31592-8
ISBN-10: 0615315925

"This is a terrific book. The veracity is undeniable, and I hope it gets broad national coverage. Our nation needs it. When you finally put *White King Rising* down, you sit back and know you have gained something of permanence—something of overarching significance. Lee Kessler again displays her depth of intellect and immense talent for seamlessly weaving fiction amidst real-time factual events and people in the current War on Terror. With a God's-eye view, she delivers a chilling shiver with the absolute plausibility of this back story aimed at America's total demise. Her insights are stunning. *White King Rising* should be required reading for all those in the military and intelligence communities. Anyone concerned with our nation's security—indeed its survival—needs to read Kessler's brilliant and revealing work."

—"Sam" Warner, former NASA Public Affairs Officer & Strategic Communications Consultant Fairfax, Va.

"The long awaited follow-up to Lee Kessler's *White King and the Doctor* does not disappoint in its fast-paced and thought-provoking journey into the highest levels of Al Qaeda's leadership, while peeling away one layer after another of our adversaries' true intent and ongoing strategy. The stunning prophetic accuracy of a book that was written ahead of real world events is enough to keep one awake at night wondering if anyone in a position of leadership in our United States is paying attention to the possibility that Lee Kessler is actually chess moves ahead in her thought process.

Her first two offerings read like the best of Tom Clancy, carry the suspense and intrigue of a John Grisham classic, and could easily be the script for the next season of *24*. My only regret after finishing part two of this journey is that there is not a 3rd installment that I can immediately dive into."

—Vince Rush, Owner of Rush International & Cincinnati Sports Photography Cincinnati, Ohio

"Wow! What a journey! The writing is brilliant. And, while I felt great relief reading the first book, this book gave me the certainty that once people read it (or see the movie), we will have conquered the two most direct threats to our survival, and without shedding even one drop of blood. *White King and the Doctor* and *White King Rising* will turn the tide most certainly, and beautifully.

White King Rising gets it on all fronts, and tells it as cleverly and enticingly as the first book. The enemy is very formidable and, with so much riding on this game, the story rises to the level of personal consequence to the reader."
> **—Ariella Kapelner, Radio Talk Show Host, KCLA-FM (2007-08) & Director of the Writers' Group Film Corp. Los Angeles, Ca.**

"*White King Rising* exposes the weaknesses of the American people that our enemies perceive, but which exist only because of our strengths: trust, intense desire to do the right thing, and warrior reaction towards anyone or anything we even suspect intends to hurt us as a nation. The enemy, though, cannot know us. We are a people of intrigue and strength, well outweighing any flaws. I was on the edge of my seat throughout this book. I was shocked many times. I learned about the terrorist mind and, in the end, was revitalized in my hope that good will win out—in real life, right now. Thank you, Lee for this exciting, emotional, and eye-opening story about our neighbors—the Americans."
> **—Marcy Sanders, VP Administration, Vision Practice Management, Inc. Clearwater, Fl.**

"By brilliantly creating a vast panorama of intrigue, Lee Kessler establishes a bond with her readers from the very first pages of *White King Rising*. Her powerful style comes through as she pits an evil international mastermind and his many cohorts against an ingenious American trio, who have devised a fascinating "game" plan. Descriptions of the dramatic struggles between these two forces are truly vivid and often terrifying. This imaginative novel entertains, and more than that, it makes one wonder about what might be next on the global horizon of evil machinations."

—**Verna Sabelle, Editor & Publisher**
New York, New York

"A very captivating book. I loved it!"
—**Rich DeVos, co-founder of Amway & Chairman of the**
NBA Orlando Magic

This book is dedicated to L. Ron Hubbard, philosopher and humanitarian. I regard him as my friend—and a friend to all Mankind. He once said, "Constant and continual alertness is the price of freedom. Constant willingness to fight back is the price of freedom. There is no other price, actually." May we all understand this now, as we face "the unwitting."

It is in memory of my dear parents, James and Reba Kessler. They taught me to love and fight for freedom—to protect the freedoms and vision for which our ancestors fought long ago. And it is in memory of Marco Conde, who imbued in me a love of reading and writing.

Lastly, it is in loving memory of my husband, Jeff Hodgson, who passed away suddenly two days after the book was completed. Though he never had a chance to read it, his dedication to *White King Rising* was unending. He lived his life to help heal others, and his purpose lives on in this work.

All five were educators.

AUTHOR'S NOTE

I have been asked many times at book signings and in radio/TV interviews about how I used my acting experience and imagination to discover the very plausible scenario, which became the book *White King and the Doctor*.

Though speculation and fiction, and written about events which had not yet happened, the theory of *White King and the Doctor* has now—four years later—proven accurate to the point of seeming almost prophetic.

Since 9/11, Americans have reached an almost hysterical level of angry reactivity. With my background in acting, marketing, and with my interest in the stimulus-response nature of a manipulated mind, I stumbled upon what I believe to be a Fifth Column attack upon the United States.

A wide range of sociological phenomena appear to be undermining our culture and its future, and I asked myself the unthinkable: "Could these seemingly unrelated sociological factors actually be connected? If so, could an enemy versed in mind control and propaganda warfare tap into that, or cause it?"

My back story research on Ayman Al-Zawahiri revealed a very good likelihood that he *is* using an old Soviet strategy to bring the United States down from within, and that he could actively be manipulating us so effectively that we are now our own Fifth Column— "dividing and conquering" ourselves!

Brilliant and diabolical, such a plan would save our enemy a great deal of time and money. Convinced now that our current terrorism situation has very little to do with "Religion" or "Military," and everything to do with the top four "games" discovered in *White King and the Doctor*, I wrote *White King Rising*.

The sequel is my answer to the question, "How do we defeat

them?" Like the first book, it is a fictional present and future, displayed against the backdrop of actual events, and it reveals a very different picture.

CHAPTER 1
THE DOCTOR

"The Doctor" stood mesmerized in front of the television in the musty hotel suite. No matter how one tried to cover it up, the humidity in Panama City left its pungent smell in the curtains, carpets, and fabrics of homes and hotels alike. Though the ceiling fan moved the air around, somewhat alleviating the repressive heat, perspiration was starting to bead and trickle down his clean-shaven face.

He would not have turned the TV on so quickly, but the bellboy had been especially eager to please. Seeing the fine alligator bags the hotel's new client was carrying caused him to believe he would receive an especially fine tip if he took some time to educate their guest on the hotel and its amenities. The bellboy was particularly proud of the new flat-screen TVs that hung over the false mantle in each of the suites. And so he had turned it on, demonstrated proudly the cable capabilities, and left it on as he pocketed the generous tip.

And there they were, captured on every channel—the Iraqi citizens defying the threats of his man, Zarqawi, by going to the polls by the millions to cast their first vote. His ulcer acted up, sending its familiar acid reflux bile into his throat as he watched jubilant face after jubilant face proudly display their purple finger.

A purple finger, he sneered to himself. *It's stunningly simple after all. I'm amazed they had the wits to think up anything that simple, let alone that effective public relations-wise!* He popped an antacid under his tongue and hissed at the flat screen, "Samir has his work cut out for him on this!"

He settled down a bit then, as the overhead fan began to cool him down. No doubt this was a defeat for Al Qaeda, and would

1

cost them dearly in the coming months, but there had been a serendipity or two along the way. For the moment, those were foremost on his mind. After all, he had successfully escaped from Switzerland before anyone could uncover the true identity of Phillipe Monet. He was safe, for now.

The Doctor poured himself a tall glass of water from the bottle left by the bellboy and sighed as he sat down on the bed, still gazing at the screen. *Zarqawi lost the first round,* he lamented. *But we'll reset the goal. That annoying old woman with her purple finger in my face won't have the last say here.*

And with that, the man the world's intelligence agencies wanted more than any other terrorist, save Usama Bin Laden, formulated the strategy Abou Al-Zarqawi would take before the second Iraqi election. The people of Iraq had defied the odds; they had demonstrated their defiance; they had won the day—today. But Ayman Al-Zawahiri knew the odds were they could not sustain their march to democracy—regardless of how inspiring it was to the international media to see thousands of them walking together from town to town to find a precinct open to receive their vote.

Quite the contrary, he reassured himself. Zawahiri was certain that Al Qaeda's Public Relations Chief, Samir, would be up to the challenge, and that he would somehow turn the media against the Iraqi people before they had a chance to form a government. After all, Samir had had his way with the White King. The Doctor was certain he could do it again.

The fact that their funds had been successfully moved to banking operations in Panama and Brazil gave him further comfort. His military commander in Pakistan had laid the plans and had successfully escaped while the world was distracted by Zarqawi in Iraq. That, at least, had gone according to plan. With Makkawi safe, and resupplied, the plan called now for Al Qaeda to open a new theatre.

The completion of his ultimate plan necessitated this next phase. And the Doctor was ready. He was more than ready—he was euphoric. For this time, he was on the doorstep of the White King himself. The various chess strategies he had deployed since 9/11 were all coming together now in what would be the explosive finale. Confident that the United States was unsuspecting, he swelled with pride at the devastation he would cause before the end of 2012. *Just a little longer now, a little longer,* he coached himself softly. *Their complete collapse is within my grasp.*

With that reassurance, he turned off the annoying image of the Iraqi people and logged onto his computer. First up was his language lesson. He had been diligent. All of them had been. Had American intelligence been more creative, they might have noticed a dramatic increase, not in the number of crash courses in the Spanish language that were promoted online but in the number of people buying and studying Spanish in the last months of 2004. They weren't, however. And even if some gung-ho analyst had spotted it, the analysis would have seemed nothing more than corroboration that the United States was indeed morphing into a Spanish-speaking culture.

US intelligence had missed it once again. Perhaps there was no way to identify it—no way to know that the increase in demand for Spanish language courses was coming from multiple nations in the Mid-East, not from the United States. But the Doctor knew. It was part of his plan. These new Internet students spoke Arabic, and they were getting ready to change location. And he, like the others, was preparing to blend in. It would begin in Panama.

CHAPTER 2
THE PLAYER

"**B**rian Carver?" the disemboweled voice called down the cell block. The tone of voice suggested the man was totally bored with this whole affair, and that he knew he wasn't exactly summoning a hardened criminal.

For Brian, though, this was the first time he had ever been arrested for anything. He'd come close a few times on the streets of Southeast Washington, and in a bar brawl after a game at Los Angeles Western University, but this time he had actually spent two days in jail—for trying to deliver a cup of water. The whole ordeal had shaken him, and he hadn't slept any. Eager to find out what was up, he jumped to his feet. "Yeah, down here."

"Carver, I've released your cell. Get your butt out here to the desk."

The County Jail in Clearwater, Florida wasn't exactly the epitome of technology, but it was automated, and Brian heard the lock release. He grabbed his coat and knapsack and exited quickly. As he came through the door into the outer office, the guard who had called for him silently pointed him in the direction of the officer in charge.

Despite the fact that Brian was well over six feet and in perfect physical condition, he instinctively lowered his head and stared at his feet as he approached the sergeant. A small voice inside him argued that this was demeaning and he should raise his head, but Brian Carver knew he was in the South, and he was in the "man's" house. So, like generations before him, he stood submissively—stealing a quick look up to see what might be coming next. He was acting submissive, but his set jaw revealed the tension and anger he was harnessing.

"Brian Washington Carver?" the sergeant asked to confirm his identity.

"Yes, sir, that's me."

"Boy, you're being released."

Brian flinched momentarily at the insult of the word "boy." *How long does it take for these people to get it?* he thought. *Surely, they've at least heard we don't like to be called that! Since my grandpappy was a young man!* But he knew enough not to say a word. They were letting him go. And he was too smart to let anything get in the way. So he did what others had done before him. He diverted his eyes and mumbled, "Thank you."

"No point in keepin' ya here."

Brian said nothing. He didn't know where the officer was going with this, so he decided to let it play out.

"She died a few minutes ago. DA says to let all y'all go." The man's voice sounded sympathetic somehow, as if fulfilling his duty these last few days had cost him, too. After a moment he added, "Brian Washington Carver. Hmm. You got a lot to live up to."

"Sir?" Brian looked up briefly.

"Your name, son."

Brian assumed he was referring to the scientist who had transformed southern agriculture by developing over three hundred products derived from the lone peanut. George Washington Carver was a hero to a lot of folks it seemed. His grandfather had told him the story of this black man who had made good, and, in fact, Brian had been named after him. Brian had never cared. It was another of his grandpa's attempts to make black people proud of being black, as if somehow the accomplishment of one spilled over onto the group as a whole. But Brian never bought that. He was more like his own dad in that mindset. The man was surly and truly unproductive, but his dad knew somehow that he was okay just because he *was*, not because some guy he'd never known had done something important. Right now, though, Brian just wanted to get the hell out of there.

"Yeah, I guess, sir. My grandma loved George Washington Carver and managed to pressure my dad into naming me after him." He forced a smile.

The sergeant, however, looked puzzled. Then he got it. "No.

I weren't talkin' 'bout him. I was talkin' about this wide receiver they got playing for LA Western University this year. The kid's got golden hands. That's his name. You got a lot to live up to if your name is Brian Washington Carver."

Suddenly Brian laughed. The whole thing was turning surreal now. "That's me, sir. I play for LAWU."

"You shittin' me? That's you?!"

Brian nodded yes.

"Son of a gun!" He just stared at Brian for a moment, looking him over good. "Yeah, yeah, it *is* you. Son of a gun!"

There was an awkward silence. Brian looked down. It ended when the sergeant handed Brian his wallet and keys, and said in a noticeably kinder voice, "Son, you get in your car out there and you leave this town. Go back to school. Forget this mess and go live your life."

The fact that a policeman in Florida was lecturing him—albeit kindly—about what he should do with his life rankled him a bit. He was not in the mood to discuss this and indeed wanted to get out of Florida. "Yes, sir, I understand." He took the keys, slipped his wallet into his pack, and walked out of the County Jail.

Driving across the Courtney Campbell Causeway, he couldn't help but admire the beauty of the bay that day. Tampa Bay lay out to his right like a gigantic mirror, and the skyline of Tampa glistened in front of him. It was beautiful and soothing, and that felt oddly creepy. For what had happened in Clearwater, Florida had changed his life. He knew that. But Brian Washington Carver had no way of knowing then just how much his life had changed. There was no way this football-playing friend of a brainy chess player could have known he was now on a collision course with a man called "the Doctor."

As he headed north on I-75, he caught the news just before he reached I-10. The Pope was gravely ill and was sinking into unconsciousness. It seemed the whole world was watching now, to see when this brave man would slip away. And finally, Brian began to cry. He needed to. He was not Catholic, but he empathized somehow with this compassionate man who had done all he could do. Through tears so thick he had to wipe his eyes to see the road, Brian wondered if he had done all he could. There was so much he didn't understand.

He had a choice now—to take I-10 west and head back to Los Angeles, or to take it east. The prudent thing was to head west and put this behind him. But somehow, he was haunted by the words his great-grandpa used to speak to him often: "If it gets tough, son, remember not to run. Face it, whatever it is." He knew he had to face something, but he didn't really know what that was. He was confused and disoriented, and he wished he could talk to Andy.

Without even knowing that he had done it, he headed east on I-10 and made the connection in Jacksonville to I-95 north. It would take him about sixteen hours if he just stopped for gas. *I can do it. I did longer getting here. I can do it.* And with that, he sped north to Arlington, Virginia.

CHAPTER 3
THE CHESS MAN

*T*here were no cherry blossoms budding as Andrew Weir pulled into the parking lot at Arlington National Cemetery. It was late in the day, and the brisk wind off the Potomac penetrated his windbreaker, causing him to shiver. Something was wrong, but he knew he had to come. He had been summoned by his friend, Brian, with an urgent cell-phone call.

Andrew Weir was no stranger to this area of the cemetery. He walked briskly and saluted the guard as he passed by the Tomb of the Unknown Soldier. Every guard there knew Andy Weir—not only as a Grandmaster chess champion but also as the son of a soldier who guarded the tomb. And they all knew or had heard of the graciousness and kindness of Kelly Weir after her husband's death. He had loved that detail, and she made sure that the men who took his place at the Tomb were cared for and respected. So Andy came and went through the years, whenever he needed to. No one was going to stop him. No one was going to tell him it was late. By birthright, Andy had privileges.

Coming down the sloping path that led to his father's headstone, he could just see the top of Brian's head. Apparently he was sitting on the ground next to the grave. *Odd,* Andy thought. *I can't imagine what this is about.* He hesitated for a moment, then called out to his friend, "Hey, how're ya doing, my man?"

Brian sprang to his feet, a bit startled. "I didn't hear you coming."

Andy just stared at him. Brian looked so different. It wasn't just that the ruby earring was missing. Andy figured he might have lost that body-surfing. It wasn't even that the famous braids were gone, replaced by a neat, trim, TV-acceptable haircut. That was attributable to the LA Western University's Public Relations department. After all, Brian was being groomed for the NFL; he was one of their stars. Andy had expected him to look like a guy who would sign endorsement contracts. So it didn't surprise him at all that his former wide receiver no longer looked like a sullen, surly street kid. *He cleaned up good,* Andy thought to himself. *Knowing his mom, I bet she approves!*

But Brian's face was oddly changed somehow. Andy felt a sudden sense of loss and sadness, and he didn't know why. Breaking the awkward silence, he smiled and said, "You look good—real good."

Whatever distance had crept in between these two colleagues, who had won a state football championship, vanished on those simple words. They had always been a team. No matter the differences in their color, their families, and their outlooks, they had always been unbeatable as the Quarterback and his Wide Receiver.

Brian let out a sigh and embraced his friend. "It's good to see you, man. Thanks for coming."

"No problem." Andy looked at him for a moment and asked, "What are you doing in this neck of the woods?"

"Long story, dude. And I should ask the same of you. What are you doing here? I was expecting you to be at MIT."

Andy answered quickly. "I was. For about three months. I just graduated."

"No way! How the hell did you do that?" Brian was incredulous.

"Well, without going into too much detail, I was building extra credits on a project I was doing down here. Then, after three months up there, they patched together enough credits to get rid of me." He laughed, hoping that Brian wouldn't ask about the project. No one but his mom, Kelly, and retired CIA analyst, James Mikolas, had any knowledge of the secret hunt he had been conducting for Al Qaeda's mastermind, Ayman Al-Zawahiri. It had nearly cost Andy his life, and it had cost his mentor his job.

Their analysis using a three-dimensional chess game had identified the layers of Zawahiri's manipulations, and had enabled them to forecast his probable location. But no one in government had any real interest in confronting the frightening truth.

Admitting the truth would have forced them to acknowledge the presence of a Fifth Column inside the United States. Andy and James were working now on a plan to warn the unsuspecting American people. And that is why Andy Weir had been in the vicinity of Washington, D.C. when Brian phoned, desperately wanting to meet.

Brian smiled politely, but really had no interest. He wanted to unburden himself to the one man he trusted. It was Andy's brilliance and patience that had put such a spotlight on Brian in the first place. And that spotlight had led to the football scholarship at one of the nation's top universities. In the absence of a coach, he needed his Quarterback. The two sat down, and Brian told Andy his story.

It was growing dark as Brian tearfully and disjointedly struggled to tell the story of his compulsive journey cross-country to try to help Mrs. Schiavo. Having failed in that attempt, he was questioning now what was happening to him.

"Brian . . . " Andy paused for a moment to get his hands around the idea he wanted to convey. "I'm sorry, I don't know if I can be much help here. I heard the news, but to be honest with you, I didn't give it much thought." Andy could see Brian looked confused, so he added apologetically, "Maybe I should have—it is odd what with Congress convening and intervening—but I just had my attention some place else."

Brian seized on that. "That's the point, Andy. I didn't have my attention on it either. Frankly, I've never paid much attention to what white people do to other white people. You're the only white friend I got."

Andy didn't know what to make of that remark. In the four years they had played ball together, it had never come up. Andy didn't see color. He saw work ethic and talent. To him, Brian was just a friend and teammate. And at this moment, he didn't know how to respond. His friend didn't look like a boy from the hood, but he was certainly talking like one, and Andy was out of his comfort zone. So, he said nothing for a moment. He waited.

Then Brian added something remarkable. "But you're not white, you're just Andy."

Somehow, Andy knew that remark was a mature one, even if Brian didn't realize it yet. He nodded agreement. "And that's the whole freakin' point, Andy! Mrs. Schiavo wasn't white either; she was just Mrs. Schiavo!"

After the outburst, Andy reached over and touched Brian's back. "Brian, you gotta explain, brother. How did you get in the middle of all this? I want to understand. I really do."

"It's like this." Brian cleared his throat to choke back some tears. "I'm sittin' in Los Angeles, eatin' pizza with some teammates, and the TV's on. And they're going on and on about this woman and whether or not she should be allowed to starve to death. There's one hysterical character after another on the screen. It was a circus, man!"

"Yeah, that part I do know."

"And I wasn't paying much mind to it, see? Fact is, I was laughing about the whole damn thing, as if it was interfering with my life somehow—this woman's dying. And then it happened."

"What?"

Brian couldn't hold the tears back now. He inhaled and grinned, as if that would hold it, but his eyes still brimmed and he shook. Andy said again, "What?"

"You know me, Andy. You know my grandpa, and how bitter he is about Viet Nam, always talkin' about how they used us as cannon fodder and all that crap. You know that's all I've heard since he used to fry me catfish and make me eat it."

Andy nodded and Brian continued. "Well, my buddies started making fun of her. They were laughing and making fun of everybody there—especially those church-goers who got their kids to try to take in water. It was funny to them." He stopped suddenly.

"And it wasn't to you?"

"At first." There was a long silence, then, "I'm ashamed, Andy…"

"Go on. I'm listening."

Brian wiped his nose on his sleeve. "I think I would have just kept yuckin' it up, if it hadn't been for her husband's lawyer. He got on the TV, with his mug in the camera, and he's going off on how he had just seen her, and how beautiful she looked. And if that wasn't perverse enough, he adds that he doesn't think he ever saw her look more beautiful. And I just snapped. It was like I'd been asleep or somethin' for twenty-one years. Somethin' snapped, and I woke up."

Brian had no way of knowing it, but his story was striking a chord deep within Andy. His friend, the chess-playing quarterback, looked subdued and attentive—and he said nothing.

"All I could see were Pappy's pictures." Andy looked lost, so Brian added quickly, "My great-grandpa is Pappy. He was in the Infantry in World War II, was one of the first blacks in a combat position, and he went through hell from all directions. But he had pictures."

"What kind of pictures?"

"Of dead people, and dying people. His unit came upon a concentration camp and mass graves. He took pictures, and he showed them to me when I was five."

"Jesus! Really?"

"Yeah. He said he wanted me to know why he had done it— why he had endured the beatings and abuse. He wanted me to know what he had been fighting for and who he had been trying to save. I was too young to care about all that, but I remember the pictures. They were of people who had been starved to death, or nearly to death, before they were executed. And I've never forgotten what a starving body looks like."

Brian swallowed several times. "And there he was, the lawyer, saying he had never seen her look more beautiful and at peace. And he smiled! He was actually happy to have produced a starving woman. I saw those pictures, Andy, and one thing I know is that starving people don't look *beautiful* and *peaceful*. It's awful."

Neither young man spoke for a moment, letting the image just hang there.

Andy broke the silence. "What happened?"

"Well, it was like I woke up or somethin'. Like that guy. Who was that guy who slept for twenty years?"

"Rip Van Winkle?" Andy answered uncertainly.

"Yeah, him. It was like I'd been asleep my whole life, living in my own dream world. And suddenly she wasn't a white woman;

she was just a woman who was starving and dehydrating. And I knew how Pappy had felt. It wasn't a color thing. They were people. And she was a person. To me, she was bein' killed by that fiend." He let out a long sigh, then added, "That's the best I can describe it. I got up; I got in my car and drove to Florida, like I told ya. Next thing I know I'm in jail for trying to take her a cup of water."

That was sobering. Andy asked, "They just let you out? They didn't do anything to you?"

"Oh yeah, as soon as she died. And they told me very politely to get my black ass out of town."

"Whew." Andy looked away, as if focusing on the distance could clear his head and give him some perspective.

Brian broke the silence. "Andy?"

"Yeah?"

"Did you ever feel like that? Like you just woke up—that the world's been going on around you, and you just woke up? And you didn't understand the issues, but you knew somehow that something was wrong? Dreadfully wrong?"

For Andrew Weir, the answer to that question was easy. Not four years ago, his golden and almost anointed life as a Grandmaster chess champion and star football player—admitted on scholarship to the prestigious MIT—had come caving in when he, too, had been awakened from a dream life. His life had been girls, games, fans, and press interviews.

Then one day, a man named James Mikolas had walked into his life and shown him a glimpse of hell. And for the last four years, he and James Mikolas had been chasing evil incarnate in an all-too-real game of chess. Though not actual chess, Ayman Al-Zawahiri, whom Andy called the Black King, had been manipulating pieces in multiple theatres of operation. And like his friend Brian, Andy too had responded to the plight of something dying. The fact that both young men had acted impulsively and compulsively, out of lessons learned from beloved warriors, allowed Andy to understand his friend's pain now.

"Yes, Brian. I have felt like that." It was all he said. It was all Brian needed to hear. Somehow, he had known that Andy had gone to a place like this. Why else would he have stayed in Virginia instead of heading off to MIT when he was scheduled to? Why else would he have dropped out of the chess world? Why else would he have faded away from his friends? Instinctively, Brian knew Andy would understand. However it had happened, the two partners had been abruptly awakened to the dangers and the confusions of the events that swirled around them.

They did not have the answers to the issues that were tearing America apart. But at least they were both awake. They had been a great team once. They would become one again.

Brian made it clear he did not want to return to LA Western—that he hoped, somehow, Andy would help him sort all this out. Characteristic of Andy, he motioned to Brian to huddle up. As Brian came closer, the two bent over as if in the huddle. As he had done so often in the past, Andy turned his head toward his wide receiver and quietly said, "I've got someone for you to meet. We're going to Cape Fear."

CHAPTER 4
THE ANALYST

"*Y*ou want some more gravy, honey?" Sadie asked, as she walked past James' table.

"Nah, I'm good," he responded. "But don't forget me for pie!"

"Deal." Sadie noticed the extra set up at the table and wondered if James' guest was, in fact, coming. "You want me to take that away and give you some more room?"

"No, he'll want it. Trust me. This guy likes dessert, so when he gets here, promote your pie…" Before James could finish the sentence, he saw Ari Ben-Gurion enter the restaurant, glancing around quickly. He didn't even get off a wave before Ari flashed him a smile and slid onto the vinyl seat. Sadie's Diner was a landmark in Cape Fear. She'd been in business since the early '70s, and many a traveler had been told to stop by there if they wanted a great Southern meal. No matter that the tables and chairs were from the '50s and the linoleum appeared even older. The meal, and Sadie's buoyant personality, were all anyone noticed.

"Hey, Ari." James offered his hand in a genuinely warm handshake. "It's been awhile, and it's good to see you."

Before Ari could speak, Sadie returned on cue with two pieces of magnificent lemon meringue pie—one in each hand. "Gentlemen? This is my recommendation for the day."

Sadie was clearly not expecting any resistance here, so she just placed them in front of the two men. Ari didn't mind. After all, he couldn't feel guilty about indulging if she was going to be that way about it. He grinned and said, in his rather thick Israeli accent, "Thank you."

Ari turned back to James. "I understand you're retired," he said, before he put the first piece of pie into his mouth.

"Yeah, well, you could say that." James paused for a moment to take in a piece of pie and then added, "It was time to go, Ari. There was no one at Langley listening to me, and I couldn't go back in the field. So, I hung it up."

Ari's years in Israeli intelligence had taught him not to ask how colleagues were handling the inside politics and confusion that clouded their work area. So instead, he simply nodded. After a short while he asked, very pointedly, "You working on anything on your own?"

"Why do you ask?" James couldn't tell whether Ari was on to him, or whether he was just being social. He assumed the former, knowing how direct and to the point his counter-part in the Mossad was.

"Because, if you're working on something, I have a hunch what it is. And I might have something for you." With that, he set down his fork and pulled an 8 ½ x 11 manila envelope from a valise on the seat next to him. He set the envelope on the table and slid it over to James.

James opened it and found himself staring at the photograph of two men at what appeared to be a social event. One was smiling and looking into camera, and the other looked startled and somewhat camera shy. James had no idea who he was looking at, or why this would be relevant to the four-year project he and Andy Weir had been working on—trying to figure out where Ayman Al-Zawahiri would be found, and what he would do next. In one of the most shocking theories ever offered at Langley, James had deduced that Zawahiri was using an elaborate chess game as a framework for his plans for Al Qaeda. He and a young Grandmaster chess champion had spent three years trying to penetrate the mind of the man James felt was responsible for 9/11. Their theories had cost them their jobs—and nearly their lives.

And now here was the same intelligence officer who, several years before 9/11, had tipped him off about Zawahiri's brilliance, and the menace to the world that presented.

"Should I know these men?" James asked innocently.

Ari was eager to respond. He lowered his voice and leaned in. "One, probably not." He pointed to the smiling character who seemed to thrive in the spotlight. But the one on his right is someone, I think, that you and your government have a keen interest in."

James shivered. He didn't know why, but the skin was crawling up the back of his neck. He examined the picture more closely. "This doesn't look like him."

"Precisely." Ari sounded a bit impatient. "That's what I tried to warn you about before. We don't *know* what he looks like! That is the reason you can't find him."

"And you think this man is him?"

"Regrettably, I do." Ari let out a huge sigh and looked out the window for a moment into the sun-splashed patio area. Then he returned to his pie. James just studied the rather tall man's face for a few moments. Then, "Well, he looks something like him, but I would have expected him to be shorter, and certainly more portly."

"Hum. Yes, you would…"Ari's voice trailed off, leaving the rest of his thought incomplete.

James ignored the sarcasm there and queried, "Where was this taken?"

It didn't take long for Ari to fill James in on the long investigation his team had been running on the finance institution in Zurich and its Director. Their money laundering operations for Al Qaeda were complex, but ultimately cracked. After the arrest of the Director, the Israeli intelligence squad that Ari headed began their customary practice of examining photos of all known associates of the target. In there they often found collaborators and conspirators. It was that routine process that had focused Ari's attention on the man in the picture.

"What makes you think this is him?"

"I assigned a new guy to identify him, as this was the first time this particular man had shown up in any photographs. We routinely then check into the backgrounds of anyone we find."

James was getting a little anxious now. "And?"

"Well, our young man comes back with a red flag. He had identified him as Phillipe Monet, a respected investor in Geneva. It seems Monet is on the Board of Directors of WHO, and a major stock holder in DECU-HEHIZ."

"Who?" James interrupted.

"DECU-HEHIZ. They're a large pharmaceutical company based near Geneva."

Had Ari been looking closely, he would have seen James turn pale. But he was into his story and continued without noticing the change in his friend. "Their President, Rudi Iseli, says the man has been an integral part of the city for more than fifteen years, and vouched for him completely."

"Do you believe him?" James asked. He was starting to breathe faster.

"We believe Iseli *thinks* the man is a legitimate businessman. But we don't believe he is."

"Why not?"

Ari ate the last piece of his pie, carefully cleaned his mouth with his napkin, and set it neatly aside on the table before continuing. "Because when our man tried to verify Monet's background, it was too thin—just too thin. That was the red flag that the 'new guy' spotted. Fortunately, he did spot it, and he brought it to me. Then we took a *good* look at Mr. Phillipe Monet, and we couldn't place him prior to his showing up in Geneva some years back."

"Jesus!" James exhaled. "But what makes you think this is Zawahiri? Geneva's a long way from Afghanistan."

"That's the reason I wanted to speak to you, James. I know you're out of the game, but I reasoned you'd be the only one who could handle this next information. We've turned it over to the CIA, but they're convinced he's still in the region where they last cornered him and Bin Laden. We aren't. You, my friend, have got some sense."

James just looked at Ari for a moment, then back at the picture. Could Phillipe Monet be the second most-wanted terrorist in the world? Was he that good that he could have pulled this off? James concluded he was. He listened closely now.

"This is confidential, James. But I know you'll be discreet. We're investigating—have been for a couple of years—a major kingpin in Lugano. He's up to his eyeballs with terrorists and arms deals. And we'll take him down in about six months. But as we followed the money lines and dug deep, the trail led to Liechtenstein and Switzerland. We'll get the top guy. We know who he is and how he's operating. We're just trying to bring in as many fish with this net as we can."

James smiled at the fisherman reference. Knowing how

18

predatory Ari was, the image of a fisherman casting his net struck James as ironic. He sobered up immediately upon Ari's next statement, however.

"But when we went down the rabbit hole, at the very bottom we found traces of a businessman—a man whose identity is so very carefully camouflaged that no one knows who he is. We know he's an investor; we know he's not on anyone's radar since he is not involved in money laundering. And we're certain from intel we've gathered, through interrogations of a key prisoner we're holding, that he is top echelon Al Qaeda. That much we know. But we don't know his name, or what he looks like, or whether he is in Liechtenstein, or whether he crossed the border east of Zurich."

James took a deep breath and started to put it together. "And you think the man at the bottom of the rabbit hole is the Al Qaeda link between Lugano and Liechtenstein?"

"We do."

"And you think your mystery man could be this financier, Phillipe Monet?"

He nodded. "I do. I can't prove it yet. But I wanted you to know right away."

"Why?"

"Because I believe, James, that I met this man."

That was a stunning revelation. James was confused. "How?" he asked.

"I was sitting at a café on the lake, indulging in a little repast before heading to Lugano. A man bumped my chair as he was trying to squeeze past behind me. He excused himself and, as he did, I looked up at him to acknowledge him." Ari stopped short for a moment. He swallowed hard, as if something were stuck in his throat and he was trying to force it down. "I'm quite certain it was him. Phillipe Monet. Ironic, isn't it, that I would be hunting Zawahiri all over the world, and he ends up standing over me in a café, looking down at me—and I didn't recognize him!"

James just waited. Missing a target under those circumstances was the stuff of nightmares for anyone in intelligence.

"Once our investigation turned up *unknowns* on this guy's past, we raided his offices."

"Please tell me he was there, and that you have him!" James

knew as he said it that it was not the case. He longed to put the chessboards away and never think of this beast again, but he knew that was a child's fantasy. Ari was, after all, in Cape Fear, North Carolina briefing James. That could only mean one thing—the rat had slipped the trap.

With a weary and sad voice, Ari said, "I only wish that was the outcome, my friend. I only wish. When we went to his offices, they were closed. The word in Geneva was that he was on one of the long business trips he customarily took. No one thought anything of his absence. When we got into his offices, they were a front."

"Don't tell me," James interrupted, exasperated, "when you opened the filing cabinets they were all empty. There was no staff. There never had been, except maybe one person who made the thing appear legit if anyone walked in."

"That's pretty much it. The single employee he did have, a woman who'd been with his company for a number of years, died in a boating accident shortly before we got to him."

James just shook his head in silent understanding of the all-too-familiar scenario. "I gather you think he killed her?"

"Frankly, yes, I do. The timing was just too coincidental. My team thinks he emptied the filing cabinets before he pulled out and destroyed the records of Al Qaeda activities and plans."

"That's bullshit!" James scoffed.

Ari smiled. "Right. Bullshit. There never *were* any records. There never was a business. It was, to my mind, merely a cover site."

There was a pressure in James' chest now, and he was beginning to feel nauseous. *He's like a phantom, this Ayman Al-Zawahiri*, James thought. *He's like a puppeteer, playing everyone on the planet from some elevated position.* "So . . . he got away."

"Yes." Ari sounded ashamed.

"And our governments?" James asked pointedly.

"They are still convinced he's in Afghanistan or Pakistan, or, on a long shot, possibly in Iran."

That was too much for James. He just started to laugh. It was so abrupt a laugh that Sadie turned from the grill to see if maybe he was choking. Satisfied that her favorite customer was okay, she returned to frying the green tomatoes. "May I keep this?" he asked finally, waving the photograph.

"Yes, of course. I thought you might need it."

James didn't quite understand the reference. He cocked his head slightly and looked quizzically at Ari. But Ari didn't hesitate whatsoever to add, "From what I hear, you're the one who got the closest to figuring him out. Word is you and this kid, Weir, theorized he'd be with a pharmaceutical company, that he'd be an investor or advisor, and that he had absolutely escaped Afghanistan. And I know that was viewed by your superiors as absurd."

James said nothing. The insult of his theory having been completely rejected by the self-serving directors above him was still a sore spot. And he could only imagine how word of this had reached Ari Ben-Gurion of Israel's Mossad.

Ari pressed on. "I missed him on the street—there in Geneva. I pray every night, my dear friend, that you get him your way."

And with that, he neatly placed his fork in its proper place on the pie plate, and exited.

———————————

James barely remembered driving back to his cabin on the Cape Fear River. As he got out of the car and turned toward the cabin, he was startled to see two young men sitting on the rickety porch. He stopped and squinted. Seeing who it was, he called across the un-mowed yard, "That you, Kid?"

"You bet, James. I brought someone for you to meet."

James had always had a great memory for faces and names. It was essential working in the field. As he came up to the step, he remembered vividly the night he'd had to make Andy "take a walk." Images came back to him clearly now of these two boys throwing a football in the streets of Arlington at midnight.

"I recognize you," James said cheerfully. "How've you been, Brian?"

CHAPTER 5

*M*akkawi was livid at the prospect of supplying more men and arms to Abou Al-Zarqawi. The tension between the chief of military operations of Al Qaeda and their superstar Zarqawi was mounting as the months went by. At first, Makkawi welcomed the respite Zarqawi's activities in Iraq gave him from the relentless pursuit the Americans and Pakistanis were presenting. He had escaped capture so many times in the last two years that he was almost accepting as normal never having more than a few hours sleep, having to plan their operations in two-hour chunks, and living with adrenalin pumping.

As Zarqawi's presence in Iraq became more dominant—both in the international press coverage and in the internal political whirlwind of the emerging Iraq—focus on Makkawi himself seemed to have lessened a bit. Though he knew the enemy's forces were skillfully searching for Bin Laden and Zawahiri, his well-developed sense of irony forced him to smile now. For Bin Laden was dead—dead since December of 2001. And their new commander Ayman Al-Zawahiri had long since escaped Afghanistan. Makkawi had been there when Bin Laden's body was taken and buried in a cave, and he had been there the night Zawahiri slipped away. Through masterful and state-of-the-art encryption technology, they communicated occasionally by phone now, and by email. Once they had met in Turkey to coordinate this past year's war activities in Iraq. The rest was done by courier.

It didn't bother Makkawi in the least that he did not know Zawahiri's whereabouts. The brilliance of the Doctor's cell strategy—which left no one Al Qaeda cell knowing what another Al Qaeda cell was engaged upon—was unquestionably providing them all with a type of security that could probably never be compromised. As long as he could communicate with the Doctor in some way, no matter how primitive, he felt confident.

And that is why he was a little startled that a call was coming in from the Doctor several weeks prior to their next planned meeting. He sensed trouble.

"Ayman? Is that you?"

"Yes." Zawahiri's voice showed no signs of strain. Makkawi relaxed a bit. Then the Doctor continued. "I need to make an adjustment in our plan."

"What is that?"

Now the coldness crept in. The Doctor laid it out. "It is apparent our man in Iraq is failing in his primary mission to prevent elections—they've successfully accomplished two now."

"Yes, true, but he has inflicted much damage and engendered great fear." Makkawi found himself defending Zarqawi's results, but in reality he was actually defending their own strategy.

"I am aware of that. In that, he has done well. But we are going to have to switch strategies."

Makkawi had inherited his responsibilities when Al Qaeda's original chief of military operations, Muhammad Atef, was killed by the Americans. He had performed brilliantly in the wake of that devastating loss. Makkawi was gifted and flexible, but sudden change of strategies had always unnerved him. Tactics he could change instantly, but he labored over a change in the base plan. So he paused and swallowed hard before asking, "Are you sure?"

"Definitely." There was no room for debate in the succinct answer.

"Very well. What do you want me to do?"

Once the Doctor was certain he was not encountering resistance, his tone softened somewhat. "It is clear to me the Iraqi people have embraced this idea of having elections and forming a government. I no longer believe we can stop them from having elections, which had been our strategy. But I do believe we can cause this new government to collapse from within. And that is the strategy toward which I want our energies and resources directed."

"Well, sir, the only way it would collapse from within is if our tactics are switched to making them turn on one another,"

Makkawi said, thinking out loud. "Given the centuries-old animosities between several of their sects, if we can convince one group of Iraqis that another group of Iraqis is actually doing the killing—rather than us—then they should start to devour themselves."

The Doctor was quick to comment. "I believe your analysis is exact. So what I want you to devise are tactics which will enflame their hatred, and fuel their distrust of one another to the point where it disintegrates into a civil war." He waited to let that sink in, then added, "Do you have a way to do that?"

Without any lag whatsoever, Makkawi responded, "Yes, sir, I do."

"Excellent. Will you need Zarqawi?"

"Not the man himself, but I will need his men."

The Doctor wanted to be sure he and Makkawi were in agreement on a plan. He asked, "What will be your first step?"

"We will need to raid, without anyone's awareness, the supply warehouses for the new Iraqi civilian police forces. If I can get hold of their weapons, and very importantly, their uniforms, I can borrow a page from Hitler's plans. We'll kill in disguise, and the civilians who are witnesses will report that it is the police themselves that are turning on a particular group of Iraqis."

The Doctor approved. Gaining in confidence now, Makkawi forged ahead. "That should create suspicion and animosity between the new government and the citizens of Iraq. Since the US military trained these police, it shouldn't be difficult to transfer some of that already-festering hostility to the Americans. We'll pick up press coverage on the atrocities, and that will incite riots and further violence. It should be quite a spectacle." He concluded, "Will your man, Samir, be able to capitalize on that?"

Had Makkawi been able to see the Doctor, he would have been relieved by the breadth of his smile. For the Doctor knew that their Public Relations chief, Samir, would not only be able to take advantage of it, but he would be able to insert the issue into the elections in the United States as well. He was delighted that this would produce havoc in the election processes of both nations. One would be violent and bloody. The other would not. But in any case, they would be able to topple the leaders who would have otherwise sustained existing US policy in the region. *Violence and electoral chaos. I'll settle for that,* the Doctor thought.

"We'll disgrace the United States once again, and hammer the Iraqis so badly they'll wish they had their bastard dictator back!" It was said with venom. "And we'll leave them with so much suspicion of each other that they will be virtually paralyzed. That should keep the Americans there a little longer."

"So that part of our strategy remains the same?" Makkawi asked.

"Yes. I want to bleed them in that arena as much as possible, and keep their press distracted with the Mid-East until we are in place for our main assault."

"Understood. Tell Samir we'll give him the ammunition, and that we're counting on him to keep the pressure on Bush."

"He's already made that the lynchpin of his strategy. Until Bush is out of office, we will see to it that he is disgraced and embarrassed time and time again. I need for them to doubt him—especially now." That was all the Doctor said. Makkawi did not understand why the urgency now, but he also knew he was not privy to the full plan. Only the Doctor knew the master plan, and the players. And Mohamed Makkawi was not going to try to cross that line. He politely ended the conversation and hung up.

The call had lasted a mere two minutes. But those two minutes had laid the foundation for a plan so comprehensive that even the world's best analysts would miss it. It would bring on an assault upon the United States from a totally different direction. With their eyes skillfully directed toward the Middle East by a propaganda machine like no other, a storm was gathering—in another direction, and with another methodology. The people of the United States would not see it coming, and they lacked the imagination even to contemplate it.

Ayman Al-Zawahiri knew one thing for certain: Good people can't really contemplate evil. And as such, they are ineffective in confronting it. His studies of the mind, and of every war of the last century, had borne that out. He was confidant *that* one fact alone would insure his ultimate victory and domination.

He repacked the satellite phone into a simple canvas bag that was then tucked into the alligator suitcase. After pulling out the one business suit he had brought along, he showered and dressed. *It won't be long now*, he told himself. *My days of having to be a prominent citizen are nearly over. Soon I will vanish.*

It was his plan to make one last visit to the Central Bank of Panama, to establish the money channels he and others would need to finance the next stage of their operation, and then to disappear into the landscape of the poorer areas of the city. As Eduardo Morales, he would commence his job as the buyer for a small import/export firm in Panama. His living quarters would be meager, and he was confident he would not stand out in any way.

Ayman Al-Zawahiri was about to merge with the rest of the hard-working, lower-class masses of a teaming city. Under the guise of a job that would keep him traveling, his next stop would be Colombia. An embryonic "cell" awaited him there.

CHAPTER 6

*T*he military plan was simple really. Makkawi and Zarqawi would keep the Americans and British occupied indefinitely in the region of their first theatre of operation. As long as they were still getting mileage out of bombings and beheadings, they would continue to hold the chaos in the newly forming Iraq in the forefront of the media's minds. Through the skillful manipulation of media opinion, and thus world opinion, by their public relations officer, Samir, the people of the United States were barely conscious that a government was in fact forming. What fixated their attention were the body count and the mounting dead, and Hollywood versions of tales of oil and corporate greed.

And with the enemy's attention skillfully controlled by Al Qaeda's own man, the main flanking operation had begun. Through all of military history, a good general knows to watch his flank. Every war college in history had addressed the vulnerabilities of getting soft in the flank. Yet, America's flank was exposed. If handled properly, Ayman Al-Zawahiri knew that an escalating menace could be set up, and that a flanking maneuver would leave the United States vulnerable for generations. What made his plan even more thrilling to him was his knowledge that this was just the military maneuver. It was the game that was second from the bottom in the eight-tiered game he was playing. The real assault—the one that would not just bring America to its knees, but which would erase it and its people from the history books—would play out in the top four layers of his complex game.

The cell that would accomplish it was in place, and had been for some time. That cell, like all Al Qaeda cells, had no idea of its mission in relation to any other. And the military commanders of Al Qaeda had no idea of the existence of this one particular cell. Only the Doctor knew of its existence. For now, he was content to leave it that way.

More immediately, however, he faced the challenge of integrating into one conspiracy Colombia's FARC, the government of Venezuela, the decrepit Cuban dictator's successors, and the ambitious politicians of Mexico. It was for this purpose that he traveled across the Southern border of Panama, into the expansive territory of Colombia that was controlled by the FARC and their heavily-armed, murderous gangs.

He would begin with the FARC, and one representative selected by, and sent by, the Venezuelans. Plausible deniability dictated that the Dictator of Venezuela not be present. It would be imperative that his name not be linked to the operations. Time alone would reveal the true intent of that country's head of state. The Doctor, however, didn't care. As far as he was concerned, the man was just another man to be used to accomplish his goal.

"Pongase esta-bolsa en la cabeza, y las manos atras de su espalda, señor!" Zawahiri's command of the Spanish language was still at too introductory a level, forcing him to guess the order he had been given. He knew it was an order by the man's barely respectful tone of voice. But he was slow in complying, and the tall man with dirty, oily hair poked him in his shoulder with the barrel of his AK-47.

They have no idea what is about to happen to them, the Doctor assured himself. *I can suffer this insubordinate attitude until we get what we want from them. I need them for a while, but not for long.* Realizing now what the man had ordered him to do, the Doctor submissively allowed himself to be handcuffed, blindfolded, and led into the jungle's darkness by the FARC. The fact that he experienced no real fear of them, or the men he was about to meet, confirmed for him just how powerful Al Qaeda was—and how feared it was. As far as these men were concerned, they were about to enter into a high-level negotiation with a senior member of Al Qaeda. Though they had blindfolded this member of Al Qaeda, he knew they were doing so to protect the location of their base. It was something at which Al Qaeda was superb. If anything, he suspected they were hoping to impress the acknowledged masters of deception with how much they had learned.

The FARC were drug lords and mercenaries. They had long ago given up the pretense of being a legitimate political rebel force. Today they had accepted the world's view of them as perhaps the best-armed, best-trained, largest group of criminals in South America. The land they controlled was nearly one-third of the land mass of Colombia, and no one in the Colombian government had the strength to retake it. Even the Colombian military had proven itself helpless in the face of their weaponry and their cunning. The long arm of their retribution was legendary, and they had successfully assassinated every judge or politician who had tried to attack them.

So, it was with some degree of arrogance that the head of their military operations agreed to meet with an emissary from Usama Bin Laden. The two forces had collaborated for years on drugs and arms deals, and had laid meticulous escape routes for terrorists moving up through Central America to the United States. But never once had there been such a high level, in-person meeting.

The man known only as La Hyena sat on a rock by the stream, waiting in the shadows. He expected that the Al Qaeda representative would be the first to be brought to him. Tonight, he was sober. Quite certain that he would need to be in full possession of his faculties, he had refrained from any drug use. It made him a little jumpy, however, and he wished he had taken the edge off. *Too late now,* he told himself. *They are coming.*

"Call me Eduardo," the Doctor offered to the interpreter provided to him for translating Arabic and Spanish. The translator conveyed the greeting. Both men, however, knew it was not his real name.

La Hyena smiled. "Call me La Hyena."

"Where are the other two?"

"They are being brought to us now. It seems their journey through rough terrain, and their quarters, have not matched the splendid lifestyle they've grown accustomed to in Caracas and Havana." La Hyena laughed at his own joke. "You, on the other hand, know what a life like ours is like."

"Yes, indeed." That was all the Doctor said. He slipped down to the ground, hoping to lean up against a rock and sip some water from the canteen they had provided him. And he prepared to wait.

It was not long. In a matter of minutes, two men and their escorts appeared at the stream. They did, in fact, appear exhausted and drained by the heat and humidity. And their European clothing was completely inappropriate for the primitive environment they were experiencing.

"Please, gentlemen, remove those jackets!" La Hyena pleaded, acting like the perfect host. "You're making me hot and tired just looking at you!" The interpreter translated all the banality for the Doctor and kept pace almost simultaneously with his translation.

Each man forced a small smile, nodded to their escorts to leave, and happily dropped their jackets on the ground beside them.

"So, we're all here to plan the end of US domination in the area, is that correct?" La Hyena took the lead, opening very dramatically. He stopped, noticing that the representative from Venezuela looked puzzled. The way he was turning around, looking down the trail they had traversed, caused La Hyena to probe. "Is there something wrong?"

"No, I was just wondering where the representative from Mexico was?"

"The candidate's representative will not be part of our discussions." This seemed to surprise the men from Havana and Caracas, so he continued. "Frankly, it is up to us to set the stage. After that, it does not really matter which one of them is elected, or even if they stage a coup. The *play*, gentlemen, is being written by us. We'll cast the lead actor later."

The Doctor liked this man's insouciance. Here they were, sitting in a snake-infested, God-forsaken sector of Colombia scheming up the overthrow of the Mexican government, and the placing of men, armaments, and hatred along the entire US border, and this drug-ravaged killer was talking to them as if they were developing a Broadway musical. *The man's right*, he told himself. *It doesn't really matter who the dictator of Mexico is; it only matters that he is a puppet of Havana, Venezuela, and the FARC. I'm here to make certain that happens.*

"Understood," the Doctor said, breaking the silence. "That is a wise choice, and one which Al Qaeda thoroughly supports." The mere mention of Al Qaeda by the interpreter seemed to bring the other two to their senses, as they realized the magnitude of the game they were playing. And somehow, they realized now who was really in control of this meeting. They all did—even La Hyena.

Less than two hours later, as the meeting area slipped into the same type of impenetrable darkness that shrouded the trails, and the sounds of night insects made it almost impossible to hear one another, the meeting was ending. The plan that the Doctor brought to the table had been accepted. Whether the participating governments were in total agreement or not, their mutual hatred of America, and the freedom it represented, allowed them to agree. In that short span of time, a sweeping military/political strategy had been adopted. Its execution over the coming years would forever alter the politics and economics of the entire region. Each knew it. And that is why they decided to "dance with the devil" that night—with Al Qaeda itself.

The plan was to forge an alliance whereby the FARC would supply arms and men to support, covertly, the political and economic goals of the Venezuelan government. With Venezuela using oil and money to extort the US economy, and with Castro supplying methodologies and ideologues to Mexico, the Mexican people were expected to succumb and place in power a Marxist/Communist government. And from there they would have limitless opportunities within the United States. With a Marxist government, rich in resources, along 2,000 miles of US border; with that government supported and funded by

Venezuelan oil and money; and with its rebels trained by Cubans and armed by the FARC, the Southern flank of the United States would be wide open for any activity Al Qaeda wished to stage.

It was brilliant actually. The Doctor had devised a way to develop an Al Qaeda staging area along the entire border. Any one of these allies would provide safe harbor for Al Qaeda—any one of them would be as competent as the Taliban had been. And the jungles were as foreboding as the mountains of Afghanistan and Pakistan. *One has to adjust, that's all,* Zawahiri reminded himself. *Being flexible is something we are very good at.* There was just one drawback that he saw, even though he felt he could control it. That was that the entire area was Catholic—not Muslim. There would be trouble with that, he was sure. But he also knew that the Americans would never expect him to be able to stage from this area for that very reason. What he was gambling on was the ruthless ambition of the men from Colombia, Venezuela, Cuba, and Mexico. With them walking point, he felt it would work. And so he dismissed it for the moment.

"Eduardo?" La Hyena beckoned the Doctor to remain, along with the translator, as the others left the area. "If you would stay for a moment . . . "

"Of course."

"There is one thing that troubles me," La Hyena said, quite somberly. His mouth contorted, making it appear as if he were sneering.

"And what is that?"

"I have no doubt of our ability to affect a political change in Mexico that will allow us *all* a great opportunity. Certainly our drug trafficking into the United States will be greatly facilitated, but..." His voice trailed off for a moment. He spat on the ground, then cleared his throat. "But this all depends on the United States closing its border, creating havoc in Mexico."

"Yes, what's your point?" the Doctor asked impatiently.

"It seems right now that President Bush won't do that—that he's keeping it open despite the danger to them. Why is that, do you think? Stupidity?"

"Hardly. I expect that he, or that witch of a Secretary of State, have guessed that the dangers of closing it are greater than the dangers of keeping it open."

"Jesus! Then our plan will fail!" La Hyena exclaimed.

"No, it will not."

The Doctor had answered with the kind of quiet certainty that generally ended debate. But, La Hyena looked unconvinced, so he continued. "You leave that to us, my friend. Whether President Bush sees the trap or not, we'll make sure that border is closed."

"How will you do that?"

"You just leave that to me. Follow through with your part. I'll take care of ours." It was said softly but so firmly that La Hyena backed off. As if a few extra feet between him and this man from Al Qaeda could help La Hyena take measure of him, he stepped back and stared at the man he knew as Eduardo. He had sized up many a man in his lifetime. Though only thirty-eight, the fact that he'd survived this long was indicative of his ability to accurately measure a man. Today, he believed this man from Al Qaeda knew exactly what he was talking about. Suddenly, La Hyena laughed. It was a high-pitched, unnerving laugh, which left no doubt as to how he had acquired his name. As his laughter subsided, he first extended his muddy hand, and then embraced the Doctor.

"So be it." Then he was gone.

A few hours later, Eduardo Morales checked into a modest hotel in Bogota. The rooms were mundane and sparsely furnished, but the hotel offered Internet connection. He removed a small computer from his bag and plugged it in. Bringing up a familiar cube, he lit up the layer second from the bottom. Labeled "Military," he moved the black rooks and knights and set them in a crescent position on the board. Satisfied that the military game was well in motion, he left it.

Smiling, he then highlighted the top four layers of the three-dimensional game. The ones labeled "Medical" and "Weapons" were brightened easily by his mouse. Though the others were lit, the Doctor's attention was clearly on these two areas. It was from these areas that Al Qaeda would deliver its fatal blows to the United States. The plan to do so was known only to the Doctor.

It had never been discussed by Al Qaeda's top leadership. It had never been considered by Usama Bin Laden. And therefore, and most importantly, it had never been contemplated by anyone in intelligence anywhere. The one nation that could have deciphered it was already blinded by it—already enmeshed within it. *They will never see it coming.*

With that, he closed the cube-shaped game out and created one email. It was to ST & Associates in Manhattan. It read simply, *"Samir, I have a project I need your help with. There is a door I want you to close. Please contact me."*

CHAPTER 7

"What are those lights in the woods?" Brian asked, peering across the river to the dense woods on the other side.

"They're fireflies," Andy answered simply.

"Yeah, man, try again!" Brian scoffed. "It's too early for fireflies!"

Andy didn't answer. He just studied them, too.

"Andy?" Brian tried again. "Seriously, what is that? It's kinda spooky."

"They're fireflies," James answered, coming up behind them. "They're early. But that's typical of this area. Things seem to be all out of season on the Cape Fear River."

"Hum. Wonder why?"

"Global warming," Andy joked.

"Very funny, my man." The three sat for a while, just watching the dancing lights flickering and jumping, bunched into a cloud shape that appeared almost ghost-like. Then Brian asked what he'd wanted to ask since arriving at this retreat on the river. "All right guys. Tell me what you're doin' here. Somehow I can't see your mom being too keen on you livin' down here."

"Actually, she likes the place." Andrew didn't seem at all surprised by the non-sequitur question, and answered matter-of-factly.

"She's been here?"

"Yeah."

"Shit, man, how'd you manage that, Andy? Your mom never leaves her shop." It was dark enough that Brian didn't see James flinch slightly at the language. Even if he had, it probably wouldn't have mattered. He had always dealt with Andy, never James. And he had never really understood why those two had seemed so inseparable back in Arlington.

"She and James brought me down here for my twenty-first. They thought I needed a break."

That did it. The subject both young men had been dodging since they left Arlington was now on the table. Brian knew Andy brought him here for a reason. He also knew, in the aching part of his soul, that he had come to Andy for a reason. He was about to find out why.

Brian took a deep breath and asked, "Why'd you need a break? Seems to me you were on one. I was out in LA, busting my butt on the football field, and my dad told me you were delivering pizza for…" He suddenly remembered his mama's admonitions not to take the Lord's name in vain, shot a glance at James, and continued somewhat lamely. "Pete's sake!" *At least Coach would be proud of me,* he thought.

"Well, I was doing a little more than just delivering pizza."

"What then?" The tone in Brian's voice betrayed his growing impatience.

Andy turned to James. "You want to tell him?"

"No thanks, Kid, this is your party."

Brian looked confused. Noticing that, Andy released him from the mystery with an opening question about the time they were sitting in Arlington National Cemetery. "Remember when you told me you felt you had just woken up—and things weren't right?"

"Yeah. Sure. I still feel that way."

"Well, I got a wake-up call, too. James delivered it to me one day, disguised as a game."

"A game? Where?" Brian had more questions than just those, but they were enough to elicit a very candid answer from Andy.

"In a meeting at the Central Intelligence Agency." Andy said it as if he'd said, "at the local malt shop we went to after a football victory." The cloud of fireflies had moved farther down the river, and it was much darker now, no longer dusk. Brian was straining to see Andy in the increasing shadows. He wasn't certain he'd heard it right. Andy just waited.

"Did you say the Central Intelligence Agency?"

"He did," James answered.

"You're CIA?" Brian asked James, his question reflecting accusation and a hint of disdain.

"I was. I'm not anymore."

"Why not?"

"The answer to that, Brian, is why I brought you here," Andy interjected. "I have a story I'm free to tell you now—at least parts of it."

Somehow, Brian sensed that this night would alter his life. He had had an ominous feeling since turning north for Washington. Seeing Andy had caused it to subside for a while, but that sense of foreboding had returned. He could feel his anxious stomach. He always felt that squeamishness just before an important game. He was used to it. However, there was something more here tonight on the banks of the Cape Fear River. There was danger here. But, for whom? Not able to handle the suspense and mystery any longer, he suddenly blurted out, "Who's in danger, Andy?"

Kelly was just finishing the blue-gray rinse on Mrs. Standish. It never ceased to amaze her how that color applied to any elderly woman instantly gave her stature and dignity. And, as she finished combing the curly hair of one of her most generous regulars, she could see Mrs. Standish squinting through her glasses, checking it out. The slight turn up at the corner of her mouth told Kelly what her vote was. She was happy once again.

Spinning the chair around so that her client could view the cut and color from the rear, Kelly saw them all entering in her mirror. She wasn't surprised to see James with Andy, but she was surprised to see the muscular, black kid with him.

Mrs. Standish stiffened slightly as the three approached the area of the chair, reminding Kelly that Virginia was, after all, still a Southern state. Though a nice woman, Kelly's client had an instinctive response to the black people who now lived in their Arlington neighborhoods. Years of listening to the nightly news about the situations and violence of Southeast Washington had left her a bit prejudiced, whether she would admit it or not. As soon as she saw Andy, though, she smiled and politely said hello.

Kelly patted her on the shoulder and excused herself with, "I'll be right back to spray it a bit. Sit tight."

"Okay, dear. I wanted to finish this article on Kelly Preston, anyway. She seems like such a sweetheart," she gushed.

"Brian?" Kelly asked incredulously. "Is that you?"

"Yes, ma'am." Brian had always been a kid of few words, especially so with adults. His mama had taught him to behave with respect for her, and for those older than himself. Whenever he was around Andy's mom, his behavior changed to that which he exhibited with his own mama.

Looking at James, then Andy, and then back to Brian, she remarked, "I honestly would not have recognized you!" That was true. Whereas Andy had dropped body mass and muscularity once he stopped regularly training for football season, Brian had beefed up. His body was denser, and sculpted, and his hair and grooming were superlative.

Andy had casually commented once that Brian was being groomed for the NFL. That was real to her now as she noted the changes in his appearance. *Today, he certainly looks the part*, she thought, and then commented admiringly, "Well, you look wonderful."

"Yes, ma'am."

"Are you on a break from LA Western?"

"Sort of..." Brian's voice trailed off, as he dropped his eyes to the floor. It was clear he was a little embarrassed and uncertain of what to answer.

Kelly knew that look. She had seen that same look four years earlier when Andy dragged James home to dinner so that James could break the news that her son, and his genius mind, were needed by the government in its War on Terror. She had agreed that night to let Andy help—and wondered ever since if her decision had been the right one. The life she and her dead husband had planned for their son vanished over the ensuing months and years. The work that Andy had done with James had left them both irrevocably changed, and had nearly gotten her killed. And, now, here was Brian with that same look of "there's something I must do"!

She turned to James with a look of, "how could you?" Though James had seen that expression of surprise and disapproval before, he merely shrugged and, in self-defense, responded, "It wasn't my idea. Andy brought him to me."

James suppressed a smile when he saw the look that then passed between Kelly and Andy. *I see she's still got that Irish temper,* he mused. *I hope she never mellows.* Truth be told, it had been quite a few months since he and Andy had moved more permanently to his cabin on the Cape Fear River. Though Kelly had resigned herself to Andy's moving out of the house, and even out of the state, he could see now how strong the bond between Andy and his mom was. And James felt a twinge of loss. He had truly enjoyed the semblance of family this widow and her son had provided him. So, he was determined not to rile Kelly, or make her anxious in any way. He'd brought enough of that into her life over the last four years.

Bravely, James volunteered, "Kelly, Brian here is taking a breather from all the hoopla out there. He's going to spend a little time helping Andy and me."

"Really?" she sounded skeptical.

"Yeah," Andy answered, without a hint of embarrassment.

Having no idea what would qualify Brian to work with these two, she felt it would be both rude and unkind to ask. So she just nodded. There was an awkward silence, as it was apparent none of these three wanted to talk about it. Switching the channel in her mind, she wondered now what they were even doing here.

"Well, Brian, it is good to see you again. I've been following your successes, and I'm very proud of you."

"Thank you, ma'am." Brian grinned broadly.

Deciding to change the subject, she thought she'd get to the point, and then get back to her blue-haired client, who seemed to be wrapping up the article that had engrossed her. "And to what do I owe the honor of this visit to me today?"

Andy responded, "Two things, Mom."

"Yes?"

"I need the computer from the bedroom at the house. All three of us will need one, and we just have two down there. I thought Brian could use my old one. Then we got to talking about the fact that it was the Pope's funeral, and thought you might enjoy seeing us—you know—maybe let us take you out to dinner."

He didn't have to say anymore. Andy was right. Kelly did

admire the Pope so very much, and was feeling blue that the man who had headed her church for most of her adult life was gone. Andy and Kelly Weir were indeed close, and he knew his mom would be experiencing yet another loss of things she held stable in her life. So, he and James had already decided to take her out and keep her company before Brian had even shown up. Given Brian's state of mind, bringing him with them seemed the best thing they could do for everybody.

Kelly said nothing for a moment. Then she looked back at Mrs. Standish and said, "Let me finish with her. She's my last appointment for the day. Then, I'd be delighted to join you three men for dinner." Playfully, she threw over her shoulder, "Brian and I have a lot of catching up to do!" She winked at James and returned to her client.

CHAPTER 8

*B*rian had noticed immediately the eight chess games that seemed to be going constantly in a corner of the cabin near the kitchen. Not being a chess player, he mostly just walked past them on his way to get a glass of juice or some salami from the refrigerator.

But as the weeks went by, and he settled into the magnificent springtime in the South, his anxiety and sense of disassociation settled down as well. He was noticing colors again, as well as fragrances, and the sounds of the birds recruiting a mate and making their nests along the river. Each day he took a long walk, just observing his new surroundings. And each day he became more and more interested in what was around him.

By mid-May, he knew he was ready to confront what those games meant, and discover for himself what it was that had "awakened" Andy and made him change course. Both James and Andy had kept the conversations sketchy around him, waiting for him to come to this on his own. Given how distraught he had been over the Schiavo case, they had no idea what his reaction would be to the reality that Ayman Al-Zawahiri was coming after the White King—and the White King was the American people.

Though they had laid it out to him in general terms in response to his question about who was in danger, and how they had come to meet and discover Zawahiri's likely plans, they had never gotten into any real detail about the actual eight games Andy had discovered, let alone the devastating sequence and overlap of the games. The discovery that "Religion" and "Military" were the two bottom-most of the games—used only to recruit and distract—had proven to be the career-breaker for James. No one at the CIA could grasp it; or if they could, they

41

did not have the stomach to explain it to their superiors, let alone the American people.

Andy's further identification that the most important games in which the mastermind of Al Qaeda had engaged were games called "Weapons," "Sociology," "Medical," and "Money," had been an unprecedented breakthrough in intelligence analysis. Their subsequent analyses, even to the point of identifying the likely location of "the Doctor" himself, were breathtaking in their accuracy. And they, too, had been completely ignored by the Central Intelligence Agency. That fact had nearly gotten them killed in a gun battle in the basement of Kelly Weir's home when a fanatical Al Qaeda "wannabe" uncovered their work. It had gotten Andy Weir interrogated for possible conspiracy against the United States government, and it had ended James Mikolas' productive and sincere thirty-four-year career in intelligence.

Since that time, James and Andy had made one last, astonishing discovery—one that altered everything they would pursue. Their initial conclusions had been that the White King, or the intended target of Al Qaeda, was the President of the United States. Instead, they had eventually concluded that the White King was the American people, and that the mastermind himself was developing a way to bring down the American people through a complicated and impenetrable weaving of eight separate game areas—all played simultaneously.

The fact that the intelligence community worldwide was fixated on military, religious, and propaganda areas had allowed Zawahiri to escalate his offense into the arenas where Americans were virtually defenseless. James and Andy had isolated this and were now consumed with figuring out how to bring this to the attention of the American people. They faced—and they knew it—not only that formidable challenge but also the certainty that they had not discovered "how" he was doing it. The fact that they knew he was scheming and moving in the areas of drugs, weapons, and sociology did not provide, on the surface, a grasp of how he would deliver blows powerful enough to obliterate any gains the United States made against Al Qaeda militarily or intelligence-wise.

They were convinced he could do it, and they were mystified as to how he would do it. And, to the agony of both men, they full well understood that if they could not penetrate it, they surely could not communicate it.

In fact, by the time Brian Washington Carver appeared, emotionally wounded, on their doorstep, they and their theories had been rejected time and time again by congressmen, think tanks, and human rights organizations alike. For months since the Inauguration, they had attended hearings, sent mailings, used the Internet, attended seminars, and used "confidential" channels to try to awaken the public and its elected officials to the menace. Each time, although they were regarded as sincere, their analysis fell on deaf ears. The picture they painted of the intentions and abilities of the man they knew to be running Al Qaeda did not match the fixed idea these sincere patriots held.

And why would it? James knew very well that unless they penetrated *how* he was doing it, and offered proof that was observable, their theories were just that. And no one risks their career, or money, or energy on mere theories. They had even approached the business world at its highest levels, hoping a visionary, far-thinking billionaire or two would grasp the possibilities of the whole thing being a money game. It was there that they were greeted with consternation. Once again, just as inside the CIA, they were regarded as "fringe."

The only way they could change that conclusion was to change people's perception of them. And neither James nor Andy had a clue how to accomplish that. To add to it, now they had a dysfunctional friend who had turned to Andy for answers. James would have preferred that Brian be coached back to his football career plans, but for some reason, Andy was letting his former wide receiver hang around, moping.

James had no way of knowing that Andy's inherent compassion would have such a profound effect on the outcome of the War on Terror—that it would be this young man who would create the greatest obstacle Ayman Al-Zawahiri would face. And the young man himself had no idea. Though he was still trying to figure out why the world had changed so much, and how he had been so disconnected from it, Brian's courage and determination were, nonetheless, a match for Andy's.

He might be disoriented now, but Brian had possessed the desire to escape from an almost-guaranteed future of drugs and prison. Very few came out of his neighborhood with any semblance of an ability to pursue the American dream. Yes, he had trained and worked hard to achieve athletic prowess. His abilities had attracted the attention of the scouts at LA Western, and four other major universities. But what no one in the sports press noticed, or even cared about, was that Brian had chosen LA Western for its academics, as well as its nationally renowned football team. Brian Washington Carver was smart, and he had been encouraged by his mama not only to play ball but also to think. Andy had yet to discover this about his friend. To be sure, Brian had much to discover about himself.

And today, James definitely had no idea. Today, he had decided to talk to Andy about sending Brian back into the loving arms of his coaches at LAWU. Fortunately for the White King, Brian had other ideas.

The encrypted code inside the Internet chess game alerted Zawahiri that his commander of military operations wanted to communicate with him directly. The chess game was a great way of sending general signals from one cell to another, or from one Al Qaeda leader to another, but it was not intended to provide sufficient detail for judgment calls. The fact that Makkawi had signaled the need for more explicit communication irritated the Doctor.

Don't you know I'm deep into our next phase of operation? the Doctor chided his commander in absentia. The truth was he would prefer to be rid of the whole Mid-East phase, and the identities he had to assume in order to play his part. He had no idea how much longer he could keep from his top-level lieutenants the fact that Bin Laden was alive. They all presumed him dead and buried near Tora Bora in Afghanistan. Soon, however, he knew he would need to reveal Bin Laden's status—if for no other reason than to keep them in line.

To do that, he would need to travel to Iran personally, and endure the risks attendant with such a journey. Not even the

Iranian government knew Bin Laden was secreted in a desolate mental hospital in the hinterlands. Then, presuming Bin Laden's overall health had remained the same, he would need once again to wean him from the psychiatric medications he had administered to Bin Laden to keep him near catatonic. The mere thought of the risks, and the annoyance of it, started his stomach on its familiar burning.

Moreover, he suspected Makkawi wanted to discuss Zarqawi. The decision to place Abou Al-Zarqawi in charge of Iraq operations was made by Bin Laden himself. And it was approved by the Doctor and Makkawi. All three knew Zarqawi to be a half-wit, nothing more than a local thug and thief. They all knew he would swallow their line about his being the best one to advance operations in Iraq prior to, and subsequent to, the removal of Saddam Hussein.

And they knew, moreover, that his myopic view of situations, coupled with his low IQ, would obscure the reality of his situation from him. Tonight he guessed that Makkawi was insistent on a communication because he was alarmed at the failed objectives in Iraq relevant to their elections and the formation of their government. And knowing Makkawi, he further guessed the man was becoming incensed by Zarqawi's relentless killing of Muslims along with the killing of Americans.

Zawahiri, in fact, agreed with Zarqawi on this issue. He was not in the least bit loathe to kill a Muslim, if that Muslim's practice of his faith was deviant from the Doctor's own concept of Shar'ia. Throughout his rise to the number one position in terrorism worldwide, the Doctor had done it by eliminating anyone who stood in his way. And that included misguided Muslims who felt that all Muslims should be treated like brothers. As far as the Doctor was concerned, if a moderate Muslim needed to be killed in order to advance his objective, they were as dispensable as an Infidel.

Nonetheless, he had his own "beef" with Zarqawi. And that, basically, was that the man had failed, and was continuing to fail, to prevent the formation of a government in Iraq. Since that was essential to Al Qaeda's goals in the region, his Black Knight was incompetent. And so it was that he sent a response in the simulated chess game he was playing.

Wanting to confuse the intelligence community, which might now have the capability of somehow intercepting their satellite phone conversations, he signaled Makkawi to correspond with him this time via courier. Their most sensitive transmissions had been handled this way, since the beginning of the US invasion of Afghanistan.

As good as their encryption was—and it was state of the art—he felt nothing took the place of a centuries-old means of getting a message from one important person to another—the courier. Communication by courier was slower, but nearly foolproof. The Doctor used his next chess move to alert Makkawi. The Black Bishop's move to within one square of the White Bishop was the signal to resort to courier. Though it might take weeks for the courier to arrive at his go-between in Paris, the Doctor evaluated that to be his wisest move.

In fact, it delighted him to imagine American and British intelligence scratching their heads, wondering why the lines had gone silent on communications between senior members of Al Qaeda. *That should put them in a spin as to where we are, and what has happened to us,* he mused. *Knowing them, they'll think we're dead!*

So, letting out a huge sigh, and with it the pent-up exasperation he was feeling, he reconciled himself to the fact that there would likely be a lengthy and demanding letter coming from Makkawi. He concluded that he'd better let his man in Paris know to be expecting a courier from Turkey, and that he could bring that pouch with him when they met in Panama City. He knew Samir would not open the pouch, that he would just let himself be a delivery boy; and that Samir, instead, would be focusing on the Doctor's cryptic "close the door" memo, which he had sent earlier.

It was late, and the family in the apartment next door was quarreling over something. His limited Spanish curtailed his understanding, but it sounded as if the father was berating the mother for something regarding the behavior of one of the daughters. He had had a daughter, but his wife Azza had never given him cause to raise his voice to her like that. The noise and the heat sickened him, but he needed rest. He lay down on the cot in his cell-sized bedroom and waited for sleep to overtake him.

CHAPTER 9

S amir was understandably confused as he made his way through the incessant traffic in Panama City. Clutching the directions to the newly-established offices of ST & Associates, he might as well have been a new client trying to find the PR firm for the first time. Although Samir had offices in Paris and New York, this was his first venture south of the border, and he was completely unfamiliar not only with Panama City but also with the language and customs of this new country.

All he knew was that he had been summoned there by the Doctor himself, and that he had been given less than a week to set up offices. Fortunately, one of his Paris staff had a cousin in commercial leasing with the Bank of Panama who was able to set up their lease and office in absentia. It provided exceptional cover for his trip to Panama City. *Of course, I would want to set up the offices and select the staff in our first operation in this new country,* he reassured himself. *Everyone would expect that of me.*

Nonetheless, he felt uncomfortable in this teeming place, where he looked indigenous but was, in fact, a complete stranger. Seeing the street address printed on his instruction sheet, he breathed a sigh of relief. Realizing he would be climbing to a fifth-floor walk-up, he admonished himself for having given carte blanche to an unknown person regarding selecting suitable office space. *Who in their right mind would want to climb five floors to talk over a marketing campaign?* he mused. His skepticism vanished, however, when the disciplined Al Qaeda operative realized that this was actually the point. High above the corner market and the bicycle repair shop, which flanked the shabby, single-door entrance to the offices and apartments above, he was confident no one would just wander in. And if they did not just "wander

47

in," there would be no danger of their operation being compromised.

The key to the office was included in the packet he had received. Carefully placing it in a lock that looked as if it hadn't been used in some time, he turned the key gently, hoping not to break it off. The latch released easily, however, and he breathed yet another sigh of relief.

To his surprise, the Doctor was already there, sitting somewhat stiffly on a fold-up chair in front of the window. Given the intensity of the heat and humidity here, he understood full well why Ayman Al-Zawahiri would be trying to capture a bit of a breeze off the rooftop garden on the building next door.

Like two friends who haven't seen each other in some time, both men enthusiastically embraced in the center of the room. Their emotion was genuine. Both lived secret lives with completely false identities and professions to mask their real activities, and it was rare indeed for either man to be able to let down his guard. For a moment, the presence of the one made the other stronger. And each man felt it.

After the official cheek-to-cheek salutation that was characteristic of men of their culture, they each stood back and eyed the other. Samir looked as he always did. Given that he frequented the finest restaurants and clubs in both New York and Paris, his impeccable dress seemed out of place in this city of linen suits and loose cotton shirts. The Doctor, on the other hand, bore no resemblance whatsoever to the dapper Swiss investment guru he had pretended to be before escaping from Geneva, Switzerland to begin the next phase of Al Qaeda's operations.

He had lost weight. His face was thinner, as was his hair. And he was dressed shabbily—business attire, but ill-fitting and wrinkled.

"Nice disguise," Samir commented, as he scanned the Doctor from head to toe. Fearing he might have been a little too familiar with his superior officer, he retracted it immediately with, "Forgive me, I meant no disrespect."

"None taken," the Doctor reassured him. "Your response is what I was intending to elicit. Here, unlike Geneva, where I was quite prominent in the community, I wish to blend in and attract no attention." He eyed Samir to see if he totally understood.

Satisfied that he did, he resumed. "I will not be in this sector long. Just long enough to direct this ragtag alliance to the point that they can be counted on. Then," he said, walking back to his chair and sitting down, "I wish to vanish without anyone noticing I am gone."

Samir smiled, looked for a folding chair that he too could use, and joked, "Mission accomplished." He passed the pouch from Makkawi to Zawahiri. Deftly the Doctor read its contents. Showing no sign of emotion or disagreement, he closed it back up tightly.

Before Samir could even settle in, however, the Doctor handed him a file with an application in it. "What is this?" Samir asked.

"A real estate application for your new offices in Los Angeles."

Having no idea what this was about, Samir just looked at the Doctor. The silence was not awkward. Samir knew very well that he was the one receiving orders, and he knew the Doctor would explain to him only what he needed to know relevant to the Al Qaeda cell he commanded. His place was not to ask, but to wait. This he was good at.

The Doctor smiled and said, "I see you're taken a bit by surprise."

"Yes, of course, as I barely figured out the directions to these new offices."

"Ah yes, I understand," the Doctor sympathized, "but you won't be using these offices. They are a relay station only for communications between you and me."

Samir had worked with this man long enough to appreciate his genius in setting up communication operations, whereby Al Qaeda's money and manpower could be coordinated. Apparently this was just another of these. Though he was puzzled then as to why he had even needed to come here, he suspected it had to do with the fact that the Doctor needed to meet with him in person, and that Zawahiri was unable to get any closer to New York than Panama City.

He had to admit, however, that the idea of doing business of any kind in Los Angeles was enticing. "May I ask what my firm will be doing in the City of Angels?"

"Your Los Angeles firm will concentrate on Public Relations to Hollywood. I've decided it's time we involved you in something more than just brilliant work for pharmaceutical and food companies."

Samir was pleased with the Doctor's appreciation of the amazing public relations work he had done for some of the country's leading pharmaceutical giants. He had no idea, however, just how big a part this supposed "cover" in the United States was playing in Ayman Al-Zawahiri's master plan. The prominence of his New York office had placed him in good stead with Bud Walker, the media mogul, and had secured him an almost permanent spot on the guest-list of some of the most coveted social events in Manhattan. For some reason, Bud Walker trusted Samir. That trust would jeopardize the security of the nation in the years to come. But at this moment, in the steaming heat and almost overcome by the putrid smells from the street below, Samir did not know the full extent of the Doctor's New York plan, let alone the Hollywood plan. *Perhaps the two are tied,* he reflected.

"Samir?"

The Doctor's tone of voice brought Samir out of his momentary reverie. "Yes, sorry, I was distracted there for a moment." He tried to excuse his lapse of concentration by adding, "The smell from the garbage below is a bit strong through the window. I've not eaten, and it just overtook me for a moment."

Without saying a word, the Doctor's right arm thrust backward. Grabbing the window, he deftly pulled it shut. The seal was weak enough to cause a momentary rattle as the frame hit the sill. But the glass held.

"My apologies, dear friend. You are right. It seems we're over the dumping spot for the spoiled fruit and vegetables!" Both men smiled. Then the Doctor added, "It is time for us to represent studios, celebrities, and agencies. I believe this will add something very interesting into the mix."

"No doubt," Samir agreed. "Do you have a plan on how I will make this transition?"

He guessed that it would somehow involve Bud Walker's actress wife. She was rumored to be staging a comeback into films, and she had taken quite a liking to Samir. More than likely he would be encouraged to explore this entry point.

"Yes, most definitely. You'll begin with the 'Black Tower.'" Samir was unfamiliar with that reference, as were most Americans. Hollywood insiders knew though, and soon Samir would be welcome there as well.

Though he had not devised a plan on how to move into the inner circles of Hollywood, Samir showed no reluctance whatsoever to the idea itself. *He's an agile and sporting player,* Zawahiri thought to himself. *I need that now—someone who can operate in any environment.*

"What's the message?" Samir inquired.

"What?"

"The message, sir." Samir waited, then added, "I assume it is something different from what we have been feeding to the press."

The Doctor laughed. "No, Samir, quite the contrary. It is the same—just an extension of the playing field, that is all." The Doctor waited to see if Samir understood. He seemed to.

"All right, let me make sure I understand." Samir reached into his briefcase and extracted a note pad. His gold Mont Blanc was where it always was—in the pocket of his shirt. The Doctor smiled at the fastidiousness of this colleague. He swore that Samir would have that pen on his person even if he were sunning on a beach in Malibu. Samir, however, was too immersed in the new strategy to notice his boss's smile.

"We already have the Media convinced that the Administration is hiding something. So, Hollywood as an extension of that..." He looked up to the ceiling, as if the answer might somehow be there.

The Doctor waited.

Giving up, he let out a long breath and shook his head. "I'm sorry, sir, I'm not quite tracking with you here. Please, enlighten me."

"Samir, there is something I discovered about *good people.*" He had Samir's full attention. "A truth."

"Yes?"

"Remember this, Samir. You will need to know this well." His voice was chillingly calm, but insistent.

"Yes, sir."

"When good people have something bad happen to them,

they believe there must be a reason. They believe they must have done something, or the bad thing would not have happened. And they will look for what they did that caused it."

"No!" Samir seemed to scoff. "You can't be serious!" As soon as he uttered it, he wished he could retract the words. Feebly, he added hastily, "Forgive me. I just don't quite get this."

"I know. But it *is* true, nonetheless. As I said, it is a truth. And with that, I expect you to hang the Americans and their government. And I expect you to use Hollywood to assist you. Never forget we have limited resources. We must compromise some of theirs if we are to seriously impinge and unhinge the Americans."

Suddenly Samir stood and paced to the window. It was too encrusted with dirt to look out, but he stood there nonetheless, as if he were standing in Paris overlooking the Seine. Slowly, he started to nod his head, and eventually rock his whole body as if in prayer. "All right, all right," he breathed. "We want the Americans to believe they caused the attacks themselves. We want them looking inward, at themselves, until they believe they themselves are the 'cause.'"

"Exactly!" The Doctor smiled.

"So, Iraq is a diversion?"

"Yes."

He hesitated to ask, but Samir felt now that he was on a "need to know" due to his assumption of the responsibilities of Propaganda Chief of Al Qaeda. "Was it always so?" he ventured tentatively.

"No. Not initially. But Zarqawi has failed us." The Doctor patted the courier pouch as if to acknowledge its contents. "Our fallback position is to use Iraq as a diversion and aggravation to the Americans. Your 'this is another Viet Nam' campaign will pay off handsomely for us."

"Hah!" Samir laughed suddenly. "All right, I see it. Their guilt over Viet Nam, their obsession with oil, their ignorance of economics…" His voice trailed off. Then, like a composer who is grabbling hold of the melody line, he continued. "So, I go for the most ignorant of them, the most self-centered, the most self-aggrandizing!"

"Right. You have it. Select them well. Not everyone in their midst is a candidate for our purposes." Then, as if to drive the point home, Zawahiri reaffirmed, "Select them well."

"I will." Samir was grinning now, eager for this new type of opportunity and challenge. "Should be fun!"

"Yes, Samir. It will be very satisfying to take the spear of corruption they used to permeate the world with their debauchery, and turn it on itself."

The Doctor's malignant comments sometimes unnerved even Samir. There was a mystery to this man—one Samir had no intention of deciphering. He knew his own survival depended on Ayman Al-Zawahiri never turning on him. Changing the subject gracefully he asked, "And Zarqawi, what will he bring me next?"

The game had been set that Zarqawi's actions in Iraq would provide fuel for Samir's brilliant propaganda machine run out of their Paris office. It had worked well for some time. No matter what Zarqawi did, or failed to do, Samir had somehow manipulated it into a Public Relations victory for Al Qaeda. He wondered now how much longer it would continue.

Fingering the edges of the pouch gingerly and meticulously, the Doctor answered quietly, "Makkawi is offering him a chance to redeem himself." He paused for a moment and added, "There are two more elections scheduled. If he succeeds in blocking either one, and prevents the formation of a government in Iraq, and the acceptance of a democratic constitution, he will remain."

"And, if he does not?"

"Then I doubt he will still be alive."

It was said so matter-of-factly that Samir did not dare ask for clarification. He did not have the audacity to ask if Zarqawi would die at the hand of the Iraqis, or at the hand of the Doctor. *Either way, it means nothing to me now,* he mused, *as I have new marching orders.*

"Samir?" the Doctor seemed to read the mind of his protégé. "That is of no concern to you. You have a new goal in front of you now." And then, as if to reassure him, the Doctor added, "Your game is far more important to our outcome than anything going on in Iraq." He paused to let that sink in, and then concluded, "Military campaigns come and go; theatres change. It is how the enemy views them that ensures victory or defeat. And that is your territory, my able friend."

Samir nodded that he understood, although his facial expression alone would have given him away. He was not fully grasping it.

Smiling now, the Doctor embraced him and, laughing, said, "Let's go have some dinner. Then we'll discuss how you're going to get the President of the United States to close the border to Mexico within two years." Samir sat motionless, as if paralyzed. "Ah, my friend, do not worry. I know exactly how to do it, and I will coach you—after you have fed your body. It's not wise to discuss such weighty games on a hungry stomach." On that note, he gently guided Samir to the door, pushed him through it, and closed it behind them.

And with that, one of the saddest and most reprehensible periods of American history began. Unknowingly, in their desire to gain the admiration of the people of other countries, the American people would soon disgrace themselves, and jeopardize the very freedoms they were trying to protect.

But, for now, the people of the United States sat down to their dinner, and their evening of reality television.

CHAPTER 10

"**I** am very angry with him." The Doctor paused for effect, then continued. "I am *very* angry with him, Samir."

Flushed from the heat and the discomfort of too large a meal, Samir sat and waited. He knew the Doctor would embellish. But, for now, it was best to let him seethe.

"Our plans depend upon his closing the border to Mexico within two years. And, he's refusing to do that!" The Doctor spat into his hand and wiped it away. "I don't know whether it is him, or that woman he takes advice from, but he must be moved off this point. And now he's presented a plan of his own." The Doctor contorted his mouth in disdain. "And it seems he's persuaded even the fat bureaucrat from Massachusetts to his argument."

Samir removed a white linen handkerchief from his back pocket and patted his face lightly to absorb the sweat that was starting to drip down his temple. He waited a moment. "Sir," Samir entered quietly, "if his enemies cannot stop him, then perhaps it is time for his friends to do so."

It took Zawahiri a moment to realize that his protégé had delineated an attack strategy. But, when he saw it, he laughed with ironic appreciation. "Ah, my friend, I was right. A little food did bring your wits back to you."

They both enjoyed the banter. Only a few years ago, the Doctor had been the mentor and tutor of Samir in the ways of propaganda, mind control, and the manipulation of whole populations. He had been a good student—so good that today the Doctor realized his former pupil was perhaps one of the most skilled propaganda operatives in the world. The fact that Samir was still submissive to him, and still eager to learn, gave the Doctor comfort. He waited for a moment, for their mirth to subside. Then suddenly, the Doctor asked, "Do you have an idea, my friend?"

"Yes. Simply put, I will turn his allies against him."

"His allies? Blair?"

"No, friend, the ones he really counts on."

Seeing that the Doctor failed, in fact, to understand, for the first time it was Samir's chance to educate the Doctor. "I have studied American politics, Ayman, and I have studied their use of media and public relations. This president cultivated, however he did it, a set of allies in the media. And they are very powerful. They have the ear of the American people. Once I turn them, we neutralize the president. He will have no one to speak for him—not even Ms. Rice."

"I see." The Doctor was looking directly in front of him, as if he were inspecting this idea, trying to look at it from a variety of angles. Samir waited, taking the opportunity to mop his brow yet again.

"And if I do it extremely carefully, they themselves will turn and devour him, like a pack of wolves on an injured elk."

"That will please Allah," the Doctor ventured.

It was the first time they had spoken of Allah, and Samir wondered if the Doctor was sincere. He was used to Bin Laden referring to Allah in almost every conversation, but since the Doctor's assumption of command, this was the first time Zawahiri had spoken of He whom they were to serve.

Samir, however, was not a religious man. Though no one in Al Qaeda had observed this fact, it was this very aspect of his character that caused Ayman Al Zawahiri to place his faith in the talents of his propaganda minister. Zawahiri, ever watchful of zealots who would usurp his power and betray him in the name of Allah, had no such worries about Samir. Not even money threatened Samir's loyalty, for Ayman Al Zawahiri had observed in Samir a true sociopath. He would wreak as much destruction in his life as he could. *And we're the only game of true destruction. He has to stay with us.*

The Doctor peered at Samir over a cup of tea he had been nurturing, and reflected, *And when the destruction is complete and it's time to construct a new world, even he will no longer be needed.* Ayman Al-Zawihiri was down-deep terrified of all of his colleagues, for he knew full well the type of mischief any one of them could and would get into. Knowing that he could be particularly vulnerable to one this brilliant, he savored this realization. *But for now, Samir's genius will advance the timeline.* Breaking the silence, he decided to commence a two-man war council.

"All right, lay it out. I'm all ears."

Deftly, Samir wrote something on his ever-present notebook, tore the page out, and slid it across the rickety table to the Doctor. It caught momentarily on slivers in the tabletop, and Samir wondered why the Doctor could not have at least created a semblance of an office. The one thing they would need, however—a safe—appeared to be state of the art. Sitting inside a wardrobe closet, he guessed his notes would remain there.

"And you believe you can compromise these people?"

"Yes." Samir was quick to answer. He added, "I'll use this button." Pointing to the bottom of the page, he looked on smugly as he watched the Doctor read the single word he had written, and then heave a deep sigh of approval.

"Brilliant."

"No matter what Bush proposes, they'll parrot the 'button' and attack him along that line. Attacked from the rear, I expect his PR team will be stunned. They'll fold, and let him down."

The Doctor looked at the page, pursed his lips as if contemplating some type of change, and said, "May I?" He reached for Samir's pen.

"Of course."

"You'll use their righteousness, is that right?" he asked, while writing that below the word Samir had written.

"Yes, as we did before, we'll turn their strength into a weakness." He paused a moment to mull that over and then announced, "Their righteousness will be turned to self-righteousness. This is a fairly ripe issue to do that with."

"And Mexico falls?"

Samir grinned. "Mexico most decidedly falls."

But Samir, nonetheless, had something nagging at him in this area—a pesky thought he had been unable to push from his mind. Deciding it had to be addressed since it still lingered, he hoped now was the correct time to discuss it. "Do you think he knows the plan, Ayman?" he blurted out.

"Yes, I believe he's guessed it."

Samir accepted the answer. The Doctor, too, reflected a moment, and added sharply, "Or Calderon and Vincenze Fox have guessed it, and persuaded him. That's why your plan must work, Samir. The attack from the rear on the President of the United States must render him incapable of a move!"

Samir exhaled. "Ah, I know that, sir. And I assure you this will work. These men have the ear of the people—far more than Bush. We'll get him."

"Good, good," the Doctor said in agreement. He was feeling better now, more confident. He debated whether to tell Samir the next phase, and decided he should. If something happened to him, this phase would be in the hands of Makkawi, their military commander, and Samir.

"After that, Mexico falls. Either this election, or the next. Without those US dollars crossing back into Mexico to feed their families, a revolution is inevitable. The target, Samir, is Mexico's economy. And your work will bring it down. Makkawi will set up bases in Mexico, Colombia, Brazil, Bolivia, and Venezuela. The Cubans will indoctrinate the indigenous people into Marxism, and our enemy will find itself with a Marxist regime on its entire southern border."

There was absolute quiet now. It was as if all of Panama City had faded. Samir's mind grasped the magnitude of the coming years, and his part in it. His pulse raced, and he was emboldened to ask, "And the FARC? Chavez?"

"They will be free to attack at will. The new Mexican regime will allow them access to any route into the United States, and to men, if necessary." Then he added another piece to the plan. "Zarqawi will keep the pressure up in Iraq. If he prevails, fine. If not—he will have provided the necessary diversion. Makkawi will fuel Afghanistan temporarily, distracting them even further."

Samir swallowed, and for a moment, the contents of his stomach seemed to lurch toward his throat. "Sir, I appreciate your confidence in me. I hope you know I will keep their attention on Iraq. Whatever happens, their eyes will be focused there. And, I shall get the American people to close the border to Mexico." Suddenly, he laughed. It was a quiet laugh at first. Then it became guttural as he let it settle into his being. "And all the while, the fools will think this secures them!"

The Doctor allowed a smile. "Precisely."

Retrieving his pen, Samir took one last glance at the paper and said, "Remind me never to play chess with you, Ayman." He shook his head in acknowledgment of his mentor's diabolical genius. "Usama chose you wisely. Thank you for the opportunity."

As he rose to leave, Zawahiri threw one last comment at him. "Samir, remember. You have no price on your head. You are the one we are counting on."

Nodding, Samir inhaled deeply, opened the door, and descended into the streets of Panama City. At the airport, waiting for his plane to New York, he called Bud Walker, President of WNG, to seek help in acquiring offices in Los Angeles—and to ask his friend Walker if the rising star of WNG, Alicia Quixote, was seriously dating anyone.

This marketing button he would plant himself. One of the areas that had fascinated him the most in his study of marketing had been the idea of marketing by definition. He had learned that you can change a person's viewpoint on an issue simply by changing the definition. It was an insight he had grasped, mastered, and deployed frequently over the years.

Smiling, he reached for his notepad and jotted down two words that would split the nation in the coming two years—two words he had discovered in the American landscape, and which he would use against them: "multiculturalism" and "diversity."

Flipping to the back of his notebook, he added a group to his "Unwitting" list. And this unsuspecting list, which had no idea it was being *played* by Al Qaeda, also had no idea the part the newly-added group would play in furthering Al Qaeda's aim. And the people on that list certainly had *no* idea of the simplicity of the button he would use to brainwash them. *Yes, this one I will have to handle personally,* he thought. Settling into the rear of the taxi, he leaned back and closed his eyes.

CHAPTER 11

*T*he pain in his stomach was unbearable. It was deeper and more cutting than anything he had experienced. The Doctor struggled to get to his feet, knocking over the night stand in his meager apartment. The sound must have awakened the husband next door, because he started to bang on the wall, cursing in Spanish.

Fortunately for the Doctor, his own muffled moan camouflaged his pain and seemed to satisfy the angry neighbor. Straightening up, he reached for his briefcase, and opened the bottle of prescription pain medication he carried to counteract his ulcerous condition. Several pills spilled onto the floor, but he didn't care. He just needed to get them into him, even without water.

He was sweating profusely now, but his skin was clammy and he knew he was getting worse. *There's only so long these bodies last,* he consoled himself. *I'm no longer young.* This thought sobered him up enough to take stock of his plans. For the first time, Ayman Al-Zawahiri realized he might not live long enough to see the final, delicious climax of his games and plans—that he might not survive the cataclysmic conclusion he had envisioned.

I'm so close, he coached himself. *I have to stay alive.*

He repeated it, this time out loud. "I have to stay alive." Inhaling deeply, he reached the conclusion that, to accomplish his final goal, he would have to advance the timeline on his most ambitious project. It did not matter to him now whether he was alive to enjoy the money. It only mattered that he remain alive to enjoy the destruction. For Ayman Al-Zawahiri was about to launch his plan to destroy the United States of America in one attack, and collapse the world economy in its aftermath. All of the other theaters of operation, which were so successfully distracting governments and news media, were a mere subterfuge—and a successful one at that. He was quite certain no one had any idea what he would actually do. He laughed suddenly, and the knife-like pain rekindled.

Gritting his teeth, he continued to breathe deeply, waiting for the pain to subside. It did, and he lay back in bed gingerly. But he could not sleep. He was excited now for the dawn. With the new day, he could summon the players and trigger a sequence of events. Smiling, he was satisfied that although his body was growing weaker, the series of games he had been playing were gaining in momentum. He was certain this next sequence had been guessed by no one—not even Al Qaeda. For Ayman Al-Zawahiri was off the grid now, and off the playbook. This next event would be his—and his alone. It no longer mattered who the United States caught or interrogated. There was no one alive who knew of the cell he had been cultivating for more than a decade.

In order to hasten the daybreak, he turned on the cable television that even the poorest of apartments in Panama City seemed able to afford, and, keeping the volume low so as not to disturb the angry man next door, watched the news. Satisfied that Americans were divided and suspicious, he knew they were also more drugged than they had ever been before. Without even having access to the reports from DECU-HEHIZ, the drug company he had financed to the pinnacles of success in psychiatric pharmaceutical manufacturing, he knew what those reports would say. Drug sales in the anti-depressant market would be up; profits would be up; and the usage in the United States would be increasing. For Americans were now angry, confused, and anxious. And that anxiety would walk them right into his arms. This thought brought a smile to his parched lips.

All channels seemed to be covering the same issues, and the networks seemed to have their attention on revved-up tension between Iran and the United States, and between North Korea and the Pacific Rim countries. *More fear,* he thought. *Good for business.*

As the pain subsided, he got up and opened the file with the cube-shaped game-board. All layers were lit, and there were chess pieces on each of the layers. The bottom-most game was labeled "Religion," and it was in an apparent frenzy of activity. Above that was "Military," and there the theaters were spread worldwide. The next two games of "Intelligence" and "Public Relations" were going exactly as he had planned. His public relations man, Samir, was brilliant, and was about to create a debilitating attack upon the Presidency of the United States.

As he scrutinized the next layer up, which was labeled "Weapons," he rejoiced at how effective a weapon *fear* actually was. Not only would the fear lead to an ever-increasing level of divisiveness in the United States, but also those divisions would split along racial lines, as well as political ones. Remembering the great work that Hitler had done, he was delighted to see the racial discord in America flaring up again.

All this leads to more despair and sickness, he rejoiced. *And with that, more drugs sold, and more money.* All eight games, playing simultaneously. But today, the game he highlighted in gold was the game labeled "Medical." For it was here that he would attack next.

Though his blinds were drawn, he felt the morning light, and knew he could place the call now. He would do it personally, via satellite phone. He would be circumspect. *Don't be overconfident,* he admonished himself. *Be cautious!*

Thirty minutes later, switchboards at five major US drug manufacturing companies had received calls directed toward the Production Managers' offices. And at that moment, the most secret cell created by Ayman Al-Zawahiri was activated. The members of that cell had been in preparation for almost fifteen years. Their existence was known only to the Doctor. Bin Laden himself had no knowledge of the cell's existence. And no other cell had any knowledge. They could not be compromised. They had been waiting. And today they received an invitation to an international conference on manufacturing technology advancements. It would convene in Panama City one month from the phone call.

Five unwitting presidents of corporations signed the financial appropriation requests submitted by their production chiefs without thinking a thing about it. Each wanted his company to be on the cutting edge of manufacturing. Each trusted his production chief. Each had been duped. It was done before nightfall.

CHAPTER 12

"All right, gentlemen, let's convene and have our leader lay this out for us." Every man in the room knew that those words, spoken by Ali Roos, signaled the beginning of the attack.

Ali Roos was the chief pharmacist at perhaps the largest hospital facility in the Los Angeles area. Its complex covered more than nine city blocks, and was at the hub of the city's busiest thoroughfares. And it was the hospital of choice for the elite and wealthy of the city. Ali had complete access to all pharmaceutical ordering and dispensation, and most definitely had the capability of putting anything into any bottle he wanted. Due to the imperative in a hospital pharmacy of zero tolerance on errors, since patients' lives depended on their medications, Ali had developed the reputation over the last fifteen years of being a brilliant, dedicated—if not a tad anal—senior manager of the pharmacy and its inventory. In all the years he had worked there, not a single incident of error in the filling of prescriptions had occurred.

For that accomplishment, he had been promoted and handsomely compensated by the hospital. And for that accomplishment, he had been recruited by Ayman Al-Zawahiri to spearhead the most audacious and deadly of his plans. The Doctor had no idea why this emigrant from Syria had initially caught his eye, but he had. Zawahiri had assigned it to "Divine Inspiration"—though he knew it was not that. On cynical days, he knew that his own eye had caught just a hint of resentment in Roos's eyes as a Jewish doctor tersely told him to have a new prescription ready in ten minutes.

That was nearly fifteen years ago, during the one visit the Doctor had made to the United States—astonishingly, a fund-raising tour sponsored by Ali A. Mohamed. Not only had he raised the money that funded the bombing of the Egyptian Embassy in Islamabad, Pakistan, but he had also inspected possible US targets. He had been in San Francisco—that was known by US intelligence. But he had also made it to Los Angeles. That was not known. There he met and recruited Roos. And for the last ten years, Ali Roos lived almost anonymously in a quiet neighborhood in Glendale. He paid little attention to his neighbors, and they, as is characteristic of California, paid no attention to him. Perhaps a neighbor walking his dog would wave or nod. But, for certain, no one really knew anything about him. Therefore, they had no idea he had been waiting for the call to come to Panama—let alone what it signaled.

There were six other men in the room, and not one of them knew the name of any other man at the conference, except Ali Roos. Quickly they took their seats at the conference table. It was a surprisingly small room for a supposed international conference—completely sterile and devoid of even a color-splashed picture on the wall. There were not even any of the usual notepads and pens that hotels provide their seminar participants. But then again, only seven men had been invited. None had ever met the others; none even knew their positions until today; and all knew they would never see each other again. The one common denominator was that each man spoke French. Command of that language had been an important part of the Doctor's selection process. Limited to his native languages of Arabic and French, the Doctor had to be certain that his instructions were carried out to the last, accurate detail.

Sitting to Ali's right was the Doctor. To his right was the production manager for DECU-HEHIZ. Counter-clockwise around the table were the production managers of the five leading pharmaceutical companies in the world. Though their companies were predominantly European, these men were in charge of production and distribution in the United States. It was for that reason they had been chosen. The man from DECU-HEHIZ controlled what was exported to the United States, and had been the last man recruited to the cell.

As they sat waiting, what was notable was that none of them had any intention of taking notes. Their full attention was on Ayman Al-Zawahiri, and they knew the content of this historic meeting would be committed to memory. They were ready. And each felt honored to have been called.

Ironically, they did not know who had "called" them—only that it was one of the highest-ranking Al Qaeda leaders, dispatched by Bin Laden himself. The Doctor's skill in deception had enabled him for a long time to move about without people knowing his true identity. He had used a double for years, confounding the world's intelligence communities to the point that the United States' FBI site showed a picture of the man believed to be Ayman Al-Zawahiri, but, mysteriously, could not provide details on his height and weight. So it was that each of the men accepted him as the emissary from Bin Laden, and the commander of their cell, but none had any idea they were face-to-face with "the Doctor" himself.

Not that it would have mattered. It was doubtful anything could have deepened their commitment. Each man had a streak of hatred driving him. That, coupled with brilliance and competence in his field, had enabled each to climb the corporate ladder in companies that demanded a certain degree of ruthlessness in their executives.

Finally, the Doctor began. "The date will be June 30, 2011—your last run of the second quarter." He looked around to make sure each man had understood. They had, so he continued. "Your method will be to insert a lethal chemical, in the final moments of production, into all psychiatric medications your companies manufacture."

Before he could continue, Ali asked, "Sir, I beg your pardon, but a clarification, please?"

"Go on."

"What chemical?"

The Doctor smiled and answered, "That, I leave to your discretion. Each of you has a tremendous background in chemistry, and I trust that you have something appropriate within your own labs." He said it with the glibness of someone discussing locating something suitable to wear in a closet. It meant nothing to Ayman Al-Zawahiri. And the men listening were too honored to have been chosen for this task to even think about what that kind of "disconnect" meant. They themselves would soon be disconnecting from their fellow man as well, for their plot would be the single most deadly attack upon man in man's history.

As if to caution them, the Doctor added, "The only thing you must be certain of is that it is a chemical that will be deadly upon ingestion, and, in combination with other ingredients, dissipate in the victims' systems prior to autopsy. You can check out the tetrodotoxin class, but the key thing is to use something that will be confusing to them."

That qualifier seemed to stun the men around the table. Brows furrowed, each moved nervously in his chair, as if it had suddenly become uncomfortable. The Doctor smiled and reassured them. "Gentlemen, gentlemen, have no concern. That narrows your options a bit, doesn't it?" He laughed as each signified yes. "But you *do* have options, do you not?" Again, each nodded agreement. "Good. Pick what you want, and substitute it when the last ingredient is being inserted. No one will know."

There was silence. He reinforced his point. "It is imperative, gentlemen, that no one know. Is that understood?"

It was.

"Once you have done that, I would suggest you turn in your resignation and depart for Switzerland or Venezuela."

Ali raised his hand somewhat tentatively. "Sir, would it not be better for us to relocate to Syria perhaps, or even Iran?"

"Yes, of course it would, Ali. But who among you thinks the United States government is going to give you a visa to visit Syria or Iran?"

That broke the tension, and they all laughed. They were, after all, scientists, not terrorists. They were not wanted men, and had no realistic idea of Homeland Security and the transactions it watched. But the irony of it did not escape them, and they enjoyed the same insidious laughter in which conspirators of every age have engaged.

Once that subsided, the Doctor advised them further. "Switzerland will be easy, and attract no attention to yourself, as you will appear to be any other tourist who wants to see the Alps. Those of you who select Venezuela will have to be a bit more creative."

"How so?" one of the managers asked.

"Well, let's just say the government of the United States

doesn't like Hugo Chavez. And it's suspicious of those who want to visit there. You'll be allowed to go. They let presidents and movie stars go; they'll let you, too—if you have a creative reason."

Zawahiri could tell by their expressions that there weren't going to be many takers on Venezuela. *That's best anyway,* he thought. *They're chemists, not spies. I'll not leave too much to their imagination.*

One of the men was curious, however, and indiscreet enough to ask, "Sir, what happens after we leave?"

Zawahiri delayed answering for a moment, deciding whether they should know this. He concluded they should and felt it would keep them motivated for the next five or six years. He pouted briefly, then relaxed his mouth and answered with a question. "How many people are on psychiatric medications? Do you know?"

Ali did. As a pharmacist, he reviewed papers on these medications and their classifications regularly. "Currently, close to 100 million, sir."

"That's worldwide?"

"Yes, sir, with a huge percentage of that in the United States. The last report I saw was nearly $25 billion in sales of anti-depressants and anti-psychotics in the US."

The Doctor let that hang in the air for a moment, then added, "Does that include all age groups?"

Ali answered, "Yes, it does."

With a sinister smile, the Doctor quietly said, "Then, on your television set in Switzerland, our target is that you will be able to watch 50 million Americans die. You are orderly men. But you will witness confusion on the part of the Center for Disease Control. Frankly, they will not be able to put together the common denominators quickly enough to save anyone. People will die in different sections of the country, in different demographic groups, all different ages, all ethnicities, and on different timelines."

No one spoke. It seemed as if all sounds had been suspended in mid-air, even the traffic noises of the city.

The Doctor paused for effect. Looking each man in the eye, one at a time, he added, "It will be months before the Center for Disease

Control manages to come out from under an avalanche of confusion, where there is no apparent weapon. A chemical that leaves no trace. Think of it, gentlemen. The goal is that the United States will have 50 million dead and not even understand why."

He paused for a moment to let that sink in. "And by the time they put it together, narrowing it to pharmaceuticals somehow, there will be an even greater panic as people stop taking *all* their medications. That will create a different type of chaos, and you will have created *the* most successful terrorist attack upon our enemies in the annals of war."

"Chaos?"

"Yes. What happens when someone stops taking psychiatric medications 'cold-turkey?'"

Apparently, these men were in shock at the magnitude of this—either that or they were stonewalling him. The Doctor became angry at their lack of response. "Come! Come! You know the answer to this!" he barked. "Your companies know the answer to this. You've seen the confidential research and test results—you performed those tests in your quality control divisions. And you kept the dirty little secret!" he hissed with venom. "It is *why* I chose you, gentlemen. So, tell me! What happens when patients go off their psych-meds suddenly?"

The Americans in the room could not speak, but each was looking at the floor. The Doctor knew they were fully "in the know" regarding the effects upon the patient who suddenly stopped taking his psychiatric meds. Before he could ask again, the manager from DECU-HEHIZ answered calmly. "The risk of suicide, violence, and even homicide increases dramatically."

"There you have it," the Doctor agreed cheerfully. "So, whether killed in your first attack, or killed later by their own hand, they will suffer. Not to mention those who will die when they stop their heart medications and blood pressure medications because they fear they may be the cause of the devastation." He let that sink in for a moment and finished with, "And that, gentlemen, is your collateral damage."

Though each had been somewhat overwhelmed temporarily by the magnitude and viciousness of the attack their cell would carry out, they got their wits around it fairly quickly. For each was Al Qaeda. And each knew that killing Infidels would honor and please Mohammed, and Allah. Pride returning, they spontaneously rose and embraced the Doctor—one man at a time. And as they looked into his eyes, each man said, "Thank you, sir, for the honor you have bestowed upon me. I will not let you down. Please inform Usama that I will accomplish my assignment in this most holy of wars. May Allah be praised."

A few hours later, sitting at the simple wooden table in the corner of his cramped living quarters, the Doctor opened up his computer and brought up the cube once again. He scrutinized the second game from the top from all angles and smiled. It was labeled "Medical," and the white king was cornered in his own first row. The only piece protecting him was the white queen, whose job it was to move at will and keep her king safe. With the flick of a finger, the Doctor rotated the white queen 180 degrees and moved her to a diagonal, one square removed from her king, in the second row. Behind her, she was backed up by the white bishop. The king was checkmated by his own queen.

And so it will be with the American people—betrayed by their doctors and their drug companies, he concluded. *And no one will be there to rescue them.*

That last thought was not exactly true, and the Doctor knew it. For one company represented that afternoon at the table was the company in which the Doctor himself was a major shareholder. Though present, and part of the cell, DECU-HEHIZ's part would not be the same as the others.

As the men were leaving, the Doctor had asked his man from DECU-HEHIZ to stay behind. The second part of the Doctor's plan was then given to that man. He was to stand down on June 30, 2011, and let his production line run un-tampered-with. There was to be no sabotage there. As the fall-out of the massacre of 50 million Americans would settle down, and the discovery of the complicity of the major American drug companies would be exposed, he knew there had to be someone the United States could turn to. That would be his company, DECU-HEHIZ.

And so now, in the stillness of evening, the Doctor

highlighted the top game, labeled "Money," and set the checkmate there as well. He sat back, satisfied that whether he survived until June 30, 2011 or not, the attack that would end the United States and its dominance would happen, and it would succeed.

The white king—the people of the United States—would be devastated, and their power and will would be annihilated. And dead or alive, that was a victory for the Doctor.

But, if I am alive, he reminded himself, *I will be a very, very wealthy man! Fitting! After all I will have done for Mankind!*

And for the first time in a long time, his gut relaxed. He felt renewed, and he started to whistle.

———————————

The next morning, as he had done so many times before, Ayman Al-Zawahiri removed his few belongings, terminated his lease, and disappeared.

CHAPTER 13

"*F* ool, get your black ass in here!"

Brian knew that voice even before he heard the security screen door being unlocked from the inside. And he knew his father, Roland, had been drinking, by the sound of it. Though it filled him with disgust, he had no fear. For Brian Washington Carver was a very fast runner. He had needed to be to get away from his father when he was in this condition. Now, however, as a grown man, he knew he could take him. Today, he felt only regret for a wasted life, but no particular affection for a man who had never been a father, let alone a husband.

I'm surprised he's even here, Brian thought, as he opened the door and stepped in. The place was as orderly as it could be given that four people lived there, and given the fact that they lived in one of the roughest areas of the District of Columbia. The finely screened door wasn't for decoration in that part of town—as they were in Arabic villages. In Islamic countries, the ornately detailed screens, which masked the interior from the sight of an outsider while still allowing light into the home and allowing the home's inhabitant to look out unobserved, were usually blue and a thing of art. Here, they were a self-defense mechanism of the people imprisoned in their own homes. For the "hood" was a dangerous place for good people.

Brian's family were good people. And it pained him to know his mother had to contend with the hood's violence as a way of life. He knew his scholarship to LA Western, to play football with one of the premier teams in the nation right now, was a chance for him—and his family—to escape this environment. His two sisters had escaped by way of early pregnancies and marriage, leaving their mother to fend for herself with three generations of

71

Carver men. But, for the rest of the family, he was their chance to get a leg up in life.

That's why he knew what was coming next. It was why he had waited so long to come. *All right, let's just get this over with,* he coached himself.

Right then his father, Roland Carver, stepped back into the light to look over his son. Brian could see he was dressed today, wearing a shirt with his name sewn on the left pocket. *I guess the man is working at least, and not just living off Mama's salary at the bank,* he allowed, somewhat begrudgingly.

Brian didn't have to worry about any form of ice-breaker. His father lit into him as soon as he was within range. "Where the hell you been, boy?" Before Brian could even open his mouth, he continued. "Your mother has been worried sick about you. Gone from school for three months! They've been callin' here nearly every damn day!"

Not knowing whether Roland was finished or not, Brian just stood there. Roland wasn't finished. "You get one chance to get your ass out of here and be somebody—one chance—and you screw that up!"

Still Brian said nothing. He knew that anything he might say to this leech of a man would only cause trouble today. So he just stood there, with his jaw set, locking the tongue inside. Brian also knew that his father's rage was not coming from any real concern for Brian, or for his mother even. It was coming from his father's own greed. For Brian knew his father was counting on his son being an NFL player so he could have something to brag about at the bar, and a reason for people to buy him drinks. And he knew Roland was counting on Brian to supply a better meal ticket than his wife Althea had. Out of respect for his mama, Althea, Brian said nothing. For he had known from boyhood who really supported the family and held it together—or tried to at least. Brian loved his mama, and he was here to make things right with her.

"Relax, man, I haven't lost the scholarship. Go back to your game." With that, he brushed his father aside and left him to sit back down on the forty-year-old furniture they'd gotten when Brian's grandfather, Lincoln Carver, had moved in after the death of his wife. Along with the furniture came Pappy, his great-grandfather. It was his dear mother and Pappy to whom Brian was paying homage today. His father and grandfather alternated between anger and apathy, and it was that environment from which Brian had been liberated by his association with a brainy chess player who happened to be one of the best quarterbacks in the region.

Their partnership as quarterback and wide receiver had drawn enough attention to Brian that a scout had offered him a way out. Without hesitation, he had taken the offer. And without hesitation, he was going to stay with Andy Weir—even if it did mean giving up football. Right now, he wanted to accomplish his mission and get out of here.

"Where's Mama?" Brian asked.

Before his father could answer, yet another voice answered from the kitchen. "She's at the Piggly Wiggly getting groceries." Brian was almost relieved to have to face his grandfather as well, and be done with the criticisms and disapproving grunting.

"Grandpa," Brian entered the kitchen, extending his hand.

"What's that?" his grandfather Lincoln retorted, refusing his hand. "Something those *fine* white folk taught you out there in *Los Angeles!*"

"No, sir."

"No, sir," Lincoln repeated mockingly. "They messin' with yo' mind, boy. Whitey is real good at telling *you* what *you* need to do to make it in his world." He paused to let this bit of grandfatherly wisdom sink in. "But they will never let ya win, boy, never. And that's the truth!"

Brian looked away, and then back. "Yeah, I know."

Suddenly Lincoln slapped him in the chest, hard enough to knock him slightly off balance. Brian steadied himself on the kitchen table. "What are you doing, Grandpa? I didn't come here for this."

"What did you come for?"

If nothing else, Brian had been raised by his mother to answer honestly. He did so today. "I came to see Mama, and to ask Pappy something."

For a moment, Brian thought he was going to get one of the thousands of lectures he'd received from this man about how the white man was still suppressing the black man; how the government had botched the military; how the white boys that went to Viet Nam got three months of duty and were sent home to their dear mamas, and the black boys got the privilege of staying the full tour, only to be sent home to their mamas in body bags. He'd heard it so many times, he barely even heard the words any more.

Once, years ago, he'd been confused by this hatred his grandfather had for his country, and for all whites. Everywhere he went, the boys in the neighborhood expressed the same rote hatred. He had asked his mother about it once. She said she couldn't speak for the other boys, but he shouldn't pay much attention to her father-in-law. "He's not been right in the head since the war, Brian." That's what she had said.

Brian was ten years old then, and to this day, his memories of his grandfather were memories of a man either depressed or angry. Some days the man was in near-apathy, and some days he was ranting about the government and what the white man had done to the black man. "He's on medication now, Brian," she had told him. "He's less angry now." Brian suspected somehow that he wasn't really less angry, but rather just subdued by the drugs. Still, his mother had lovingly preached to him, "But don't you be that way, son. You're a good boy. You'll have a good life."

That was the mantra that Brian had clung to—"You'll have a good life." When times were tough, he thought of his mama, and her Herculean efforts to raise him and his two older sisters in a ghetto, in a household with dysfunctional men.

He was feeling a little anxious now. He wanted Mama to be home. And then, there she was, coming up the steps with her arms full of bags. Brian could see her resolved countenance, but she could not see him through the screen. When he opened the door and stepped out to help her, she screamed, first with alarm, and then with joy.

"Baby, baby!! Oh, my beautiful boy is home!" She held his face between her two hands, as she had done since he was a baby, and examined him as if he were a piece of fruit she was considering. "You look okay," she commented, nodding her approval. "I was so worried."

"I know, Mama. I'm sorry I didn't tell you where I was."

"He's been with that white boy, Althea, that's where he's been," his grandfather's voice bellowed from the living room.

Althea looked at him quizzically. "Andy Weir?" She seemed stunned.

"Yeah."

"For how long?"

Quickly he answered, "A few weeks. He's been helping me sort out a few things."

Althea loved her son too much to challenge him on this. And she knew the other men in her family too well to fail to understand why Brian sought coaching and advice from someone else. Any twinge of regret that he hadn't come to her was just that, a twinge. For Althea Carver was realistic enough to know that there is only so much advice a woman can give a young man—especially when that woman, though bright and competent, has justified staying with a man that basically never took care of his family. She did what many women of her race were doing. They were loving and taking care of their families despite the absent dads. They were feeding their families even without financial support.

That was the only thing she agreed with the Reverend Lewis Farracon about. But she was resigned to her lot, and too exhausted to change now. Her hopes were pinned on her son, Brian. "So, are you sorted out?"

Brian smiled. He knew she had just elected to keep this conversation superficial. No one could be hurt that way. *She's a wise one*, he mused.

"Yeah," he started to say, then corrected himself. "Well, not totally. Andy's just been a good friend, letting me hang out."

"You shouldn't be hanging out with his kind, Brian." Brian spun around, not realizing his grandfather had entered the room, or somehow overheard the conversation. "He's not your people. Do ya hear me?"

Althea was looking right at Brian, and her eyes were pleading with him not to pick a fight. He knew that look. And he knew she was right. After all, he'd be gone in a few hours, and Althea would still be there with two angry men. Still looking at his mama, and with his back to his grandfather, he answered quietly, "Yes, sir."

"Humph." Then he was back to the ball game.

Funny, Brian concluded, *there's no difference between the way that jail guard in Pinellas County spoke to me, and the way Grandfather speaks to me.* Suddenly he laughed. *I don't think I'll try to explain that to him though.*

He just shook his head and gave his mama a big hug. She clung to him, refusing to let go, as she always did. The day he'd left for Los Angeles, she had held him so tight, and so long, he thought he'd have to take her with him. Eyes misting, feeling that soft bosom that had comforted him for years, he said, "You're the best, Mama. I'm glad to see you."

Releasing him, she straightened her business attire up a bit and said, "I'll make your favorite." He knew that meant collard greens and fried chicken.

"Thank you. Mama, where's Pappy?"

"He's upstairs taking a nap," she answered. "At least, he was when I went to the store."

"Is he okay?" Brian was worried.

"Yes, yes. He's *old,* but he's fine," she reassured him. "You know him. He doesn't like that kind of talk. So, he stays in his room a lot. Go wake him."

"You sure?"

"Sure. He'll want to see as much of you as he can. Talk to Pappy. *He* won't be mad at you," she joked.

Brian laughed. She was so right about that. Escaping, he bounded upstairs.

If Washington Adams Carver had been asleep, he couldn't have remained so with the sound Brian made going up those stairs. Althea put on her apron and began humming as she started dinner.

"Pappy?" Brian spoke softly as he entered.

"You don't need to whisper, Brian, what with all that yelling goin' on downstairs."

Brian felt guilty now that the family squabble had awakened Pappy. At eighty-five, he should be allowed to rest. "Sorry."

"No need. I'm used to those two by now. I just come up here and enjoy my own room."

Brian looked around. It was the first time he'd been in his pappy's room in a long time. The room had the neatness of a barracks. The bed was meticulously made, the only mussing being the outline of the old man's body where he had been napping.

His foot locker was at the foot of the bed; water glass, glasses, and Bible on the night stand. And his rocker sat by the window. There was no TV. It was austere, but comforting somehow. Below, despite Althea's best efforts, there was no order in the downstairs area. The house was not a mess, but there was confusion there—a disharmony that reflected its occupants. Here, however, was a different story. Pappy was not confused—had never been. His room reflected the quiet dignity of the man.

Though small and frail physically now, Pappy, as Brian called him, was a giant of a man in Brian's eyes. Pappy and Andrew Weir were the two most influential men in Brian's life. And that is why Brian needed to talk to his great-grandfather, Washington Adams Carver.

"Did you quit?" Pappy's question was blunt and unexpected.

"No, sir, just taking a bit of time off."

"Why?"

"I needed time to think." Brian did not want to get into the whole cross-country sojourn, but he did want to get some insight, or maybe just some comfort, from him.

Pappy snorted. "That sounds like something your father would say! Next thing we know, he's gone for two, three months, and your sisters and mother are having a fit."

"No, no, it's nothing like that," he reassured him as he sat down on the bed next to Pappy. "I need to decide whether I want to play football, or do some other career, that's all."

"Football's all you know, son."

"Not anymore, Pappy," Brian said, defending himself gently. "You have to actually take classes out there you know, and pick a major. All that stuff."

"I apologize, Brian. I only meant I thought football was your dream."

"It was. But my eyes have been opened to other possibilities, and I'm looking them over."

"You said *was*."

"I beg your pardon?" Brian queried.

"You said it 'was' your dream. Sounds to me you made up your mind already."

Brian just nodded, looking at this for the first time.

"You planning on doing something with the Weir kid?" The

question was innocent, but Brian's reaction was overly defensive.

"Not you, too! Why is it everyone in this family is so bigoted?" The instant Brian said the word, he knew he had crossed a line black people do not cross with one another, let alone with Pappy, whom he respected so much. Before he could apologize, however, Pappy sat up, swung his legs over the side of the bed, and moved over next to Brian.

He felt Pappy's hand firmly on his knee. "Son?"

"Yes, Pappy." Brian was contrite.

"What's troubling you?"

That opened a floodgate. "Everyone in this family seems to be mad at me for not being in school, and for spending time with Andy."

"Yeah?"

"Yeah, Pappy. But I know why—at least why my father is mad. He doesn't give a rat's ass who I hang with. He never has. All he cares about now is my being his next meal ticket when I'm playing pro ball. Mama hasn't given him enough, and he's counting on me to take care of him. And that's why he wants me back in school. It has nothing to do with my welfare. Hell, he'd have me hanging out with that 18th street gang dealing drugs if it was going to give him something to brag about!"

Pappy squeezed his leg a little harder, but said nothing.

"And Grandfather! All he sees is white versus black. The only reason he doesn't want me hanging with Andy is that he's white. Forget he's my best friend. Forget he got me into shape so that I'd get noticed by LA Western. If it hadn't been for Andy, I would probably be dealing dope in the neighborhood—or scrounging for jobs now and again like my father."

The vehemence of the outburst caused Pappy to withdraw his hand. Without saying a word, he got up, pulled a straight-back chair over in front of Brian, and sat facing him.

"Brian," Pappy began softly, but strongly, "those are true words. I'm sad they are. But they are."

Brian looked up, surprised.

But Pappy wasn't finished. "I'm not concerned about those boys. They're men. They've made their choices. I do wish your grandfather had never gone to Viet Nam, trying to follow in my footsteps. If I could change that, I would. But not for the reasons you think."

"Why then?"

"The drugs, Brian—the drugs. I'm an old man now, and can look back. When you're your age, you got nothing to look back at really. But now, I see."

"What?"

"The drugs started there, son, both in Viet Nam with the military, and with our precious young men and women at home. We've never been the same. So, *that* I do regret. If I could re-enlist, I'd fight the drugs as hard as I fought the Nazis."

"Hmm." Brian was turning this over in his mind.

"But, not because of color, Brian. As far as I can see, white folk are just as messed up as black folk."

This was why Brian loved Pappy. Brian was a man now, and Pappy was the first man he'd actually heard dare to say that "black folk," as he put it, were messed up, too. He'd heard plenty of talk about how wronged they were, and how victimized, but he'd not heard it said quite like Pappy. It wasn't even *what* Pappy had said, as much as it was *how* Pappy had said it.

"I assume, since you came here after disappearing for these many weeks, and scaring your mother, that you want some advice from me. Is that true?"

Brian nodded vigorously. "Yes. Absolutely. I already apologized to them for scaring them. But, truth Pappy, I came to see you."

"I have only one thing to say, Brian."

Brian waited, hopeful.

"I learned one thing for sure during the War." The War was Pappy's term of endearment for World War II, where he had been one of the first black men in America allowed into a combat position. Prior to that, it was blindly and prejudicially assumed "colored" men were inferior somehow, and could not be counted on to fight with courage, skill, and persistence. Washington Adams Carver had not let that deter him. Regardless of what the government said, this was his country, and he knew he had to defend it and win if his own family were to be able to stay free. Washington Carver had not gone to war to prove the white man bigoted and wrong. Washington Carver had gone to war to protect and save his family, and to save the lives of men and women in distant lands who had begged for help.

That right choice had influenced his career, and all his subsequent perceptions. It had influenced his common sense, and set him on the path of a productive, rational life. He was, in fact, the sanest man in Brian Washington Carver's boyhood. He did not have money to speak of; he did not have an estate to leave behind. What he did have to leave behind was a legacy of personal integrity, responsibility, and fair play. He had been grossly and maliciously mistreated by fellow soldiers during the War. Because his purpose was right, however, he had not been degraded. And today, sixty years after his triumphant return to America, he still had the uncommon certainty that what he had done had saved lives.

"Yes, Pappy?"

"Take men one at a time, Brian."

"Sir?" Brian wasn't quite sure he knew what Pappy meant.

"The man in front of you, son. Look at the man, not some 'group.' If you can learn not to classify people by a group, but rather assess them for who they actually are, you will be fine."

"I think I understand."

"I know you do, Brian." Pappy smiled. "I know you do. I've seen it with you and Andrew Weir. I don't know the boy personally, but I know he's white, and that didn't mean a hill of beans to you. He was your friend."

Brian nodded. "That's right."

"Keep it that way." Then Pappy's voice took on a stern edge. "If you don't, son, you'll be bitter like that pair downstairs. They live their lives talking about how they've been mistreated by the *government,* the *military, white people.* When they talk to a man, they don't see the man—they see the group. And if they hate the group, they hate the man."

Brian was quiet, and growing calmer.

"I fought a war long ago to overturn a bunch of thugs who looked at people that way, son. Now, it seems the same type of folk are back out there, bent on killing people, and knocking buildings down. And now, it's your turn. It's your responsibility now. Bigotry is bigotry. And a fool's a fool. And it don't make a lick of difference what color that fool is, Brian. You remember that. And it don't make a lick of difference what religion he is either."

"I will, sir. I do see that."

"The way I look at it, it's purely a question of responsibility. I upheld mine. I got rid of that murdering bunch we faced back then. Your grandfather didn't uphold his. Instead, he made excuses for using drugs, and frying his good brain. To him, it was the white man. As long as he could blame 'Whitey,' he didn't have to face it."

Brian took a long, deep breath and let it out slowly. He was listening.

"Maybe he was right. Maybe white people are all alike. I don't know. But I do know we are responsible for our own condition. And you know what, Brian?"

"What?"

"I decided a long time ago that even if that is true, I'm not going to let that bad white seed infect the black. It's about you, son. It's about who you gonna be, not who you gonna blame for *not* being."

Smiling, Brian was reminded of times years ago when his grandfather, Lincoln, made fun of Pappy for his "philosophizing." "The old fool thinks too much," he used to tell Brian. "Pay no mind. Just take care of yourself; watch your back."

How different can father and son be? he thought. Four men—all carrying the same last name, all sharing genes—and each one lived a totally different life. He was the fourth. He was making choices now that would determine his story. And somehow he knew that story did not include football.

Brian Washington Carver had no way of knowing that this calming conversation in the subdued lighting of afternoon, in a run-down house in the ghetto, was the beginning of the end for an evil man, who saw all people of the West as something vile to be exterminated.

And while that man studied Hitler's tactics of extermination and domination, Brian decided simply to enjoy his family's company, and most especially his wonderful mama's cooking.

Althea, to keep the conversation away from inflammatory subjects, asked her son what he was majoring in while playing football at LAWU. His answer, surprisingly, was, "Marketing, Mama, I'm studying marketing."

"What the hell is that?" his grandfather bellowed. "Sounds

like a white man's word for gettin' us to do what we oughtn't."
Surprisingly, though they lagged for a second, everyone found
that funny. And for a brief moment, the Carver family was
united.

CHAPTER 14

S amir was just unpacking the last box in his new offices overlooking the Sunset Strip. His view of the city of Los Angeles was magnificent on days clear enough to see it. But, for him, that made no difference. Bud Walker himself had extended the lease to ST & Associates, allowing him to use an attractive but small space in one of Walker's holdings.

Since he wasn't using it himself in his WNG activities, Walker, like any good businessman, was happy to have the space occupied. *Besides, having a good PR guy close by can't hurt,* Walker had reasoned. And he was pleased to see what he guessed was a relationship developing between Alicia Quixote, his LA anchorwoman, and Samir. He'd been instrumental after all in getting the two of them together after Samir's ill-camouflaged expression of interest in her. They seemed a good match in Walker's eyes—both superbly ambitious and competent. He'd told his wife that himself.

Excusing himself, he informed Samir he had to get to the studio, and left. And that was perfect timing. For Samir's emails today from his Paris office had notified him to expect transmission in the early evening of some art work for his approval. The email said there would be three attachments, with two of the three being very large files. That email was code from his Al Qaeda cell that the second of the three held the coded message.

Al Qaeda of late had turned to steganography when they had to use the Internet. Short of looking it up in a computer dictionary, almost no one knew the term. Steganography was a picture held within a picture, and had become a method of secret communication in which messages are hidden by disguising their presence in the picture within a picture.

Makkawi was aware that analysts were watching chess sites, hoping to pick up coded messages in the chess moves. Zawahiri himself used that form of communication. Satellite phone was also used. Though Makkawi, Al Qaeda's military commander, preferred to use courier, some messages were too urgent. The one coming through today fit that category. Knowing that the US intelligence agencies would be looking for cryptography and ingenious encryption as a tool of information security, he had recently turned to use of pictures. Since the recipient of these communications was usually their propaganda officer, Samir, it was more appropriate to forward art work and graphics that fit within the legal business activities of a prominent Public Relations firm.

On a fragrant summer evening, just as the lights of the City of Angels were coming on in the dusk, the files came in. Samir opened the first document, casually glancing at a handsome male model caressing the hair of a luscious female model on the second level of the Eiffel tower. The ad, scheduled to run in Le Monde—the longtime top newspaper of France—represented very effectively the smooth whiskey it was promoting. His response was to accept it, issue go-ahead authority, and then file it. Then he opened the second file, knowing full well that this was the steganography file. The insurance company it purportedly represented would have been pleased at the drama of the French coastline near Mont St. Michele. Floundering in the distance was a boat, seemingly unable to make it to the safety of shore. *Fitting,* he mused. Overlaying a program to strip away sections of the picture, pixel by pixel, the hidden message emerged.

Makkawi was insistent upon speaking with Zawahiri, grumbling that he could not raise him on the satellite phone. In a somewhat desperate manner, he had turned to their propaganda officer, Samir, to make his concerns known regarding Zarqawi's death campaign in Iraq. Though the strategy had worked initially, Makkawi was concerned that Zarqawi was indiscriminate about who he killed, and the toll he was taking on Shi'ite and Sunni alike was recoiling on Al Qaeda. All he needed was for the people of Iraq to start cooperating with the US military, and their meager numbers would be depleted. The whole point had been to establish a new base of operation, and now, no matter what the media was reporting, Makkawi felt Al Qaeda was losing ground. This he attributed directly to the brutal killing of indigenous Muslims by Zarqawi. Ultimately, Makkawi decided it was a public relations problem in the making, and that Samir would be the senior Al Qaeda official to inform.

The message that emerged, letter by letter, in Arabic was succinct. "Inform the Doctor that a tape by Bin Laden needs to be released. Offset negative PR of Zarqawi killing Muslims. Redirect attention to anti-US and Israel. Priority—Urgent."

That was all. Samir committed it to memory, and then used the second phase of his computer program to restore the original image, pixel by pixel. As the plea dissolved into the advertisement, Samir knew he would need to locate the Doctor. For he knew Makkawi was right. It might be some time before it unraveled, but it *would* unravel. How much time he had, he could only estimate. *A year—maybe a little longer. That's my evaluation,* he affirmed to himself.

"Maybe longer—if the Doctor can reign in our pit bull."

The next day, Samir flew unexpectedly to New York and went immediately to their safety deposit box at Continental Bank of North America. Using his personal DVD player and earphones, sequestered in the customer room provided for safety deposit box holders, he reviewed the remaining footage of Bin Laden. Many possible scenarios had been recorded by their Film Production chief, Nanda, before his death, and before Bin Laden's death. What Samir was praying for was one that would approximate the world scene sufficiently that they could release it through Al-Jazeera news media. If it were believable enough, Al-Jazeera would run with it—after that, the Western media. His hopes of quashing the public relations debacle Zarqawi was creating were dashed, however. Though they had dramatized, and recorded on audio and video, nearly everything they could think would happen, it had never occurred to them to film something to protect them from the actions of one of their own cell commanders. Nanda would never have thought of this, as Zarqawi had not even been selected to mastermind Iraq—let alone become the superstar of terrorism—when they had taken Bin Laden into their film studio. The decoy films designed to make intelligence agencies believe Bin Laden was still alive, and, more importantly, make the news media believe he was, were brilliant. But there was a gap—a scenario they had not anticipated. And this would cost Al Qaeda.

Samir left the bank's vault subdued, knowing he was going to have to inform both the Doctor and Makkawi of his inability to handle the situation. His responsibilities included taking the military victories that Zarqawi achieved and converting them into public relations victories as well, and, in the cases where the military news was not good, still somehow creating a public relations coup.

He was sweating noticeably as he left the bank. It was an oppressively sultry afternoon in Manhattan, and most New Yorkers were sweating as they made their way up Fifth Avenue, so he did not stand out in the crowd. Samir's discomfort, however, was produced by feelings of impotence with regard to handling this problem. He was not a man who was accustomed to having no ideas or moves that he could make. Dreading being the messenger with bad news, he bolstered himself to tell the Doctor.

A continent away, not even knowing of this situation yet, Ayman Al-Zawahiri would suffer the most from the actions of his hand-picked commander in Iraq. But, that was a year away.

CHAPTER 15

"*H*ey." Brian greeted James and Andy, slipping through the screen door to the cabin on the Cape Fear River and into the congested room in which James and Andy were working.

Andy got up first and embraced his friend the way they did on the football field. "We wondered if you'd be back. Thought maybe you'd headed back to California."

It was the middle of July—that time of year when it is a steam bath in Washington, D.C. and in North Carolina as well. And it was the time of year when football teams were commencing their training, getting ready for the season ahead. For Los Angeles Western University, the coaches were suiting up their best players right now, bringing them back in advance of the school year. For this year, the university was planning on not only taking the Conference title but also receiving an invitation to the Rose Bowl. And for that, they would need Brian Washington Carver.

So, Andy's words were appropriate, though Brian was non-committal about it. He just shrugged his shoulders and turned on his computer. "Nah, I went to see my mama, and Pappy, that's all."

Brian's answer satisfied Andy, but not James. While Brian was gone, James had strongly urged Andy to send his friend back to California—partly because Brian was exceptional at sports and it seemed a waste to James for him to be hanging out with them, playing computer games all day. And partly because James felt that a third person in their close environment was slowing them down. Liking Brian was not the issue. He liked Brian. In fact, he felt like he had two kids of his own here—one brains, one brawn. He just felt uncomfortable somehow, and he felt uneasy having a kid around who seemed to be hiding in computer games, unable to confront and handle his own life.

It was draining too much of James' attention, and distracting him from the urgency of their own mission. As he observed the two of them now—seeing that Andy was not going to change anything in the arrangement—James confronted the issue head-on. "Brian, I know you're assessing a career in football."

"Yeah, man." Brian perked up. "In fact, I've pretty much decided against it."

That was not what James wanted to hear, but he pressed on, swallowing before speaking. "I'm sorry to hear that, son. You're gifted in that area."

"Thanks." Brian grinned.

Amazing! James thought. *I have no idea what to do with that. It's a blessing I don't have kids!* But he'd started it, and he knew, given the stunned expression on Andy's face, that he had to finish it.

Divine inspiration prompted James' next remark. He almost couldn't believe he was hearing himself say it, since he had given no thought whatsoever to how he would respond. "Fine, Brian. That's fine. And it is your choice, son, but..." His voice trailed off for a moment.

Brian took the opportunity to fill the silence with, "You got that right, James. You got that right," he repeated more belligerently.

"Yeah, yeah, absolutely." James regained the initiative. "But there's something else for you to consider, I think."

"What's that?"

Andy seemed to be asking the same question, by the looks of him. Andy, however, trusted James completely, and if James wanted to discuss this—in his house—then Andy was going to hear him out.

"Whether you want to play pro-ball or not has nothing to do with whether or not you should help your school win a trip to the Rose Bowl this year. They are not the same thing. Seems to me, the team needs what you have. And you owe it to them."

"What you *mean*, I owe it to them?" Brian asked testily.

James was into it now, no turning back, so he just plunged ahead. "Honestly, Brian, I think you owe them this last season because they gave you an education. And, NFL or not, they need that Bowl and all it means to them."

Brian was chewing on his lip, eyeing James from his cocked

head. He was nodding now, with that familiar rocking back and forth that accompanied his affirmative nods. "You right, brother. You right. I never even looked at it that way." As he said this, he straightened his head up as if he were looking at the issue straight on now, and not from some cocked angle. "You are *right*."

No one knew what to say after that—least of all James. Andy just waited. He knew Brian, and he knew there was more. That was pretty obvious since Brian looked as if he were about to cry. Incongruous as that seemed, he looked rejected. Finally he said, "I just wanted to stay here and work with you guys on... on..." He was looking for the right words, since he had no idea *what* exactly they were working on. "On whatever it is that you do— are doing."

Understanding now that Brian, like so many of his generation, just wanted to belong and to work with his friend again, James spoke kindly. "I appreciate that, Brian; I really do. Not too many people have been willing to help us at all. But, as good a kid as you are, and as good a friend as you are to Andy, I'm not sure you can help us—other than gopher stuff. And you've got way too much going for you to do that."

It had been a completely honest answer. Brian knew that. So did Andy. What James did not know, however, was what talents and abilities Brian Washington Carver *did* possess. And neither did Brian. All he knew now was that he hadn't left California and tried to save that poor woman for no reason. And he was smart enough to know that this confusion he was experiencing might just be the fog of misdirection blowing off—that his true talents weren't being used well. His next sentence surprised even him.

"Well, why don't you tell me just what you *are* workin' on right now, and you let me be the judge of that."

Now where do I go with that? James looked to Andy for rescue, but Andy was taking stock of his friend. There had been many a time when he led their football team that, while in the huddle, he would see something in the eye of one of his players, and decide on the field to change the play and call an audible. Their coach had always allowed him that latitude because he knew that the Quarterback on the field, if he's good, has a sense of who has his head totally in the game at that moment. He decided, once again, to call an audible.

"James, Brian's right," Andy interjected. "Yeah, he's a football player, but do we really know, or does he even really know, what else he is?"

"What do you mean, Kid?" James asked sincerely.

"Well, when you met me, I knew I was two things—a chess player, and a football player. But we didn't know what else I could be. Working with you brought that out."

"Yeah?" James was trying to put it together.

"So, all I'm saying is, all we know is Brian is a football player."

"And a computer game player," James added somewhat sarcastically. Brian, however, didn't seem to take offense.

"Yeah, that, too," Andy conceded. "But what else is Brian? That's what I'm thinking."

Turning to Brian, Andy silently put the question to him.

"I don't know, man," Brian responded without hesitation. "I just got a feeling you and I are meant to be together. So, why don't you just fill me in on what you are working on, and I'll see if I can help. Okay?"

That was simple enough—a reasonable request from a disarmingly reasonable kid. Now James was nodding. Gesturing to Andy to begin, he said, "Fair enough. Andy, do me the honors of explaining what exactly you and I are trying to do."

It didn't take long, actually, for Andy to explain to Brian that he and James, while still working at the CIA, had theorized that Ayman Al-Zawahiri was playing a multi-leveled type of chess game in order to bring down the United States. Though it had been proved later that he was not really playing chess, it was evident to them he was using chess models and pieces to keep track of his multi-faceted strategies and tactics.

Brian was extremely attentive when Andy laid out his final conclusions that there were eight arenas in which Zawahiri was playing—and that they were in a sequence of importance. He seemed fascinated by Andy's conclusion that Zawahiri had duped the world into thinking this was all about religion and military, when his real game was money and domination—and that he was using propaganda in a unique way to brainwash the American people remotely.

James was certain he was creating, or had created, a Fifth Column inside the United States, whose purpose would be to sabotage internally, especially to break the solidarity and unity of the country.

Brian was nodding, as if he followed that reasoning especially well.

Andy concluded by telling Brian that they felt Zawahiri's main avenue of attack would be using propaganda to create fear, in order to influence the sociological factors that the United States was struggling with, and to increase the demand for drugs, thus ultimately dominating financially—weakening the American people physically and mentally at the same time.

Though he couldn't elaborate on how Zawahiri would do that, or who would help him, Andy finished by telling Brian James' latest theory that the White King of these seeming chess games—the opponent Zawahiri wanted and indeed needed to destroy—was not the President of the United States but rather the people of the United States themselves. And that he and James were trying to warn the American people that they were the target of Al Qaeda's strategy, and that the attack would come from within.

"That makes total sense, Andy," Brian said, without even raising an eyebrow. "You're right, James," he added, turning to James.

James was taken aback that Brian understood all this, let alone that he seemed to just slide right into the analysis. He didn't know what to say. *Did I miss something here?* he asked himself.

But Brian didn't need an invitation to participate. He had been engrossed. Listening to Andy now was no different from listening to Andy when he and Coach used to plan out strategies to defeat their opponents back in Arlington, Va. And he was used to this type of evaluation from the brilliant coaches he was experiencing at LA Western.

One other thing though made it possible for Brian to understand this, and to complement it—something neither James nor Andy would ever have thought of. Brian played computer games, constantly. Andy and James had observed this when he first arrived at James' place. They had assumed he was just hiding—playing games to avoid facing his life, and the confusions in it right then. Later they concluded he had somehow turned into one of those game junkies who waste away their life sucked into the computer.

That was not the case, as it turned out. Brian just happened to be one of those under-rated kids who liked to play games; and he liked to play them on the computer. The more challenging they were, the better he liked it. What neither James nor Andy could have known was that Brian had evolved into a very high level of strategic thinking. He won the games because he could strategically think with the game, and he *knew* what the game's creator was hiding, and what he was doing to make the game difficult. Knowing that, Brian won.

But for now, not even Brian knew how important that developed skill would be. All he knew right now—on this very sticky night, as mosquitoes whose wing-wash could flip a Cadillac attacked the screen door—was that he was tracking with his friend, and he felt he could help.

"Yup, you're right." He opened up the vintage refrigerator James still nursed along, took out a soda, and popped the top. Nearly downing it in one swig, Brian added, "To take down the President or the country, you take down the people." He plopped down onto the sofa, nodded his head as if agreeing with his own thoughts, and then added easily, "But there's more. In football, Andy, how many times you get sacked?"

That question came out of nowhere and caught Andy completely off guard. He thought for a moment, smiled, and answered, "Enough." Then, seeing Brian wanted a less flippant answer, he conceded, "Not many."

"Bet your white ass!" Brian exclaimed. "They 'sacked' me!" He laughed. "I was the one the ball was going to. If I didn't get past those safeties, they had a license to tackle me right after I caught the ball. Now that's where the real pressure is! Give me five, bro!" he said, slapping Andy's open hand with zest. "You had protection. The receiver has to catch that thing and immediately get decked, or he has to slip away and outrun those fools."

Now it was Andy's turn to "get it." James, however, was clueless. He was completely out of the loop as these two talked their game. Seeing that, Brian embellished a bit. "Yeah, it is simple, my man. Just look to see where the ball is goin'. That's who they will tackle."

He let that sink in for a moment. James ruminated on it for a moment and assumed Brian's comment confirmed their theory about the White King.

What Brian said next, however, shocked them both. Working in the Ivory Tower of analysis, they had missed this. "It's brilliant, really. The ball is going to our generation, Andy. You know, 'pass the baton' and all that. They'll come after the young." Nodding vigorously now, he seemed to endorse his own theory with, "Yup, they'll smash the young!"

Andy was grateful the screen door was closed, because as wide open as James' mouth was, it would have taken in a whole swarm of mosquitoes. The truth of it hit James so hard his endocrine system didn't even have time to send out any adrenalin. The game had just changed in front of him, and a new picture was emerging.

Andy was on it first. "How do we stop them?"

"For starters, stop playin' chess," Brian answered quickly. He rose, crossed the room to his computer, and swiveled the monitor toward James and Andy. "*We* don't play chess." He said it kindly, but it was pointed at Andy.

"What?" Andy didn't get it right away.

"It's video, baby, video! And when you graduate, it is computer games!"

James was a little blinder here than Andy, but in looking at what Brian had just suggested, he figured it out faster. "You know, Andy, he's right."

"How so?" Andy challenged.

James laughed. "We missed it, Kid. And we would have gone right on missing it!" He turned to Brian with a new respect. "Amazing, Brian, thank you."

Brian nodded, smiled, and finished off his soda.

Seeing that Andy had missed something, James added, "Andy, chess is your personal preference. Quarterbacking is your preference. These involve intellect—a different type of intellect."

Suddenly, Brian clapped his hands, as if applauding the conclusion James had just reached. "But not me, Andy. You two don't exactly represent America, you know." That was an unusual truth, but it made Andy smile. He knew that to be true. Brian continued. "Let's keep this in football terms, okay?"

"Okay. Sure."

"The key is—don't resist! Let me show you."

"Please." Andy had been a great quarterback, but he was humble enough to realize now that his friend had just had four years playing with some of the best talent in the country, coached by some of the best. Brian knew a great deal now, and it was time for Andy to catch up.

"When you passed the ball, Andy, there was heavy coverage on me."

"That's right. They knew you were my receiver of choice."

"Damn right! Here's the point. If I resist the fact that they are going to be all over me, they block it or intercept it. And no first down for our side. But, get this," he continued triumphantly. "If I go with it, contribute to the coverage—remember you have your eyes on *me*—I catch it!" He grinned.

"All right, all right. I follow you. You're saying we need to *not* resist."

"That's right, my man. You been doin' a lot of that. Seems like the whole government's been doin' that, too."

"Yeah, so we don't resist. We contribute." Andy's voice exposed his uncertainty.

"But, how do we contribute?" James and Andy asked at the same moment. "How do we 'go with' the Fifth Column attack?"

"Simple," Brian answered. "Do what kids do."

"What? Drugs?" Andy scoffed.

"No, Andy, not the stupid stuff that losers use. Games, man, games—computer games." Brian waited for a moment for them to digest this. "Once you find out where they are attacking and how—how they are planning on 'sacking' us Americans—you make a game. Teach us through your game. Seems to me that's better than trying to get those old farts in Washington to figure it out, or some pinhead do-gooder to listen to you."

Brian persisted, admiringly. "Andy, it's been awhile. But one of the things I remember most about playing with you was how much Coach trusted you to just look at the line, and call the play yourself. You wait for the guys up in the box to figure it out, you would have been sacked a whole lot more—and you wouldn't have kept your gorgeous puss, not to mention we wouldn't have scored! Remember how many times we won running that Buttonhook? That was a beaut, man. Just when I'm turning to catch it, and they commit to the tackle, I'd fake, and I'd turn and run away downfield. It always worked, bro', because they went where they thought you were going to throw it. Only we surprised 'em!" He cuffed Andy playfully on the side of the head.

Andy was laughing now. He felt such a sense of release, as if he'd just been freed from a mental prison. "Amazing stuff, Brian. Amazing. I got to look at this a bit, but thank you, man. This was an eye-opener." With that, he got up and almost apologized. "I gotta hit the john."

Brian turned to James as if to check his pulse on the whole revelation. James was just sitting there, scrutinizing Brian. He was looking at him as if he didn't recognize him. Suddenly Brian asked, "What you lookin' at, man? You look like you examinin' some bug under a microscope or something."

"Sorry, Brian, sorry. I meant no offense."

"Then none taken, James—none taken."

"I need some air," was all James could say.

James didn't hear the screen door open behind him. Thankfully, the mosquitoes had given it a rest, or been scared off by the citron candle James had lit. He didn't know how long he'd been sitting on the porch step, but it must have been awhile.

It had been a long time since he'd had his head realigned so severely. There were times—working a problem for the CIA—when he had had to assume an entirely different viewpoint in order to make sense of something. He'd done that right after 9/11, with the information the Mossad had given to him about Ayman Al-Zawahiri.

This was different though. He felt he had severely misjudged Brian. *No, not misjudged. More like underestimated,* he reflected. *He's really on to something here.* "Suppose the target *is* his generation—

95

not the American people as a whole," he said out loud to no one. *That would explain why no one listened when Andy and I knocked on the door of just about everyone. They were too old to see it. They were the wrong target.*

"We always were an arrogant bunch," he mused.

"What's that?" Andy asked.

"Nothing, Kid. Just thinking out loud, is all." He motioned for Andy to sit beside him.

"Where's Brian?"

"Inside, playing a game."

"For real?" James just shook his head.

"Yup, says it challenges his mind." Andy paused a moment, then added, "He also reiterated that you're right. He should go back and finish this season. So, he's leaving at the end of the week."

James let out a big sigh and shook his head from side to side. Andy knew something was up.

"What?"

"Well, Andy, I've been thinking Brian's on to something. And if he's right, I sure as hell don't know how to reach kids—you either. No disrespect, Kid."

"None taken."

"So, I'm thinking you and I better pack up and go with him. I got a hunch we're going to need what he knows."

"You're not joking."

"Nope. He may be our best chance. I just got a feeling about this."

Now it was Andy's turned to exhale. "Wow!"

"What?"

"Telling Brian's no problem. He'll be thrilled. I just *really* don't know how to break this to Mom!" Telling Kelly about their adventures and future plans had been almost a running joke between these two. It had begun when Andy decided to help James in the first place, back in 2001. Not knowing how to tell his mother he would be working with the CIA, James had offered his help. Both remembered how that had turned out.

Five years later, with memories obscured by the apparent tranquility of their lives today, they could laugh about the anxiety their decisions must have caused Kelly, and how well she had played the role of the protective mother. But this new scheme was so absurd, they both started to laugh. It was mild at first, and then finally convulsive. Clearly, they needed to blow off some steam, and laughter was the right thing.

Regaining control, James offered, "This time, Kid, let me do the talking. I've got a good idea I think." Rising, he patted Andy on the head. "You're a good kid."

CHAPTER 16

James took a long, deep breath before he knocked on the door. The neighborhood was as familiar as his own had been. He'd spent so much time here in the last four years that he knew every street light and garbage can. It was one of those Washington, D.C. July evenings when the air doesn't move and the humidity is so oppressive emotions bubble to the surface.

He'd heard once, years ago, that the murder rate in the city nearly doubled on these hot summer nights. And he knew why. People already on edge, and unstable, were pushed over by their inability to shake the oppression. He was sweating, as usual, but tonight it was from fear, for he didn't exactly know what he was going to tell Kelly. Quite the contrary, he was more or less winging it. He'd told Andy he had a plan—convincingly, too. At least, it was convincing enough that Andy had let James come up here by himself. Truth was, he *didn't* have an idea—at least not one he knew she'd accept.

The longest journey starts with a single step, he told himself, quoting from some Hallmark calendar he'd seen. *Here goes.*

He saw the hall light come on before he saw Kelly appear in the screen door. She didn't ask who was there. Having heard the knock, Kelly peered out the window, spotting James' Mustang parked out front.

"James, my goodness, come in," she exclaimed, opening the door. "What on earth are you doing around here so late?"

"Well…" he hesitated. "I was hoping to catch you. I'm sorry to just show up, you know, without a call or something."

"James, that is never a problem, you know that," she said. "Let's go to the kitchen. I've got an extra fan there, and I'll fix us some iced tea."

"Great," he agreed, grateful to have a few more minutes to get oriented and come up with a foolproof plan.

Her hair was pulled up to allow some air to reach the back of her neck, and she had on a youthful, yellow cotton sundress. *She looks so fresh,* James thought. *I don't know how she does that.*

Handing him a tumbler full of ice and fresh-brewed peppermint tea, she sat down in the chair opposite him. Right then and there James knew that the only foolproof plan was simply "the truth." Kelly had never been one to bullshit. And he saw no reason to be condescending now.

"Okay if I just set this on the table?" he asked nervously.

Laughing, she replied, "Uh, yeah, James—it's Formica!"

He laughed, too, scratching his head and pulling his shirt away from his chest, as if that would enhance his breathing. It did cool him down though, and he finally began. "Kelly, Brian's decided to go back to Los Angeles and finish this last football season."

"That's great, James. Congratulations on getting through to him," she added admiringly. "I hope you got him to complete the school year as well as football season."

"Oh, yeah, sure," he answered somewhat vaguely. Actually, it had never crossed his mind. Events had turned so suddenly that James only remembered knowing he needed Brian to help *him*— in addition to whatever else Brian did at that university.

He must have paused a bit too long because Kelly was now prodding him. "James?"

He looked up from his glass, and straight into her green eyes. "Huh?"

"You stopped. You just stopped talking."

"Oh. Sorry."

"James?" The way she said it made him know the jig was up. "You didn't come all the way here to tell me just that, did you?"

"No, Kelly, I did not."

She let out a deep sigh and asked, with resignation in her voice, "All right, what is it? What are you and Andy into now?"

"We're going to California with Brian." He said it; then he just waited. *Some plan, you moron,* he chastised himself.

"Well, okay." She smiled and added, "How long are you going to be gone?"

Seizing on that, James walked through the door Kelly had

opened. "Now that's what I came to talk with you about. We don't know exactly. It could be short; it could be long."

"How long is long?" she asked, afraid of the answer.

"Long."

He let that sink in, watching her closely. "Brian has stumbled onto something that may help Andy and me—so we've decided to move out there *temporarily*, so that we can be near him."

She looked down at her glass, nervously squeezing more lemon into it. Without looking up she asked, "Is it really necessary?"

"It is, Kelly, it is." There, he'd said it. He knew she was wise enough and brave enough to ask the question she didn't want to ask, and accept the answer she didn't want to hear. She hadn't disappointed him. She squinted, as if to stifle a tear. Very quickly, he said what he had really come here to say. "And we want you to come with us."

James was proud of himself for conceiving the idea of getting Kelly out of this house, with its treacherous memories. He actually felt time in the sun away from "Disneyland on the Potomac"—his less-than-affectionate name for Washington—would be good for her. And he guessed she could use her beauty skills anywhere. He was optimistic she would see it his way. That's why he wanted to leave Andy in North Carolina and handle her himself. The less mother and son issues to present themselves the better, he had reasoned. He had reasoned correctly.

"Are you suggesting I move out there with you two?" she asked, more to confirm than understand.

"Absolutely."

She just looked at him.

"Absolutely, Kelly. I hear LA's a great city." She looked at him skeptically, which made him laugh, and add, "Okay, okay, it's not such a great city. I admit. But wouldn't it be fun for a short time to try something new?"

"What would be fun, James, would have been for Andy to have continued on the path he was on before 9/11—to live the life he'd created." James looked somewhat fidgety. She continued before he could protest or debate. "But none of us has that luxury now, do we, James?"

Resigned, and subdued, James calmly answered, "No. I wish we did, but we don't. You know that, Kelly. You've always known that. It's why you let Andy work with me in the first place."

Tears welled up now in her eyes, as she nodded her understanding. He finished softly, firmly, "We've got just one shot at this, Kelly. That's lousy god-dammed news, I know, but it's the truth. We miss here, and we lose our life as we know it."

Before he could say anything else, Kelly raised her hand and gestured for him to stop. "I know that, James. I didn't know it that day Andy dragged you home to strong-arm me into that project of yours. But I knew it by the election last year. We're losing, aren't we?"

He nodded, waited a bit, and then added, "Right now, yes, I think we are. I think the enemy's cleaned our clock. Their propaganda machine defies imagination. Nothing I ever saw in the Cold War comes close."

Pouring another glass of tea, Kelly asked, "And you think Brian can help?"

James smiled. Kelly knew that particular smile. He looked like a man with a secret, who was caught with it before he could speak. "Yes, ma'am, I believe he can! And that is why I want you to come to Los Angeles with us. This is a show you won't want to miss!"

"You are such a *recruiter*," she teased. She paused for only a moment, then, extending her hand across the table, she shook James' hand and said, "Where do I sign?"

CHAPTER 17

This is a daunting task, Samir reminded himself, as he reviewed his next Public Relations moves. Though the world's media did not report it as such, and America's political leaders seemed unable to grasp it, Al Qaeda was suffering extremely in their military fronts, in their intelligence activities, and in their financial resources.

Looking over the number of accounts he could no longer access, he was grateful the Doctor had created a warning system for any of his men who might use pass codes to secure money from Al Qaeda's accounts. One by one, for four years, the intelligence communities specializing in finance had been locating and seizing accounts and the millions contained in them. Any Al Qaeda operative authorized to access the accounts, who tried to do so, was being apprehended. The failsafe was the Doctor's warnings that came in steganography to Samir, and through chess sites for the others.

Fortunately for the Doctor, Samir's activities were self-sustaining, financially. Infusions of money for military activities were not necessary here. The reality was ST & Associates and its owner, Samir, had become independently wealthy through their many-pronged, and very effective marketing and PR avenues.

Zarqawi's rabid attacks, however, were providing a great intellectual challenge to him, as he tried to figure a way to turn the butchery into a propaganda victory. What he settled on that day would confound governments for the next three years, and create confusion and complexity where there actually was none. *The simple truth is, Zarqawi is an animal,* Samir thought. *I can disarm him by a diversion. I'm probably the only one who can.*

The strategy he settled on was to divert attention away from Abou Al-Zarqawi and his bloody but ineffective recruiting efforts in Iraq, by placing the media's attention elsewhere. This proved fairly simple, as American politicians—for some unfathomable reason—had decided to launch presidential campaigning right after the next year's mid-term elections. Samir had no idea why they would waste such money and energy, but he knew it was a tremendous advantage for him.

For all of them—senators, congressmen, governors—would be looking for something to complain about, to stake a claim about, to roust an opponent with. His stealth media attack upon their reason had so energized their political testosterone that none of them seemed to have any idea anymore *who* their enemy was. *And that,* he joked, *is a masterful Fifth Column. Since they can't think for themselves, I'll do their thinking for them.*

That thought, never even voiced, was as bold a tactic as any military commander was deploying in the Afghanistan and Iraq theatres. *Speaking of that . . .* He jumped up and grabbed a notepad. *I'll get Alicia to change the term from "campaign" to "war."* Pouring himself a sherry, he laughed and settled in at his desk. *That should confound their generals. It's a little hard to report information on a military campaign when the political leaders think it's a war. They'll misevaluate the significance of everything that happens from here on in Iraq. That ought to help our little superstar,* he concluded malignantly.

The second phase of his plan involved turning the world's attention to the political chaos that would naturally unfold in Iraq. *Stupid Americans! Don't even know that when you set people free who have never been free—and you do it too fast—they can't handle it. It backfires.* Samir knew that Al Qaeda's only hope militarily now in Iraq was that the political chaos that would develop with feuds and mistrust between tribes would also devour the finances and political resources of the United States and Great Britain.

His cell phone rang. Alicia Quixote, anchorwoman for WNG in Los Angeles, was smitten with Samir. He knew it was her by the special ring he'd programmed into his LG. He certainly didn't want to keep this lady waiting, for it was this "mark" who would profoundly influence public opinion. Believing she was a developing journalist and newswoman, she was in fact a mere pawn in Samir's game.

She is so dim, he thought disparagingly, as he answered her call. "Alicia, dear, how are you? Are we on for dinner?"

She must have said yes, for Samir closed his computer and started to straighten up his wet bar. "Yes, our favorite. I'll meet you there. Half-hour?"

It was done. Alicia had suggested they eat quickly between shows at Ugo's on Santa Monica Blvd. Hovering between Hollywood and West Hollywood, it was a very popular place—not just for the locals but also for celebrities who liked to remind themselves of what it was like in New York. For all of them seemed to either miss the neighborhood coffee houses where they could hang out and "be seen," or they pretended to. Either way, it was good for Samir.

He had taken the opportunity to have Alicia introduce him to some of the more vocal and influential of Hollywood royalty who came in to dine, and he had fed them with marketing buttons and propaganda bites that went unrecognized by the unwitting star. After his phenomenal success in planting the button "Viet Nam" with Alicia's boss, Bud Walker, he had seen Walker take that button and turn it into an almost insane equation. The Doctor and he both knew that Viet Nam and Iraq were not the same, but brilliant marketing and PR is brilliant marketing and PR. Unwittingly, Walker himself had set the nation on a path of irrationality whereby they were not looking at actual facts and situations in present time, in the context of the present. They were looking at those facts in the present through the filter and mindset of the past. It was genius actually—to foster so much mental confusion. And it camouflaged the actual present-time intentions of Al Qaeda. America was falling for it. Samir had estimated that by 2007, the market penetration would be at "saturation," and Americans would be virtually unable to differentiate between Viet Nam and Iraq.

"Time to give my insipid friend another morsel," he told himself out loud. This one would be an appetizer, albeit a juicy one. It would be the public relations foreplay for the assignment he had been directly given by the Doctor in Panama City. Success in that would mean a huge success militarily in the coming years. So tonight, he planned to insert a gradient step, which at the very least would foster divisiveness—and at the very best would destroy the winnowing solidarity of Americans. He needed Americans weak and succumbing before he planted the one that would truly devastate the country by 2007, and would render the Administration virtually impotent.

Though Samir's taste in clothes was distinctly European—most especially Italian—he knew Alicia admired the Banana Republic look. With that in mind, he selected Dockers and a khaki safari shirt. The night was warm, so he rolled up his sleeves and opened the top two buttons in the hopes of igniting her Latin fires. The lights of the city were beginning to filter through the late-afternoon smog as it dissipated. Turning off the lights, he got into his yellow Porsche and drove down Sweetzer Ave., parking behind Ugo's.

She was already there when he entered. He almost missed her, as she was deep in conversation with an A-list actor, who spent most of his days now agitating against the current political regime. *Perfect,* Samir thought. *Let's see if this sycophant will take the bait.* As he waved casually to her, and walked to her table, he couldn't help but reflect that this was working out better than expected. If he could get the actor to take up the marketing button he was about to punch up, Alicia would pounce on it, too. *After all, she's got that beast of a newsroom to feed, and needs special reports to build her ratings. She'll be looking for something to report on as her own.* And what better way than using an unsuspecting celebrity. It would be good for his publicity; it would attract the "E" network crowd as well; and it would look like she had a scoop. After all, Alicia Quixote was the darling of WNG West Coast. She was also ambitious. And she had her sights on the Big Apple.

"Hello there." Samir caressed her hair as he slid into the seat beside Alicia, and opposite the unwitting actor. *I knew I liked this restaurant for a reason,* he thought. *They put the tables close together, like New York or Paris. Such pretense!* Extending his hand to be officially introduced, he said, "Hello, I'm Samir."

Alicia completed it with, "Samir, meet Thom."

"Thom, my pleasure."

Thom never knew what hit him. Congenial, intelligent, and lively, he was a nice guy, who, unfortunately for America, was stuck in the past. He was more committed than most—certainly not apathetic like a preponderance of baby-boomers. He believed he was a reasoning individual. And, like so many stars, he believed that what he thought mattered. It was not what he knew that would trip him up. It was what he had *opinions* about—unsupported by fact—that would entangle him.

He had no way of knowing that he was sitting opposite Al Qaeda's senior propaganda officer. He had no way of knowing that the man opposite him knew more in his baby finger about the mind than Thom knew, despite his ability to compellingly create characters—despite the Oscar nominations.

For Samir had been trained by Ayman Al-Zawahiri. Though his understanding of the mind was thankfully incomplete and sometimes inaccurate, he knew enough to be out in front of the intelligence communities, eluding them at every turn. And he knew enough to straightjacket the naïve American.

This will be fun, Samir thought, as he smiled and ordered one of Ugo's famous omelets.

"Samir, where are you from?" Thom asked. His smile was insincere, but it did offset his dimples.

Condescending prick! Samir returned the smile. *You won't like the answer, you arrogant bastard.* "Originally, from Egypt. But I was educated here in the United States, and have lived until recently in France."

Not even noticing the origin Egypt, Thom continued the social chat. "France, huh. Paris?"

"Of course."

Thom didn't know what to do with that, so he continued, checking to see if Alicia was responding to him appropriately. "Yes, yes, it's a magnificent city—so intellectually honest. My wife and I adore it."

"I'm sure," Samir agreed, pleasantly. "I enjoyed my time at Princeton, but Paris has always held a fascination for me."

Thom nodded complete agreement as he sipped his herbal tea, adding a bit more honey. "Yes, she's a seductive city. When were you at Princeton?" The actor asked it more to be polite than to run a time line.

"Ten years ago. I did my graduate work in Public Relations there."

Alicia decided to enter the conversation at that point. "Thom, Bud Walker feels Samir is the best in his field. You two should exchange cards, as he might be very helpful to you in the future. Who knows?"

"Right, absolutely," Thom agreed. He had a press agent, but he did have to confess he was intrigued by this confident man. And it wouldn't hurt to have a public relations person who was "in" with the news media. After all, he had a big picture due out next summer. And then Thom fell into the trap. With no prompting whatsoever, he asked the question that was inevitable. "Alicia, what are you working on now?"

She brightened up immediately. "So glad you asked. I've really got my attention on this campaign in Iraq, and how it's all going to play out. My gut tells me we aren't being told what we need to be by Bush."

"So you're looking into that?" Thom asked.

"Yeah, absolutely. You know, Thom, that I do more than just anchor?" He nodded that he did. She smiled. "My passion is special investigations and journalistic pieces. Bud started me there, and that's what I love."

Thom instantly responded with a cliché. "Awesome."

"And that's what I need my friend, Samir, for," she said, turning toward him and patting him on the back. "He's helping me to get perspective, insights we Americans might miss. You know."

"Absolutely, absolutely. I can see how important another perspective would be," Thom concluded.

And for that condescension, my friend, you get to be complicit, Samir thought. *Now that the foreplay is over, let's see how you handle the real screwing.*

Three years earlier, Samir had learned something very valuable in his game of mind control. He learned that the term Public Relations is very innocuous. What no one really understood was that it was mind control, practiced well or poorly, practiced intentionally or innocently. And he had received quite an education from the Doctor.

He remembered the lesson vividly, as they sat together in a

café in Paris. "People get stuck in the past, Samir," the Doctor had begun. "I do not know the mechanics of how it happens, but I have seen it enough to know you can cultivate it."

Samir had been attentive, and the Doctor had persisted. "When bad things happen to a group of people, they get stuck right there—as if they were frozen in the moment it happened."

"Really?"

"Yes, Samir, and they can't get unstuck unless they are released somehow." He had paused for a moment to see if Samir was getting the implications of this on Public Relations. He was.

"And now they see the bad things again in all things they are viewing, whether they are there or not." Looking at this phenomenon himself, Zawahiri had added, "It's a type of insanity, I think—to think that something happening today is the same as something which happened forty years ago. Wouldn't you agree?"

"Yes, I can see that."

"Well, Samir, here's what you can do with this piece of insight I've given you." Samir was all ears. "I have no idea how to fix it. I have just observed that it is a trait of humans, and I have learned to exploit it."

Samir's memory was very vivid on this subject because that was the day the Doctor had provided Samir with the tool to plant the "Viet Nam" button into Bud Walker's mind. Most of the reactions of media and politicians alike were coming from this insane equation he had persuaded people to run. Viet Nam equals Iraq. It was diabolically deceptive. And it was confounding the American and British military. They were keenly aware they were in the year 2005, fighting in Afghanistan and Iraq. They were aware today that they had two military fronts open there. They had two campaigns going. And they found themselves reporting to petulant, argumentative politicians that were unconsciously reacting as if they were in the year 1968.

Yes, Zawahiri had stumbled on an oddity in the mind. Unfortunately for the free world, no one in politics or government had bothered to explore the area. And it was through this blind spot that Al Qaeda was attacking—at least if Ayman Al-Zawahiri was spearheading it.

Tonight, Samir would confuse the area even further.

Thom did exactly what was anticipated. "So, Samir, what perspective do you have on this whole debacle in Iraq? What's your take on our invasion without cause?"

He had assumed Samir saw it the way he did. It was a natural mistake for a movie star to make. Thom spent most of his time pontificating to crew members and actors on his movie sets. Occasionally, he'd appear on a talk show to promote a new movie, and like any good patriot, he'd find a way of inserting his opinion about Iraq. He was good at it. He got a lot of extra applause for it. And it guaranteed him other bookings. So, he was keenly interested in anything this guy Samir might give him.

Smiling, Samir slid into it. "Thom, I'm glad we're talking. You have no idea how much of a relief it is to talk to someone in this country who 'gets it.'"

"I bet," Thom responded, accepting the compliment.

Touching Alicia ever so gently, he continued. "Bud Walker thought Alicia would be good for me. And he was right. She doesn't accept oatmeal handed out to her."

"Pablum," Thom interjected.

"I beg your pardon?"

"You said oatmeal. I think you meant pablum," Thom corrected him.

Samir laughed. "Yes, yes, of course. Forgive my metaphors. I get my languages mixed sometimes." He looked to Alicia to confirm she was enjoying this joke at his expense. She was.

"All that aside, there is one thing I think you are confusing."

"What's that?" Thom asked eagerly, leaning in.

"This is just my perspective of course," he said, with false humility.

"Of course, of course. Tell us."

Sighing, he spoke as if they had dragged it out of him. "Well, your terms. I think you have the terms wrong." Before they could ask, he added, "By that I mean you refer to the *campaign*, or the *fighting* in Iraq. You should be referring to it as the War in Iraq."

"Really?" Thom was looking at this, really scrutinizing it.

"Certainly. By definition, it is a war that the United States is waging inside Iraq, and your people would be better served to call it that. I don't know what they feel they gain by calling it a campaign, but I can guess they think it has some PR value."

"Sons-o-bitches!" Thom exclaimed. "Those criminals think they can dupe us. That's it. If they devalue the war, calling it fighting or a campaign, they think we'll be more subdued about it—not take it so seriously."

"I wouldn't know their intentions, Thom," Samir said, sounding sincere. "I only know what I see from the Public Relations angle."

"But you're right, Samir," Alicia chimed in. "That makes total sense. I just knew they were hiding something from us. Well, there you have it. They've been telling us a partial truth, hiding the real weight of it from us."

"Bingo!" Thom was buying it now, too.

"They want their war, and they want us all to go along with it. So they're duping Congress into thinking it's just a battle, or a, what was it you called it again, Samir?"

"Campaign."

"Yes, yes, a campaign. I like that word. I've used that word on the air." She savored it a bit. Then abruptly, she looked at her watch. "My God, I have to run. I've got to be back at the studio. Sorry to stick you with the bill."

Before Samir could say "no problem," Thom reached across and took the check. "It's on me. This has been awesome! It would be my privilege."

Samir assented. *Pompous,* he thought, as he suggested Thom and he continue their conversation a bit further. "No need for us to rush off just because the lady has to work!"

Kissing her discreetly on the cheek he said, "Have a great show." She winked at Thom, and threw off the suggestion, "Enjoy yourselves."

"Right. I agree. I've got some time." Thom seemed to relish the idea of talking further with Samir. Being naturally curious—as he was a gifted actor—he wanted to see if his ideas about Europeans, most specifically the French, were accurate. "Do you like America, Samir?" he asked very directly, never taking his eyes off the man opposite him.

That was what Samir wanted. It was an open door to the answer he had been dying to give. After all, the Doctor had specifically told him to compromise some Hollywood types. And tonight he saw an opportunity to add Thom to his "Unwitting" list. Leaning in, he said, in confidence, "I like working here fine, but I've not quite adjusted to…" He was about to say American Imperialism, but checked himself before he used the term. *Too much of a cliché. This guy is too smart for that. Use something else.*

He continued, looking right and left to make sure no one was listening. "Forgive me, I mean no offense."

"None will be taken, I assure you." Thom leaned in. "I'm sincerely interested in your viewpoint."

"This American conceit of wanting a melting pot is a bit grating." He stopped and let that settle in. Thom looked a bit puzzled, so he drew the picture more clearly for him. "Yes, you seem to expect all people to want to be like you—to just jump into the caldron and be happy in the melting pot. It smacks a bit of superiority—yes, that's the word."

"How so?" Thom liked a good discussion.

"Well, doesn't the melting pot idea imply that Americans are superior, and everyone should want to give up the identity of their culture, and merge into the greater American one?"

"I don't know," Thom said slowly. "I've always rather thought we merged our cultures and became one stronger one."

"Hum…" Samir's tone implied doubt. Thom took the bait. "You disagree?"

"I don't disagree, Thom, that you would feel that America got stronger with this melting pot. It did. But I'm afraid those who came here and who were dissolved in it got weaker. I'm not sure it's such a fair trade for them."

Thom rubbed his chin thoughtfully for a minute. Something inside made him feel as if he were being criticized, but Thom prided himself in being open-minded, and he could see the viewpoint, just a bit at least. Sincerely, he questioned, "All right, all right. I never looked at it that way, but I can see how someone coming here might feel put down."

"Yes."

"So, what do you think we should emphasize? I mean, that would be more fair?"

Gotcha! Samir was salivating now. "Well, it's just my opinion, of course, but I relate to those who promote multiculturalism—who are happy with and promote the real diversity of the immigrants to the United States. Just a thought, of course, but I think it is more consistent with Europeans to cherish the many different cultures, and to encourage them at every turn."

Had Thom been a bit more literate, had he studied marketing and learned about marketing by definition, and had he really looked at the definition of terms, he might have spotted the subtle shift this term, which Samir promoted, would make in one's viewpoint. But he didn't spot it. Nor, unfortunately, would the rest of America. What they missed was that the term "multi" means "many," and if one promoted many cultures, not only would there *not* be the melting pot effect that had created a fluid American culture, but the term itself would be divisive. Instead of blending and cooperating, America and its immigrants would divide—proud of their "diversity." In another time and place, it might have been innocuous enough.

But in the year 2005, it was not. For the Fifth Column that Ayman Al-Zawahiri had unleashed would feed on "words"— planting concepts, and repeating them and repeating them until they were just "generally accepted," thereby fulfilling his strategy of divide and conquer.

Thom was congenial enough. He was sincere, and intelligent. Tonight, however, he was no match for Al Qaeda's best. Nodding, as if he were looking at something for the first time, he spoke excitedly. "You know, I never quite looked at that. But, you know, you're right about it. It really is condescending of us, isn't it?"

Samir shrugged, as if his answer would offend his new friend.

And if there was one thing Thom was really good at besides acting, it was being politically correct. He did not want to offend people—least of all 35 million new Americans. They parted, shaking hands, and exchanging cards.

"Samir, it has been a *pleasure*, and I hope to see you again."

With that, he left and drove over to Burbank for his guest appearance on a late-night TV show. Still excited about his new realization, and wanting to inject something new and significant into the otherwise-banal interview, he suddenly voiced the idea, "It's really arrogant of us to expect people to just dive into our melting pot. Maybe they want to be who they are, and not *melt* just because we think we're the greatest country in the world. It's our diversity that makes us great. So, I'm a champion of multiculturalism!"

The stunned host didn't quite know where to take that next, so he patted Thom on the arm, groping for a joke. Not finding one, he nodded as if in agreement, and changed the subject. It had been subtle, but the seed was planted.

Later that night, as she was introducing the headlines of the day, Alicia Quixote lined out the copy she had been handed during the break and inserted the word "war." She linked it to Iraq. And, in an instant, without anyone paying attention, what military officers had for centuries called, and waged as, a campaign, became popularly known as a war.

Within days, other networks had picked up the term. Anchors in major cities, and their affiliates, began the rote duplication of the term War in Iraq. The marketing button had been inserted, and it was now spreading like wildfire. Before long, Fox News changed the slide leading into Breaking News segments to read: "The War in Iraq." CNN copied. WNG had led with it, however, and that pleased Bud Walker immensely. His faith in Alicia was increasing.

"Yup, that little gal sees things the big guys don't," he told himself. "One of my best decisions, making her anchor." He patted himself on the back.

To the networks, it was just a "catch phrase"—a way to identify the topic. To political analysts, it meant a little more. To those who had already succumbed to what the Doctor had spotted—equating some past experience with a current one—it gave rise to strident and harsh criticisms. Polar opposites were emerging.

But the real losers that night were the intended targets—the American people. For, in war, campaigns are won and lost. They are part of the larger war, but they do not define the war itself. The outcome of one campaign does not mean the outcome of the war. Military professionals know that. What they didn't know, and didn't spot, was that somehow the larger global war involving finance, intelligence, politics, and military had been reduced to just one thing—Iraq. Instead of being just one area of activity, albeit an attractively violent activity, Iraq had been elevated to the status of *the only activity.* All other arenas surrendered in importance to what happened there. And the American people's attention and will was now focused solely on Iraq.

The consequences of that masterful Public Relations move would have devastating consequences for the United States and for its allies.

Thousands of miles away, the Doctor sat alone in a hotel lobby watching the international news scene. When he saw the words War in Iraq come onto the screen, he smiled. *Well done, Samir, well done. You are a most remarkable student!* He delighted in anticipation of the pain, anguish, and confusion that single, small change in reporting would produce. *And their growing desperation leads me closer and closer to June 30, 2011. With any luck, there will be 50 million Americans swallowing our "happy pills" by then.*

Sobering a bit, he looked forward now to Samir's accomplishing the task he had set out for him when they met in Panama. For military operations, the border between the United States and Mexico needed to be closed. Samir's next move should lead to that end, in time. His estimate was that it would take six months for the issue to fester and explode. Depending on when Samir planted the button, he could project from there. It would be sooner than the Doctor thought.

He had to scramble to get the light on before the phone stopped ringing. It was unusual for anyone to call his home number. Even Alicia used his cell phone.

"Hello?" Samir asked, hoping he hadn't missed the call.

"Samir?" she giggled.

"Alicia! What on earth! Are you all right?"

"Perfect, darling, perfect!" It was the first time she'd used that term with him, he noted.

Before he could ask, she posed the question, "Guess what?"

"What?"

"I've been invited to the Correspondents' Dinner in Washington. And, *you* are escorting me!"

He sat up in bed now. "I'd be honored, Alicia. And congratulations." Then, he added, "When is it?"

"April."

"That's quite a few months away, Alicia. It's not even fall yet. But, I'll put it on my calendar."

"Thank you. It gets even better. Bud will be sitting with us, and he guarantees we will be sharing a table with the number two radio/TV talk show host in America."

Samir was fully awake now. *This is it!* Instead, he said, "I look forward to it. And now, dear, I hate to be rude, but would it be all right with you if I went back to sleep? I'm so sorry, but I have some early morning calls to Europe, and I must rise in just a few hours."

"Oh yes, I'm so sorry. I just wanted to let you know. I'm so happy," she squealed.

He laughed. "You deserve it. I'll talk to you tomorrow."

"Great! Good night. 2006 is going to be *so* awesome."

"Yes, I believe it is," he said, totally sincere.

CHAPTER 18

*T*he move had not been as difficult as she had expected. Closing down the house on the familiar street in Arlington, she had told herself that if it didn't work out, she'd be back. So Kelly had not really discarded anything, not packed up a great deal. She had not even said final goodbyes to her neighbors. All she did was cover the furniture with drop cloths and pack one box of pictures and mementos to keep with her. The rest of the boxes shipped were clothes.

And it had been relatively easy to find a furnished apartment in the foothills of Glendale. The streets there reminded Kelly of Arlington, and she felt better having lots of neighbors. The fact that she personally liked the apartment manager had been the last influence. For some reason the woman was so keen on having Kelly rent the last apartment in the rear that she had offered her a month's free rent.

The other deciding factor was the fact that a salon and spa located a mere ten-minute walk from the apartment was seeking a beautician and hair stylist. Years earlier, when she resumed her career following the death of Andy's father, she had simply contacted a woman she knew, and been invited into the woman's salon for the mere price of renting a chair.

But, here in Glendale, the proximity to Hollywood and its San Fernando Valley studios rubbed off in more ways than one. She had to audition for the job. Two days of testing her on color and cutting, as well as on her interaction with the clients, had eventually ended with the owner saying he'd give her a go. Kelly was thrilled. She was starting again.

Her transition—in fact James' and Andy's, as well—had been assisted by a very shrewd Brian. Once the university knew he was on his way back, he knew he'd be thrown headlong into the fall schedule. So before "Katrina" had shown her ugly head, the three of them had arrived in the City of Angels. Brian was in his dorm, and James and Andy had taken an apartment in West Hollywood.

But on their first day in the city, Brian had taken them all to Santa Monica to get a glimpse of the Pacific Ocean from the bluffs of this old, character-filled city. It was one of those beautiful August days when the view of the Pacific seemed limitless, and the ocean was as serene as a lake. Oleander bloomed along the drive, and the smell of orange blossom and jasmine still permeated the air, despite the lateness of the season. And, it was warm.

Driving them back into town, Brian brought them past the sprawling country-club campus known as UCLA. An arch-rival of his school, he knew better than to take them past LA Western, as it, frankly, was situated in a ghetto. Like a metaphor, the great educational institution stood like a fortress surrounded by the outcome of generations of ignorance, crime, and drugs. But that was not so with UCLA. Looking like a dream residential area, the students there were oblivious to anything but their pursuit of fun.

And, if that were not enough, Brian drove them down the fountain-lined Avenue of the Americas before heading into the lush, stunning residential blocks of Beverly Hills. Certain that his friends and passengers were appropriately impressed, they stopped for a brief lunch at what looked like a happening place—Ugo's. Then they moved on to Los Feliz Blvd., with its stunning views of the downtown skyline.

For the best views of Los Angeles and the mountain ranges that divided it, Brian took them to Glendale. There, higher in the hills, they got out to ooh and aah over the magnificent city views below them—first of Glendale itself, and behind it, downtown Los Angeles.

That was what had cinched it for Kelly. She had been impressed and seduced, she knew, by the ocean and its lifestyle. But something about this bustling town, and the vistas it offered to the skyline and lights of Los Angeles, had attracted her more. When she investigated the apartment on the magnolia tree-lined street, the rear apartment had a large picture window in the bedroom. And from that window, she could see the city lights. She decided this was the spot to begin.

"Mom, what's on your mind?" Andy asked Kelly, as the three of them waited for Brian to join them at a neighborhood haunt not far from the stadium.

"Nothing," she lied unconvincingly. And that caught James' attention.

Wanting to help her out a bit, he pushed Andy, "Hey, Kid, why don't you wade through the sawdust here and see if you can get someone to bring us a menu. Okay?"

"James, this is a pizza parlor, they don't have menus," Andy retorted.

"Well, then, get us a round of beers." Andy complied, and James called after him, "And a root beer for Brian!"

Knowing it would be a few minutes before Brian joined them after showering from yet another spectacular autumn football victory, James decided to take the opportunity to probe Kelly's reticence.

"Your answer was unconvincing, Kelly."

"What answer?" She dodged the question, turning to look at the rows of football helmets and jerseys lining the walls.

"There's something on your mind, Kelly. I can almost see smoke coming out," he joked, hoping that would open her up.

It did. She laughed, looked straight at James, and shook her head. Sighing and squirming, she answered, "No one spoke English."

That was all she said. James had no idea what she was referring to, no idea of the context. He nodded, frowning. Waiting a moment to see if she would embellish it in any way, he finally concluded she needed a little coaxing. "I don't follow."

Now she was ready to say it, and be done with it. She was almost embarrassed to be thinking about this, let alone to be talking about it. But it was bothering her. She tried to shake a sense of menace she had been experiencing, but she couldn't. She was trying to expand her understanding of her new hometown, but Kelly Weir was a survivor. And in her heart, she sensed that something was threatening her survival. But even thinking about it made her feel small somehow, as if she were intolerant. She did not want to discuss it. So, she answered as succinctly as she could.

"Yesterday...I noticed no one spoke English."

"Where? At work?" James was curious.

"There, too." She shook her head. "But mostly, it was everywhere else."

"Kelly, can you be more specific?"

She looked up, and James saw that flash of eyes and compressing of lips that signaled she was angry. He chided himself now that he had pressed her, and had overstepped his bounds a bit.

"James, I really don't want to talk about this. But you asked, so I answered."

"Right. I did."

"It's nothing. Just *me* being stupid is all. But when I was shopping, and running errands yesterday, I noticed no one spoke English," she concluded, ready to move on.

"All Armenian?" James asked, guessing that would be the case in the neighborhood Kelly had chosen.

Again, her eyes flashed. "Armenian, Korean, Chinese, Spanish—all of them. And then some." Then, feeling that odd sense of embarrassment again, she added, "James, it's nothing really. Let's just drop it. I just thought it odd that even when I was their customer, no one even tried to speak English. I don't think they really wanted my business."

"Stranger in your own land..." James commented casually, and changed the subject as he spotted Brian entering the college restaurant. "Brian, over here," he shouted, not certain whether Brian could see them in the dim lighting.

But he had, and was already on the way to their table. Just then Andy returned with four beer mugs—three Guinness and one root beer, which he ceremoniously handed to Brian. "Great game, Brian, great game!"

Brian took the root beer, examined it before swigging, and hoisted it for a toast. "To the season! And to the Bowl!"

"Here, here!"

"Number Nine?" the announcer at the counter shouted into the now-crowded restaurant.

Andy jumped up immediately. "That's us." Weaving his way through the exuberant LA Western crowd, he made a beeline for the pizza pickup window, grabbed the extra-large supreme, and delivered it safely to their table.

"Brian, it was a joy seeing you play today," Kelly said sincerely. "It brought back a lot of great memories."

"I bet!"

"Well, you've gone on to another level now, Brian. We're proud of you."

James and Andy nodded their heads in complete agreement—James especially. What Kelly didn't know was that James hadn't paid attention to anyone but Brian in the game. He was studying today, to see what he could learn and observe about Brian's statement that he "contributed to the coverage," and thereby avoided failing to catch a ball. After watching multiple plays, he had finally seen it. Brian seemed to know what the "safeties" and other "backs" were thinking. Moreover, he *didn't* resist what they were thinking. He moved right along with it, keeping his eye on his quarterback and his field location. In the end, the passes were caught and the tackles were foiled—but due to Brian's intention to receive the ball more than to his desire to avoid the opponent.

It's about purpose and intention, James had concluded. *And not getting distracted. I think I'll get my wits around this in a few more games,* he had told himself at the stadium.

"Yeah, Pal, you were a sight to see!"

"Thanks, James."

"So how have you been otherwise, Brian?" Kelly asked. Of the four, she was the one most out of the loop. Living several miles from the others, and working nearly every day, she needed the small talk to get caught up.

"Fine. Classes are great."

"And how are things at home?" she added politely.

"Same as usual I guess. I hear mostly from Mama." He shoved a bite of pizza into his mouth, swallowed it almost whole, and continued. "You know the drill—who's fightin' with who, who's lookin' for work, who wants to get off his meds—the usual."

"Who? What meds?" Kelly asked. "Your great-grandpa?"

"No, ma'am, not him. He's as healthy as a horse, frankly. It's my grandpa. He's bi-polar, turns out, and they gave him some meds so he'd be less angry." He scarfed another whole slice of pizza. "You know, one day he's up, one day he's down. And his down days ain't so good. The meds help I guess."

Kelly was a bit confused by this, so she queried, "And he wants to get off them?"

"Yes, ma'am, near as I can tell."

"Why is that, Brian, if they are helping him?"

"To be honest with you, Mrs. Weir, I don't know. Grandpa and me aren't close at all, so I don't know. But if Mama says he should be on them, I'll stick with Mama."

It was said simply, yet emphatically, so Kelly dropped it. Changing the subject she asked, "So, any nice young girl you're dating, Brian?"

Brian laughed. "Now you *do* sound like my mama!" Turning to Andy, he joked, "Will you please tell your mama, Andy, how between football and classes, and working with you two jokers, I don't have time for no woman!"

"Mama, Brian ain't got time for no woman!" Andy obliged, mimicking his friend's delivery.

James eyed Kelly to see if she was handling this teasing all right. She was. So, he offered, "Another round?"

CHAPTER 19

Ayman Al-Zawahiri was credited correctly by the intelligence community with developing the cell structure of Al Qaeda, wherein no one cell knew what the other cells were doing, or who the members of each cell were. His brilliant intention was to make Al Qaeda impregnable—and to make certain that the failure of one cell's members to accomplish their mission would not jeopardize others. Men and materiel were precious to the group, now more than ever. The last four years had been devastating to the terrorist organization financially, as their money laundering operations were being ruthlessly and systematically identified and dismantled.

Financial reserves were drained, and Al Qaeda was forced to look for alliances with other terror organizations. For the Doctor this was troubling, as he knew that none of them had the audacious plans that he and Bin Laden had formulated. And he knew that none of them had top-level leadership with half the wits of his key men. Yet, here they were—working with men who could become a liability to them in the future.

Well, I'll handle it when the time comes, the Doctor reassured himself. *After all, once June 30, 2011 has come and gone, our supremacy will be obvious and unchallenged. I can wait until then.*

Feeling a little better, he passed up looking in the cracked mirror in the Panama City offices of ST & Associates. He knew what he would see there. Age was creeping up on him. His hair was graying, and his face was gaunt. His long-time ulcer flare-ups were increasing, and he knew it would not be long before surgery might be required. And the thought of undergoing surgery in a country he barely knew—with absolutely no support system around him—made him a bit anxious.

Steady, steady, he told himself. *Just a little longer now, and it will be the United States that will be tied in knots. Once Samir engages, their next two elections will be a shambles.* He smiled. Ayman Al-Zawahiri liked destruction. In his mind, the world had tilted so far off its axis because of the influence of the United States that only a plan as sweeping as the one he had created could rid the world of this great menace called America.

Just a little longer.

Unbeknownst to the Doctor, however, the pharmacist Ali Roos had other plans. Emboldened by the masterful plan that would launch on June 30, 2011—taking with it the hoped-for 50 million Americans—he had taken to heart the concept of being self-motivated. Ali had conceived of a plan he could implement faster. And, in his mind, Bin Laden was sure to approve. After all, hadn't they called for all Jihadists to form their own groups, and strike the United States and Britain at will? Wasn't that the logical extension of Zawahiri's cellular structure?

Ali Roos was a fine chemist and pharmacist. But he was not a military man. Nor was he a propagandist. Though he thought self-franchising was what the Doctor and Bin Laden were intending—and it may have been—his next move would expose a flaw so profound in the command-level reasoning and communications that it would nearly sink the Doctor's secret plan.

For in their zeal to encourage and embolden spontaneous attacks upon American and British interests, the Doctor had overlooked something. Independent cells were a brilliant idea. But they were conceived to be operating under the command intention of Ayman Al-Zawahiri or Usama Bin Laden. The ramifications of some lone ranger operating completely on his own had never been thought through. And that oversight would cost Al Qaeda dearly.

Unfortunately, Ali Roos was too naïve to even consider it. Acting on his own, he had created a "celebrity cell." It was not comprised of celebrities, but it would target celebrities. However, before he would launch an attack in the United States, he got the bright idea that it would be better to test it in Great Britain.

And so it was that, just as the Christmas decorations were coming out to drape the palm trees of Los Angeles, Ali Roos invited friends from London to visit him over the holidays. Since they were all in the medical profession, and were in fact classmates, their visitors' visas were granted without a second thought. Two were doctors, one a microbiologist, and the others were pursuing careers in Britain's health care system.

They arrived at LAX and, first, took a cab to one of downtown Los Angeles's elegant hotels. Its cylindrical towers graced the skyline and could be seen from Ali's house in the hills of the quiet, but growing, city of Glendale.

The cabbie then easily located the address they had given him and dropped the five men at the foot of the stairs to Ali's front door. It seemed as if no one was home, as the blinds on all windows were closed. Given that Ali's house faced out over one of the most breathtaking views in Southern California, and given that the people in that neighborhood paid a fortune to acquire those views, it was unusual to see a home with all windows closed off. No one could see in from any direction.

"Do you want me to wait, just in case no one's home?" the cabbie offered.

"No, no, not necessary," one of the men assured the cabbie, while his partner paid him. "He'll be here."

"Suit yourself," the cabbie retorted, not really caring anymore, since his tip had been a good one.

As he drove away, he almost grazed a woman who was walking—apparently getting some late-afternoon exercise. He honked the horn, which drew the men's attention to her.

They looked over their shoulders in both directions to make certain no one was watching them. Then they removed their shoes and entered the house.

Stabilizing herself after losing her footing a bit with the closeness of the cab, Kelly Weir looked up just as the last man looked around and disappeared inside.

Thousands of miles away, another rogue began to defy his orders as well. Abou Zarqawi was tired of being chastised by Makkawi from his safe house in Pakistan. He had trained his men, and he had seen as many of them killed as he had trained.

And he was growing increasingly resentful of the Doctor's exhortations to accomplish the political mission in Iraq. He had failed twice already to prevent elections, and he feared that the Iraqis' final election in December would enrage the Doctor. Zarqawi, however, felt that their tactics had been too weak. He had been told to create enough fear and resentment that the Iraqi people would not dare venture out on election days, even if their quarrelsome leadership managed to pull off elections.

But that plan had failed. Not a day went by that he didn't squirm at the image of the women of Iraq, proudly displaying their purple finger. Hindered by a less than average intelligence, Zarqawi reasoned now that the Doctor's plan was flawed. And, on his own, he concluded that what was needed was a little old-fashioned Lenin.

Pulling his men together, he pontificated. "The purpose of terror is to terrify." Though a direct quote from Lenin, Zarqawi felt no need whatsoever to credit him. As far as he was concerned, he was more important than Lenin had been. *Lenin, who was he?* he scoffed. *He was busy enslaving people. I am returning the world to Shari'a law.*

Shortly after, Al-Jazeerah network aired a tape by Abou Zarqawi, issuing his own threats. In the weeks to come, without the advance knowledge or approval of the military commander of Al Qaeda, Zarqawi commenced relentless attacks upon Sunni and Shi'ite alike. Hoping to incite a civil war between these two forces and the Kurds in the north, he had concluded that was the best way to topple the vulnerable government the Iraqis had been determined to form—and to redeem himself for his inability to terrify the Americans to the point where they left, or the Iraqis to the point where they would abandon their tentative steps toward a representative government. Making the Iraqis collateral damage to attacks upon the imperialistic Americans and Brits had been the Doctor's strategy.

Clearly, the old man doesn't know what he's doing. I'm the one with the price on my head. He was breathing deeply now, exhaling equally deeply. *I'm the one with the most to lose!*

And with that self-serving reasoning, Abou Al-Zarqawi

embarked upon a strategy that would reshape Iraq, the people of Iraq, and the future of Iraq. He had decided to attack the Iraqi people themselves—including the Sunnis, who had been looking the other way, refusing to give up Al Qaeda's safe houses and weapons' stashes. That single choice would cost him his life, and the lives of thousands of his men, and jeopardize the entire Iraq project.

Ayman Al-Zawahiri may have been half the globe away, but he watched the news. And he could always count on the American media to cover news from Al-Jazeerah. He saw the chink in the armor before Makkawi had even been informed. Once news reached the small town in Pakistan where Makkawi was holed up, the Doctor knew he would receive a communication. He expected nothing less.

———————————

This development disturbed the Doctor greatly. Not only did he know he would have to meet with Makkawi personally—despite the terrible risk that entailed—the Doctor recognized that it was imperative now that Samir plant the marketing button needed to turn the Americans' attention away from Iraq and on to another subject. Al Qaeda was going to need a new home. He knew that. Makkawi probably recognized that. Zarqawi did not. *And with any luck, the Americans won't know it,* he encouraged himself.

What had to happen now was the closure of the border between the United States and Mexico, and the attendant chaos that would follow in the Mexican economy. *With the flow of illegal workers stopped, and the flow of American money back to Mexico stopped along with it, Mexico is doomed.* The Doctor felt no remorse for what that would mean to the Mexican people. Quite the contrary, he was counting on the economic and political fall-out from the border closure to create havoc throughout Central America. He smiled malevolently, as he contemplated the millions of potential recruits to Al Qaeda, and to terrorism, which the imminent economic duress in Mexico would produce. *What a great incubator of terrorists Mexico will become!*

All that was needed was for him to advance Samir's timeline.

Samir's chance to do that came just as planned. Right before Christmas, Alicia Quixote and Samir received a personal invitation to ski and snowmobile at Bud Walker's ranch. The festivities, which were spread out over the long weekend, were to conclude with a buffalo barbeque and square dance.

Alicia's Hispanic background, and her years in the southwest, had left her a little uneasy about the skiing part of this trip. And Samir, a world-class skier who had used his skills often in Afghanistan, was somewhat skittish about the square dance.

"Darling, I'll teach you to dance. You'll like it," she reassured him, as she helped him choose the appropriate clothes from his closet.

"I'm sure," he responded, unconvincingly.

"No, seriously, it's easy. The guy calling the next steps does all the work. We just have to follow instructions." Then, to really convince him, she added, "I'll teach you what dosido means and you'll be good to go."

Samir grabbed her waist and pulled her close. She laughed, pulled herself away, and teased, "It's not that kind of dancing."

"No?"

"No. You'll be lucky to touch me at all." She paused to see what he would do with that.

"Pity."

That was what Alicia hoped he would say. She smiled.

And to her surprise, Samir made an odd recommendation. "And you, my sweet, will sit in the lodge and drink some brandy or cocoa. But you will not ski."

He had said it gently, but firmly. Normally, Alicia would have bridled at the audacity of a man telling her what she could and couldn't do. But tonight, she felt this was actually a romantic and protective gesture—that he was sparing her the risk of a dangerous fall.

"Alicia, I'm truly looking forward to this."

"Me, too."

"Do you know who will be there?" Samir tossed this off innocently, while packing sweaters into his bag.

"As a matter of fact I do." She smiled, delighted with her secret. Then, with no pressure from him whatsoever, she relented. "All right, I'll tell you."

Samir paused and turned to look straight at her.

"I'm all ears."

"Well, Samir, you are about to see just how broad-minded and moderate Bud really is—and how well-liked."

"How so?"

She could hardly contain herself, for Bud Walker had decided to make a reputation for himself as the reasonable media mogul—the one news celebrities could trust regardless of which side of the media bias they were on. He wanted them to view him as a temperate man, a reasonable and fair man, and a man they could trust to get it right when it came to reporting matters that were vital to American interests.

For months, he had made phone calls, had lunches, hosted parties, and picked the brains of the leading radio talk show commentators in America. Gaining their trust, he had been encouraged to call in and discuss issues they were debating. And, according to his plan, most were Conservative talk show hosts. There hadn't been that many even available who were Liberal, so Bud Walker had decided to earn the friendship, and perhaps indebtedness, of the most powerful people in the news media.

No matter what CBS, NBC, or ABC thought, Bud Walker had concluded that the power rested with the talk radio giants. And, one by one, they were getting to know Bud Walker. When his invitation to them and their families arrived, inviting them for what promised to be a truly American experience in some of the nation's most magnificent country, none of them turned him down.

To them it promised to be a "down-home" and refreshing change of pace from the stiff Correspondents' Dinners where they usually saw each other.

With pride, Alicia listed off the names of those she knew would be attending. Bud himself was proud of the number of men and women who were gladly accepting his hospitality.

Samir listened, and smiled appropriately. Inside, however, he reasoned ecstatically, *Perfect! The number 2 and 3 ranked Conservative Talk Radio hosts. And just about everyone else I've ever heard talk. Ayman will be thrilled. It will happen in the Northwest.*

"You look so happy, darling." Alicia mistook Samir's enthrallment. "Can you imagine what wonderful contacts you will make?"

Coming around he responded, "Yes, yes, I was just thinking of that. Wonderful opportunities, actually."

"Well, knowing you, you'll make the most of them."

And with deadly earnest, Samir added, "You can be sure."

Hours later, Samir sent a coded message to the Doctor. It read simply, "His allies will turn on him. It will happen shortly."

Upon receiving this reassuring communication, Ayman Al-Zawahiri notified the cabal in Cuba, Mexico, Venezuela, and Colombia that the ball was in play. And, agreeably, they waited.

All Andy heard was Kelly scream. He didn't hear the glass crash to the floor. He only heard a desperate cry from his mother. He and James both bolted to the kitchen where Kelly was preparing them a Christmas Eve dinner. It had become a tradition of sorts with the three of them during the three years Andy and James worked on the Zawahiri project.

Brian had been invited, but he was tied up with practices—in anticipation of his Bowl appearance in a few days. No one expected to see much of him 'til the game was over.

"Mom, what is it?" Andy yelled, as he caught his sneaker on some broken glass. James stopped right behind him, surveying the room before entering. He wasn't going to get caught in a trap again.

Kelly said nothing. She was shaking, with tears streaming down her face, staring at the television news. Fearing there had been another terror attack, James and Andy turned to the screen. James had no idea what had disturbed Kelly.

But Andy did. "No, God no," he sighed, inhaling deeply and

bracing himself. Before James could ask, Andy signaled for him to be quiet, that he needed to listen to the Breaking News that was coming in from Southeast Washington, DC.

The scene in the background was chaotic, with multiple ambulances parked outside a small house in a ghetto neighborhood of the District of Columbia. There were red lights flashing, sirens, shouts of police and medical people overtop one another as they rushed to do their work. The journalist dispatched to cover the scene was reporting what he had gathered from bystanders.

Other than the fact that Kelly and Andy were in shock, James saw no difference between this scene and thousands he had seen on national news shows. When the news around the world was light, it seemed the news shows created their daily quota of fear with shots and stories of fires and murders. Juicy interviews with victims and families always accompanied, and were guaranteed to upset the viewer. He wondered if this news story was just another one of these. Save for Kelly, he might have dismissed it and gone back to stringing lights on Kelly's tree so she could hang the sentimental tree ornaments she had transported with her to Los Angeles.

But he knew Kelly Weir. Something was drastically wrong. So he waited and watched. The reporter, reading now from his notes, said, "WNG has confirmed from local police at the scene that the victims are Althea Carver, Roland Carver, Washington Adams Carver, and Lincoln Carver. Details are not fully known, but neighbors report hearing multiple gunshots at this address. When police arrived, they found Althea and Roland Carver shot to death in the living room of the residence, Washington Adams Carver shot to death in his upstairs bedroom, and Lincoln Carver—the victim of an apparent self-inflicted gunshot wound—in the basement. No one knows at this time why Lincoln Carver shot and killed his family and then himself. Neighbors say he had suffered from depression throughout the years, but they never thought anything like this could happen. Back to you, John, from this sad, sad location—at what was to be a joyous time of year."

There was silence. Andy looked at the floor, saying nothing. Kelly sat down at the table, openly crying. James, realizing this must be Brian's family, was trying to find words. But he couldn't.

His mouth was *so* dry. The best he could do was clear his throat.

Andy broke the silence. "Mom."

"Yes?"

"Brian doesn't know."

She didn't quite get it. "What do you mean? How could he not know?"

"I don't know, Mom, but if he had been told, he would have called me. I know this. I know Brian." It was said emphatically.

"You mean the bastards released this on national television before the family was fully notified?" She was so stunned, she added, "Is that possible?"

James knew it was possible, so he answered for Andy. "Yes, Kelly, it is possible. There's a pressure to fill the hour, to get the story out. It is possible they failed to find Brian first, or his sisters."

Andy bolted for the hall closet and grabbed his windbreaker. "I've got to get to him before he sees it on the news. James, you coming?"

"Absolutely."

"James, Andy," her voice was quiet, but resolved. "I go."

"What?" Andy asked, uncertain of why Kelly felt she needed to do this.

James understood though. He had watched military wives throughout the years. And one thing he knew was there was almost a code amongst them. If there was bad news to be delivered, it would be delivered by an understanding woman. "Andy, Kelly's right."

Andy still looked confused. James persisted. "This is going to be the worst night in Brian's life. Tonight he needs a 'mom.'"

Andy nodded. He understood, though his heart was breaking for his friend. *Dear God, how will he bear up to this?*

Calmly and authoritatively now, Kelly guided the two out of the apartment and into the car. A few minutes later, when they pulled up in front of Brian's dorm, James and Andy waited in the car. Kelly went to the reception area, leaned in to the young man who was monitoring the dorm switchboard, and said something to him. He looked up, startled and upset. She smiled kindly. Then he gave her the room number and pointed toward the elevators.

Thankfully, Brian's room was across from the elevator, so she didn't have to walk far. She wasn't sure how she was going to do this, and she was grateful it would be over soon. As she approached his door, which was loaded with encouraging signs about the Bowl game, she saw a light under the door and knew he was there. She knocked.

Brian opened the door, was surprised to see her in this arena, and then grinned. "Mrs. Weir, my goodness, what are you doing here? Come to give me one last pep talk?"

"Brian, if I may come in, I have some very, very bad news, and I wanted to bring it to you myself." With that, she stepped in and closed the door.

CHAPTER 20

*T*he year 2006 hadn't started the way they had expected. James and Andy both felt as if they had been gut-punched. With no wind behind them, the mission they had set for themselves seemed beached somehow. Their minds, as disciplined as they were, kept wandering to their friend, Brian.

Trying to watch bowl games had made it even worse. Brian, of course, had missed his. But somehow, the enthusiastic crowds, the vibrant colors, and the bands jarred the sad reality that blanketed their world. In the end, they'd given up and taken a long walk. It had helped.

And now they were back at work. James sensed that this new year would be pivotal for America, and for Al Qaeda. So, once again, they sat with fresh paper in front of them, ready to begin a new analysis. Because they were focused finally on that task, they hadn't heard him enter. If it hadn't been for the cross-breeze that scattered some of their worksheets as the front door to the apartment opened, James and Andy wouldn't have known he was there.

"Brian…" Andy began, not really knowing what to do from there. He started to rise and move toward his friend, but a quick look from James told him to hold back and be cool. He sat back down at the butcher block table they used for eating and working. James was looking right at Brian, assessing him.

It seemed a long time, but then Brian woodenly said, "Hey."

Andy hadn't spotted it yet, but Brian had a suitcase and knapsack with him. Guessing that he had just come from the airport, and the funerals of every member of his family whom he had known and cared about, James thought, *I gotta get this next sentence right. This is pretty critical.* He could tell by the way Brian was

133

jutting his jaw forward that he was struggling to keep it together, and James wondered if it was that countenance that the Brits referred to as a "stiff upper lip."

James was no father. But he had watched men suffer the better part of his life, in every part of the planet—and he knew what had to come next for Brian. *Please, God, let me say this right. Let him make this next step.*

"Son, I don't know if this is the right time or not, but we could use your help with something." There, he'd said it. Andy got it. There was a hint of a smile and an ever so slight nod of his head.

It was the opening move of a new game. James knew that Brian would have to step up now and create new goals, making a new purpose, or the next years of his life could be bleak indeed. No one spoke. Andy didn't dare turn around. He closed his eyes, as if expecting a blow and not wanting to look. And he held his breath. *Come on, bro. I pray this isn't too much, too soon.*

James saw it first. He engaged ever so slightly. Though Brian's countenance was still wooden, and his face revealed the haunted, empty look of men who are shell-shocked, the slight backward tip of his head, exposing the jaw even more, told James he was about to move. And then, quietly, he put his bag down on the floor near the door and walked to the makeshift desk where James and Andy were sitting.

"With what?" Brian's voice showed no keen interest. It was a sad monotone at best. But, he had *engaged.* It was a start.

Andy had no idea where James was going with this, so he just looked to James. Without even a beat, James picked it up. "Well, you know I've been an analyst most of my life—even when I was out in the field. The last four or five years that was all I did for the CIA." Brian's head nodded slightly as he stood a few feet away from their table. "And I'm beginning to think Andy and I have been barking up the wrong tree."

There was a lag, but, at the same time, a hint of interest. "How so?"

"Well, it was something you said back at Cape Fear. I can't get it out of my mind." He expected Brian to maybe ask. He did not. Rather he just stood there, waiting. So James expanded. "Andy and I had figured out that this SOB Zawahiri plays games; he's after the White King."

"That's a chess reference," Andy inserted lamely. Andy could tell by Brian's look that it was a stupid remark. After all, they had been over this many times during the spring and summer. "Sorry."

"Well, anyway," James added, "as you know, we concluded, too late, that the White King was the American people themselves—that Zawahiri's strategy is to bring down the American people, and with that, the whole thing topples like a house of cards."

"I remember that, James." Brian's tone was somewhat defiant now, as if to say "get on with it."

"Right. Well, you used a football analogy, and suggested the real target would have to be the youth of America."

"James, I remember." Brian was growing more impatient now.

"Good, Brian. Because that's what I haven't been able to get out of my mind—for months. I think you're right. But I need your help."

"How so?" Brian's jaw relaxed a bit.

"I need you to help us figure out how he's going to do that—or what he's going to use that's already here. I—" he corrected himself, "*we* need you to help us discover what he's likely to use."

"And when you do, wha'cha going to do then, tell the President?" The question was belligerent. Andy's eyes widened, but James smiled. Their friend was moving in the right direction. He was getting some fight back.

"No, son. Then we're going to have you help us with what you're really good at—what we need *you* the most for." James challenged Brian, looking directly at the young man standing above him.

Given that Andy had no idea what James was referring to, he added a faint, "Right."

"All right, all right, I'll play," Brian said. "And what exactly is that?"

"Marketing. That's your major, isn't it?"

Brian was shocked. He had no idea what this had to do with the global war on terror, but he had always followed his friend's lead, and he remembered that back at Cape Fear, he *had* asked to work with them. "Yes, James, it is. But what the hell does marketing have to do with this?"

James smiled now. "Frankly, Brian, I don't know yet. I have this theory that it does, however. And I'm going to need you to help me prove it."

Five years earlier, James Mikolas had spoken similar words to Andy Weir. Andy's next choice had changed his life forever. Brian's next choice would do the same. There was a somber silence, for fear and death were part of all three of their lives now. They had that in common. What each sensed, but didn't speak about, was the almost idealistic hope that a synthesis of their separate experiences and talents would form a group more powerful than any of them could be separately—that their common ground would empower them.

Brian knew his football days were over. He had fulfilled his responsibility to his school and to his team. And he knew at the joint funerals of his family members that all choices he made now had to be his alone, and not choices made to fulfill others' expectations of him. Though he still had two sisters, they had been disconnected from the family for so long that they had no real need, or even interest, in him.

Oddly enough, as he stood there looking down at Andy and James, he wasn't surprised at all by what James had said. He was inexplicably calm. He was free now. With the keen sense of responsibility and loyalty with which he had been endowed, he had already resolved to somehow, someway, make the seemingly meaningless deaths of his family count for something. And, like his two friends, who operated on a highly intuitive level, this somehow felt like the path to take to accomplish that.

"All right," he said, as he sat down at the table with them, "I'm in. I don't exactly know what you think I can do, but I meant it back there at Cape Fear. I want to work with you."

"You hungry?" James asked. It was a complete non-sequitur, but James didn't see any point in getting maudlin here. He was just grateful the kid had responded. He felt good.

"Yeah, I could eat."

A few minutes later, James put tuna fish sandwiches, pickles, and chips on the table. Since it was his staple, it had become a standing joke between him and Andy. "James is great! He loves to make dinner!" Andy said, with a poker face.

The look on Brian's face told them he was wondering *what's wrong with you two?* But he didn't say anything. He just grabbed a sandwich and started to eat.

"All right, guys, rise and shine!" James rousted Andy out of his bed, and Brian off the living room sofa, which was now, apparently, his home. "I've set us up, and the first thing we're going to do is a little brain storming."

Five minutes later, on a magnificent sunny Southern California morning, they commenced their analysis. "Here's what we're going to do—however long it takes us, okay?"

"Okay."

"Okay."

"If we accept our theory that the strategy is to destroy America by destroying its youth, we're going to start with the outcome of a destroyed generation, and trace backwards until we find the root cause or causes. First, let's list the symptoms of a dying generation—you know, what's upsetting you, killing you—and then we'll trace back to conditions or professions involved with that, which could have precipitated the symptom. Then, and finally, we'll look for common denominators in those areas until we locate the source points. And then, gentlemen, we will *solve the problem.*"

Andy was the first to respond. "Got it. This is quite a puzzle." He didn't realize it, but he was smiling, ever so slightly, as he looked into the distance. James was betting that Brian's competitiveness, coupled with his intelligence and love of games, would urge him on. He was right.

"We're not seriously doing this on paper?" Brian asked incredulously, looking at the tablets and pens James had set on the table.

"Sure, why not?" Andy retorted.

"Well, for starters, my man, here you are this MIT grad— with God knows how much programming ability, or whatever you want to call it—and we're hand-writing this stuff!"

"Brian, whoa," James interjected. "Here's the deal. This is

how Andy likes to work. Drove me nuts, too. I wanted everything on the computer. But, no, he insisted. And friend, thank God he did. If we hadn't, we would have missed what Zawahiri was actually doing."

"For real?" Brian looked to Andy.

"Yeah, it was a real fluky thing, actually. But, yeah, let's write it down first. We'll bring it onto computer at a later step. I get where James is going with this."

"You're my quarterback, man. You lead. Just let me know when you're throwing me the ball, okay?"

"You bet." Like the young men James had seen back in Arlington, Virginia, these two partners of his were in the spirit of play once again. He was very optimistic.

"Okay, okay," Andy began. "Page One. Symptoms of a dying generation . . . "

By lunch, they had quite a list. What had proven fruitful was to first start with conditions that they had observed or experienced—the emotions, sometimes the actions. Then they were ready to start into "contributing factors" or "professions." It was daunting, and very difficult to confront. Most people want to turn away from it with the dismissive "things were different in my day" mentality. To look right at it, dispassionately, was challenging. But James' job was to keep them looking. It had gotten easier each minute, however. The more they looked, the more they saw—and the freer they felt.

About the time Andy wanted to take a break to call Kelly, James collected the papers and started the review. The list was handwritten by two different people. Andy's handwriting had that formality and clarity with which engineers print and write. Brian's was cruder, more unpredictable—more spontaneous. But each had gotten the job done. Now it was time for one of the finest analysts the CIA had ever fielded to take a look, and see what jumped out—if anything.

Blowing on his coffee to cool it down a little, James read the shocking list of symptoms. "Apathy, hopelessness, anger, violence, suicide, crime, abortion, promiscuity, unwed mothers, deadbeat fathers, obesity, addiction, sickness, racial hatred, intolerance, disease, mental illness, depression, no money, no self-respect, loneliness, class separation, bigotry, status." It was quite a list. For a moment, James was overcome with a sense of sadness. He had asked two really bright young men, who were high achievers in life, to list what they had observed and experienced—and this was that list. Because it had been done clinically, and dispassionately, the list battered James even more. Until that moment, he had not known the true platform from which this generation was launching its future. *If this is what they feel and experience now, is there hope? Has Zawahiri already won?*

He shoved those thoughts out with a monumental effort, and turned to page two: "Contributing Factors, Institutions, Professions, etc." Bracing himself, he read, "Education, Television." Then, there was a footnote written by Andy, which said, "James, these are activities all of us engage in or are exposed to. We leave it to your genius to analyze this. Like before, pal, this is just the data. We'll supply what we see, but we are disciplining ourselves not to evaluate. Okay?"

James smiled and read on. "Educational failures, Drug usage—street and prescription, Religion, Military, Divorced parents, Gangs, Underemployment, Law Enforcement, Medicine, Video games, Sports, Internet, Sex, Sexually transmitted disease, Fast Food—poor eating."

That was it. It was as far as they had gotten. To James, this list was a good start. Young men and women in America, he had to admit, were exposed to everything on this list to greater or lesser degrees. *Should we lengthen it, or do we start here?* he asked himself. He decided to start his analysis, and as in the past, let Andy and Brian add in new things if they thought of them. What he had to determine now was whether or not there was a connection between the "Outcomes" list and the "Institutions" lists, as he preferred to think of them. Did one contribute to the other—in part, or in total? And if so, were there common denominators? And, if they were addressed, could a reversal be achieved? And, moreover, could he find where Zawahiri would strike? Would it even be necessary?

These were the questions that occupied James the remainder of the day. Later that night, he asked Andy to create a computer program that would allow them data entry and evaluation, with metrics to weigh and measure each of the data pieces. And, then, as they had done before, they began to collect news items involving all aspects of American life. It was a much broader view than they had had to take when they were looking at a simpler military-only picture. *But if we're "going down" through the enemy's use of our sociology, our own way of life—we start here.* Somehow, having braced himself for that, James was ready to begin. A sense of calm had come over him.

Andy and Brian took the rest of the night off. They needed something more substantive than James' chili. They went to Kelly's for a good meal, and so that Brian could thank her for that night when she had helped him so much.

None of them knew it, but on that list was a seed, which—if nurtured properly—could become the beginning of the end of Ayman Al-Zawahiri, and his dreams of deadly glory. And a thousand miles away, Ayman Al-Zawahiri lay pinned to a small cot, stricken with a resurgence of his ulcers, and terrorized by the recurrent dream of the white horse.

CHAPTER 21

"*L*adies, gents, we'll be taking a thirty-minute break." The square dance caller's voice cut easily through the applause, laughter, and heavy breathing that ended the last dance. It had been a real workout, and he knew the crowd could use another beer, a trip to the can, or a smoke. "We'll be back," he added. "So, don't none of you bail out on us now, you hear?"

Obligingly, the chorus of sweating dancers cheered, "We'll be right here for you, Sid!"

Alicia took the opportunity to head to the ladies room, and Samir headed outside to clear his head, and figure out how he was going to plant the seed before the night ended, or before his targets decided to call it a night.

Frankly, this has been an exhausting day, he concluded. *A ski slope is no place to get into a conversation. Let's see if I can find someone sitting down, catching his breath, like I am.*

And he did. Just as he was rubbing out his cigar with his brand new Tony Lama boots, Bud Walker walked past. "Hey, Samir, got some people I'd like you to meet."

Samir responded immediately, hoping this wouldn't divert him. Noticing that Bud's hands were full of beer mugs, he offered to assist. The two approached a small group of men who were seated in the cedar Adirondack chairs surrounding the open fire pit. All were leaning in to warm their hands and faces. Despite the exertion of the dance, the night was chilly enough outside to warrant huddling up around the fire.

"Gentlemen, these look like beer mugs, but I assure you there is something in here better suited to warming you up," Bud Walker joked, as he and Samir passed them out. "And I'd like you all to meet Samir. He runs one of the best public relations firms in the world."

It was quite an endorsement. Samir knew that would help with credibility once he decided to speak. *And this is the time*, he coached himself. *Number 2 and Number 3 are right here. Birds of a feather.* He sat down, listened, and waited. He didn't have to wait long.

The conversation was a bit tentative at first. Each of these men was a giant in his industry, and none of them were really used to keeping each other's company. In fact, they rarely, if ever, had met. Each had a healthy respect for the others' intellect, and ratings, but there was a natural reticence. After all, one wouldn't want to say some profound thing here around the campfire, and then have a competitor pick it up and use it to enhance his ratings.

But Radio talk show hosts can't stay away from politics and government for long. And the warmth of the toddy that Walker provided began to loosen them up. In a few minutes, they were skating back to familiar territory—conversations where they pretty much knew they were all in agreement.

Sitting next to Samir was the number two ranked Conservative talk show host in the United States. Across from him was number three. Samir thought of them as Number 2 and Number 3 in his mind to keep his focus on the high value of the target. The two had started to converse innocuously about their networks, the rising ratings, and the keen interest Americans were taking in talk radio.

That alone would have been an interesting discussion, and Samir was fascinated to hear why each man felt talk radio was climbing, and why the liberal talk shows didn't seem to make it.

Before long though, the talk turned to President Bush and his proposal or plan to handle the immigration and border issues. The man to Samir's right said, "I for one give him points for bringing it up. Every other President has passed it on to the next."

There was a pause, followed by general agreement, and then the man who was chasing him in the ratings added, "But, we're going to need more than this. There are so many holes in the thing. I just can't see how he's going to round up the 14 million who are already here!"

"Or is he thinking of letting them stay, and somehow just fix the thing from here forward?" Bud Walker chimed in.

"Nah, Reagan tried that. He was a true believer. But it still didn't work."

"And I just don't see how Bush could expect it to work. He's been the Governor of Texas, for Pete's sake. Surely he knows how impossible that whole thing is."

Bud Walker nodded, getting the point. Then he added, "And I just don't get why Ted Kennedy is in on the thing!" There was a round of laughter on that one. Somehow the idea of George Bush and Ted Kennedy on the same side of anything sent them into peals of laughter. "Now hold on there, fellas, we don't know Kennedy will be aboard, do we?"

The man to Samir's right answered, "You're right, Bud, we don't. That's the point. It's too fuzzy now, too many unanswered questions. But we'll hear more, you can be sure of that. Heck, we're just starting the year. This will heat up for the mid-term elections, don't you think?"

On that, they were all in agreement. Then Bud surprised Samir with his next comment. "Well, to give the man credit, he did say it was just an idea, a beginning proposal. I was right there when he said this wasn't carved in stone—that what he wanted was for the bright guys to sit down and talk, and create something even better." All eyes were on Walker as he continued. "And you know, he was right. It's really about the intention, isn't it? Don't we start there—by saying 'this is something we need to get done; now get it done; you figure it out?'" He paused for effect; then added, "That's what John Kennedy did. Hell, we hadn't even made a rocket that could leave the launch pad without exploding when he told Americans we would land on the moon before the decade was out! That sure left a lot out!"

"You're right, Bud," Samir's next-door neighbor said. "JFK set the goal—and he left it to the ingenuity and creativity of Americans to get the job done. And we did!" The man smiled and sat back in his chair, as if he'd won a debate point. Unfortunately, they were not debating. Samir eyed him closely, and decided he was the one.

This one. This one right here. Even if he changes his mind, when he thinks he's right, he sticks with it—he holds his ground. He's the one I'll use, and he'll persuade the others. If the man to Samir's right had been a little more observant of Samir, and a little less of his colleagues, who seemed to be listening to him, he might have noticed a fleeting, malevolent smile. Not noticing, however, he had no idea he was about to be struck.

Bud Walker added, "Well, it's going to be a hell of a debate on this one. I mean this 'path to citizenship' thing, the whole pay a fine, register, send your money home, pay your taxes thing—that's a humdinger!"

"So true, Bud. This is wisdom of Solomon time!"

The man opposite Number 2 posed the next question. It was asked innocently and intelligently. And the answer that would finally stick, after their fireside chat, would reshape American politics for the remainder of the decade. It would become the litmus test for every candidate in 2006, and in the Presidential election to follow. He began by emptying the last of his mug into the flames. They sizzled briefly, and released a wisp of smoke.

"It's a real complex and emotional thing, I think. I mean you have the millions who are already here and how to deal with them. How do you make them legal? Jesus, we'd have to have a Gestapo to find them all and deport them. And I just can't see Americans putting up with that."

"Exactly!" all of them answered in chorus. The man continued. "And you got the need to ferret out the criminals and Al Qaeda—somehow separate them from the Hispanics who are breaking the law, but, you know, they're good people basically, just trying to feed their families. I mean, we've got to separate out the really bad from the little bit bad, right?"

There was silence now. These men were struggling with this. Their sense of goodness and fair play was causing them to stumble over this. They didn't know what the right course of action was. And unfortunately, uncertainty was not something to which any of them was accustomed. They were paid to be certain—and persuasive—and tonight they were all floundering.

Samir knew his moment was nearing. He waited patiently. The man went on. "So, is this it? Is this a brilliant idea—this, however they work it out, guest worker, path to citizenship option? Does this solve the problem—finally?"

Samir shifted his weight in his chair ever so slightly, to attract Bud's attention. It worked. Bud turned to him and said, "Samir, what's your take on this? With your background, what's your perspective?"

Dropping his head slightly in deference to his benefactor, Samir calmly inserted the marketing button the mastermind of Al

Qaeda had commanded him to introduce into the American debate. *And what better way than through the men the people of the United States listen to more than anyone else?* he mused. *Once again, Americans, your love of free speech and free press will be your undoing.* And without so much as a batting of the eye, he responded, "Yes, yes I do. If you will be so kind..."

They all asserted they were most interested in his input. After all, Bud Walker himself had placed the stamp of endorsement on this man. They leaned in as Samir quietly said, "Of course, I have a different perspective being in public relations. But it seems to me that some brilliant public relations have been exerted here."

"How so?" the man to Samir's right asked.

"Well, to paraphrase some poet or other, 'amnesty by any other name is still amnesty.'" That was all he said. He let it settle for a moment, to see if it was sinking in. It was. Although the President and his team were suggesting formulating something quite original and new, in that one moment Samir had artfully punched a button—and it brought up painful memories of defeat and failure. An American president twenty years earlier had tried amnesty. It had not worked. And there was one thing Samir knew about Americans—they do not like to fail, and they do not like to be wrong. And if there was one thing Conservative talk radio prided itself in, it was in being right, courageous, and outspoken in its protection of the American people.

One man took the bait that night. A hero of his had tried and failed before, and he wasn't going to let that happen to his people again. He had heard one other thing that night—"basically good people breaking the law." He would hang his argument on "the law is the law." They had broken one in coming to the United States illegally. That would become enough for him. In calmer, more rational times, he would have spotted that an illegal border crossing is not the same magnitude of crime as murder. What the President of the United States and a few senators could differentiate, and upon which they had built their suggestions, became a mass of confusion and equations of "the law is the law is the law."

These were not rational times in the world, however, and neither the President of the United States, nor the Conservative talk show celebrities, nor the people of the United States would be able to identify just how a reasonably-begun debate got turned into the most inflammatory, emotion-creating issue of the next three years.

Samir knew. Standing up and stretching, he was certain he had succeeded. All he needed to do now was wait, and listen, and watch. It wouldn't be long. Excusing himself, he said politely, "Gentlemen, it has been a pleasure meeting you, and a true honor listening to your discussions. I hope we get to do this again in the future."

They all smiled and overlapped each other with assertions of, "Likewise, Samir. We may call upon you on the air from time to time. You have a fresh perspective."

"That he does. That he does," Bud concluded.

"Good night. I think I'll see if I can persuade Alicia that we're 'danced out' for the evening."

CHAPTER 22

A bone-chilling cold penetrated the Doctor as he arrived in Miran Shah, Pakistan. *I must admit, there are advantages to Panama,* he told himself. *I'd forgotten what it is like to barely be able to breathe.*

But he had made it—and that was the important thing. What could have been a most treacherous crossing into the Taliban area of Pakistan, where the ferocious Haqqanni Clan still protected Al Qaeda, had gone almost uneventfully. There had been one moment, as he and his guide walked down a steep street in the border village, where he noticed a young boy peer out the window, and then fade back into the room quickly—away from the window. The Doctor's instincts were honed, after years of being on the run, and his powers of observation were legendary. In that moment, he had seen fear in the boy's eyes, and the Doctor wondered if they were walking into a trap. The Pakistan Army maintained a significant presence in the area, and he had cause to consider a trap.

It had not been one, however. Once they cleared the narrow, almost medieval stone-paved street and came into a small square, the Doctor hissed and made it very clear that he wanted to stay in the open, in relatively busy areas. His guide willingly complied. A few minutes later, Zawahiri entered a small mosque and exited the rear.

Behind the mosque was a building that appeared to be a renovated livestock stable. Made of clay blocks, there was barely even one block removed for air and light. The Doctor had to stoop to enter the building. This startled his guide for the moment. He had been told he would be escorting a high-level Al Qaeda commander into the area. Looking at his charge as they came into North Waziristan, he had assumed him to be Ayman

Al-Zawahiri, since he bore some resemblance to photos he had seen of the Al Qaeda leader. But now he wasn't so sure.

Everyone in Al Qaeda knew that the Doctor was a short man, and the guide pondered fleetingly how much taller the Doctor was in person, as compared to how he appeared in pictures—if this was indeed Zawahiri. Fortunately for the Doctor, the man chosen was an excellent guide, and fierce body-guard, but he did not have much of an intellect. He didn't know who this man was, but he concluded it couldn't be Zawahiri.

If he had been a bit brighter, he might have unmasked the ruse that had been perpetrated even amongst Al Qaeda circles. For everyone—other than Bin Laden, Samir, Makkawi, and Abou Al-Zarqawi—had been duped into believing that the now-dead double Zawahiri used was the Doctor himself. The Doctor didn't need disguises, as no one really knew what he looked like. And that was still holding, apparently. No one had given him even a second glance as he and his companion had made their way into Taliban territory.

"You may go, my friend," the Doctor said sincerely, excusing his guide. "I'll be fine from here. Alhamdulillah!"

"Alhamdulillah," the guide responded dutifully. He could not discern whether his charge was just informally using the word to say, "Thank goodness," or whether he meant it more piously and was truly saying, "Praise to God." Given that he was in Taliban territory, he concluded the latter, and mustered up a response of equal reverence.

Once the man was gone, the Doctor allowed his eyes to adjust; then he entered the room, moving to the opposite side so that his back was to the rear wall, and so that he could see anyone moving in his direction. *Old habits,* he reflected. He began to warm up, and removed the outer layer of clothing, exposing his familiar robe, with the western vest over it.

"Are you well, Ayman?"

The Doctor was startled by what seemed like a disemboweled voice. He was sure no one was in the room, yet he had been addressed. Peering into the shadows, now he saw yet another man with his back to the wall, facing out. The Doctor laughed and embraced the man as he rose. "I am very glad to see you, my friend."

The man nodded and smiled. "And you as well." He paused

for a moment. "I wish the circumstances were better. Nonetheless, I welcome your reassuring presence."

"We have little time, I fear," the Doctor said, launching right into it. "I would have preferred to do this by courier, but I felt I needed to be face to face with you." It had been said without malice, but Makkawi knew that this meeting—as dangerous as it was for both—would be definitive for Al Qaeda's plans in the coming years.

"I agree. Where do you want me to—"

The Doctor cut him off. "I want you to tell me first why President Musharraf still breathes."

Makkawi sighed, knowing this was the likely first topic. After all, the order to assassinate the Pakistani president had been issued immediately following his alignment with the United States and Britain. Attempts had been made, but each had failed. In fact, the man and his security teams seemed as resilient as a reptile's tail, which might be cut off, and yet would grow back quickly and stronger. After each failed attempt, the President's security forces seemed to penetrate the veil of secrecy more and more, gathering more information on hiding places and potential assassins.

"Sir, I have no excuses. And I will be very direct. We have tried, as you are aware, several times. We are no closer. We could even be farther. He has built a network of informants."

"And how is he doing that? Blackmail?" Zawahiri asked.

"Yes, most likely. He is a dictator, after all, and most dictators I have known have a very thick file on nearly everyone they might want to exert influence over."

The Doctor laughed. "Yes, well, I have used that as well." Then his demeanor turned stern. "And what is your recommendation, my friend?"

This time there was a hint of danger in the question, and Makkawi knew his next answer needed to be the correct one. Without hesitation, he said, "Our strategy I believe is still valid, but a change of tactic is warranted, I think."

He never has liked changing strategies, the Doctor thought. *How I miss Atef! He was so flexible in strategy and tactics.* Then he reminded himself, *Still, the man is loyal, and the one Atef personally chose to succeed him. I'll hear him out.*

"I believe our strategy is to destabilize the American coalition, and to destabilize the government of Pakistan, thereby weakening Musharraf, and possibly causing a coup, or at least insurrection."

"That is correct," the Doctor confirmed. "But, in our last plans I made it clear I wanted to force the issue in Pakistan by killing the man. The Americans would be deprived of their 'ally,' and we would have an opportunity to increase our presence and dominance in Pakistan itself."

"I know that, Ayman, but I'm suggesting that we have been unable to accomplish that, and that I have another way to bring about the same effect—causing civil insurrection, and possible civil war within the country."

The Doctor mulled that over for a moment. It was, in fact, the goal—a Pakistan too torn apart to be counted on by the Americans, and one which would pull their attention away from Iraq because of the nuclear weapons capability Pakistan already possessed. Nothing frightened the West more than the idea of a radical Islamic country with nuclear weapons—nothing. "All right, how do we accomplish that?"

"I've been watching the politics of the country. And I think there is an opportunity developing."

"Yes?" The Doctor was interested now. "Continue."

"Musharraf has had to tighten controls on his people, using force and his intelligence community in fairly brutal ways, in order to placate the Americans and to insure his whole country doesn't turn into an Al Qaeda haven. And here's what is delicious, Ayman. The people in the country are taking up the mantra of 'democracy.' They are almost giddily taking on this preposterous concept."

The Doctor listened, showing no expression whatsoever on his face. "And?"

"There is word that Bhutto and others in her Pakistan People's Party will challenge him in the next year, seeking election in 2007."

"Is she seriously considering this?"

"I believe so."

"I would have thought losing her father and two brothers to the political machinations of this area—not to mention her imprisonment—would have disabused her of politics!" Ayman laughed.

Makkawi laughed as well. "No, sir, not her. She's arrogant—

and reckless. And she's emboldened by the amnesty Musharraf has given her."

"Most assuredly, if she's even considering pressing Musharraf for democratic elections here."

"I believe she is. And, sir, this is where our opportunity lies." He paused to make certain he had the Doctor's full attention. He did. "She will have to challenge the President directly. She will have to provoke him in the hopes of gaining public support and sympathy. And in doing so, she will expose herself in public. She will become a target for assassination."

Makkawi continued. "We will assassinate her. The press, and the people of Pakistan, will believe she was assassinated by Musharraf—and I believe civil war will erupt."

The Doctor tilted his head, first to one side then the other, as if examining this idea full circle. "That would certainly accomplish our goal of destabilizing the area and securing our position—and of destroying Musharraf."

"Yes, sir, I believe so."

The Doctor liked this plan. *After all, it is very difficult to kill someone as well-protected as Musharraf. But a political opponent, even with security, is far more vulnerable.* "I like it." Then he added, "But what if it is not her?"

"Whoever it is will be someone who challenges the President's dictatorial powers. They have to, because the influence of the United States is an influence of democratic reform, and greater rights to the people. The next candidate, whether it be Bhutto or someone else, will be someone the United States secretly wants to challenge Musharraf."

"Do you think the United States wants Musharraf gone?" the Doctor asked.

"Not necessarily gone, but more under their influence for sure."

Suddenly, the Doctor laughed. It was genuine, and robust. For the first time, he felt they might be making some headway here. "Very well done, my friend. Here's the new order. Kill Musharraf if you can." Seeing Makkawi's look of surprise, he added, "I don't like the man, my friend. If we can still accomplish it, then do it. But begin immediately to implement the plan to assassinate the first serious political threat to Musharraf—

151

whether it be this presumptuous, ambitious woman, or someone else. And you are correct. I believe it accomplishes our strategy—perhaps even better than the original plan." He concluded and smiled. Remembering that he had not eaten, he said, "Were you planning to feed me?"

"Yes, sir, most definitely. Would you prefer to address the second issue now, or after our repast?"

One of the things the Doctor admired about Makkawi was his courage. He was a no-nonsense military commander, with almost no axes to grind. He believed in the cause, and he had proven trustworthy. Though his mind was nowhere near as brilliant as Muhammad Atef's, his loyalty and certainty were greater. Atef had had to die. Makkawi could remain. *I wonder if I even have a second choice?* the Doctor suddenly asked himself. *Is there anyone who could plan the global operations at all now?* That was such a dark thought that he waived it off as being the result of hunger and lack of sleep.

"I think our meal first, my friend. From your demeanor, I believe you have guessed the true reason I am here."

"Yes, sir. And I too need to fortify my body to prepare for this next discussion."

"Do you need rest as well?"

"No, Makkawi, I am ready now. Let us finish this."

"I am deeply concerned about Zarqawi, and whether or not he will be able to sustain and accomplish his mission in Iraq." There, he'd said it. Now Makkawi waited, knowing how much faith the Doctor seemed to have placed in this man, and how much in agreement the Doctor had been with his strategy of tearing Iraq apart by turning one religious sect against the other.

"I agree." The Doctor said nothing more.

Emboldened by his apparent agreement, Makkawi laid it out. "His insistence upon escalating the attacks upon Muslims within that country is backfiring. And I fear the people of Iraq will actually unite as the 'People of Iraq' rather than remain the bickering smaller groups we have successfully cultivated. And that, I believe, jeopardizes us all."

"How so?" the Doctor asked, watching his man closely.

"My fear is that the degree of his violence will turn the people against *us*, and toward the Americans. If they fear us more than they fear or dislike the Americans, the backlash against us will be profound. His mission was to create chaos and confusion—to the point they could not form a government. That failed. Then we amended the mission to destabilize various sections of the country to the point their new government could not stand. That would be a colossal defeat for the United States, and a great victory for us."

The Doctor needed confirmation on something. "We are losing a great many men there, are we not?"

"Far too many. The Americans seem to know now what towns they are in, and worse yet, what safe houses. That tells me there are informants. And they seem to know when they are rolling in vehicles, given the number of attacks upon our caravans."

"Do you mean they know where we are going?"

"It's beyond that, Ayman." Makkawi used his familiar name now. He was growing in confidence. "Anyone could probably guess where we would go. But knowing *when* and *how* we're moving tells me our security has been compromised. I believe there is a backlash of the Iraqis themselves. And that is untenable for us."

"Agreed." Now came the tough question the Doctor had risked his life to ask in person. "Have you spoken to Abou about this?"

"No, sir, I have not."

"And, why not?" the Doctor pressed.

"He is no longer responding to communiqués from our headquarters here."

This was what the Doctor had feared, that his man was isolated—or worse. "Is that because he is perpetually on the run these days, do you think?"

"I wish I could say that," Makkawi answered, with a weary sigh. "No doubt he is under extreme pressure. But he is also no longer answering the satellite phone we provided. In essence, he is completely out of communication."

Both were military men, and both knew that to have a major commander out of communication with the central command would be disastrous in this vital Iraq issue.

The next question was the hard one. "Do you believe he is still in possession of the phone?"

"Yes, sir, I do. And that is the alarming thing. If he would speak with me, I could relay your views and directives. I could even get him out of there—if he would speak with me."

Ayman Al-Zawahiri remembered now a conclusion he had reached years ago, when he first decided to give this command to Zarqawi. Knowing the man was hot-tempered, and not too bright, the Doctor had known Zarqawi would not survive this war. He would die in the fight.

"And sir, I fear one other thing."

"What is that?" the Doctor asked in resignation.

"Knowing that Nanda, his propaganda officer, is presumed dead, we can no longer rely upon Nanda's ability to choose the exact right films and videos to release to Al-Jazeera. He was truly a master at propaganda, and I believe his films and the timing of his releases have sustained our fight, and increased the fear of the whole world."

"I agree. And Nanda's loss was one of our most profound. The loss of Usama ranks as paramount, but there is no question Nanda and his films were vital to our strategy."

"So, Ayman, here's my fear. The man is off the grid; we do not know where he is. He is not communicating, and does not appear any longer to be implementing your tactics. He seems to be implementing his own. Not only do I feel they are not working, I fear he will continue to release his own videos—acting on his own timing."

"Allah, Allah, Allah." The Doctor rubbed his hands through his hair and held his head, as if in pain. "No, no, that *would* be disastrous. I and I alone control the releases. His mission was to create an environment of fear, and Samir's is to weave that fear into the fabric of America, Great Britain, and any other enemy who stands between us and the restoration of the Caliphate."

"Well, that's my apprehension—that he will be recording his own audio and video tapes, and releasing them on his agenda, regardless of how it will affect our political, financial, or military plans."

"Can he be brought back, Makkawi?" The Doctor asked it rhetorically, not literally, and Makkawi understood him completely.

"No, sir, I do not believe so. We are entering 2006; we are losing men in Iraq. And the chosen commander does not seem to care. The absence of communication tells me we have a rogue commander operating our most vital military theatre at the present time."

There was silence for a moment. The room appeared darker and gloomier than the late afternoon shadows would normally have created. There was a muffled sound of prayer horns summoning the good Muslims of Miran Shah to prayers at the Mosque. A block or two away, there was the barking of a dog. And, in the quiet of the moment, Abou Al-Zarqawi's fate was sealed.

"That is unfortunate." Again, the Doctor paused, twisting a button on his vest. "He will die in Iraq." Makkawi was holding his breath, not even knowing how to form the next question. He didn't need to. Ayman Al-Zawahiri was in command of Al Qaeda. The next order would be his. "If he releases any additional tapes of his own—not prerecorded by Nanda, Usama, or myself—he will be signaling to the United States that there is internal dissention in Al Qaeda. It would be tantamount to telling the Americans that their strategies are working, that they are dividing and conquering us."

"Yes, sir."

"So, my friend, send written communication to him of this by courier. And then, if he fails to understand this, and does anything that makes him appear to be in charge of Al Qaeda—or foments divisiveness in any way—you, with a heavy heart, will do your duty."

"I understand." Makkawi waited respectfully; then he pressed the issue. "Will there be a replacement, if such an action is necessary?"

"I think not, my friend. Sadly, I believe—if he cannot be contained—that we have lost Iraq." The Doctor said it quietly, and almost sadly. But he was a master game player, and he knew this was just one game in a series of games. And they had done huge damage to their enemies. The next games would be fruitful as well. He was sure of that.

Embracing his friend warmly, he donned the heavy winter

wear and head garb, and approached the door. Before he reached it, Makkawi quietly, and with resignation, said, "I don't think you should come here again, my friend."

Without turning, Zawahiri's mind raced to decipher the true meaning of Makkawi's remark. The Doctor's innate suspicion of everyone never allowed him to take any statement at face value. He always had to inspect it, probing it for any perfidious motive. Tonight was no exception. Slowly he turned to confront his commander. "What do you mean?"

There was just enough suspicion in his tone to warn Makkawi. Immediately he clarified. "Forgive me, sir, I did not mean you would not be welcome. I meant it is not safe for you here. It is a great burden on my heart to recommend as your military commander that you keep your person away from us."

Realizing they did have more to cover, the Doctor took a seat once again, and motioned for Makkawi to do the same. He had, of course, noticed that Makkawi looked tired, but now, upon closer inspection, he saw it was more than that—the man looked haunted, and besieged. Uncharacteristically, he asked rather kindly, "Is it the Americans?"

"Yes, sir. They are pretty much everywhere, and ruthlessly persistent."

Trying to reassure him, the Doctor interjected, "Perhaps it is time for you to take your three advisors and move to a safer location."

"With respect, sir, flight is no longer an option. No, it is safer to remain here, and pray there are no traitors amongst the Haqqanni who would reveal our identities or location."

"Why can you no longer run?" the Doctor asked impatiently. "Surely the Americans are not in this section of Pakistan?"

"My friend, the Americans are dug in." Pausing for effect, and seeing the Doctor's brow furrow, he added, "They have hundreds of teams operating in the entire border area. Their satellite capability allows them to identify and stake out the passes and safe areas the Russians never penetrated."

The Doctor was calculating with this. "You are speaking of Special Forces?"

"Yes."

"How many?"

"Thousands. Our informants tell us they are basically burrowed into a cave or pass, waiting for one of us to come by." Makkawi laughed disdainfully. "The curs are taking a play from our own book. We mustn't forget they fought with the Afghan resistance against the Soviets. I fear we miscalculated that. They *do* know the terrain, as well as where we successfully attacked and hid before."

Why did I not think of this? the Doctor chastised himself. *Makkawi is right. That is not good.* Trying to conceal his complete chagrin over something this fundamental being overlooked back in 2001, he probed further. "So, movement in Afghanistan is impossible?"

Makkawi quickly responded. "Not impossible, but extremely dangerous." He waited for a minute, and then delivered worse news. "And they are here, too."

"Here, inside North Waziristan?" he asked, in disbelief.

"Yes. They have a distinct public relations advantage in this matter, Ayman."

"How so?"

"Their media has no idea how many of them there are—how many units—let alone where they are deployed. They're all focused on the poor scum we're killing with improvised explosive devices in Iraq. Not even the mighty American press has guessed the true, and secret, configuration of the military's special forces."

There was a very sharp jab in Zawahiri's stomach at this disclosure. *This means the whole debate about pulling out of Iraq is moot,* he told himself. *Even if they do it, it will all be for show. The real threat remains. Damn Bush!*

"You see, Ayman?" Makkawi said. "It is wiser for us to stay here and hope we remain undiscovered. The odds of us running into the Americans, or informants of the Pakistan Army, if we move within this once-safe area, are too great."

"I see."

"And you understand now why I do not feel you should come here again?"

"I do." The Doctor doubted Makkawi's motives, however. He suspected the man was more concerned about his presence attracting attention, thereby exposing Makkawi and his men, than he was about his safety. *The advice is well-given, however, no matter the motive. I will not return to this place again.*

"You are right, of course, my comrade. I will not jeopardize you or your position again."

Quickly, Makkawi said, "I meant you no disrespect, Ayman. Please, I pray you understand that."

"Of course, of course. You would be a poor selection as military commander if you did not advise senior commanders where to go and when. Your predecessor would have done no less." He paused for a moment, thinking, and then offered, "I will have a Bin Laden video released shortly. You know, see if we can put some attention back on Iraq, and deflect it away from Pakistan." Suddenly, he laughed. Given the rarity of such an occurrence, this caught Makkawi by surprise.

"What?"

"I appreciate irony. Do you appreciate irony, my friend?" Makkawi answered that he did. The Doctor smiled. "Good, because I'll release the video with Bin Laden offering a truce, an 'honorable exit' from Iraq." Now Makkawi smiled as well. The Doctor added, "That should serve as a burr under their skin."

Makkawi nodded, and the two men embraced once again. "I will pray that Allah protects you."

"Allah Akbar!" And then he was gone.

Before Zawahiri could return to Panama City, he heard the news of the air strike near the Afghan border, which, according to the Pakistani officials and the BBC, killed four militants in a remote village. He had no idea whether Makkawi was among them, or if it was even the same village. *If it was, was I the target? Or Makkawi? Did they know I was there?*

There was no answer to be gained from the news media. They seemed to have nothing but speculation. So the Doctor resigned himself to waiting. A few days later, he received a communication from Makkawi that he was unhurt, and not involved. The short message just underscored, however, the accuracy of Makkawi's evaluation.

I can use this, the Doctor thought. For the first time, he smiled cunningly. *The Americans didn't get any of my main team, and they've irritated the Pakistanis. A gift—a small one—but one I will take.*

Then, shortly before the end of January, 2006, the BBC reported that, "Al Qaeda's number two man, Ayman Al-Zawahiri, has appeared on a video tape taunting the United States about an air strike in Pakistan which failed to kill him."

Once again, no one knew where the tape was made, or how it had been delivered to Al-Jazeera TV. And just as the Doctor hoped, it proved a tremendous opportunity to dupe the intelligence community into believing he was in that region of Pakistan, eluding them still.

Ensconced once again in the offices of ST & Associates in Panama City, sleeping on a rickety cot, he wondered if the Americans would be angry at his defiant statement in the tape. "Do you want to know where I am? I am among the Muslim masses." *No matter,* he assured himself, *I'm sure Samir can make this wound "smart."*

CHAPTER 23

*U*nlike the cramped quarters and small workspace James and Andy had used in the basement of Andy's Arlington home, where they had developed the probable sequence of multiple games being played by Zawahiri, this next analysis required every bit of space in their apartment in West Hollywood.

Even the furniture had been rearranged to facilitate the flow of information toward the central computer, which was set up in the middle of the living room. With its monitor facing the front door, it was the featured item in the room. A soiled, beige armchair had been dragged in front of it, to make it comfortable for whoever would be doing the data entry.

On the sandwich bar that separated the kitchen area from the dining area were three laptop computers, each with an Internet connection, and each with a stool in front of it for whoever was searching for data at any given moment.

To the right of the central computer were three televisions. None were flat screens; none had any fancy bells and whistles. James and Andy were not on vacation. They were in a race now to identify the Fifth Column inside the United States, whose purpose was to destroy the solidarity of the country, and to overwhelm and sink the nation before any successful attack could commence from outside. They had evaluated that the Fifth Column would attack through the game of "Sociology," and they, therefore, were poring over and evaluating all sociological phenomena and their recent history.

Each of the 19-inch TVs was set on rather unstable TV trays, and each was always on—tuned into WNG, CNN, and FOX. James didn't even want to know what his cable and phone bills were going to be for this operation. *What does it matter?* he told himself. *What good's retirement income if you don't spend it on something?*

To complete the research area, Andy had bought Rubbermaid tubs to house the collections of newspapers and magazines they were amassing. He had to admit, there was a stunning variety. They had subscriptions to everything from *O* to *US News & World Report.* They had started out with the usual suspects—the *LA Times,* the *San Francisco Chronicle* and the *New York Times*—but had quickly expanded their reading research into the more tabloid newspapers as well. And then there was a specialty section. One box held *The New England Journal of Medicine,* another *Psychology Today.* Nutrition and wellness magazines were all in one as well. One box held law journals from major California law schools. Then there were the local papers in gang-ridden cities like Compton, Long Beach, and Santa Ana. And there was even a religious section, which held magazines and newsletters from various churches in the metropolitan area. And, finally, the box that held *Cosmopolitan, Us, People,* and *Time.*

The bathroom was down the hall, along with two small bedrooms, which looked out over the courtyard and second-floor walkway that connected all the units. Andy and James each had their own personal computers in their bedrooms, and a few personal items. Andy's dresser had pictures of his mom and dad on their wedding day, his mom and him on his graduation day, Brian and him receiving the MVP award at the state championship, and James and him eating hotdogs—mustard on their chins and all—at one of the last games Brian had played. Kelly had taken it surreptitiously, but it was a great picture of the two of them trying to cheer and still handle their sodas and "dogs."

James' room had that same picture of Kelly and Andy on graduation day. It was the only picture he had. The truth was they were the only family he felt he had. So much had been sacrificed during the Cold War, as he'd lived undercover in the nations of Eastern Europe. Images of his mother and father were retained in his mind and heart, and seemed a part of another man's past. His life seemed to have just started when he met this brainy kid in Arlington, Va. So, it was fitting that there would be just one photo. James was in fact just beginning his life as a civilian. The rest were just years of being a CIA analyst and agent. And that was as artificial a life as he could think of.

Their routine was a pretty simple one actually. Daily, James would listen to TV, monitoring for segments that involved the sociological phenomena Andy and Brian had listed as relevant to their generation. Likewise, he would read the newspapers and magazines. When he found something, he would go to one of the Internet-connected laptops on the counter, and Google search to see any other related incidents, discussions, or articles. The full body of that was then transported to the central computer.

While online, James also explored any related Internet sites that came up. *Man, there are a lot of bloggers out there!* he told himself. *And, then, the websites people create! It's overwhelming.* And, to make matters worse, for the first time, he had to explore Facebook and MySpace. For James, it helped him get an insight into the minds of the generation he was now trying to save. And that was perhaps the most disturbing of all. Still, he struggled to remain objective.

Andy was still developing the program on the computer in his room, but the data banks were filling, ready for the program that would search for common denominators to the problems that plagued the young men and women of America.

Upon hearing Breaking News about a school shooting in the Northwest, a Google search quickly revealed other, earlier school shootings. The full articles, with an indexing of terms and words used within the articles, was then fed into the central computer. This was their routine. It was a daunting task.

"Frankly, Kid, I'd rather be looking through war-related chess moves than this haystack of unrelated stuff," James lamented one afternoon. Unlike their earlier analysis, which had unearthed Zawahiri's likely moves and whereabouts, they were not just evaluating news stories to see if the recent news event was the Doctor's latest "move" following a "move" by the United States or Britain. Back then, through brilliant and creative analysis, they had discovered the eight different layers of games the Doctor was playing, and had sequenced them in order of importance.

Now, however, knowing that the aberrated social conditions manifesting themselves in the United States—particularly with its young generation—were the likely avenue being used by the enemy to bring us down, the scope of their investigation and analysis was immense. They were looking for common denominators—someone or something—that might explain all of the areas of travail. Whether the enemy was using these common denominators, or merely benefiting from them, was what they were trying to discover.

James' background assured him that even if Al Qaeda was merely benefiting from the social breakdown, one of the best ways to damage Al Qaeda would be to identify, isolate, and dismantle whatever causes existed that were in fact weakening this vital generation in America's history. Should they be deliberately using them, then dismantling the causes would be devastating not only to Al Qaeda but also to any future enemy of the people of the United States.

Sensing that this study would be definitive, James felt the pressure. Any self-doubt he had, he tried to set aside in order to stay focused.

Andy, as usual, seemed to know what James was feeling. "I know, James, this is huge." For a moment, Andy just looked at the magazine in his hand, but then he added, "But, you and I both know they aren't unrelated. They're connected somehow—if we're right."

"Oh, we're right, Kid. We're right. What I'm sore about is the fact that we're doing this like a couple of lab rats using a prehistoric computer system, instead of one of the Super Crays the Pentagon or CIA are equipped with." He cleared his throat, as if something were stuck in it, and continued. "*They* should be looking for this, not us. It's a Fifth Column, for Pete's sake—ought to be of interest in a military fight!"

"James, James, I know. They just don't see," Andy said, trying to console him. "People don't know what they don't know, and they can't see what they can't see."

James shot him one of those, "Don't say another word" looks, and Andy knew it was time for lunch. "All I'm saying is that they're looking for the Fifth Column to be an Al Qaeda cell or something; they're looking for saboteurs. It's a paradigm, that's all. We'll have to shift the paradigm, and then they'll give you your super computer."

"Guys, guys, I can hear you all the way down the corridor," Brian chided, as he walked in and dropped his duffle bag near his make-shift bed on the sofa.

"We didn't hear you coming."

"Small wonder, Andy, with all the racket comin' outta this place!" He looked around to examine the area and concluded, "It's growing, every day—like a tumor."

James was the first to respond. "Yeah, we're nearly through with collecting data though."

"Yeah?" Brian seemed a tad doubtful.

"Yeah. We've got material from the last six months—and we're researching back to 1964 any items that stand out."

Brian scoffed at this. "What for? That's way before our time, bro! Shouldn't we cut this off in '82, '83?"

"Nope." That was all James said.

"No?" Brian still seemed mystified.

"No, Brian, we need a context, a statistical comparison, an ability to graph any trends. We need to see what my generation encountered on these topics—if we did—and what your generation is encountering, and if there is anything that got added. The common denominators could be recent. That will show up."

"Huh. I see. You got to see if there is something going on with us that wasn't with you. Or if something got worse."

Andy smiled. "You got it, Brian. If so, then we look to see what's in there, influencing it. Our theory is that some destructive things have been added."

"It could be *someone*, not *something*," James reminded them.

"Yeah, we won't know for awhile, Brian. All three of us have to do the analysis from here out." Brian looked around the room at the seemingly insurmountable amount of data, looked down for a moment, and asked humbly, "And you think I can actually do this?"

"Without a doubt, my friend, without a doubt," Andy joked, slapping him on the back of his head.

"I hope so, Andy. My job was always to run like hell and get away from the boogie man so I could catch your pass—not run headlong into him."

Brian was smiling, which reassured James that Brian was ready. *It'll be good for him*, he reasoned. *It'll keep his mind off what happened to him.*

As optimistic as that thought was, it would not prove to be

true. Neither James, nor Andy, nor Brian could have known that day that one of the subjects they would soon research would smash Brian right into the greatest tragedy of his life. And no one could have known that Brian's reaction to that would be devastating to the plans of the Fifth Column.

But, for now, they were just three hungry guys who no longer had anywhere to sit down and eat in the apartment. So, they headed for Ugo's.

CHAPTER 24

"James, could you come here for a minute?" Kelly whispered. She was leaning over his shoulder as James, Brian, and Andy were engrossed in a Lakers' game on the TV. Like every other sports fan in Los Angeles, they had caught Lakers' fever, and with football season over, this sport had grabbed them.

James looked up questioningly and saw Kelly beckon him to follow her to the kitchen area of her apartment. Theirs was too crowded to enjoy watching anything—let alone get away from work. So, they had all gladly accepted her invitation for some corn beef and cabbage on St. Patrick's Day. Joining her, he, too, whispered, "What's up?"

"Is he okay?"

"Who? Andy?"

"No, James, don't be dim here," she said, chiding him lightly. "I mean Brian. Is he okay?"

Honestly, James had no idea, and he wished Kelly wasn't bringing this up. His whole relationship with Brian was what he would describe as indirect. Andy had chosen Brian; Andy had brought him along. Brian was Andy's partner, and by virtue of association only, James'.

"I don't know. I don't know just how okay one can be with something like that." She nodded. "But, he's working, if that's what you mean. He's got his head in the game."

"Truth?"

"I think so, from what I see. But we should ask Andy."

"Ask me what?" Andy inquired, as he darted into the kitchen to get some more ice from the icemaker.

Keeping their voices low, James said, "Your mom was

wondering how Brian's doing, and I told her I thought he was okay." Then he added quickly, "But I also said you were the one with the best vantage point and comparison."

Taking his glass to the sink, Andy turned the faucet and filled it with tap water. Gulping some down, he shivered and made a distasteful face. It didn't go unnoticed and Kelly retorted, "I know. I know. It's lousy water. But I can't afford the good stuff yet."

"Some day, Mom, I'm going to buy you the best water filter in the country." He kissed her lightly on the cheek and added, "And to answer your question...I'd say he's okay. But, he's not great."

"That's what I thought," Kelly said.

"James, some days when he's working, you know, poring through magazines, Internet blogs, all that, he looks inside."

"You mean, like off into the distance?" James asked.

"No. Like, inside. He's not out, he's in." Seeing that neither Kelly nor James fully understood, he explained. "It's what a coach means, I think, when they have to tell you to keep your head in the game. They mean, stop looking in—stop thinking, or criticizing, or regretting. Just get out, put your attention on the game, on your teammates, and on the opponent."

"Oh, I see, and he's doing that, you think?" James was the first to ask.

"Sometimes. Yes. Not all the time, James. As I said, most of the time he has his head in the game, but every once in awhile I'll feel him turn in."

That's what James loved so much about this kid. He had said he'd "feel" him, not "see" him. Andy operated on a level of awareness about people, and ideas, that was far beyond anyone James had ever encountered in the field of intelligence.

Andy continued, in a low voice. "I mean it's natural I think. How do you just put out of your mind that one day you have a family—even if some of them are deadbeats—and the next day you don't. And then, the big mystery about why it happened. I mean, I'd be concerned about him if I *didn't* see him withdraw and turn in."

"Do you think he is depressed?" she asked innocently and sincerely.

"I don't want you to go there, Mom. I don't want you to

167

speak of that again!" His defiance and tone of voice was something James had never experienced between Andy and Kelly.

"Hey…hey!" he interjected. "What's goin' on here?"

Immediately, Andy apologized. "Sorry, Mom, really. But you—both of you—need to understand that Brian is a champion athlete. And, it appears, he's really smart, too. I don't think he's ever really stretched himself there. And he is stretching himself now, I promise you. I see him really work. No one but James has ever really told Brian that he had the gray matter, and that he should use it."

"Well, that's true," James admitted.

"And," Andy continued, as if there had been no interruption, "you have to understand that champions know how to win, even if they are playing hurt. And he's playing hurt right now."

They said nothing, but they were both listening closely. "I've known Brian a long time. He's tough. He grew up tough. By rights, he shouldn't have come as far as he has. God knows what he's witnessed living where he did…" Andy's voice trailed off for a moment. "Well, anyway, he's a winner. And winners know they can't change the past, but they sure as heck can change the future. So, to me, when I see him turn inward for a while, I just ignore it. I know he'll be back out shortly."

"And you don't think this is just a game face?" James asked.

"I don't care if it is. This is a walk Brian's got to make by himself, James. And none of us white guys are in a position to be helpful here."

James had no idea what Andy meant by that, but given the intensity of the way he set the glass down on the counter, he knew his partner well enough not to press. Maybe it *was* a "black" thing. He didn't know. *Surely there are experiences that one race knows that another race doesn't. Surely there are some areas where there is no common ground.* Maybe this was one of these. But, even as he thought it, James doubted it. His gut told him that the sudden and tragic loss of family, and the devastation that follows, is something common to all men, regardless of color.

What James, Kelly, and Andy couldn't see was that Brian *was* looking inward. He was looking for what he had missed, what he could have done. There was, in fact, a mystery there that kept him awake at nights. There was anger at knowing his entire family had been victimized by his grandfather, and he had no idea why. Brian's gut told him there was a cause—that something had happened to his grandfather—that his grandfather was not born a mass murderer. Something must have happened.

And, every day when he went to work with James and Andy, even though he didn't want it to, a wave of fear and apprehension would wash over him. It was during those moments he was looking inward. Something in his immediate environment, something he was researching perhaps, was frightening him. And Brian Washington Carver did not like the vile taste of fear. Truth be told, he was looking inward to muster up enough courage to cast the fear out. On those days, he wondered if Andy had felt that, too.

Concluding that he had, Brian was always able to pull himself back out, and return to work. What Andy never heard was Brian quietly saying under his breath, "Andy needs me. Stay focused. Stay focused."

"Am I the only one watching this game?" Brian asked, interrupting them suddenly in the kitchen.

Kelly recovered first. "No, Brian, no. I'm going to snag James here to help me bring supper on, but Andy's free to indulge in some TV."

Andy picked up on her lightness and quipped, "Spoken like a true mom!" As soon as he said it, he realized it might have been a faux pas to remind his friend of the fact he didn't have a mom anymore. But Brian seemed un-phased. *Whew, thank God*, Andy thought.

"Well, you'd better get in here, pal, cause the Jazz just scored twelve points!"

"What? Twelve points?" James asked incredulously. "What the..."

Kelly knew she was outnumbered and that James, too, would be worthless in the kitchen now. She rescued them with, "All right, James too. He's free, too. I'll turn the heat back and slow this dinner down 'til the game is over."

"Thank you. You are an angel. Thank you." It was a chorus, and Kelly couldn't distinguish who said what. She laughed, and was happy thinking, *Boys will be boys.*

The Lakers lost, and the next day all three were back at work. Something was developing at Gitmo.

CHAPTER 25

"*I*'m sending Alicia out on this one," Bud Walker told his editorial chiefs in their morning meeting.

"Why not one of our New York investigators?" his Manhattan bureau chief inquired.

Bud Walker was taking a gamble here, but every time he had used Alicia before, it had paid off. His reasoning was simply articulated. "Because the presence of a woman down there might just cause these 'good-old-boy Marine brass' to make a mistake."

Seeing that his team wasn't quite following this, he added, "They'll think they can put something over on her—you know, given she's from Los Angeles and all. But she's shrewd, and she'll spot it. No, gentlemen, it's Alicia, and she's en-route now. We'll get a live-feed in a few hours."

Less than twelve hours after two of the detainees at Gitmo had committed suicide by hanging themselves in their cells, Alicia Quixote had, in fact, gotten her story. The military, predictably wanting to put a quick end to this story, had graciously offered Alicia the opportunity to visit the quarters, and to personally witness how humanely the detainees were being treated. And they were quick to point out that a military investigation was already underway.

She had even been allowed to video in Camp One, the highest security section of the prison. Having shown the original chain-link outdoor cells in which the first detainees had been harbored, as well as the newer, almost-windowless, concrete cells now in use, she stood in

171

front of the facility with a condescending colonel, delivering her report via satellite to the salacious audience of WNG.

The New York anchor skillfully questioned her about the young men's deaths, and what was being reported at the scene. He then asked a question or two of the colonel, who seemed noticeably stiff and ill-at-ease. He was the public relations officer for the base, and, in fact, was somewhat disarmed by Alicia's charm. Standing in front of the camera, he doubted now whether it had been a wise choice to accept Alicia's offer to be on camera with her, and to answer, as she had put it, "a few questions."

The colonel's instincts were sadly correct. Though the questions posed to him by the New York anchor were innocuous enough, Alicia's last question would produce a profound impact, and further complicate the War on Terror.

Alicia Quixote was a product of an American upbringing. In fact, she was only a few years older than Brian and Andy. Her viewpoint was distinctly American, and she knew next to nothing about the Arab mind, let alone the terrorist mind. To her, suicide was a sad ending to a life, and it meant something terrible had been done to the person. To a young, Arab male, however—who had been recruited, programmed, and trained by Al Qaeda—suicide meant something altogether different. But her final question arose from her own personal reality, not from a deeper understanding or expertise. She asked the colonel, "Colonel, given this tragic occurrence, will the United States military be providing mental health care for the detainees?"

The colonel swallowed hard before he answered, knowing he had just walked into a trap. There was no way, in the remaining five seconds, for him to adequately address that. And so, he did what all bureaucrats are trained to do—he answered curtly, "We'll look into it."

It took Amnesty International and Human Rights Watch less than twenty-four hours to respond. They were not only concerned about the legality of detention at Guantanamo Bay—one calling for the closing of the facility—but one group commented to the BBC on the depth of despair that must have driven these young men to take their lives. By the end of the day, inspired by the sincerity of these organizations, the mental health of detainees now became a "cause célèbre."

CHAPTER 26

"*J*ump, Abou, jump!" Zarqawi's bodyguard screamed at him, hoping Zarqawi could hear him over the deafening and painful rocket and machine-gun assault on their caravan.

Zarqawi had had one narrow miss after another over the recent months as he and his newly trained men launched unfettered, and deadly, attacks upon US military and Iraqi civilians alike. Tonight was to have been a routine placing of some improvised explosive devices, known as IEDs, and a quick escape back to Fallujah.

But a tip that came into the military base had forewarned the Americans of the attack, and the hunter was now being hunted. Abou Al-Zarqawi, commander of Al Qaeda forces inside Iraq, was a coveted prize. And the team that deployed that night was bent on capturing or killing the terrorist super-star.

Still yelling, Zarqawi's bodyguard struggled to take control of their vehicle. The driver was shot, and had slumped to the left. Climbing from the passenger side to a precarious position where he could at least reach the accelerator, and maintain a degree of control over the steering wheel, he told Zarqawi, "I'll get along side the gully up ahead, but I won't be able to slow down. You'll have to jump anyway. Roll when you hit!"

Zarqawi signaled that he understood. He could hardly breathe. There was so much smoke and dust. The screaming of the men who were dying was over-riding. *I've gotten away before. I can do it again,* he reassured himself. Then, screaming "Allah Akbar!" at the top of his lungs, he dove from the vehicle as it careened near the road's edge.

With all the smoke, debris, and crashing vehicles, the Americans in pursuit never saw the door open, let alone their prey escape. Quietly—injured, and on his stomach—the man the Americans regarded as vermin, crawled away. He wasn't finished yet.

CHAPTER 27

*F*ragrance from the jasmine in the courtyard below wafted up
into the apartment. Since June in Los Angeles is usually gray
and overcast due to the inversion layer off the Pacific Ocean, it
was possible for James, Andy, and Brian to leave their windows
and doors open.

All of their neighbors worked during the day, so, other than
the apartment manager, they were usually alone. The only liability,
if you could call it that, of leaving their door open was the visit it
invited from Barney, a black cat with white boots and whiskers,
owned by their neighbor on the opposite side. Barney loved to
"crash the party." If the door was open, he took it as an
invitation to come for a visit. Today was no exception. Barney
was comfortably curled up on the sofa, oblivious to the work
going on around him.

They were nearing the end of six months of research and data
entry. It had even been necessary to rent a storage facility down
on Olympic Blvd. to hold the boxes upon boxes of material they
had gathered. Though entered into the computer, James and
Andy insisted upon keeping the hard copies—to prove to what
they knew would be doubtful CIA directors that the research was
valid, and to revisit if their initial analysis was too thin.

As they entered June, however, James was quite certain there
was enough to go to the next step. Brian was relieved to help
move all the boxes out, as it gave him more than just sofa space
as his living quarters. On days when it had gotten too
claustrophobic, he had slept on the floor of Andy's room, small
as it was. Truth be told, he liked having a roommate, and seeing
the picture of him and Andy made him feel good.

One of the first areas of data entry had been the decline of education in the United States. As America turned into the 21st century, literacy levels continued to decline until nearly 40 million adult Americans were considered to be functionally illiterate. With continually declining SAT scores as well, those test scores had been recalibrated and standards had been lowered to give American students a better showing. In math and science the United States, moreover, had dropped to seventeen and sixteen out of twenty-three developed nations participating in international testing. James wondered what could have caused the nation to drop from the top to near the bottom. Therefore, he had looked into educational systems, philosophies, and any written explanations for these devastating phenomena.

You don't have to be a rocket scientist to know that if kids aren't educated, they can't participate, James had told himself. *If they can't read and write, they're left out of the game of life. What a bleak picture of the future these kids must have.*

And starting from there, James knew that most of the rest of Andy and Brian's "Symptoms" list would follow. He was reviewing that list right now, to run a final check. Dropping out, apathy, hopelessness, anger, depression, teen pregnancy, drug usage, no self-respect, no money, loneliness—all of these phenomena were natural consequences, James felt, of someone left out of the game of life by an inability to learn, think, and apply. *Jesus, this topic alone would be enough for a PhD.* He chastised himself. *Stay focused, James, stay focused. There's more.*

Television and Internet institutions were an obvious check-off. TV watching hours and Internet usage by this generation would have to be described as pervasive. James knew this was influencing values, interaction, relationships, communication ability—and that all of that would affect and possibly promote promiscuity, deadbeat fathers and mothers, obesity, intolerance, loneliness, class separation, and a host of other "symptoms of a dying generation."

The proliferation of drug usage was almost a cliché. It had begun with James' generation in the '60s, but was now so pervasive that all legal, educational, religious, athletic, military, and even business enterprises had to factor it in. Pharm parties—where kids snatch all prescription meds from their parents medicine cabinets, pouring them into a large bowl at a party, then popping pills randomly while consuming alcohol—had so shocked James the day he stumbled on it that he had had to take a walk for more than two hours to clear his head, and stop shaking.

On his own, he had added in "no parental supervision" to the list. That had made him feel better, and he was quite confident Brian and Andy would agree that it was a phenomenon that should be addressed, even if they had not personally experienced it.

Because of gangs, which James felt emanated from the loneliness and hopelessness of the educational failures, and because of the violence that followed when gangs were coupled with drugs, the law enforcement/legal profession and all legal practices—starting from the moment of arrest, to trial, imprisonment, and probation—had been included.

Given the fact that there had been a spate of lawsuits brought in recent years against churches, the area of religion was also examined. James was particularly interested in any personnel or practices, which might have been added in the last decade or two to the institution of religion itself. He had not limited it to the obvious articles and exposes relevant to the Catholic Church, but had expanded it to any and all religions under fire—or not prospering as they had before.

One of the most prolific and overwhelming areas they had researched was the field of Medicine. Since "Medical" had surfaced as the game second from the top in the hierarchy of games they believed Zawahiri was playing, James had insisted that microscopic attention be given to this category. Given the fact also that Ari Ben-Gurion had confirmed the presence of high-level Al Qaeda in the Swiss pharmaceutical industry, most probably Zawahiri, this "game" never left James' mind.

Upon first research, there was so much evidence of decline in the health of Americans that James wondered if we had just suddenly become one of the sickest nations on Earth, or if there was a change in the documentation and diagnoses, making us *appear* sicker. What had once been a healthy and prosperous people had turned into what the World Health Organization classified, by the year 2000, as number 72 in the world on "level of health"—just below Bosnia and Argentina, and just above Bhutan, Nicaragua, and Iraq.

Again, it was easy to look at the "Symptoms" list the boys had put together and connect depression, illness, abortion, miscarriages, apathy, hopelessness, no self-respect, obesity—almost the whole list—to this category.

Though Brian was unaware of the magnitude of this area, James and Andy were keenly aware that their initial analysis had led them straight into the Medical and Pharmaceutical industries earlier. Now, however, they were not doing analysis, just data entry—a mental discipline Andy seemed to accomplish easily. James, however, was struggling to keep a clear head amidst the mounting data, and experienced ferocious nausea and an anxious stomach whenever they dealt with this material. He longed to begin analysis, but knew now was not the time.

Underemployment was most likely linked to Education and Economics. But, it had been included as well, as the statistical links between money and divorce were unequivocal.

And even the Military and its practices had been scrutinized. James' introduction to the military had been the Viet Nam era. But all recruiting, training, indoctrination, disciplining, and maintenance practices of military personnel were looked into. It was clear to James that bigotry, hatred, violence, pregnancy, abortion, disease, anger, and even class separation and self-image could be symptomatic of problems there as well.

Just before he closed out his checklist, James sat back in the overstuffed chair in front of the main computer, sighed deeply, and closed his eyes. It seemed evident to him now that all of America's institutions were besieged—that the entire American culture was under attack. Proof of that lay in the devastating symptoms in each of the major categories that engage people. Religion, education, military, law, health, medicine, economics, family, entertainment—these were the woof and warp of our American culture. Andy and Brian had, on their own, listed all of these areas as ones that were plaguing and befuddling their generation.

James knew in his gut, as he continued to breathe deeply, that the Fifth Column would be found somewhere in here. He had no idea whether it would be a person, a concept, a group—he didn't know. But he knew instinctively that for this much to have happened, so broadly and so fast, there was a sinister source.

James Mikolas was not a religious man, but he haltingly said under his breath, "Dear God, please, please. I love these boys. Please let this work."

Awkwardly concluding his prayer, he called out to Andy, "Are you ready?"

"Yep!" Andy answered, before James had barely finished. Holding a flash drive in his hand, he looked off into the distance for a second, out the dining room window toward the Hollywood Hills, smiled, and added, "If you'll turn over control of the 'Pilot's Seat,' I'll install the program on this computer and run the database through it."

Rising deftly, James smiled through his anxiety and said, "Be my guest."

It had taken months to research and enter the voluminous material. It took less than a minute for Andy to insert the flash drive and install the program. The next step would commence the filtering of the entire database through Andy's program, as it would search, winnow, and find any and all common denominators.

"Let's get Brian out of the shower so he can witness this," James joked.

"Right, right."

A moment later, Brian emerged from the bathroom wearing his LA Western workout sweats. Looking a bit wild now that his hair wasn't as well-groomed as his football coaches would have liked, he asked, "What's up?"

"We're ready to launch, Brian."

"Seriously?"

James walked over and offered his hand. Brian shook hands vigorously with James, grinned uncharacteristically, and exclaimed, "Seriously!"

"Okay, here we go," Andy interjected, as James walked behind him. The program started. For a moment, all three stared at the screen as if they were expecting something to happen. Laughing, Andy rose saying, "Guys, this will take hours! Let's go eat."

"Sure." James suddenly had an appetite. "Why don't we call your mom and take her to brunch at the Pacific Dining Car? I hear it is a great place to eat."

"It is," Brian affirmed. Still fascinated by the screen, he sat down in the armchair and offered, "I had a protein shake this morning, and a couple of those B-12 energy drinks Andy always drinks. If you don't mind, I'll just stay here and baby-sit this."

Andy knew what was going on, and he signaled to James not to argue with Brian.

"Sure, Brian. Sure. Can we bring you anything?"

"Nope. How long you think this will take?"

"It could take eight hours, maybe longer. I don't really know."

"That long?"

"Yeah, Brian, so don't feel you need to monitor it every minute. The fireworks won't come 'til the end."

That reminded James. "Hey, Kid, how will we know it's done?"

"It'll say 'Done.'"

"That's all?" James and Brian were both incredulous. Clearly they felt that having put so much time into this warranted something with a bit more fanfare.

"Well, yes. But, in the lower half of the screen, it'll print out the list of common denominators." Andy offered that up, hoping it would placate them a bit.

"That seems simple enough," James concluded.

"It is. Now let's pick up Mom. I want to take her out to Huntington Gardens this afternoon as well. She's been wanting to go out there, and I had to keep putting her off. What do you say, James, that we indulge her a bit today?"

"Sounds great. Let me just change my shirt." James darted into his bedroom.

Neither Andy nor Brian had any idea why James needed to change a perfectly good shirt, but Andy did note James looked spiffier when he came out, and he'd changed to pressed trousers, too. Brian winked at Andy as he coaxed them out. "Go on, now. Be good. I'll man the fort."

It was dusk by the time James and Andy returned. Not only had they taken Kelly to the Pacific Dining Car, which had been a great hit, but they had also toured the gardens, library, and museum of the very prestigious Huntington Gardens. By the time they finished there, they had all worked up an appetite, so James had suggested their new favorite fast-food place, the In-And-Out burger in Glendale.

They bought dinner for Brian as well, certain that he would be hungry by now. It was a little after 9PM when they returned.

When they entered the courtyard down below, they were surprised to see no lights on in their apartment up above. Maybe Brian had gone out after all, losing patience with the process. But, when they came along the walkway, they could see that the door to the apartment was open.

James had a terrible sense of dread, fearing there had been some type of break-in. He tried to steady his nerves by reminding himself that no one knew what they were working on. That only made things worse when he realized their apartment was full of valuable equipment. To them the data and program were paramount. But to a burglar, multiple computers, TVs, and laptops might have been the enticement. *No, no, it can't be,* he repeated to himself, as they rapidly approached the door.

"Brian, are you in there?" Andy shouted, as he stepped into the dark apartment. He knew immediately there had been no burglary, because the only light in the apartment was coming from the monitor facing the front door. The computer was on, and the screen was lit, casting an unearthly light in its wake.

James entered, regretting he'd left his ankle weapon in his bureau drawer. "What the..."

Neither could see if Brian was in the chair, as its back was tall, but as their eyes adjusted, they saw that nothing appeared disturbed.

"He's probably asleep," Andy concluded. "It's pretty boring, and I expect he's asleep in the chair."

"No, I'm not," Brian responded quietly, emotionlessly.

Turning on the light, Andy spoke first. "Wow, you gave us a scare!"

"Sorry, didn't mean to." He didn't say anything more.

James was quick to re-orient. "So, Brian, is it finished?"

"Yup. A few hours ago." Again, Brian said nothing more. There was an odd quality to his voice. James couldn't quite identify what it meant. He and Andy approached the chair from behind to look at the screen.

"Did it find some common denominators?" Andy asked.

"Oh, yeah." Brian was almost flippant.

"And it printed them?" James added.

"Oh, yeah." He repeated the phrase exactly the same way.

"How big is the list?" James grimaced. He was hoping it wasn't too long to be of value. It had to be short enough to confirm their theory, and propel their approach to a solution. If it were too long, there would be no way for them to create something pervasive enough to affect the sociology of the United States, let alone dismantle the destructive line it created for the Fifth Column.

The answer was immediate. "Short."

James and Andy both let out a huge sigh of relief. "Great!" Their voices overlapped. "Let's see what we've got!"

Looking over Brian's shoulder, Andy's eye reached the bottom half of the screen first. Since he'd designed the program, he knew exactly where the data would appear. A second later, James' eye focused there as well. What they saw stopped them cold, riveting them to the screen.

"That's it? That's all there is?!" Andy asked almost belligerently.

"Yup, that's all she wrote," Brian responded quietly. Then, finally, he added, "I thought it was odd myself, so I ran it a second time—finished an hour ago. Came out the same both times."

"My God." James was just standing there, looking at the screen. His jaw was proverbially dropped. He had hoped for a short list. But this was stunning. There was but one word on the computer screen in the box labeled COMMON DENOMINATORS.

In his gut, he knew the program was accurate, that it had given the right answer. He'd been in the intelligence game too long not to have spotted the hint of it as he did his research over the last six months. Yet here, now, was the empirical compilation spanning every sector of the American culture. And one word was common to all the institutions to which this generation was exposed. One word was common to all the articles related to the symptoms Andy and Brian felt were devastating their generation.

Man, this is going to be hard to sell, James thought despondently.

If I thought I was pilloried for my first theory, wait 'til they get a load of this! Almost immediately, he recovered, however, as he remembered an old Bible concept his mother had taught him—that "knowing the truth shall set you free." *Well, this is certainly "knowing the truth" time. Wonder how the Kid is taking this?*

Slowly, Andy's hand slipped onto Brian's shoulder and squeezed it. Brian tipped his head back and looked up at his friend. "Well, I got to say, friend, this wasn't the pass I was expecting you to throw." There was a look of irony in his eyes as he smiled ever so slightly. He was resigned.

Brian had always had absolute faith and confidence in Andy. It was Andy he had turned to after his wake-up call, and trip to Florida to intervene in a mercy killing. It was Andy he had chosen to stay with. And it was Andy's project he had chosen to join. He had even promised James and Andy that once they found the sources of this decline, he would create a computer game to defeat them. At the time, it had been offered as a way of assuaging their fears that he spent too much time on the computer playing games, and not enough time playing in life. That promise, however, was on his mind now.

"Guess I've got a job to do now, don't I?" That was all Brian said. But now there was firm resolve in his voice.

"We all do, son, we all do," James added.

Just then, Barney the cat jumped up onto the back of the chair, as if he too wanted to see what had the three men so mesmerized. At the bottom of the screen was one word—Psychiatry.

CHAPTER 28

*T*he Doctor sat alone in the sparse office of ST & Associates in Panama City. It had been some months since he and Samir had met here, and in that time no one had wandered off the street and up the five floors to the meager office. Once again, sitting with his back to the window, he was aware of the fact that the only illumination in the room came from the light that filtered in between the buildings and through the dirt-encrusted window.

Confident that no one knew he had moved in here, and that no one could see into the office, Ayman Al-Zawahiri was certain he had successfully disappeared off anyone's radar screen when he had closed out the small apartment from which he had been operating. Without his Internet capabilities, he was forced to rely more on the satellite phone than ever, but he was satisfied their advanced encryption technologies afforded him some security—at least for now.

He was expecting a call, and waited patiently, fanning himself occasionally. The satellite phone was on the floor, as neither he nor Samir had even brought up a proper desk. The table, which was left over from the previous tenant, was the only work space. None was needed, however, as Eduardo Morales, as he was known in Panama City, rarely ventured out. His walks outside in the neighborhood were also so sporadic that he doubted anyone would even recognize him. And that was the way the Doctor wanted it. With every plan laid in place, operating on its own time clock, he rather looked forward to disappearing into obscurity. *If I outlive the destruction of the United States, then I'll return, free to use my given name,* he promised himself. *And if I don't, well...* He smiled. *The mystery of where I am will haunt them for a long time to come.*

Taking pleasure in the degree of control he had attained, and

184

the power he wielded, he nonetheless was growing impatient. *It should be done by now.* "I do not wish to wait here all evening!" he exclaimed out loud.

And then, as if it, too, was under the orders of Ayman Al-Zawahiri, the phone rang. Bending over and picking it up, the Doctor recognized the incoming number, and gingerly pushed the receiver.

"I have bad news. It is confirmed." That was the entirety of what Samir initially said.

Keeping his subterfuge going, the Doctor asked, "What is?"

"Sir, it is coming over the wires now, and will be announced by CNN shortly. Abou al-Zarqawi was killed yesterday."

The Doctor, of course, knew what this call would be about. Actually, he had known all along that Zarqawi was too independent and hot-headed to survive a protracted assignment. But, what he didn't know specifically was who had ordered it. To be sure, the man was no longer operating under the command authority of the Doctor, and was becoming a liability to Al Qaeda itself, and to its mission in Iraq. *Did Makkawi do this?* he asked himself. Then, so as not to arouse Samir's suspicions, he asked, "Was he out in the open?"

"No, sir, he was in his safe house in Baquba."

"How did it happen, do you know?"

Samir quickly responded. "According to the media, he was attacked by a bombing raid perpetrated by the Americans. F-16s I believe." Samir knew what question would be next. In fact, he knew there would be two, so he was prepared.

As expected, the Doctor asked first, "Was anyone else killed?"

"Yes, his spiritual advisor, Sheik Abd-al-Rahman, and a woman and a child."

"His?"

Now that question was unexpected, and it surprised Samir.

He answered quickly and honestly. "I do not know, sir. I have no information whatsoever." The Doctor seemed satisfied, but Samir couldn't help but wonder why he had asked this. *Surely, Zarqawi would know the penalty for illicit sexual behavior. Surely he would,* Samir pondered momentarily.

And then the question he dreaded, but knew was coming. "How did they find him, do you know?"

"There's conflicting information coming in on that, sir. The Iraqis say one thing, the Americans another. The person who confirmed the story for me says it appears someone tipped them off about the Sheik, and they followed the Sheik to the meeting." Samir waited, trying to guess how devastating this event was from the Doctor's reactions. But he wasn't even able to guess. *I may just have to ask,* he told himself.

"We have a man captured in Jordan, do we not?"

"Yes, Makkawi's second-in-command."

"Do we know what's become of him, Samir?" The voice was calm, but Samir knew right then that the Doctor suspected Zarqawi had been betrayed by a senior level Al Qaeda figure, and that this man had given the Jordanians the name of the spiritual advisor. It would be simply a matter of cat and mouse until Zarqawi showed up.

"Regretfully, sir, we do not." He paused for a moment and then plunged in. "Sir, I had been relying upon Abou's Iraq activities to inflame the Americans here in the States. What does this mean? How are you evaluating this?"

Without even a second's hesitation, the Doctor responded forcefully, saying, "It does not impact anything, Samir. The man's actions were turning the Iraqis against us. He was unreachable, and intractable. It is regrettable that another of our brave warriors has had to die, but our cause will not be diminished one iota by this." He paused for effect and then added, "In fact, it is probably enhanced."

"I see." Samir didn't quite see it that way. But it did confirm for him suspicions he had had that there was a split developing between Makkawi and Zarqawi. Recently he had developed a growing concern that Zarqawi was becoming a rogue. He responded quickly. "Well, that is good news at least."

"Indeed." The Doctor's tone indicated he did not want to stay on their satellite phone much longer. "Was there anything else?"

Sighing slightly, Samir ended with, "Not really...I can actually see how I can use this right now to foster the idea here in the States that with Zarqawi dead the United States has even less reason to remain in Iraq—what with the sectarian violence, which I'm sure will continue." The more he looked at that, the more exciting the prospect became of planting that "button" with the already-growing anti-war movement in the country. *Why stay and endure the violence of the Iraqis if the man you were after in Iraq is dead?* He mulled the idea over, and a propaganda thread was forming nicely.

The Doctor interrupted him with, "Excellent. I'll leave that in your capable hands. And thank you for the report." Abruptly he disconnected the call, and sat back in the chair, smiling. It was done. His Iraq problem was solved.

Releasing the straps on his leather briefcase, he pulled out his laptop and checked the battery charge. There was enough juice remaining, so he booted up his laptop and brought up the familiar cube. The second level from the bottom, highlighted in blue, showed two black knights. One was Makkawi, and the other had been Zarqawi. Adeptly, he deleted the Black Knight labeled Zarqawi from the electronic three-dimensional chess board. There were two questions in his mind now—*Who replaces him? And who ordered this?* Though it made him uneasy to contemplate the possibility that a member of the inner sanctum had ordered the elimination of another member, he knew very well it was something he himself might have ordered in the near future, and he assumed Makkawi felt that their earlier conversation about "duty" had been his authorization to handle the situation. Surely, in all his years, neither he nor Usama had hesitated to eliminate obstacles to their objectives. *Abou was becoming an obstacle.*

There was a sudden, sharp jab in his gut, and a simultaneous rising of acidic fluid from his stomach up into his esophagus. He knew what that meant, not only physically but also psychologically. Something was bothering Ayman Al-Zawahiri— not knowing for sure *who it was.* Something more elusive was bothering him as well, and it was his inability to grasp *it* that terrified him. There was danger, he was sure of that, but he could not tell its source.

———————————

On that day in June 2006, a common denominator to a host of devastating social and cultural phenomena had been identified. And on that day, someone collected a $25 million reward for information leading to the death of Abou Al-Zarqawi. It had started out as an innocuous day in an otherwise ordinary June. But Al Qaeda had been dealt two blows that day.

One was known, and would be talked about and evaluated by experts, journalists, and politicians throughout the world for weeks. The other was unknown, and unobserved—for now.

CHAPTER 29

James had fallen asleep easily after their discovery. The relief of the long months of initial research ending, followed by the confirmation of what his "gut" had told him, left him feeling affirmed and ready for the next step. Not long after he'd gone to his room, he'd heard Andy's door close as well, and seen the lights go out in the living room.

Suddenly, he awakened. There were no unusual sounds. He could hear the usual steady hum of traffic on Santa Monica Blvd. During the day, no one would notice, but late at night, when all the rest of the neighborhood was quiet, the sound of traffic was the only sound that stood out. It acted like white noise for James, making it possible for him to sleep soundly.

Getting up to see what had awakened him, he noticed a light on in the living room. Quietly, he opened the door and peeked out. The light was coming from the end table near the sofa where Brian slept. Curiosity getting the better of him, James came down the short corridor and entered the living room, almost tripping over some of the cables to the counter-top computers.

Brian was sitting up on the sofa, looking straight ahead, as if studying something. Seeing James enter snapped him out of the reverie sufficiently to grunt, "Hey."

"What's up, Pal?" He sat down next to Brian, trying to look comfortable. He sensed this was going to be another one of those conversations where his wisdom and understanding might be taxed.

"I got a question for ya. Been keepin' me up."

"All right. I'm up, too. So, what is it, Brian?"

Brian hesitated for a moment, as if trying to phrase it right; then he said, "You and Andy didn't seem surprised by our *discovery*." He looked at James to measure his reaction.

Nonplused, James answered quietly, "We weren't."

"Well, I sure as shit was! Why weren't you?" he asked defiantly.

"We had a bit of an advantage over you, Brian."

"How so?"

"You remember we explained to you the project we had been working on trying to figure out what Zawahiri would do next, and where he might be?"

"What kind of question is that?" Brian stopped for a moment to suppress his rising anger; then, losing that battle, he abruptly added, "You know, James, I may have seemed a little 'out of it' back there at Cape Fear, but I followed you—and I've been working with you everyday for, what, six months? How the hell wouldn't I know what you were working on?"

Taking that outburst in stride, James quickly added, "Good, 'cause that isn't what I meant!" He stared back at Brian, equally defiant. Finally, Brian laughed. James continued. "Well, once we figured out the sequence of these games Zawahiri is playing, and once we figured out that he would use a variety of weapons to influence sociology, that led us to pharmaceuticals and medicine. So, we had a bit of a head start. We'd confronted some of this data before—just not so much of it."

"I see."

"And remember, I'm a 'mind guy.' That wasn't in your curriculum."

Brian jutted his jaw, looking James right in the eye and challenged, "Is that a joke?"

"Kind of…it's more irony I think. You and your buddies missed a bit in your world history courses. Let's just put it that way."

Pausing for a moment to stretch his neck from right to left, he added, "Also, Pal, Andy stumbled on the TV ads promoting all the meds—psychiatric meds more than the others—and put two and two together on how television indoctrination was penetrating the marketplace with that crap, creating a demand. We knew somebody stood to gain from all those drug sales. It wasn't too long a jump to guess who."

Brian sat back a bit now, just nodding his head. Then, as if to reconcile this in his own mind, he asked, "It's the fact that we found just one common denominator, James. Is it possible—

really possible—that the only thing common to all those areas we studied is the field of psychiatry?"

James didn't hesitate for a second. "Yes, it is, Brian. It may be that, with an even more comprehensive database, more time, a more scientific extrapolation of data, perhaps a few other common denominators might appear. But, given what Andy had already discovered, and given Zawahiri's background, this is the one that makes the most sense. This is the likely avenue he *would* use to attack. It fits him."

"Right. I see. This doesn't contradict your earlier conclusions."

"That's correct," James affirmed.

Brian was still chewing on it, mulling it around a bit, and added, "So, are they all evil then?"

James had no idea what he meant. "Who?"

"All psychiatrists. Are they all in on it?"

James had not ever looked at that, and was somewhat shocked at the way the question was phrased. It was expressed with the kind of hurt feelings a child has when he's been disappointed by someone, and now he's wondering if everyone is like that.

"Uh…" James stumbled for a moment, squirming a bit on the sofa. "No, I doubt it. Seems to me a lot of people go into those fields because they want to help people."

"Yeah, well this sure as shit ain't helpin'!"

"Right, right, it isn't." Then, to clarify, he added, "Brian, I expect for a lot of them it's just ignorance. The problem is the *field* of Psychiatry. It's the infusion of a highly flawed pseudo-science into all sectors of the society that is the problem." James paused for a moment. "To my mind, they're just unwitting accomplices. Their ignorance makes it possible for the bad guys to do their work."

"What do you mean, 'bad guys?'"

James really wished he wasn't having this conversation at 3AM. But he could see Brian was struggling with this, so he pressed on. "You know my background, right, Brian?"

"Yeah, Andy says you're a 'spook.'"

James laughed. "Yeah, that sounds like the Kid. Actually, I…" He was fumbling for a way to explain this without breaching confidentialities. "There's a part of that profession—a section of the field—that are *really* bad, Brian. Hitler used this part; Stalin used this part. We've used this part. And these guys are really good at mind control. Their expertise is psychological warfare, and it is stunning, and devastating—especially once drugs are introduced into the mix. And the people I've fought my whole life paid handsomely to acquire this *expertise*."

Brian just looked at him. James reminded himself that "wake-up calls" can be disconcerting, leaving the person destabilized, not knowing what to embrace or do. So he decided to elaborate, in the hopes that it would flesh it out and make it more possible for Brian to swallow. "Anyway, I got to looking at the idea that Zawahiri might somehow be exerting a type of mind control using PDH remotely. That God-damned intrigued me, brother."

The bewildered look on Brian's face told James right away he'd better explain a few terms here. Brian beat him to it with, "What's PDH? I don't remember that in your little briefing back at Cape Fear."

"You're right. You sure you want to get into this now?" James asked, pointing to the clock.

"Yup, I do. This is a mystery to me, and I need some information."

"It's a technique used to exert control over an individual by taking command of his mind and actions. Basically, you combine pain with drugs, and then introduce hypnosis. Once the hypnotic command is driven in by the force of the pain and the drugs—you've got the guy where you want him."

Brian brightened up and concluded, "That's like what they did to those kids, those child soldiers in Sierra Leone. You know, like in the movie, *Blood Diamond?*"

James knew the movie, and he knew exactly what scene Brian was referring to. "Yeah, you got it. It's fast, and deadly."

"Wow. Pain, drug, hypnosis—I got to remember that."

Now it was James' turn to stare at Brian. He didn't know quite how to interpret that last remark.

Then, Brian added, "And you think this Zawahiri guy is using this, what'd you call it again?"

"PDH."

"PDH." Brian repeated it, obviously wanting to assimilate this data. "He's using this against us, you think?"

"I do." James looked down and swallowed hard. "Yes, I think he's smart enough that he figured out how to do it remotely. And that he intends to have all of us under his control."

Suddenly Brian grinned. It was such a non-sequitur, given the seriousness of the conversation, that James asked, "What?"

"James, brother, let me give you a piece of advice. Don't tell that *little theory* to anyone, or they'll think you're a couple of sandwiches short of a full picnic." Then he laughed, and continued to laugh.

"All right. All right. Very funny!"

Once Brian's laughter subsided, he settled back and, surprisingly, asked James earnestly, "Okay, tell me how that could work? What's the pain part?"

"Our theory is that the weapon of *fear*—the media's engendering of fear and anxiety—is producing an emotional pain. The longer emotional pain goes on...well, it won't be long before there is even physical pain. But either way, the person isn't at his optimum."

"I'm with you there. We do that in football. We try to scare the opponent into making mistakes." He paused for a moment, and then added aggressively, "You know what, James? Marketing would be the hypnosis part of your theory!"

Brian took a moment to tell James that he had realized, because of his own study of marketing at the university, that television ads designed to create a demand in the public for some product create what's called a marketing button. You push the button, and an automatic response is engendered in the audience. What was also causing Brian's agitation was his realization that if the ads were about pharmaceuticals and psych meds, along with sleep aids, there would be an automatic response developing in the public. "Feel bad? Take a pill." And it was at that moment that he put it together. All three—the pain, the drug, the hypnosis.

"Once you're drugged, you can be controlled, right?" Brian knew the answer before he even asked it. Adding, "I mean does it matter what the drug is?"

James shook his head a bit, equivocating, "Well, I don't think we're talking about aspirin here, Brian. But—"

Brian interrupted before he could finish. "What class or type of drugs are we talking about?"

"The kind that affect the mind; the kind where the drug is

doing something the body normally does for itself."

"Like Prozac? Like that kid a while back who shot those folks on his Indian reservation?" Brian remembered having read about that fiasco the year before, and learning that the boy had been on anti-depressants. But what he really wanted to ask had to do with his own family.

He knew he wasn't going to be able to suppress this grief forever. But ever since their discovery a few hours earlier, Brian had this terrible sense of foreboding that his family had somehow been the victims of this snake James and Andy were trying to defang. He confided in James, "You know, my grandfather was on one of those drugs. He was angry and agitated, and they prescribed something for him. He hated it, you know?"

"No, I didn't know," James said softly.

"Do you think it was this drug that made my grandpa shoot my mama, my daddy, and my pappy?" Brian was breathing quickly now, clamping his lips together, trying to maintain control of himself.

"I don't know, Brian. PDH is used to subdue, but it is also used to subvert the reasoning of the person, making it possible for him to do terrible things." He wanted to say more, to find some way to make it easier for Brian to face this very real possibility. "I'm sorry, son, I don't know the answer to that question. But what I will do is make that the first priority of the extended research we'll be doing, now that the common denominator is located."

"More research?"

"Yeah, to confirm. Now we look for date coincidence of the introduction of Psychiatry into the sectors of our society that are degrading—those institutions you boys identified. We'll be looking to see when Psychiatry was introduced into Education, into the Justice System, into the Military, Business, and Religion. You'll be looking for worsening trends following that introduction, and you'll especially be looking for presence and impact of the drugs that are so rampant with that profession."

"And what will *you* be researching, James?"

"I promise you I will look into whether or not being on these drugs, or—as in the case of your grandfather—coming off these drugs causes the person to become violent. I promise."

194

That seemed to satisfy Brian enough that his breathing became more normal, less shallow. They sat silently for a while. Brian started nodding his head again, as if agreeing with something inside himself. Not long after, he came back out and added, "And you think Zawahiri is using his knowledge of this area to attack us Americans?"

"I do. And we're in a stranglehold."

Brian was rocking back and forth now, chewing on something. "And you think anyone will believe this?"

"They have to, Pal."

"Or what?"

There's that defiance again, James thought. *Or is it fear?* Deciding to risk the answer, he responded, "We lose."

"Lose what?"

"What Pappy fought for." Before the impact of that could depress Brian down again, James added, "But I believe they'll get it."

"Why?"

"Well, it's something Andy taught me. People are basically good, and in their gut, they *know.* We just have to find a way to reach them and point it out. When they look, they will know." Reaching out, he patted Brian on the knee reassuringly.

Pappy always did that, Brian reflected. Softly and innocently he asked, "James, why do you call Andy, 'Kid?'"

"I don't know, really." James didn't. It wasn't that Andy was the kid he'd never had. He'd never thought of that. "Maybe it's because when I met him he was this truly amazing All-American kid—you know, football hero, Grandmaster chess champion, decent—everything you'd want a kid to be. He gave up a lot for this, Brian. Not many men would sacrifice what he has to help. So, I don't know why I call him 'Kid.'"

"I see. So, why do you call me 'Pal?'"

James had not thought of that either. He didn't know what to say really. So he shrugged his shoulders, cleared his throat, and answered honestly, "I don't know, Pal. Somehow I just think you *are.*" He looked to Brian to see if he was satisfied. He appeared to be.

And as abruptly as Brian had changed the conversation to personal questions, as if those answers were more important than the rest of this education, he changed it back. "Then, we're just going to have to attack him, James. If he thinks he's going to drug us, and enslave us in the process, we're going to have to dismantle that entire game plan—you know—reverse the stranglehold."

He had said it with such assertiveness and confidence that James wondered who he was actually talking to for a moment. He just didn't get this kid sometimes. One moment the boy was morose and vulnerable, and the next minute upbeat and articulate. And now, he was on his feet, dancing from right to left as if dodging someone who was trying to interfere with his catching a pass. He was excited, and to James' surprise, seemed truly genuine in his enthusiasm. He wondered what Brian knew that he didn't.

Standing as well, he asked, "Okay, okay. You got my attention. Just how are we going to do that? You got a plan?"

"Yes, I do, my man. Yes, I do!! I told you and the Kid in there that if you found me the common denominators, then I would make a game that dismantles them. You say this fool Zawahiri is coming after the White King. Well, he may know medicine and mind control, but he doesn't know what I know!"

Brian was leaving the room, headed toward the bathroom, when he turned around and fired back into the room, "And, James?"

"Yeah?"

"If you find out that those meds caused my grandpa to do what he did, and they are part of this bastard's strategy, I promise you we're going to hurt him. And hurt him bad. I know how to reach the White King, James, and I'm going to help you do it."

Grinning, he exited the room, leaving James to wonder how surreal this evening had become. Somehow, though, he had a quiet confidence that Brian *did* have a way to help. He had no idea why he would believe that exactly, but he did. *Maybe it's because Andy has such faith in him,* he told himself. *Man, I got to get some sleep! These kids are wearing me out!*

CHAPTER 30

$\mathcal{M}$uhamad Ibrahim Makkawi, military commander of Al Qaeda, was about to change strategies. Subsequent to his meeting with the Doctor, he had concluded that Al Qaeda had to develop not only a way of procuring more young men to replace the thousands who had already been sacrificed in Afghanistan and Iraq, but also a workable program for training them.

The days of the almost campus-like facilities Bin Laden and Zawahiri had used in the past—where the training grounds and residences were spread out over huge acreage, protected by their host countries—had come to an end. Al Qaeda in late 2006 had no true home. Certainly the group had sanctuary in the tribal areas of North Waziristan, but merely being protected was a far cry from the kind of liberty they'd enjoyed before 9/11. The debacle in Iraq with Zarqawi's ultimate failure, and his provocation of the Iraqi people, threatened to curtail them even more.

And though Makkawi was not naturally a strategist, his five years of command were maturing him. There had been many successes. Not the least of which was that he was still alive. That is what gave him the idea.

Before Zawahiri left their meeting, Makkawi had sincerely warned his mentor of the dangers of returning to this area. Makkawi, at least, was not on the run every few hours, as he had been before Samir had masterfully exercised a public relations ploy to distract the American media. The American military was still seeking him, but there was less of a chance of being turned in for the reward by the people harboring him, since there was less focus on their activities inside Pakistan.

Indeed, Samir had diverted so much attention to the "War in Iraq" that the mainstream media had nearly forgotten about

Afghanistan. In the minds of most Americans, Afghanistan was a settled affair, with Karzai solidly entrenched in their new government.

This was a fortunate turn of events for Al Qaeda in general, and for Makkawi in particular. For he had been shuttling back and forth between Afghanistan and Pakistan, attempting to fulfill his mission of helping the Taliban regroup, surge, and return to power. That was the obvious ideal goal. An Afghanistan with the Taliban, rearmed, retrained, and reinstated would be the ideal safe harbor once again for Al Qaeda. They had some success with this strategy, but the perils of movement and being out in the open had slowed them down considerably.

Knowing that the Doctor was totally committed to the continuation of his "suicide bombers" and, knowing the absolute workability of small cells, Makkawi had devised a way to recruit and train, and yet elude the pervasive United States Special Forces. Today was the first day in a long time that he rose feeling confident. *I didn't realize how much I missed the association with Ayman,* he concluded. *Truly, our greatest successes everywhere have been produced by our suicide bombers, and the independent cells they came from.* "I'll merely continue our successful actions," he affirmed out loud.

Finishing his morning prayers, he signaled to his aide that he was ready for the interview. Moments later, a young man entered Makkawi's modest quarters. Calmly Makkawi greeted him, and suggested he sit. Given the magnitude of this interview, the young man was remarkably serene.

I like that, Makkawi observed. *He's confident.*

"Do you know who I am?" he asked his guest.

"Yes, sir." Then the young man added politely, albeit superfluously, "My name is Rhamad."

Makkawi laughed, appreciating the irony, as it was obvious he knew who this man was. After all, he had sent for him.

"You are Taliban, are you not?"

"Yes, sir. Most decidedly."

"Rhamad, you come highly recommended to me by some of your Taliban commanders. They say you are very bright."

Rhamad answered graciously that he did not know about being bright, but that he was most certainly committed, and he worked hard. That pleased Makkawi—not Rhamad's modesty, but his certainty of where he was strong. For in truth, the recommendation had not been about his intellect; it had been about his relentless commitment to whatever assignments he had been given, and about his stealthy ability to vanish, even when his enemies thought they had him in their grasp. He was very agile. And that was primarily why Makkawi was recruiting him that day.

Makkawi's plan emanated from the fact that he himself could no longer get around easily. Instead of resisting that fact, he had concluded the best way to proceed was for him to stay in his safe house, where he was absolutely certain of his protectors, and not to venture out at all. It was in venturing out that he could be observed, and stalked by one of Musharraf's informants. But, sequestered, he was free to plan Al Qaeda's global terror objectives uninterrupted.

Once he had received confirmation of Zarqawi's death, he knew the Doctor would be looking for a replacement—if not in Iraq, at least in talent. Rhamad fit the bill. So, he explained to Rhamad, "This is not an interview. I have actually selected you for something. What we want you to do, Rhamad, is spearhead the recruitment of all our new suicide bombers, and conduct their training. We want you to do that in a very covert way, however." He paused just long enough to see if Rhamad was tracking. He was, most definitely, so Makkawi continued. "You will keep each of the groups very small—"

Rhamad interrupted him before he finished. "Forgive me, but *how* small?"

"Perhaps just a handful. Perhaps ten. But small. And even more importantly, Rhamad, you are to remain very mobile. The concept we want executed is to abstain from any fixed training locations, which could be located and attacked by our enemy. Instead, we want the training to be done on the move."

Rhamad was nodding in complete agreement. The project was already his, given his immediate grasp of the concept and his next statement. "That will be very doable with a very small group. Anything too large, and just the presence of that many young strangers will cause suspicion. Small, I can manage."

Makkawi was satisfied, and spent the next few minutes briefing Rhamad on the necessity of remaining mobile, thereby being hard to find. Both the Pakistanis and the Americans would be looking for him and his trainees at all times, and he would need to be able to pack up and vanish before an already agile enemy could attack.

Suddenly, Rhamad laughed. Not knowing why, Makkawi asked, "What? Did I say something humorous?"

Reassuring him, though still laughing, Rhamad said, "No, no. It's just I think you must have discovered in your background check on me that I am both a sprinter and a hurdle jumper!" Makkawi saw the humor immediately, as he *had* noted Rhamad's sports background, and his own physical agility. It had in fact played a part. For Makkawi was now in his mid-forties, and his body was weary from the punishment of his fugitive life. He knew a young man's passion, and body, would be very helpful to them now.

"Yes, I did. And I'm quite confident, as is Usama bin Laden, that you will not let us down." Even though Makkawi knew Usama to be dead, he was well aware that none of the rank and file of Al Qaeda, nor the enemy, knew that. *Have to keep up appearances,* he warned himself. Eyeing Rhamad, he could see this pleased the young man. Then, before he dismissed him, Makkawi added, "There is something else we want you to do for us."

There was a momentary pause, and Rhamad turned his face completely to Makkawi. He did not want to miss a word.

"In a year or so, we expect Benazir Bhutto to seriously challenge Musharraf." He stopped, watching Rhamad closely, then continued. "We will tell you when, but we want one of your teams to assassinate her."

In fact, Rhamad was Taliban. Being a young man, and a militant one at that, he had little time for, or appreciation of, politics—let alone the politics of Pakistan. His life obviously had been completely disrupted by the political changes forced upon Afghanistan when the Americans and British came to overthrow the Taliban. That political arena had direct bearing on him, but Pakistan was not in his periphery. So, he had no real appreciation of who she was. He did have some vague recollection of someone else by that name being assassinated, but nothing else caught his attention. His answer then was immediate. "Of course. Just tell me when."

And with that brief, quiet conversation, a deal was struck, and a new superstar would emerge. It would be some time before the world's press would know his name, but when that time came, it would be a result of his success in training suicide bombers and eluding all his enemies, without interrupting his training whatsoever. That would prove disconcerting to the governments of Pakistan, Afghanistan, and the United States. And, it would prove fatal late in 2007 to Benazir Bhutto.

For now, however, all that was in the future. Not even Rhamad could have guessed he would be nick-named "Rock Star."

———————

Hours later, a message was relayed from Makkawi to Samir's office in Paris. The entire staff in the Paris office was part of an Al Qaeda Public Relations cell. And the manager there forwarded an email to Samir with the message, "Have recruited successfully."

Samir, upon decoding the message, relayed it to the Doctor. Relieved, and smiling, the Doctor once again logged into his three-dimensional chess game and highlighted the military level. In the space vacated by Zarqawi, the Doctor dragged a Black Knight forward and dropped it onto the board. Satisfied, he then logged off. Al Qaeda once again had two knights "on the board."

CHAPTER 31

*J*ames and Kelly were sitting outside, having lunch at the renowned Yamashira restaurant, high in the Hollywood hills overlooking the city of Los Angeles. Its gardens were lovely at any time of the year, but the view would be sporadic, depending upon the degree of smog in the Los Angeles basin. Today was one of those clear, December days, and their view extended well past downtown to a sliver of a view of the Pacific Ocean at Los Angeles Harbor.

The last few months had become quite a sojourn for James. Keeping his promise to Brian to research the area of psychiatric medications first, James had stumbled onto facts and research that had shocked even him. Years of familiarity with psych-ops, and study of the techniques and experiments conducted by Cold War enemies, still left him unprepared for what he had found.

For James had lived his adult life outside the United States. And regardless of the activity in which he had been engaged, to his mind, he was protecting America. As long as he and his colleagues did their job, his own people would be safe. Until this past six months, James had clung to the belief that their work had kept Americans safe. But that is not what he had unearthed. There had indeed been an undermining of the people of the United States, accomplished right under the noses of every agency assigned to protect them—and worse yet, usually with their approval and endorsement. Without his knowing it, James had uncovered some of the infamous "Unwitting" list that his unknown adversary, Samir, had created long ago.

Samir and Zawahiri had long since realized that the United States could never be taken down militarily, unless it had been undermined to its very bedrock by an internal force. Then, and only then, could a combined strategy involving economic attacks and military attacks become capable of taking down the world's most powerful nation.

Until now, James had been under the delusion that he had kept America safe. But now, his research was revealing an insidious and covert attack upon an unsuspecting public. Not only had he confirmed to his satisfaction that there was a link between certain types of psychiatric medications and a rise in suicides and homicides by people taking them, but initial indications were that the drugs themselves produced the violence.

Nothing could be more politically unpopular than to tackle that subject. Everyone from Government to Industry to Media would circle the wagons and decry the lunacy of anyone even investigating in this area. They would be pilloried. And, it was for that very reason that James knew it was likely to be true. His years of training in mind control, and the audacious usages of that by Hitler, and by the Soviets and all their subsequent sycophants, had taught him one thing about truth. If the truth was outrageous—too outrageous, and outside the ordinary person's ability to accept—it was regarded as a lie.

This was an "outrageous truth," and James had no idea how to begin to tackle it. He had no way of knowing that a medical study was being conducted and would be published in the *New England Journal of Medicine* by December of 2007 confirming fraud and deception by a pharmaceutical company regarding the known, negative side effects of two of its blockbuster antidepressants.

He was aware, however, of the controversy swirling around the FDA's refusal to order a Black Box warning about the negative side effects of certain drugs. He was aware they had yielded to pressure from the Administration, and had finally done so. But, he had no idea whether patients or doctors were even looking at the warnings—let alone backing away.

It would be a year before a FOX news journalist would do exposés on the link between the drug usage, and the subsequent death or violence of the user. The journalist discovered every "school shooter"—the new vernacular for sudden, unexpected mass murder/suicide—would be found to have been using one of these drugs, or just coming off one of these drugs, prior to their radical shift to violence.

It would be a year before a beloved member of the Hollywood community would die tragically in his apartment in New York City from a combination of prescription drugs. But on this splendid, sunny Southern California day, James was seeing a bleaker picture than he had ever looked at. *At least in the Cold War we could shoot them,* he complained to himself. *How on earth do we stop this? It's epidemic.*

"James?" Kelly asked. "Are you all right?"

Realizing he had drifted off into that fear zone again, he brought himself around as best he could. "Yeah." Then, knowing he could not conceal anything really from Kelly's eyes, he added, "Not great, truth be told."

"Yeah, I can see that."

Forestalling any questions she had about whether or not he and her son were once again in danger, he explained, "We're all safe, Kelly. It's nothing like that." He noticed that she relaxed slightly, and seemed to rest more comfortably in her chair. "It's just this research project we're doing has...*is* keeping me upset, that's all."

"What, exactly, are you working on?" She knew that none of this was classified, of course. So she hoped today that she'd be allowed into *the know* on this. Andy had been very subdued of late, and he and Brian were inseparable. The looks they gave one another alternated between combativeness and cooperation, and she wondered if this had always been part of their relationship, or if this was something new.

James helped her out here, as he really needed a friend, and Kelly was the best friend he had—other than the Kid, of course. "We're doing a study on the influence of Psychiatry in the culture, to see how far reaching it is..."

Before he could finish, she interjected, "And how dangerous?"

Her question startled him, since he couldn't tell whether she was asking if the study was dangerous, or if Psychiatry were. He must have had that frown of incomprehension because she immediately added, "You're looking into the *dangers* of Psychiatry, right?"

"Yes, yes, we are." He was perplexed by this. *How? What does she know of this?*

She nodded as if she understood, and just sat there, hands

folded in her lap, waiting for him to elaborate. "I was familiar with psychiatrists in the intelligence game of course, in the FBI, even in the military. We all, I think, are aware of the forensic psychiatrists, maybe even the penetration into industry. But—"

Once again, Kelly interrupted him. "But, James, you never really looked at the drug side, did you?"

"Am I missing something here?" he asked helplessly.

"Ritalin." That was all she said. She just dropped the word on the table, picked up her chop sticks, and selected another sushi item.

Deciding to help him out, she now elaborated. "James, there is not a parent in America today that hasn't had some educational bureaucrat in their face pushing Ritalin on their kids."

Suddenly James realized that, of course, Kelly would have a perspective on this issue. He'd been too many years cloistered inside the CIA, doing dry analysis. These issues, especially the ones related to the generation he now believed was under direct attack by Al Qaeda, would have played out for real in households everywhere in the country. Now it was his turn to set down his chop sticks. "So, this is real to you?"

She smiled, but it was a sad smile. He probed. "You knew something was wrong?"

Her answer was barely audible, but it was unequivocal. "Yes." Eagerly now, Kelly told James of the time years earlier, before her husband had even become sick, when they were called in for a parent/administrator/teacher conference regarding Andy. At the time, Andy was eight. It had been the "professional opinion" of the administrator and teacher that Andy was suffering from ADHD, and that it would be best for him if he were medicated. They had suggested a drug, which was reputed to be very effective in *helping* children with this type of mental problem.

"You mean, *subduing* him," her husband had spat back. Kelly smiled wistfully as she recalled how shocked the principal had been when challenged by Greg. Apparently, the principal was used to getting his way. He had hesitated long enough for Greg to attack again. "You wish to modify the behavior of my son?" Greg had set the trap.

"To the degree that he is a disturbance to the other children, yes. I believe that if you cannot control your son's behavior, it should be handled by us."

Greg was in commanding physical shape, and the moment the insipid remark escaped the man's lips he knew it had been a mistake. Kelly finished the story proudly, asserting that Greg had *explained* to the man in terms he could not fail to grasp, that Andy was a very intelligent boy, a very creative boy, a very athletic boy, and a born leader. The argument ended when Greg hurled a question at the stupefied principal. That question had won the day for Andy. And it had become the mantra for Kelly in later years when she, by herself, had been the boy's defender.

James looked out over the city. It seemed clearer down there somehow. He wondered if the air had cleared up a bit in the last few minutes, or if it had been the incisive logic, and obvious truth, Greg Weir had uttered years earlier. He mulled it over in his mind. "Have you ever known anyone highly intelligent that didn't talk and have an opinion? Have you ever seen a creative person want to 'paint by the numbers?' Have you ever seen an athlete sit around dormant? Have you *ever* seen a born leader want to only *follow?*" Her eyes glistened with tears now as she recalled the final thing her husband had hurled at the principal. She repeated it to James now, albeit rhetorically. "When did America cease being the land of the free and the home of the brave and become instead the land of the free and the home of the mentally ill?"

That question from the grave rocked James. He looked at it for a long time. "Compliance," James breathed almost under his breath.

"What?"

"Lenin. I was thinking of Lenin. He said the purpose of terror is to terrify, and he practiced the concept that the purpose of indoctrination is to reduce the individual to compliance—reduce the gifted and independent into mediocrity and compliance. Then they no longer pose a threat to the regime." Suddenly, without warning, he choked up, and could hardly hold back the tears. For James had just come to realize why the drugs were being promoted everywhere. In the absence of the ability to forcibly restrain an enemy through brute force, you tactically use drugs to subdue him. This was straight out of James' own playbook. And never, until today, had he had the slightest idea that the application of this was occurring inside the United States, delivered by people of trust.

He turned his head away as far as he could, hoping Kelly would not notice. She had, however. Reaching across the table, she gently laid her hand on his and asked, "What is it, James?"

Because she was his friend, James answered. "I have never been so afraid in my whole life."

CHAPTER 32

J ames took a long time getting back to the apartment after dropping Kelly off in Glendale. He was mulling over what he had realized, trying to make his stomach settle down, and bracing himself to re-engage the Kid and his pal in the work they were doing. He just didn't know how he was going to camouflage the fear. *I wonder if they'll smell it on me,* he tried to joke. Then finally, he'd just given up, parked the car, and walked up the sidewalk to their building.

"James, could you come here for a minute please?" the manager of their apartment called out from his doorway.

"Sure," James responded, wondering what this was about. Like a kid being called to the principal's office, he was trying to figure out what they'd done. The man looked concerned about something. "What's up, Billy?"

Billy was a hefty guy in his mid-fifties who clearly spent a little too much time in front of the TV. Since the apartment building was only about thirty-five years old, and in good condition, he didn't even seem to get much exercise going up and down stairs. His own apartment was conveniently the first one on the left as you entered the courtyard. It was below and in front of James' second floor, two-bedroom unit.

"You know I like you guys," Billy said, almost apologetically. "You pay your rent. You seem like a nice enough group..." James interrupted him, wanting Billy to just spit out what was on his mind. He was in no mood now for pussy-footing around. That seemed to make it okay, and Billy continued firmly. "Can you get those boys up there to pipe down and make a little less noise? They're bothering people."

James was stunned, as Andy and Brian were always quiet

when he was around them. There was never even any roughhousing in the place. If they wanted to throw balls, they went to the park. Granted, James spent a lot of time away from the apartment making calls and doing research to corroborate their findings. He'd pop into the Los Angeles FBI office on Wilshire, if he got a chance, to use their database. James had the clearance to look into most anything, but he had not really had a database to tap into to see what the enemy was up to these days. A chance meeting with a couple of buddies from Washington who had been reassigned to the Los Angeles office had led to an open invitation to stop in. As far as they were concerned, if the computer was not in use, he was welcome to do research.

He must have looked mystified because Billy added, as if to paint a picture, "Yeah, they've been yelling a lot lately, James. I can't tell what about, but they're arguing and the yelling is interfering with 1B's sleep." He was referring, of course, to a nurse who worked graveyard at Cedars Sinai, and who slept in the afternoons. Billy had a habit of personifying the apartment number.

James was about to get into it a bit, when, as if on cue, Brian's voice could be heard yelling something at the top of his lungs. At least, it drowned out the TV James could hear in the background just behind Billy. Then, on top of that, sure enough, there was Andy, arguing at the top of his lungs, "I'm telling you that won't work. It just won't work!"

Billy just looked at James, shrugged his shoulders, and tilted his head in the direction of the squabble.

Patting him on the shoulder, James reassured him. "Billy, don't worry. I will take care of this. I have no idea what's going on, but I will handle this."

He took the stairs two at a time, barging through the open door, closing it behind him just as Andy was stomping into the kitchen area yelling, "This is just stupid!"

"Guys, guys," James slid in assertively. "What is going on here? I could hear you all the way to the street. And Billy is officially complaining." That stopped them for a moment, and both of them stood sheepishly in the kitchen, looking down at the floor, and then up at James somewhat defiantly. "Do you want to explain this?"

There was a deafening silence for close to thirty seconds, as one after the other they started to talk, and then cut themselves off. Finally, Andy started again. "Sorry, James, truly. I didn't realize we were loud, honest I didn't."

Then, to defend his pal, Brian jumped in. "Yeah, that's right. We really didn't know we were, you know, upsetting anybody. Honest." No doubt they were sincere, but that still didn't explain why the ruckus. James stood there expectantly.

Andy grabbed his glass of milk, headed toward the breakfast bar, grabbing the stool at the end. "Here's the deal. Brian's got this idea of how to reverse the stranglehold these bastards have on us. Good one, too."

"And that's something to fight about?" James asked incredulously.

"Nah. It's a good idea, I think. Obviously the government isn't going to fix this. And we figured the best and fastest way to fix it is to reverse the demand for the damn stuff."

"Right."

It took awhile, but finally James coaxed the whole story out of them. Both young men had concluded that to save the White King, as they referred to their generation, from the threat of drugs, and the ravages the drugs bring physically and psychologically, they would devise a game. They had reasoned that if the game was good enough, and if enough people played it, there could be a kind of grass roots movement of kids rejecting drugs—most specifically prescription meds—and at the same time rejecting the arguments of "authorities" for taking them. Both young men knew economics well enough to understand that if you dry up the demand, the supply also dries up. The mind control being practiced by proxy upon Americans was designed to create a demand in the American people for more and more medications. It was working brilliantly—a brilliant Fifth Column attack and sabotage.

Somewhere in there, James completely forgot about the fighting and yelling, and became engrossed in this possibility. Brian cleared it up even further. "Yeah, James, we figured to do an 'end run' here. Can't run this one straight up the middle—too much of a line with the pharmaceutical industry and AMA and those 'johns.' And we don't figure there's enough time to get any of us downfield for a 'Hail Mary' pass, so best thing is to run a reverse, and sweep around the end."

Now, all three of them were on stools in a high-tech huddle, surrounded by computer monitors. Brian reminded him that he had promised James that if he found out these psych meds could have changed his grandfather from an angry, bitter, harmless man into the man who had murdered his whole family, he would find a way to dismantle the whole mechanism. It was a few minutes before James observed that his own anxiety had vanished completely. There was something here that made sense.

He might not have known much about chess, or some of the complicated plays Andy developed and had spotted Zawahiri playing, but he did know football. The medical/pharmaceutical establishment was indeed too foreboding. To try to run straight into them would take power and money, and guts. They had the guts, but lacked the others. And the urgency that was developing, with more than 40% of Americans now diagnosed as "mentally ill," left no time for Andy or Brian to pass the ball to some congressional receiver down field, even if one could be found.

The best play was to run a reverse, and then sweep around the end. "Son of a gun," James said, exhaling, "you boys are going to run the opposite direction they expect you to run."

"Yup, we're going to fake to the right; pull their whole defense with it; then hand off; reverse to the left and sweep past them. By the time they even know we went past them, we'll be in the end zone." Andy was grinning.

"And the 'end zone' is?" James asked, making sure he was tracking.

"The end of the pharmaceutical cartel inside the United States, and the freeing of all children from the threat these drugs represent. They are a threat to their minds, their bodies, and to their futures. The end zone is a clear future. No bad guys in it." Brian had given the answer, and James turned to him almost in disbelief.

"Brian, were you also studying political science while you were studying marketing?" James had intended a little levity, but he was closer than he knew.

"Nope, just marketing. But, it's my marketing that made me see this maneuver." Brian explained that if the "bad guys," as he preferred to call them, were using direct marketing, as Andy had discovered, to cause Americans to seek out these various drugs— by promoting directly to the public in snazzy TV ads, games, etc.—then he would use an equally powerful direct marketing tool to reverse that demand. What they used, he would use. Only he wanted to use a play which only the young ones would relate to. That way he was confident the "old fart bad guys" wouldn't even know it was coming.

And the tool he and Andy had settled on was a computer game. They had agreed to develop a computer game to undermine the "under-miners." Every gain in yards the "bad guys" thought they were making by utilizing TV propaganda, and written propaganda, would be reversed by the young generation's proclivity for video and computer games. An attempt to gain sales through conventional advertising could be obliterated by means of the computer game propaganda Andy and Brian were dreaming up. And they had gone one step further. They weren't going to settle for just waking the kids up to the danger, and arousing their rebellion and refusal regarding taking meds; they were going to teach them how to beat it—literally how to defeat the enemy that was duping them and their parents.

James was up pacing, putting this all together. "This could work. This could work," he repeated first to himself, and next to them.

"Damned straight," Brian agreed.

Then James remembered what had started this whole conversation in the first place. Inquiring into why they were fighting and yelling, he was not prepared for the answer.

"First, James, we honestly didn't know we were yelling," Andy explained. Seeing that wasn't getting through, he added, "Brian and I are used to yelling at one another regarding placement on the field. I was always spotting for him, waving, yelling, telling him where I wanted him. And he'd yell at me to get my attention if I had my finger in my nose and missed the fact that he was wide open."

"Right," Brian confirmed.

"So, honestly, we didn't know. But we'll pipe down from now on. Honest."

"Okay. But were you arguing?"

"Oh, yeah, man," Brian responded immediately. "Andy just wasn't gettin' the play, and I had to keep drilling him with it. But he's got it now I think, don't you, Andy?"

Letting out a huge sigh, Andy confirmed that he was finally

willing to take the ball in the direction Brian wanted to go. Any misgivings he had were assuaged somewhat by Brian's persuasiveness.

Andy felt the best way to explain that to James was just to show him the game concept they had created. Reminding him that they would most certainly need a graphic designer, and better animator, they nonetheless had a working model. Brian's job had been to create the concept, and Andy's was to develop the program.

"Now, remember, James, this is rough," Andy reminded him.

All three were huddled around the computer in the center of the room. It had the largest monitor, and allowed all of them to watch. James demurred from actually playing the game, as he had never really gotten into computer games. So, Brian was in the driver's seat. And Brian was an expert gamer. He'd played every day for years—a fact James now vividly remembered about his first months spent with Brian at Cape Fear. It had annoyed him, frankly, to see Brian so immersed in the games. And he had wondered what they might be doing to him. Somehow right now, one and a half years later, he was grateful for it.

The blue screen lit up with the graphic, "White King Rising."

"That's just a working title," Brian explained. Andy thinks it's funny." Pausing the game for a moment, he turned and asked a question of James. "So, James, you know football pretty well, right?"

"Pretty well. Why?"

"Well, we're opening this game with a Buttonhook."

Though James in fact did watch a lot of football, he wasn't too sure he recognized the terminology. Turning to Andy for help, he asked, "Do I know this?"

"Sure you do, James." Andy came to his rescue. "At least you've watched it, even if you didn't know what we called it."

"Well, enlighten me, Kid, because it's just not ringing a bell."

"Okay. Let's say I'm going to pass to Brian, and he runs straight ahead 5-7 yards, then wheels around to face me for the pass. But, instead of me passing to him, I wait for the defenders to commit; then we fake. Just as the defender approaches him, Brian breaks and runs downfield, and I toss it to him deep. It's a bread and butter touchdown."

"Sweet, man, sweet," Brian said, punctuating the description.

James reflected on that for a moment and remembered seeing

this play often through the years, even though he didn't know its name. He knew also that for that one to work you had to have a poised quarterback who could wait, and then accomplish the fake. It always aroused the crowd though. "Yeah, I see it now. It's a real crowd pleaser."

"Surprises always are, my man." Brian grinned. "And that, James, is what we are going to do to the enemy. We are going to fake them out, and run the Buttonhook in a computer game."

Releasing the pause button, Brian let the game begin and did a running commentary through the beginning segment. "Right here at the beginning, James, the player goes interactive with the game. He's creating himself as a character, with the traits he admires in himself, and which project the type of image he wants others to see. He can even choose wardrobe, weapons—the whole nine yards."

Before James could even ask why that might be desirable, Brian continued enthusiastically, "And now the kicker. The player has to create something to save—something worth saving."

"Suppose he doesn't have anything worth saving?"

Andy smiled. Brian responded with, "James, everyone has *something*." Immediately he appended it to say, "Or *someone*."

"You think?"

"Yup!" Brian paused, then continued. "And that's why we're going to kick ass! Now James, this is important to point out to you. Once they've created that thing, it vanishes. It's gone." So James could follow the game, Brian created a mock-up of the image he was going to use for himself as the player, and one of an adorable young girl whom he said was his sister at age five. Sure enough, as soon as he created her, she vanished. Smiling, Brian looked up to James to check the pulse. "Nice mystery, isn't it?"

Then almost immediately, a violent scene erupted, which forced Brian's "character" to shoot a rather vile-looking man in an alley. Brian noticed James flinch and scowl disapprovingly. "Now this is what we've been arguing about, James." Brian explained further. "Andy's delicate sensibilities didn't want to create a game with any violence. This guy thinks he can stop this global debacle with some highfalutin game of *reason*!" It was said more playfully than critically, so James concluded that the fight must be over.

"Now, I know you and Andy both operate up there in this airy-fairy intellectual stratosphere, but I have finally persuaded Andy that this is *not* where the White King is. He is way down here, playing violent, sexy computer games."

In truth, Brian had successfully argued that to create a game that did not match the reality of the generation to which they were trying to market—and influence heavily—made no sense. It would limit their market too much. Both had finally agreed that to have any chance of success at all, they had to create something that would have a mass-market appeal, and which would take the computer game industry by storm. And to do that, without arousing the suspicion of the enemy, they had concluded they had to start this game the way any other mindlessly violent game started.

But there was *one* difference, and it would go unnoticed. That difference would eventually tilt the balance of the War on Terror. However, on that December day, none of the three knew it for sure. The difference was that, although the game did begin violently, and repugnantly, the player was a teenage gang member shooting a drug dealer, instead of shooting another gang's member, or, worse yet, an innocent bystander in a drive-by.

This was their start point. From there, the game advanced to other levels. Each level involved the player thwarting someone's drug pushing. But, as the game progressed, the player, in order to win, had to use less and less violence. He had to figure out how to take out the opponent who presented himself, without killing. If he resorted to a violent choice at that level of the game, he failed, and was ejected back to the beginning, losing both points and time.

The level with the school nurse fascinated James. He prayed he wasn't going to see a "school shooting"—with the kid shooting the nurse. Fortunately, in order to win at that level and stay in the game, the winning action was in the vein of using a mild defiance, like spitting the pill out after the wicked witch turned her back. This was the first level of the game where the player's opponent had turned from being an obvious bad guy, like a drug pusher, into a real, as Brian called it, "civilian"—just a typical, innocuous authority figure with whom all kids eventually have to interact. The fact that she was passing out valium and

215

Ritalin, and that these meds were being spat out and destroyed, would go unnoticed by the casual observer.

The reason for that was indeed cunning. Andy and Brian, once Andy had agreed to the violent opening, had left enough beginning layers requiring less-than-civilized solutions to turn off anybody scrutinizing the game. They would either be repulsed by it, or they would assume it was just another, albeit cleverer, version of an old theme. After all, everyone knew that "these street punks weren't capable of anything higher." That was the mindset Brian was counting on.

As Brian continued to play the game, Andy admonished him to slow down just a bit so that James could follow. Reminding him that James was a newbie, Andy occasionally had Brian pause the game to point out a cute option or two they had inserted. It worked. James was stunned at the magnificent way the game unfolded for the player. In order to win and advance, the player had to become progressively more reasoning and less violent and reactive. He had to think. He had to make judgments, whether to shoot, to take a pill, to listen to an "authority"—you name it, they had it covered. Each "rational" choice, by Brian and Andy's standards, advanced the player.

What they hoped was that the unsuspecting player who was used to the programming of his peers, his school, the media, his doctors, etc. would start to *learn*. They hoped he would go off the automatic compliance or rebellion he was set on, and make new decisions. And, in order to win, those decisions had to be ones that advanced his health and sanity, and the sanity of others.

The game's final layers put the player to the ultimate test. He had to choose amongst opponents who represented the absolute most-trusted authorities he could identify. Once he had selected the authority figure, that figure presented his "true colors," as Brian referred to them. It was here that actual realizations should occur in the public he and Andy were targeting. It was here they hoped to have challenged the player sufficiently that his perspective was actually shifted, and he was different. He was making different choices in a game, but that game paralleled his life. The characters he created in the game were characters in his actual life, but he was seeing them differently.

The final, winning level, which was very arduous to reach,

involved the stunning revelation that behind the door—entrapped, and needing to be freed—was the thing the player had created at the beginning of the game that he wanted to save, the person he truly loved and had tried to help, who had vanished. Imprisoned by lies spread by the true purveyors of insanity and violence; imprisoned in the bogus diagnoses of "ADHD," "Bi-polar," "manic-depressive," "delusional," "paranoid," "acute depression," and any of a thousand others dreamed up by quacks; in danger of being drugged, and forever altered, the victim cowered helpless and weeping. And only the game's player could save him.

They surmised that most players would create some innocent child, or person they loved. And in order to rescue what they held dear, the White King had to advance from the depraved, violent attitudes and actions with which he began the game to the calm, compassionate reason and steadfastness of a true hero. A child would rescue a child.

That was the concept, and the beginnings of its execution. Andy was happy now. When he saw it actually play out, he knew Brian had been right. "Sorry, bro, I… You were totally right."

"I know."

"So, what do you think?"

James was at a loss for words. He was stunned at the level of creativity and intellect that had been involved here. No wonder these two had been formidable on a football field. But at this moment, more than anything else, he understood the foundation of their friendship. Each was an extremely gifted young man, with a profound ability to create. And it was this propensity for creation rather than destruction that would be so devastating to Ayman Al-Zawahiri, and his dream of destruction.

All James could sputter out, however, was, "Can you market this?"

Brian laughed suddenly. "Oh, yeah, that's my specialty!" Then, he slapped both friends on the back and added, "But first we test it. Let's face it, we're preaching to the choir here. Let's see if this thing actually works with kids on the street—or better yet, in my dorm. I seem to remember a few of them telling me they were *depressed.* Let's start there."

"Right. Good idea," Andy said, nodding. "First, Brian, take this to a guy I know who is a really great designer. This thing has got to be *bad*. With killer packaging, animation and graphics, we can make this the hottest ticket in town come spring."

"That fast?" James asked, hoping it was possible.

"Sure," Brian responded confidently. "Production's a piece of cake. First, we test. Then we launch." And then he added, "And Ayman Al-Zawahiri, if this is one of the ways you were counting on beating us, you can shove this up your ass!"

"Geez, Brian, would you lighten up!" Andy pushed him out the door.

"I was being light, pal. Where's your sense of humor?" There they were, yelling again. Given that James had promised Billy, he called out to them, "Guys, guys, remember the volume!"

"Right, got it!" they whispered, heading out the door to Ugo's before tackling Brian's former dorm mates.

Andy and Brian sat quickly at one of the small window tables along Santa Monica Blvd. They'd come to rely upon this place for omelets—good ones—any time of day. And playing the game had worked up an appetite.

While they were waiting for the waiter to serve them, Brian looked around to see who was in the restaurant. He'd heard that celebrities often hung out here. But he'd never seen any. Either that or he didn't recognize any he had seen. But tonight he thought he recognized one.

"Hey, Andy," he whispered, "isn't that Alicia Quixote over there to your right?"

"Who's Alicia Quixote?" Andy asked innocently.

"That WNG anchor I told you was such a hotty."

"Oh yeah." Now Andy looked at her. Having never seen her, he asked Brian, "Is it her?"

"Yup. It sure is. Wonder who that guy is with her? Looks like she's taken."

Andy looked around, catching sight of Alicia just as she was reaching over, holding her companion's hand. "Yeah, I'd say she's taken. Wonder who he is? Sure is good looking."

CHAPTER 33

*A*s it turned out, the project took longer than expected. Brian waited impatiently to test this on a variety of gamers. While Andy hired a first-rate game designer to design the intricacies of the game, and to create an image that was a knockout, he wrote the programs that would make this game a great mystery, a real tease, and a real workout for the player.

Finally, he was satisfied that it would grab the attention of any serious gamer, or anyone who used the Internet for interactive chats, blogs, research, gossip, voyeurism, and any other of the reasons millions of children were at home in their rooms, exploring a world from which their parents were excluded— creating relationships with complete strangers that were more intimate than those within their families.

This was a game for the generation James, Brian, and Andy believed would be the target of anyone wishing to bring down the United States. It was for the most technologically advanced generation in US history, and perhaps the weakest generation in exercising its own mind and developing the imperative skills of communication and relationships. The most intimate, outrageous conversations would occur on the Internet, and yet the persons engaged were unable to engage face to face.

James knew that an enemy that dealt entirely in deception, stealth, and striking suddenly from the shadows would need a target that also lived in the shadows, for the faceless enemies of the United States would find comfort and fertile territory in the minds of young men and women who also remained faceless to one another. He took some comfort in the newest trends of Facebook and other sites where at least a picture was posted, but the content of what was posted left him wondering nearly every day if what they were doing would be too little, too late.

About once a week, he would watch Andy or Brian play the developing game, to see how it was shaping up. And he had to admit, it was suspenseful, action-packed, and gripping. It unfolded almost like a movie, but with the outcome being written by the player and his skill.

Brian did in fact test it on classmates in the early spring. The results were stunning.

Then, he solicited some UCLA students. Finally, he was ready to test it on some parents who had admitted to enjoying computer games as well. It was here that they had perhaps their most unexpected results. Eight out of ten times parents were reduced to tears by the time they reached the final, inner sanctum—realizing for the first time just how much danger their own children were in.

Then one night, Brian couldn't wait any longer. His exasperation with the length of time the design and redesign had taken was at a fever pitch. The testing he had done established clearly that the game impacted part of the target group. But, he was restless to identify whether the game could reach to the deepest limits of that group, affecting those considered "lost" by society.

With trepidation, he was headed out to test that very group, and knew he had to do this alone. It would be dangerous enough even for him. *This one I do by myself,* he thought, trying to build his courage.

"Hey, Pal, where you going?" James surprised Brian as he was sneaking out the front door at dusk, with a backpack slung over his right shoulder.

Shit! Brian paused in the doorway for a moment, deciding to tell James the truth. "I'd feel more confident about releasing this, if I can test it on the street. I'm going to make a run to Compton to test this on some brothers."

"Great idea. We'll go along," Andy chimed in, apparently having overheard the conversation from his bedroom. He reached for his jacket.

"No, no, I don't think that's such a good idea, Andy," Brian responded almost defensively.

"Why not?"

"This is not the kind of place you should be hanging around."

He said it, expecting Andy to just get it and back off, but James now insisted on going along, and that changed the dynamic.

"Kid, just in case you don't get the picture, our friend here is planning on testing this with a rough crowd. Right Brian?" he asked, as he strapped his ankle gun on, pulled his socks up over the bulge, and lowered his right pants leg.

As soon as Brian saw that, he wailed, "Aw, man, now, that's why I was sneaking out. If I do this, just me, I can get this done and be satisfied." He knew it was no use though because Andy and James were both already out the door, motioning for him to follow them. "Man, oh man, sometimes you guys piss me off!"

Slapping him on the back, Andy flashed him a grin. "Yeah, well, what are friends for?"

An hour later, on South Vermont Avenue, deep inside the 118th Street gang's territory, Brian parked the car and headed around the corner, walking west. His car was an older Oldsmobile and didn't have the "panic" button the newer models had on their keys. For a moment, he deliberated whether or not he should just leave it unlocked, in case he had to high tail it out of there. Deciding he might just need that margin, he purposely left the vehicle unlocked. James and Andy were right behind him as he turned the corner, wanting to keep Brian in range. By now, with the streetlights on and menacing shadows in every alley, Andy was having second thoughts.

James, however, seemed cool as a cucumber. In fact, he was the only one who didn't seem phased by their presence in a clearly proprietary section of Los Angeles. *It won't be long now,* he told himself.

He was right. Just after the three turned the corner and about a block from their car, they almost collided with seven young African-American men. This was clearly their neighborhood, and they instinctively reacted to the interlopers, expecting some imminent violence. That was, until they stopped long enough to actually look at the three men facing them.

While James was making a quick count of the visible weapons the gang members were flashing, and memorizing the gang insignias tattooed on their forearms, the leader of the group held up his hand, motioning for Brian to get his black ass over there. Brian stepped to the front immediately, leaving the bag casually slung over his shoulder, purposely making no threatening moves.

"What are you doing here, man?" The first question was asked belligerently. "And what the fuck are you doing bringing them two with you?"

Deciding to ignore the last question and just get to the point, Brian fearlessly responded, "I want to show you something, have you take a look at it."

If this is a sting operation, this dude's a real babe in the woods, the leader joked to himself. *Who goes out looking for a sale with a couple of missionary types with him?*

Turning to his friends, who were suspiciously silent, waiting for him to take the lead, he ridiculed Brian with, "Can you believe this shit? The man thinks he can come down here and try to make a sale!" He turned around menacingly and added, "Doesn't he know what kind of business we're in?"

To his surprise, however, Brian not only didn't flinch but he also took the lead and pushed back. "That's not what I'm here for. I need your help with something, and word on the street is you're the man in these parts."

This clearly disarmed DeSean, the gang's leader. He frowned. "Yeah, well, if you want to talk to me, what'd you bring those two goons along for?"

Glancing over his shoulder, Brian smiled and responded without hostility. "No fear. Andy's a brother. James, too."

Suddenly, one of the gang started laughing, feeling emboldened to the point that he could now engage. He moved out from behind and flanked Brian on the left. James did not move but was following the move, never taking his eyes off the surly youth. "Did you hear that? This motherfucker is so dumb he doesn't even know these two are white. And he thinks they're brothers!" Spitting on the ground, he added, "Shit, man!"

DeSean, however, had decided that although he did not know what the hell *was* going on here, he was not going to greet these three the way they probably deserved. He didn't smell cops here at all. Not knowing what this trio was doing, clearly out of their league, he decided to be magnanimous. He relaxed his posture just enough to signal to the others he was standing down.

"Man's got a point there, brother," he said to Brian, not even looking at Andy or James. "You are a pretty dumb nigger to be coming down here, dressed like that, dragging these two with you."

Brian stood firm, saying nothing. It was a gesture of respectful submission, and certainly a demonstration of no fear, which caused DeSean to relent even more. Ending the game of chicken, DeSean asked, "All right. What you want? You know we ain't got no drugs here. We're clean, man," he lied, making certain he wasn't going to be entrapped tonight.

"I know. That's not why I'm...*we're* here." Brian nodded in the direction of James and Andy and continued, un-phased. "Any of you home boys into computer games?"

Surprisingly, Brian saw all seven heads dip slightly, indicating they were. "Okay. Any of you *really* good at it? I mean *seriously* good?" Immediately, one hand shot up from the back row, and the others pushed him forward.

The only thing James noticed was the size of this guy's biceps. They were nearly the size of an ordinary man's waist, and had tattoos all around the circumference. His attention was brought back to the scene though as DeSean informed them, "Yeah, he's the best. Rest of us are what you'd call wannabes."

Slowly lowering the bag from his shoulder and offering it to DeSean, Brian smiled and said, "Good, 'cause I've got something for him to try. It's a new game, and we want the best to test it."

DeSean turned to his friend as if to see if he wanted to play, knowing full well he would. Before he handed off the backpack though, he turned back to Brian and directed a question to the three of them. "What's in it for us?"

"You'll see," James responded provocatively, before Brian could even answer.

Swinging his gaze around to James somewhat hostilely, he looked him up and down, noting easily that James was packing. But DeSean Williams wasn't the leader of this gang for no reason. He knew danger when he saw it, and he recognized a non-threat when he saw it. Whoever this white guy was, he was no threat to any of them, and DeSean knew that. He knew the man was cautious, given that he had an ankle weapon concealed, but clearly he wasn't looking for a fight. And with that conclusion, he tossed the bag to the eager player.

Two hours later, DeSean escorted Brian, James, and Andy back to their car. He'd posted one of the gang members there to make certain the interlopers didn't have their ride stripped while they were all in the gang's crib playing the game. Shoving the guard aside with a shoulder brush, he personally opened the door, signaling to Brian that he could get into the driver's seat.

"You two designed this?" he asked simply, almost in disbelief.

"Yeah," Brian responded.

"And you're going to sell this?"

"Absolutely!" Andy added enthusiastically.

Slowly, DeSean walked around to the passenger's side of the car to confront Andy and James. No one said a word. "Then, I wish you well, brothers," he said to Andy pointedly, and to James, looking him straight in the eye, "I wish you well." DeSean paused for a moment, making certain they understood his meaning. Satisfied they did, he grinned suddenly and added, "Even if you is white!"

Starting to leave, he turned back. "One thing though…" he added.

"What's that?" Andy asked innocently.

"You might want to rethink the name of this thing." DeSean paused for a moment, but seeing that Andy didn't seem to get it, he added simply, "You don't want to offend the 'brothers' now, do you?"

Andy's jawed dropped slightly as he struggled to grasp the meaning of DeSean's advice, but James, clearly understanding that the game's title was potentially provocative, bailed him out with, "Right. Good point." DeSean smiled, this time with no teeth showing. "We'll take a look at that. Thanks, man."

Now DeSean showed some pearly whites. Returning to the driver's side, he closed the door once Brian was behind the wheel and, patting the door panel twice, signaled for them to drive off. Then, without a hint of his customary menacing bravura, DeSean Williams disappeared into the shadows.

On the day that Brian Washington Carver received his diploma from a university that had treated him well—with James, Kelly, and Andy proudly watching—he turned the page of his life and put out the word that they were looking to hire a Public Relations and marketing firm to launch the game. Before the year was over, the game would be one of the great success stories in the computer game industry, and Andy and Brian's lives would be forever altered.

But the year 2007 held a considerable variety of seemingly unrelated incidents. Only a God's eye view could possibly have connected them. They *were* connected. The average person, though, would not have drawn a line from one to another, nor would they have been looking for someone possibly pulling the strings of all these incidents. And that was exactly what the Doctor was counting on.

Waiting patiently in Panama City, feeling freer than he had in a long time, he took pleasure each night in watching local television covering the news as it unfolded in the United States. Of particular delight was the fact that no one seemed to have noticed or cared about why sixteen of the most talented politicians that the United States had—in both parties—had "somehow" gotten the idea that a two-year long primary season was a good idea.

In years to come, even if they tried to find out who had planted that seed, it would remain untraceable. But there they were, right after the 2006 elections, throwing their hats into the ring for the Presidency—turning American presidential politics into reality TV. Their handlers would have benefited from some training in the entertainment industry where there is such a thing as "over-exposure." Every actor has to guard against being seen too much. The audience, even though they still like the actor, gets tired of him, and switches to someone else. And a career can flounder, or even vanish. Yet, beginning in 2006 and continuing on into 2008, not one of the campaign managers thought to wonder whether it was a good idea to spend this kind of time, campaign money, not to mention time away from their responsibilities as governors and senators, and run the risk of being overexposed and contradicted in one's views and emotional opinions by history itself.

Zawahiri knew government well enough to know that politicians never want current history to catch up with them. The worst thing that can happen is for a forthright pronouncement, which seduces the voter one day, to be contradicted by real current events the next—making the politician look foolish or naïve. The propaganda campaign that caused these men and one woman to be so far out in front of history, exposed for such an endless period of time, and ultimately betrayed by history as it happened, was one of the best pieces of work Samir ever did.

And only a God's eye view would have allowed someone to see that the true beneficiaries of the hysterical ranting and ravings over the border issues, and the tension that created, would be Al Qaeda, the FARC, and Venezuela. The combined voices of Conservative talk show hosts, Minutemen, concerned citizens, and confused politicians created an extremely precarious situation in Mexico.

Vincenze Fox's candidate won his election by only the narrowest of margins. And the shriller the debate in the United States became, and the greater an issue border control and immigration became in the debates of the unwitting political candidates, the closer Mexico came to having its government overthrown by a socialist/Marxist regime. Whether the people did it violently, or through elections, mattered not at all to the Doctor. All he cared about was regime change in Mexico, leaving Mexico dependent upon Venezuela, Cuba, and Colombia—since it would no longer be able to count on the kind and generous people of the United States.

Perhaps Samir's greatest accomplishment, however, was the turning of Conservative Talk Radio against their Commander-in-Chief in a time of war. Their limited view of the situation, and their persuasive arguments about the incompetence of the administration's State Department, the Department of Homeland Security, and any poor soul who ventured a contrary opinion, gave Samir a powerful, articulate, and unwitting army. And that army worked earnestly every day to enlighten the American people.

And every day the Doctor smiled. For, despite setbacks in Iraq and Iran that he could not have foreseen, Samir was winning for him. On his computer, the fourth level of the game, labeled "Public Relations," was perhaps the single most stunning accomplishment of that year's tactics. By mid-year, it seemed the Doctor was winning in all of his games.

But the Doctor had no way of knowing that his nemesis, too, was launching a game. It was a game designed to annihilate the Doctor's most devastating playing field. They were on a collision course—and a fight to the death—in the top four layers of his three-dimensional chess game.

CHAPTER 34

*H*e was running in sheer terror, knowing he was blinded by the darkness—not knowing what obstacles or traps lay there for him. But he had to run. The presence in the shadows must be real. It was calling to him, "Ayman, Ayman, I see you."

Who could it be? Who had penetrated one of his plans? Who had compromised him? There was no time to think. He had to escape; he had to hide. But no matter what turn he managed, shuffling forward into darkness, the voice followed him, quietly, patiently.

He was out of breath now, and pain wracked his entire upper body as he struggled to breathe. Suddenly, without warning, his knees and shins crashed into a hard, immovable object, causing him to fall. He screamed—and woke up.

The Doctor found himself alone in the makeshift offices of ST & Associates. The nightmares had returned. This one had been particularly intense—so much so that he had actually gotten out of bed and started to flee, injuring his left leg on the small table in front of his chair. Groping for the light, he tried to remain as quiet as possible, hoping he had not awakened anyone in the apartments across the alley.

Once he had the light on, he calmed down a bit and the intense anxiety dissipated. Fortunately, the wound wasn't bleeding; it was just a large contusion. So, he sat down to relieve the pressure a bit, and to take in deep breaths. Soon, his breathing was normal, but his mind was agitated.

Why is this happening? What am I missing?

Believing his nightmares were always a warning about something, he compulsively started to review all the areas of games he had going. Robotically he listed all the plans and arenas in which he and his group were engaged, searching for any hint of what might have triggered this anxiety.

Zarqawi's dead, but Makkawi's plans for Afghanistan are materializing, he encouraged himself. *Iranian influence in Iraq is increasing. That fills the void of Zarqawi. Best to let the Iranians do the investment.* "No, no, that's not it," he told himself out loud. "The military plans in that area are still advancing."

Suddenly he turned his attention to Bin Laden. For more than five years, he had successfully kept Bin Laden under wraps in the mental facility in Iran. Fueled by the infusion of capital the Doctor had given the remote, derelict hospital, he was confident the Administrator there was grateful enough for his hospital funds that he would take exemplary care of the patient whose identity he didn't really know. Drugged, and unable to communicate, Bin Laden himself could pose no threat. *No, he's fine. He's available if I need him.*

He knew immediately that his anxiety couldn't be coming from the fact he was still listed as missing and at-large by British and American intelligence. The fact that he and Bin Laden both had just vanished from the scene, and remained hidden for all these years, was turning them into almost mythical proportion in the minds of people all over the world. US and British intelligence had failed to find them, and had discredited themselves in the process. *No, it's not that. That's one of our greatest victories, one of our greatest propaganda victories.* He examined it a little more closely, though.

Since he was still on the run, using false identities and living out in the open, with no support system, he took a good look at it. Concluding that hiding in plain sight was still one of the most successful aspects of their terrorism, he looked elsewhere for the source of the dream.

My doomsday scenario is in play. We have only to wait. Ali Roos is capable all by himself—even if the others fail—of delivering a huge blow. Reassuring himself that the clock was ticking on America's supremacy, and that nothing could stop it, he moved on to the more dominant war games.

Knowing that his propaganda chief, Samir, was performing brilliantly, he was certain this couldn't be the cause of it. *The United States is tortured and devouring itself,* he confirmed. *Border and*

Immigration issues are huge, and the resentment and hostility being generated in that arena represent psychological warfare at its best. The Doctor could see that Mexico was getting nervous now. Fear of overthrow was palpable in Central and South America, and while the Americans watched their border, the rest of that hemisphere watched the changing political winds.

Stupid Americans. I have them right where I want them. Concluding that everything was going according to plan, the Doctor affirmed, "Venezuela, Cuba, the FARQ—they are all ready to exploit the opening we are giving them."

He smiled and sat back a little in his chair. Dawn was coming, and he could see a faint light outside. Deciding to try to catch a little extra sleep before the noises in the neighborhood began, he lay back down. His review of all their plans started again in his mind, like a tape playing itself over and over—stuck. For the Doctor had no answer for one agonizing question: If all these things were going so well, why did he feel so anxious? Why did he feel someone was stalking him in the shadows?

Finally, he concluded it was just the residual of his years of torture. Reminding himself that this had become the psychological profile of almost everyone incarcerated and tortured during his imprisonment in Egypt, he forced himself to be resigned to it, and not fight it. Mercifully, sleep returned, and he dozed off.

Ali Roos woke an hour or so later in his home in the Los Angeles area. Convinced that a test run would be necessary if he were to pull off this catastrophic attack on June 30, 2011, he had decided to act independently. On his own authority, believing he was acting in the best interest of Al Qaeda, he contacted his friends in London and gave them a go-ahead on the plan they had formulated when they had visited him the year before.

Because all of the conspirators had medical backgrounds, and had access to government labs or programs, they had developed a sabotage program. Ali wanted to see if trusted, higher-level employees could operate undetected. In and of itself, his idea was not a bad one. But, it had never been reviewed by the Doctor, and certainly had never been approved by anyone with command authority.

Ali Roos was a scientist, and a dedicated terrorist—but a novice. And his lack of experience would haunt him for some time to come. On that day, his decision would hurt the Doctor's plan incalculably. Two factors were unknown to him, and out of his control. How could he have known? After all, he was just a pharmacist. How could he have been expected to know that someone else would use the Chinese pet food industry to float a trial balloon? Someone was probing to see how much damage could be done with an insertion at the final stages of production. Ali Roos knew neither who they were, nor even that it was being planned.

Also out of his control were the true intentions of each member of the London team. Though medically and scientifically trained, one of the conspirators was ambitious and impatient. Feeling that Ali's plan was mere child's play, he decided to create something far greater than just a test run and minor sabotage. He decided—and persuaded his colleagues—to participate in an actual bombing. Wanting to strike an immediate blow, and keep the British people off-center, he devised a plan for simultaneous car bombings in Glasgow and London.

Novice that he was, and having no awareness whatsoever of the real conspiracy Ali Roos was involved in, this "friend" imagined that his bold plan would engender the admiration of Ayman Al-Zawahiri. After all, wasn't it Zawahiri who had masterminded the simultaneous bombings already executed with great devastation in other parts of the world? Consulting no one, he launched on June 30, 2007.

Regrettably, the Chinese dog food scare, and the London/Glasgow bombings, coming on the heels of one another, would arouse the attention of every intelligence agency of substance. Ayman Al-Zawahiri would, in fact, have cause to be anxious. At that moment, however, he was not even aware of the bombings.

CHAPTER 35

*A*ndy was a little out of his element on the campus, having only been there for a couple of Brian's games. Depending on where he parked, he could get disoriented on the park-like grounds, and unlike his Alma Mater, where everything revolved around the chapel steeple in the center of campus, here he couldn't make out any landmarks.

"Excuse me." He finally gave up and addressed a co-ed and her friend, who were out walking. "Can you direct me to the Adsit Center of Commerce?"

"Sure," the blonde co-ed said cheerily. "You're almost there. About fifty yards on your right."

"Thanks." *I thought I was close,* Andy thought, commending himself.

That was it for sure. As he got closer to the building, he could see the bench under the three hundred-year-old California oak tree that was a campus landmark. And sure enough, there was Brian. Andy could tell by the expression on Brian's face, as he got close enough to see him, that Brian was contemplating something.

"Hey, Brian, you okay?"

"Absolutely!" Brian exclaimed, as he stood up to shake Andy's hand the way they always had before they went out onto the field. That gesture hadn't meant anything to anyone else, but it had grown to be a symbol of the connection between the two when they played football together. Almost as if saying "from my hand to yours," that connection had foiled the ambitions of many a defensive tackle and safety.

"Yeah?" Andy said, scrutinizing Brian's demeanor. Brian Washington Carver had always been a hard man to read. That was why he had been so effective in out-maneuvering most of the men assigned to cover him. He just didn't telegraph much of anything. Even his speech pattern and walking habits belied his incredible speed. Brian spoke deliberately; he walked rather slowly and stiffly. But, on the field—knowing his objective—he moved with lightning speed, and calculated mentally with astonishing accuracy.

"Yeah, pal. I think I'm figuring this last couple of years out."

Andy didn't know where this was going, so he just dropped down onto the bench, enjoying the shade, and the expansive view of the campus from under the tree. Now and again, someone would pass by who knew Brian. They would wave or shout out his name, but none intruded upon the conversation. It was as if they knew this particular conversation did not include them. So, Andy and Brian had some private time, surrounded by 30,000 students.

"Andy, I been thinking about dreams—you know, people's dreams." Andy just listened, nodding. "Pappy told me to follow mine, and to be true to them. Mama, too. Those two were my anchor." His voice broke ever so slightly. He hesitated, then swallowed.

Andy smiled slightly, waiting. Then, Brian opened up. "I was thinking today how much had changed for me. You know, down there in Florida. Then, again with what happened in D.C."

He continued firmly. "And, now, with what you and James discovered, it's *personal*. I'm a man on a mission," he joked ironically. "And, now that I'm graduated, I'm beginning to understand why I picked Marketing for a major."

Andy laughed, appreciating the joke as well. He didn't speak; he didn't need to. He just nodded affirmation. Surprisingly though, Brian's conversation took a turn. "Do you miss it?" he asked almost wistfully.

"What?"

"Your life, man," Brian responded with feigned exasperation.

Andy repressed a smile. "You mean football, chess..." and glancing at a pretty co-ed passing by, he nodded in her direction, "girls, school?"

"Yeah, Andy, that's what I'm talkin' about."

Dropping the cavalier demeanor, Andy answered, "Yeah, sure, but not for long." He paused a moment to choose his thoughts, turned to his partner, and said, "Brian, you need to understand I'm playing the chess game for keeps here. I didn't ask for James Mikolas to come into my life, interrupt every plan Mom and I had, and lure me off on this mission. But he did." Looking squarely at his friend, Andy added, "And I'm aboard."

"You mean it's 'your mission, Andy, should you choose to accept it' time?" Brian irreverently referenced the old *Mission Impossible* line.

Andy couldn't help but smile. "Yeah…no regrets though."

Brian accepted that, slapped Andy gently on the back, and then added, "Okay. Okay. It's definitely *personal* for you, too. But, I wanted to ask you something about James."

"Shoot."

"Is it *personal* for him?"

Without any hesitation, Andy answered, "Oh, yeah, it's personal, Brian. But on a different level."

"What do you mean?" Brian didn't seem to get it.

Andy, characteristically, looked off in the distance; then he smiled. *How do I explain this?* he asked himself. He took a stab at it. "James is *old school*. He's been at the intelligence game since the '70s and, I don't know if you knew this, but he was a field operative in Eastern Europe."

"No. I don't think I did know. To be honest with you, pal, I didn't really have much interest even if I did," Brian admitted. Then, quickly, he added, "Until now. Now, I have interest!"

Continuing gingerly, Andy added, "Well, those were dangerous times, Brian—more than you or I ever knew or studied about. James has been trying to save everybody for a long time." He paused for a moment, reflecting on his growing awareness of the shadow warrior who was his friend. "To be honest with you, I think Mom and I were the first people who actually really helped James. Hard to imagine, I know, but he *sees* things others don't. And I think the jealousy of his colleagues blinded them to what he was telling them."

"And, what was that?" Brian leaned in, apparently keenly interested in this answer.

"Well, he could probably tell you this better than me. But, I remember a conversation James and I had one day down in our basement. It had to do with what he believed to be the Soviet Union's strategy to take down the West—especially us."

"What did he think it was?"

"The way he put it, it was, 'to take down the West, you take down the American people.'"

"Yeah, I follow. *Your* White King," Brian concluded.

"Right. And he believed they would do it by inserting a propaganda line, and then accomplishing a form of mind control, but done remotely."

Brian was listening intently, so Andy continued. "He realized they would use education—our education—against us. James says their goal was to weaken the minds of America's youth. They would couple that with an increasing reliance by Americans on so-called authorities—news media, doctors—you know, authority figures. The stupider we become, the more we rely on someone else's opinion. Then, all the Soviets had to do was compromise the authority figures."

Brian was struck by this. Remembering the conversation he'd had with James months ago about Pain Drug Hypnosis, he reached out and touched Andy's arm, as if to ask him to slow up a bit. He examined this in his mind, turning something over and over, trying to make sense of it. Then, abruptly, he said, "Which they have done!"

"Which they have done, yes," Andy said, turning to face Brian more directly, "by overwhelming them. Plain and simple, they did what you and I did all the time on the football field— and most certainly what I did to defeat every opponent in chess."

It was said with such certainty that Brian felt he needed clarification. He had never liked to be behind Andy. "Overwhelm?"

This was an invitation to paint the picture, and Andy embraced it. "Yeah, with options—too many options. Faced with too many, there is a paralyzing effect. That instant of lack of decision, or poor decision, is an open door. And the propagandist walks through it boldly, with *his* solution. His *answer* sweeps away the confusion of too many choices, and the target readily accepts it. You see, he's eager for some relief of the tension, and the feeling of being overwhelmed. That's what I learned from James."

"Shit, man!" Brian exclaimed. He did see. Then, he laughed. It was the first time in months Andy had heard his friend really laugh. In fact, it was so loud and vibrant even the passers-by caught it. Andy could see them look over at Brian, then look back at one another as if to ask, "What's he so excited about?" Then, they too got caught up in it. Just as misery is contagious, so, too, is laughter.

Brian had no intention of making other people happy. In fact, he was completely unaware of the phenomenon. For it seemed to him a tremendous weight had not only been lifted but had also just plain blown up and left him. He felt very light, and very giddy.

Whatever it was, it felt good. Andy waited. A few minutes later, the laughter had subsided enough that Brian could add, "And that's what our mysterious Ayman Al-Zawahiri is doing. Yup, I can see it, too. He's laying his own propaganda along the line James' Soviets opened up. Only this time, it's *his* message. And it's a form of remote mind control. Man, that's *brazen!*"

"You got it. And what James and I had concluded was that he was using not only weapons but also fear to influence the society, and thereby producing a demand that enabled the medical and pharmaceutical people to stride in and offer their simplifying, mind-numbing solution. They make money, and Ayman Al-Zawahiri completes what the Soviets failed to do."

"He takes down the people." Brian's right leg was bouncing now. Andy knew that meant Brian was eager to receive the ball, and to run like the wind.

Now it was Andy's turn to laugh and add, "I see you've seen an opening!"

"Oh, yeah, brother, oh yeah! You could say I do!"

Andy gestured as if to say "and that is?"

"You just put the last piece of the puzzle in for me, bro—the *last* piece." Seeing Andy still didn't fully comprehend, he added, "That's the only thing I was struggling with. I been pretty much tracking with you two on all this intelligence stuff, and War on Terror threat—all that. I knew the game ideas I had were helping you." Andy nodded vigorously his agreement on that. Brian rode over that, however, with, "But, what I didn't fully know was what this compulsion I had to major in Marketing was all about."

"And you do now?"

"For sure, pal, for sure. Marketing is—forgive me for saying this, Andy—the white man's form of propaganda. I like business, when it's done right. I like Marketing. And when it's done wrong, me and every other thinking person gets pissed off. Huh!"

"What?"

"Well, Andy, thanks for showing me that side of James. I feel good. He earned his spot on the team, as far as I'm concerned." He was grinning now, showing those incredibly perfect, white teeth. "And I'm your man, once again! I *feel good*, as James Brown always said." Brian was up now, dancing in imitation of the legendary singer, singing at the top of his lungs, "I feel good..."

Andy just shook his head. He had seen this exuberance before. It felt good, truth be told. For five years, he and James had been roaming a dark and dangerous world, on a rescue mission. Alone, and taunted, they had clung to each other. And now, Brian was with them. Before Andy could even finish the thought, Brian abruptly stopped dancing and said, in a magnificently playful tone, "We are going to have to match this Mr. Ayman Al-Zawahiri at his own game. And I'm your man! And Marketing is my game!"

With that, Brian started off without even a goodbye, prompting Andy to call after him, "Where are you going?"

"To meet with the head of my department. I got a question for him, pal. See you later at the apartment."

Brian's meeting with the head of his department did indeed go well. His natural gift for strategic thinking, and his disarming honesty, had made him a star at Los Angeles Western University, even when he was not on the field. Whereas many of his classmates thought in clichés, and offered slick formula presentations with enough technological pizzazz to assure them slots with most of America's mediocre advertising agencies, Brian's original approaches—driven by long-term thinking—had earned him the respect of a businessman-turned-professor.

Not only was the head of his department a man with years of experience in marketing, advertising, and public relations himself, but he had also maintained all of his business connections.

Known as a straight shooter, who had executed his own strategies with integrity over his thirty-year career, the professor's list of friends extended into the very wealthy. Many of them had studied with him over the last twenty years, deployed his teachings, made fortunes, and were very grateful.

Brian's market research on the beginning game was well thought-out and well-targeted. His sampling was accurate, his follow-up testing and feedback lines were impeccable. And his former roommate, whose degree was in Statistics, had helped him tabulate and evaluate the game. The game had proven to be exciting. It was sufficiently difficult to expunge dilettante parents and onlookers. Challenging to real "gamers," they had naturally spread the word to friends.

This phenomenon was one of the most encouraging to Brian. For them to produce the effect in society that he and Andy intended, the word of mouth had to be strong. To his relief, and yet completely unexpectedly, he was receiving text messages from "gamers" who raved about the game and its crescendo to the shocking final victory—all the while tooting their own horns that they had made it to the level where they'd solved the final mystery. And they were asking permission to bring friends in on it; demanding to know where their friends could get it.

Two categories of calls came in, each identical. One category was the large demographic of inner city youth. Whether in gangs, or merely living in the environments marauded by the gangs, their response was huge. And the other was the category of upper middle-class youth—both white and black.

"You know, I don't know anything much about video games, or computer games, Brian," his professor had told him.

"I know, sir. The game, frankly, wasn't designed for you. Its mission involves another generation."

That simple statement had intrigued the professor. The research he was looking at clearly showed which generation, and it showed a huge demographic spread. What had caught his attention was the word Brian had used to describe the purpose of the game—*mission*.

Had Brian been at Harvard, or George Washington University, or some other exemplary school, it might have gone unnoticed. But Los Angeles Western University, a private university despite its name, had attracted through the years an elite faculty. Most were entrepreneurial in nature, and most of them drove the business school in which Brian had enrolled.

Kindly, his professor asked, "Tell me the mission."

"I'll do you one better, Prof. I'll introduce you to it!" The grin on Brian's face was an invitation his mentor could not refuse.

"Why do I get the feeling the roles are about to reverse here, Brian?" his professor and mentor joked.

"Because they are, sir." It had been said simply, but with such certainty, that all sense of joking vanished. Only once in his life had this Professor met with that certainty in a student. That other student had transformed the world of business with innovative marketing strategies. And today, Brian's professor willingly sat down in a chair while his student loaded the software so that he, too, could play the game "White King Rising."

Determined to finish, the man labored at the game, occasionally turning to Brian for help on a strategic or tactical choice that would help him advance and win. Finally he did. And when he was done, red-faced and teary-eyed, he turned to Brian. He tried to speak, but words would not come. Brian just sat patiently. Finally, the man who was a father of three, grandfather of seven, and survivor of the suicide of one of his grandchildren, found the words, "This is an important game."

It was all he said. His next action was to pick up the phone and punch in a number. A moment later, without even identifying himself to the person who had answered on the other end, he simply said, "I have someone you need to meet."

And that one phone call, placed by a dedicated professor on behalf of a brilliant student's project, would shake the United States to its core, and would short circuit the top four games Ayman Al-Zawahiri was counting on for victory. Innocuous as it seemed, the tide had turned.

"This is a pretty snazzy place, Brian," James commented, as the three of them stood on Figueroa St.—straining to see the top of the building they were about to enter.

239

"Yeah, out of my league for sure!" Brian retorted. "Looks more like Andy's style to me!"

"You gotta be kidding," Andy answered immediately. "Whew, I have never seen anything this elegant. Wonder how much the rent is in this joint?"

James cut it short. "All right you two. Now that we are all properly impressed, let's not be late. What do ya say?"

Signing them in, the uniformed security attendant politely smiled and escorted them to the elevator. Opening it with his key, he ushered them in, punched in the floor code, and said, "It's the top floor. You are expected."

Stepping out of the elevator, James, Andy, and Brian felt suddenly as if they were suspended above the entire Los Angeles basin. They were in the Penthouse offices of the luxury building, and the entire office area was glass. Whoever occupied these offices could view any section of Los Angeles, from any direction. It was a magnificent day—uncharacteristically clear for the smog-plagued city. That was prophetic.

A middle-aged woman approached them, smiling. "Magnificent view, don't you think?"

"Yes, ma'am," James answered. "I'm James Mikolas. And these young men are Brian Washington Carver and Andrew Weir." He offered his hand in greeting.

She received it firmly and said, "And I am your Investor."

CHAPTER 36

"Was this us?" the man's voice was uncharacteristically demanding.

The Doctor had immediately answered the satellite phone when the call, with their emergency code, had come through. Disoriented by the sense of urgency in Samir's voice, he calmly asked, "To what are you referring, Samir?"

Realizing that the Doctor must not have seen the news reports coming in from London and Scotland, he consciously altered his tone before saying, "I beg your pardon, sir, but I gather you have not seen the news."

Before the words had fully reached him, Ayman Al-Zawahiri had reached for the remote control, instantly bringing up CNN on his television. He had very little in this office space where he was hiding out, but his wealth had recently bought him the most state-of-the-art wireless television technology. The upgrade from the neighborhood's limited TV gave him the ability to watch without anyone knowing there was even a television on that floor.

"I'm looking at it right now, Samir. You're referring to the bombings they are reporting on, correct?"

"Yes, sir, I am. I need to know if this is Hamas, or Hezbollah, or us. Who planned this one?"

As the Doctor was just coming up to speed, he didn't fully grasp why Samir felt this was so urgent. Surely they were all used to allied terrorist organizations striking their own targets for their own reasons. *This is probably just one of those,* he thought, reassuring himself.

"Because it looks like us—and they botched it. And I need to know, so I can figure out how and where to respond, media-wise."

As the Doctor turned up the sound a bit, the BBC reporter was commenting on the capture of the car-bombers. *They surely did botch it if they got caught,* he thought. In his eagerness, the BBC reporter added that, although the investigation was on-going, initial reports were confirmed that most of the bombers had medical backgrounds—and they seemed to be employed by the British government in its health services area.

If this had been just another low-level car bombing with a modicum of damage, the Doctor would have dismissed it out of hand. But, the similarities to his use of simultaneous attacks and suicide bombers meant it was either Al Qaeda, or a copycat.

Regardless, he had no idea which group or person *had* authorized this, nor whether it was one of his own. And, knowing that Samir had no idea of the secret cell that would attack through medical and pharmaceutical lines, he admonished himself, *Be careful. Watch what you say to Samir.*

"Samir, I do not believe this is anyone from our team," he said reassuringly. "The competency level is too low, and I am not aware of any of our good men being in that area, with an attack on this timeline. I assume it is a copycat."

But Samir pressed further. "And what if no one takes credit for it? What do you want me to do?"

"Nothing."

"Not even if the media asserts this is you?" Samir asked.

"Not even if they assert it is me." Then the Doctor laughed out loud and added playfully, "Besides, my friend, I think they have more respect for me than that. They will recognize this is an imitator—and an amateur one at that! After all, the point of a suicide bomber is to be a suicide, not a prisoner."

He heard Samir give out a long sigh, and he assumed this had satisfied him. Waiting, it was a few seconds before Samir concluded with, "That's excellent. Thank you. I am sorry to have disturbed you, but I felt it was important."

"No problem, my dear friend," the Doctor assured him. "Thankfully it is nothing."

Once the line was dead, however, the Doctor's demeanor shifted significantly—to one of fury. In truth, he had no idea who had done this. What he could not tell Samir was that this was, in fact, deeply troubling. Whoever it was, the fact that there were medical and government people involved could jeopardize the security of his plans for June 30, 2011.

The Doctor was angry with himself now. He thought he had foreseen everything with regard to keeping this one cell and its intentions a complete secret. He planned no similar attacks prior to 2011, and he had been confident that the United States and Britain would be looking for the obvious ways of staging a terrorist attack of a biological or chemical nature. They would look at infrastructure targets, and delivery systems. He had been confident they were too unimaginative to conceive of a chemical attack from medicine cabinets inside every home in America.

That was, until now. Though he knew the intelligence community to be behind in the game, they were not witless. *And when they realize these attackers were doctors and the like, they will ask themselves questions. And those questions could lead them to contemplate an attack from another direction. They will ask themselves, "Where could doctors or health services people attack?"*

The acid reached his throat very quickly as he contemplated this scenario. In pain, he slumped into the chair closest to the television and numbly stared at it. Cursing the images of the men as they were being taken away in chains by British authorities, he prayed to Allah that no one in British intelligence would get creative and conceive of a scheme that could compromise the manufacturing integrity of pharmaceutical companies. If they did, his entire plan could be corrupted.

At that, he almost passed out. Gripping the table near him, he prayed, "Let them conclude this is just another terrorist bombing cell with members who *happened* to be educated in medicine and science; that it's just a coincidence, please! Let them not conclude it is a medical cell."

He paused for a moment, examining the ramifications. Too weak to speak, he thought, *If they conclude the latter, they might just be smart enough to run an analysis, and get right answers.*

For the sake of Shari'a we must all pray now.

That appeared to calm him. The pain abated, and he sat up, looking around the room at the barren, cracked walls. Then, almost as suddenly as the pain had started, an idea pressed on him. He wondered now if, somehow, this did have something to do with his own plans. The Doctor had known all his adult life that people were against him, that none could really be trusted. His natural suspicion of everyone, and his fear of what they could do to him if he did not remain in control, enabled him to look more closely into his own plot and plotters.

After all, what do I really know about him?

"Pharmacy…" Ali Roos answered the phone himself, as it was his assistant's lunch break.

"Did you have anything to do with this?" an unrecognizable voice hissed into the phone.

Startled, Ali struggled to comprehend. "I don't know what you are referring to," he said, stuttering a bit. "Who is this?"

Then, in his normal voice, the Doctor said, with deceptive calm, "It is I, Ali, and I wanted to know if you were in any way involved in the events in Glasgow and London?"

Ali recognized his cell commander's voice now, and he also suspected the man had drawn the same conclusion he had—that he had somehow compromised the brilliant attack scheduled for just four years from now. He was sick about that very possibility when the Breaking News had started coming in. And, sneaking a quick glance at the TV screen that was always on in the pharmacy to see what he could find out, he had recognized one of his friends.

Furious and afraid, he deliberated frantically now over what to say to the Doctor. Had he more experience, were he a long-time collaborator with the Doctor, he would have known never to lie to him. But Ali Roos lacked that experience. Quickly concluding that the Doctor didn't really know, or else he wouldn't be asking, Ali decided to lie to Ayman Al-Zawahiri.

His answer was technically not a lie. After all, *he* had not been involved. Had they asked him, he would have told them to stand down. Reassuring himself of that fact, he quietly answered, "No, sir, I was not."

There had been a fraction of a second's hesitation, however, as he had mulled it over in his mind. It had been noticed by the

Doctor. Giving no sign of noticing, the Doctor answered reassuringly, "Good. I didn't think you could possibly have risked compromising our plans. Thank you for your candor. Good day, my friend."

And, as abruptly as the call had begun, it ended. Ali Roos was still afraid, however. And, on the other end, the Doctor was contemplating how much of his plan had been, or would be, compromised. He had concluded that whether Roos had been involved or not was a moot point. The point was—would it raise enough of a red flag to attract the attention of intelligence analysts, and, if it did, would it arouse their suspicions and imagination enough that they would probe it?

It was a question he could not answer, and he did not like the feeling of hopelessness that washed over him at that moment. The chess move was now someone else's. But it was done already. There was nothing he could do about it—except make sure nothing else like that happened again between now and 2011. With help from Allah, intelligence analysts would drop it like an old bone, and move on to something fresher. *Yes, they are impatient. They'll drop it, even if they do sniff it out.* Then he got it. *We'll just have to create a diversion.*

Feeling relieved, he now turned his attention to a more pressing aspect of the problem and asked himself rhetorically, *What to do with Ali Roos?*

CHAPTER 37

"Mr. Weir, Mr. Carver," the limo driver said, as he opened the door for them to exit, "I called ahead, and they are waiting for you."

The way the driver treated them, the respect with which they were greeted at the downtown office and premier restaurants throughout Los Angeles, was almost surreal to Andy. He had intended to create a game that would convey the message to American youth of a danger, and of a solution. He had believed in his game once his partner, Brian, had persuaded him to reach that generation on the level at which they played. He prayed nightly that their strategy would work, so that he and Kelly could return to Virginia and resume the life so abruptly interrupted by James Mikolas when he had asked for their help.

What he had not considered, however, was how meteoric their rise would be in business celebrity status. Andy Weir was not a businessman; nor was James Mikolas. Brian Washington Carver had aspirations, but lacked connections. That is what made the link to the investor so profound. One person's presence on the project had made all the difference. Their investor had money, and she had connections. Believing in their game, she had introduced them to a team of attorneys, accountants, consultants, and graphic arts personnel.

A project of this magnitude could have taken years. But with her help, it had taken only months. Brian got the brilliant artistic director he needed to make the game so compelling visually that anyone seeing it would want to try it. He got a genius game designer who took Andy's rudimentary design to a level of game that would challenge the best, and yet be playable by a novice—if they had drive and tenacity.

Carver and Weir, Inc., as their company was legally known, also had a game production facility, and a design facility below it in a manufacturing complex in West Los Angeles. Brian had always heard that the speed of a project is directly relevant to how much money you put toward it. Now, he knew that to be true. Their investor, whom they affectionately referred to as "the Investor," had been very specific that she would provide the necessary funds to develop, manufacture, and distribute this product—all within the year 2007.

Now, under her guidance, Andy and Brian were planning to hire their marketing and public relations team. On their own, they had been considering a marketing team from a committed local human rights organization who were inspired about their insights, and their message.

Ironically, he knew a few of the team from his university. But, in the years he had attended, his practice schedule had been so intense he usually raced from class to the football field, and had never once engaged in conversation with two young men who were eagerly mastering the field of Marketing and Public Relations. In order to draw attention to human rights abuses globally, they were being trained in the American version of propaganda as well.

At the moment, however, their Investor had arranged a lunch at an elegant, palm-studded restaurant on the Sunset Strip. The purpose—to interview another candidate she was recommending. With no parking, only limousines were permitted to stop long enough to allow their occupants to step out and be escorted into a restaurant, which had perhaps the tightest reservation list in the Los Angeles business community. Deals involving billions were being discussed daily at nearly every table. It was here that projects launched onto the landscape of American business. It was indeed an elite atmosphere, made even more special by the expansive view of the mid-Wilshire district of Los Angeles. Through the palms that graced an all-glass patio, one could also view the skyline of Century City.

"Are you ready for this?" Andy asked.

"Sure!" Brian responded quickly, then he added, "This has been a rocket-ride, I admit, pal, but this is the last piece. We're ready in manufacturing. All that remains is for Carver and Weir, Inc. to select its public relations firm."

Though they were expected to enter, Andy reached out, pulling Brian gently on the arm, and guided him off to the side for a moment. Clearly, he was struggling with something. Finally, he dove in. "Well, that's why I'm a bit uneasy today."

"Why?" Brian asked sincerely.

"I know this is your field and all, Brian. You're the man. You've been brilliant..." His voice trailed off.

Before he could continue, Brian interjected, "But?"

Andy smiled. "But...I'm a chess player, you know. And we're about to hire the Bishop in chess terms."

"Pal, you're losing me here! You know I never got through a game of chess in my life."

"Right, sorry. The Bishop is the spokesman, the one who advances what the king stands for." He stopped momentarily. Brian was just looking at him blankly, waiting for the punch line. "So...I like your guys from the university. Seems to me they understand the mission, and are reflective of us, and our target market. That's all."

Brian got it immediately. "Oh, yeah, man, I know what you mean. But 'she' wants us to interview this firm she heard about from that media giant she pals around with." Then, as if to reassure Andy, he added, "You know, she's been spot on so far, so I'm willing to give them at least a shot at it. What's the harm in that?"

Obviously, Andy knew there was no harm in interviewing another team, and having a great lunch to boot, so he smiled, punched his friend on the arm, and said, "You're right. No harm at all. I just wanted you to know my feelings. You know, we want somebody like us in the Bishop's slot."

Brian nodded agreement. Just as they were about to step inside, James' familiar voice caught their attention. "Mind if I join you two?"

Andy brightened up immediately. "Hey, James, I am *so* glad you are here!"

"Me too, Kid," James added enthusiastically. "I appreciate the invite." Looking around quickly, he added, "Where the heck does anybody park around here? I thought I'd missed you."

James had no idea why Brian and Andy found this funny, but he was looking forward to lunch. Though he would have absolutely no official involvement in the business meeting, and would have to be passed off as their technical advisor to even get him into the place, he didn't have any qualms about being a fifth wheel. He was simply planning to watch.

What he had not told Andy, however, was that his insistence on being there had to do with a slight racing of his pulse, and the small surge of adrenalin he'd experienced this morning. For this old Cold War warrior, the heart rate and adrenalin had always been a signal of something in his environment that warranted his attention. It "caught his eye" as he was prone to explaining. But for now, he was just happy to be with the Kid and his Pal, as he called them. Their newfound income, as they assumed ownership of Carver and Weir, Inc., had allowed them to move out and into a house up above Sunset Blvd. He had remained behind in the apartment, continuing his research.

Tousling Andy's hair slightly, he simply asked, "Who are we meeting with again?"

"Some PR firm. ST & Associates, I believe." And with that succinct answer, Brian disappeared inside.

CHAPTER 38

S amir didn't really like this restaurant. Despite the fact that he needed to be in social environments, meeting the men and women who controlled or influenced America's top industries, the nature of his real work made him ill-at-ease in too public a place.

He knew, of course, that no one in US or British intelligence was looking for him. Mossad did not know of his existence. His mentor, Ayman Al-Zawahiri, had often joked that he was the one man of the upper command circle of Al Qaeda who did not have a reward on his head.

Smiling now, he reflected on those harsh times several continents away, when they all had fled for their lives, and, at the same time, had planned multi-pronged attacks over several decades to come. But, they had been dangerous times, and Samir was truly happy to be pursuing his goals in a land that admired dreamers. Imbued with a sense of irony, he couldn't help but sneer that prominent people, self-righteous people, were the ones most eager to advance and promote his ambitions.

If they had any idea, he thought, as he looked around the room to see who was dining here today. *Any idea at all.*

At that moment, his reverie was interrupted as he saw the maître d' escorting three men to his table. *I expected two. What's this, I wonder?* With European manners and grace, he rose to greet them, extended his hand, and said warmly, "It's a pleasure to meet you. My name is Samir."

"Hello." "Good to meet you, too." "Hi." The three voices overlapped as they all four sat down. One of the voices sounded less enthusiastic than the others, but the overlap made it difficult for him to determine which one of these three was more conservative about their meeting.

As lunch progressed, it became obvious that the odd-man-out was the one named James Mikolas. Samir was experiencing an unusual sense of discomfort with the man. Doubting that he was really a technical advisor, as he had been introduced, he finally concluded he was there only to observe. The question was, for whom?

Sensing no malice, however, Samir finally dismissed it, concluding that James was there protecting some interest of the female investor Bud Walker had told him about. He relaxed even further when he decided that he did not have to take this client if he did not want to.

Bud had only wanted him to meet these two young guys, in the event their company's project turned out to be an area that might expand ST & Associates' visibility. With no pressure on him to have to pacify or impress Walker, Samir was free to make his own evaluation. Truth be told, his client roster was swollen to the maximum as it was. Leads into the entertainment industry had opened doors to stars and studios alike. Samir liked that crowd, and he was filling his pockets nicely with the fees they were willing to pay.

His own "first impression" was that taking on a start-up company, albeit a well-financed one, might be more work than he wanted to do. *After all, my real work is in Paris,* he reminded himself. *I have to stay free enough to leave for France at a moment's notice—and not have it draw attention.*

For that reason, his interest was polite, but mild. He feigned interest in the game industry, as he had no real background in that. But he was interested in seeing the game, based upon the enthusiasm demonstrated by the young black man.

Samir turned to Andy. "Do you perhaps have the game with you?" Samir asked.

Grinning, Andy responded without hesitation. "Always, Samir. My friend here never lets it leave his side. He sleeps with it!" The humor of that escaped Samir, but he joined in convincingly anyway.

Suddenly the table jolted slightly as Brian slung his wireless laptop up onto the table. An anxious waiter eyed the noise of glass tingling. Not wanting any of their china or glassware to end up on the floor, he adroitly scooped up any unnecessary pieces, freeing up a perfect place for Brian to demonstrate the game.

Even more upsetting to the waiter, and to the other hushed business negotiations going on nearby was the explosive sound of gunfire as the game opened up. "Oops, sorry." Brian flinched and kicked off the sound. "Forgot about those speakers."

Pulling his chair around slightly to get a better view of the action, Samir politely watched as Brian opened the game and started to demonstrate it. But Brian recognized almost immediately that without sound, and without Samir playing the game himself, he wouldn't have an appreciation of it—let alone an idea on how to market it.

Brian, James, and Andy had all agreed months ago that they would not describe the game to anyone. Even the university public relations team they had interviewed had had no advance concept of the game's purpose. All they knew was that it was a new game two guys had designed, that they had money backing them, and they needed somebody creative to turn them into the next big cover story on *Inc.* magazine.

They wanted to observe, personally, the reactions of the people who would hold the game's fate in their hands. The human rights activists had passed muster. Now, they all wanted to see if Samir would.

But, in fairness, Brian knew it wasn't going to be possible for Samir to make a good assessment without being in a position to actually play the game, and examine it. And he knew, too, there was no way they could honestly evaluate Samir. So, as suddenly as he had dropped the computer on the table, Brian shut it down, folded it quickly, and slipped it into his computer bag.

Samir looked up in question. "Samir, I just realized there's no way you can get the real idea about this without playing it. So, what I propose is that we all finish this great lunch, and adjourn to our factory so you can see the whole deal."

"Agreed," Samir answered. Having nothing else to talk about now, Samir seized the opportunity to probe James. "So, James, what is your involvement in this affair?"

"None, really, other than technical advice," James answered immediately.

"What kind of technical advice?" Samir asked, challenging him slightly.

He's a smooth one, James observed. *Wonder why he really wants to know?* Equally smoothly, James answered, "None of the hard stuff. Computer programming's not my forte. I advised mostly on strategy—of the characters in the game."

"Oh, you mean, like a military advisor on a movie set? For authenticity, etc.?"

"Exactly," James affirmed, smiling.

That seemed to satisfy Samir, as it provided him with something to talk about while they concluded their meal. It seemed his questions were, in fact, only aroused by the need to find something to fill the silence.

Shortly, the limousine picked them all up and headed out Olympic Blvd. to the factory.

"This is an amazing facility!" Samir exclaimed, as he caught his first glimpse of the spacious production house and computer laboratory. "Extraordinary, really!"

"Thank you," Andy answered. "Our Investor is very astute, and our business development team really made it possible for us to do almost everything under one roof."

"Hum," Samir said, nodding. Though the facility was truly a bustling, state-of-the art game production house, his own lack of interest and experience in this area made him a little more of a superficial observer than a true evaluator. But, he did want to explore it thoroughly enough to justify his decision yeah or nay to Bud Walker.

One room particularly caught his attention. Behind interior glass windows, which allowed Brian and Andy to watch what was going on, was a room with rows and rows of tables. Set up in aisles, the long tables had multiple PCs placed about four feet apart, with a chair and person at each PC. Headers on the wall above each row of tables indicated what level of skill the player was—from beginner to advanced, and from young to old.

This was their testing room. Eight hours a day, they had men, women, boys, and girls sitting in those chairs testing the game.

What Andy and Brian were developing were varying skill-levels of the same game. The purpose was the same, the content of the game was the same, and the outcome for the winner was the same—but they were creating several versions that allowed different entry and learning curves in the game.

Intending to make this a game for anyone, they were now making it possible for anyone to enter—and not quit. All four of them stood outside and watched through the window.

"Wow, those people are serious about this," Samir commented innocently.

"You bet," Andy responded. "Wait 'til someone wins. That's a 'party,' let me tell you!"

And then, as if on cue, a young man sitting at the beginners' table won his game and started screaming and shouting, "I did it! I did it!" Running up and down the aisle, the exuberant young man high-fived the others, and bounded back to his seat, staring at the screen with an almost serene look of satisfaction.

"Is that typical?" Samir asked.

This time James answered. "Oh yes, yes it is. People like to win this game." There was a look of satisfaction on James' face at that moment, but Samir was pre-occupied with the activity inside the testing room, and failed to notice it.

"How 'bout you? You want to try?" Andy offered.

"Me?" Samir tried to mask his uncertainty. "Sure." Then, to qualify his response, he added, "A bit anyway."

"Great. We'll do it in our office where it's quieter." Brian led the way and opened up an office with two rather sparsely bedecked desks, a PC on each. There was a picture on one wall and a mirror on the other. "You a beginner, Samir?" he asked.

"How'd you guess?" Samir joked. They all laughed at that.

"Well, we won't pressure you, so we'll leave you alone, to play a bit at your own pace."

"Fair enough. What do I do?" Samir asked, as he slipped into the chair in front of the PC on the first desk.

"I'll just slip this CD in, it'll fire up—and it's pretty much self-explanatory after that." Then, as if to reassure the novice a tad, he added, "We put a little tutorial on the front for the beginners." Grinning, Brian exited before Samir could enjoy the joke with him.

"Thanks," Samir called out to no one in particular. Then, he started the tutorial. Accustomed to computers and learning complicated applications—including codifying and hiding top secret communications—Samir picked up pretty quickly how to engage the game.

Behind the mirror, in an adjacent room James had had specially built for observation, Brian, Andy, and James watched Samir study and start. Brian felt really uncomfortable "spying on folks," as he called it, from the hidden room. But Andy had assured him it was just a little quirky thing with James, and to humor him. A few weeks earlier Andy had convinced him, "Some old habits are hard to break, Brian. I don't get it either, but James has his reasons. And, if he wants a 'spook' room, as he called it, then let's let him have it." And so they let James have it. Samir was now the second candidate they had observed play the game in the room.

If Samir had known the purpose of the game, his choices might have been different that day. Certainly, if he had had any way of knowing the ramifications of this game upon the plans of the Doctor, he would have decided differently. But all he saw, once he got used to the images, was yet another violent scenario being acted out by American youth in their entertainment forms. *Typical American garbage,* he told himself. He had observed this violence; Al Qaeda exploited the degradation this type of violence had produced; and he whole-heartedly supported American youth frying their brains, and becoming mindlessly addicted to games. But he himself had no real *chemistry* with it.

Arrogant by nature, and somewhat complacent after a few years of living and working in the sterile world of public relations in the United States, Samir rather disdainfully looked down upon a game, which started with one gang member shooting a dope dealer. Out of respect for Bud Walker, he played for a while. In fact, he actually got to the point of disarming the school nurse, but he didn't really comprehend any particular significance in that act.

Samir had a natural disrespect for women, so nothing in his sensibilities thought the type of disrespect that was handed to this unfortunate character was unusual. If anything, he subliminally agreed. Tiring now, and having made his decision, he decided to politely disengage.

"Geez, he's done," Andy whispered. "We'd better get in there."

Just as Samir stepped out of the office, the three came around the corner, feigning surprise at seeing him. "Done already?" Brian asked innocently.

"No, no, my friend, I don't learn that quickly," Samir demurred. "I just realized that as brilliant a game as it is, and as great a start-up as I believe you have here, I don't believe I'm the one best suited for taking it to the top."

No one disagreed with him, so he finished with, "I know you will be very successful, and I appreciate very much the opportunity to meet you, and see what you've done here. My best." It was said totally sincerely, and his handshake with all three was warm and genuine.

As Samir stepped into the limo they had called for him, James breathed a sigh of relief. He couldn't put his finger on it, but Samir had made him uneasy. James had tried to shake it throughout lunch and at the factory. Surely the man was smart, articulate, and professional, but still there was something nagging.

Anyway, it's a moot point now, James told himself. *The guy's gone.*

Andy caught James' eye and asked, "Are you happy?" James grinned and nodded yes.

"Me, too."

"Me, too." Brian was the last.

"So, are we agreed?" James paused a moment and added, "It's your pals from college?"

"Yup. I don't see any reason why not."

As quickly as that, it was done. The firm chosen to launch Carver and Weir, Inc.'s computer game was an unknown duo—well-trained, young, and eager to make an impact. The firm that had turned it down was brilliant, experienced, globally positioned—and arrogant.

Perhaps Samir had been exposed to the American media too long. Perhaps the media's arrogance—which he had ridiculed and despised while in Afghanistan and Paris, and which he himself had exploited—had permeated him unknowingly. Whatever the reason, the choice he had made seemed insignificant to him. A man in his position had the privilege of exploring many opportunities. They were abundant, and he had to turn down most of them. This was just another one of those.

Samir didn't give it a second thought.

CHAPTER 39

"So, that's it then? We're agreed?"

Andy and Brian were alone in their office. Despite the wall of glass, which allowed them to view the production lines and game testing area, the fact that they were closed off allowed them some privacy, and most certainly some quiet. Frenetic would be a good description of the activities behind them.

Briefly, Andy turned to survey the ever-growing number of personnel in the area; then he looked back at Brian and winked. "Almost a metaphor, isn't it?"

"For what?" Brian retorted. Brian Washington Carver had a keen intellect, but he was also street smart. And he had a burning desire to avenge the deaths of his family. Not being a violent person, he had resorted to the most rational way he knew—find out why it happened, and tackle it. For that reason, he didn't let his mind wander off into intellectual thoughts or introspection.

The last year with Andy had taught him to come out of himself, and to apply himself to the mission. Once he fully understood what that mission was, he excelled. Noticing that Andy was still watching the young men and women playing the game, he repeated, "Hey, Bub, for what?"

That ended Andy's moment of reflection as well. "Oh, nothing, really." He let out a short, cough-like laugh. "I was just thinking you and I are in here, hopefully out in front of this thing, watching from behind our glass wall, as we plunge others into a brutal awareness of the traps they are in, and then challenge them to get out."

"Right, gotcha," Brian quipped. "Now, Andy…"

Before he could finish Andy snapped out of it. "Sorry."

Wanting to reassure Andy, Brian sat down for a moment and

took a deep breath. "Andy, we're doing the right thing here. Adding the section where, if they go to the Pharm Party and make the wrong choice, and continue to make the wrong choice, they die, is a real wake-up call."

"Do you think we'll lose a lot of them there—that they'll give up playing?"

"No, pal, I don't. Any more than you chess geeks give up when somebody whips your ass with a slick sequence. You know what you do. You figure out how he suckered you in, and you write a damn book about it!" At that they both laughed. Andy had to admit that *was* a good description of the chess world. Brian continued, upbeat. "Well, these kids aren't any different. They'll pass the word around—'watch yourself in the Pharm party; it's a killer.' I promise you, man, they want to win. They'll come back. Only the next time they'll be smarter. That's what it's all about, Andy, making them smarter."

He had said it with enough conviction that Andy sat a bit straighter, eyeing his friend. "Yeah, I know," he conceded.

Brian was on a roll, however; he had more to say. "Andy, we're not going to get these kids the first few times. They're not gonna stop drugs with just one pass through this thing. They're gonna have to fight to win. I'm banking that they just keep coming back 'til they win. And by that time, they'll be shrugging the drug scene—all of it."

"You're right, Brian." Andy seemed restored now. "You are right! I don't really think I got it 'til now that they're competitive as well, and that to win this game, they have to try to be stellar."

Feeling they were back on track now, Brian added, "Exactly, pal. We—all of us—want to win. They are no different. We're just helping them remove a huge impediment, that's all. And, man, I'm jacked!"

With almost all strategic decisions behind them, and tremendous results coming in from early sales, Andy wholeheartedly endorsed the part of their business plan that called for them to pour almost all their investment into marketing. The Investor had been told there would be hard assets purchased to sustain a major game business. But, she would also be told that to create that major game business meant they would have to market aggressively.

That level of dollar commitment would be necessary if Carver & Weir were to continue to implement a strategy whereby every time there was a new "shooting," and psychiatric drugs were involved, they would allocate additional advertising money immediately and promote the game. That strategy had come from James. Given his certainty that Ayman Al-Zawahiri would use pharmaceuticals and medicine to achieve his blatant financial objectives, James had suggested a counter-move.

Persuasively, he had reasoned that if the greedy activities of these manufacturers were being used—wittingly or unwittingly— against the people, then their counter-attack should be right there. The plan was simple. Every time one of these drug-induced shootings occurred, Carver & Weir would drive its sales revenues up by piggybacking on the blanket news coverage the media was already providing.

Every Internet tool would be used to promote the link between the shootings and the need for people to play this game. A mystery as to the content of the game was created and exploited—all to issue a come-on to the generation that needed to reach that final, inner chamber, and discover the secret. If the enemy struck through the cultural deterioration of the US as it spun into a drugged oblivion, Carver & Weir would strike back. The slogan "Find Out Why He Did It" was the link from the shooting to the game.

That was James' strategy, which they had already begun testing. And it was working. Their PR team of Tate and Donovan worked diligently to investigate, corroborate, and attack along those lines. Though Seun-Hui Cho was reported to have been on a depression medication, Tate and Donovan could not confirm that, since his recent medical history was never released. They left that one alone. But, months later, they were prepared when Asa Coon stormed through his school, shooting and wounding four before taking his own life. He was on the antidepressant Trazodone.

It was an outrageous and gutsy strategy to shove the issue in the faces of the generation they were trying to rescue. While talking heads on cable news debated, argued, and wailed about the audacity of Carver & Weir to even suggest a link between drugs and tragedy, Carver & Weir—under the patient and skillful guidance of Tate & Donovan—promoted their game.

Critical editorials in major newspapers did not slow them down; skeptical television talk show hosts did not slow them down; screams of protest from psychiatrists did not slow them down.

The reason was simple. Despite what the adults of America were oblivious to or cognizant of—depending on your view—the young men and women of America, who were in fact being victimized by the drug culture in its entirety, apparently had no doubt about the possible validity of Carver & Weir's game theory.

Word spread like wildfire on every social networking tool that generation used—from YouTube to Facebook, to chat rooms and blogs. Truth was impinging. And for the first time, a generation was grabbing on to something they believed to be true. It appeared to be a catharsis of some sort. By the millions, teenagers began playing the game, feeling vindicated that their suspicions of the motives of the "pill pushers" seemed to be founded in fact.

They eagerly played the game and relished the struggle to solve the mysteries it presented. And as they played, and as they won, a generation found its voice. Instead of it being the harsh, strident, violent voice of recent history, it took on a calm, rational tone. Agreeing with one another, and righteously disagreeing with "authorities," had allowed them to find themselves. And what they found, they liked. For, at the very top level of the game, when one succeeded in getting there, they found a hero. "From Zero to Hero" became their war cry.

And the PR firm of Tate & Donovan did not miss a beat. Picking it up on blogs, with one kid endorsing it to another, the slogan emerged and started to duplicate. Said once, then repeated, and repeated again, it became the advertising slogan of the year. Unwittingly, the generation itself was using the propaganda techniques that Ayman Al-Zawahiri and all the doctors from past repressive regimes throughout recent history had used. Only this time, the techniques were being used to free, rather than to enslave.

The unexpected serendipity of it all was that, ultimately, their parents liked the "new view" their children expressed; they liked their attitude; and they began to listen to their sons and daughters. They, too, joined the revolution.

So, the counter-attack advanced unfettered. Not only did "White King Rising" become one of the top four games in the world for that year, with its stats still soaring, but the underlying strategy was working as well. For James Mikolas and Andy Weir in 2004 had correctly analyzed that the enemy would use *fear* as a weapon against the people of the United States, in order to exacerbate a host of cultural and sociological maelstroms. Knowing the United States had degraded to a society of violence, James had evaluated that the enemy would try to capitalize on that.

Their analysis was that the enemy would strike with fear, creating a demand for drugs of all kinds, and the drugs would contribute to the continued creation of a violent society.

Unfortunately for the Doctor—and unknown to him—his plan to do just that was compromised. Instead of violence and drug usage increasing, for some mysterious reason drug sales were about to go down. Pharmaceutical revenues were about to plummet, and would continue to plummet into 2008. However, Ayman Al-Zawahiri would not connect the dots of the root cause of that for some months.

None of the presidential candidates that year were watching the phenomenon either.

What Andy, Brian, and James had created was becoming immensely popular in the gaming world, and was flying completely below the radar screens of any of their enemies. It was the perfect covert op.

James breezed in, plopped down into one of the conference room chairs, and leaned back. "How's our Fifth Column coming along?"

"Pretty good, James, my man." Brian high-fived him, danced past him, and added, "Pretty good. We've agreed to keep the design change allowing the player to get killed off if he screws up too badly." James nodded his agreement on that.

"We've agreed to exploit the shootings through our marketing until the people wake up to this issue, and look to the real cause of the homicide. And, James, we've agreed to another design change to give the player an option of a partner in the game."

"Partner?" James wasn't quite following.

"Yeah, we're gonna let them choose a partner—if they want one. And, this is the diabolical part—their choices affect the partner. If they screw up, the partner is screwed. If they win, the partner wins."

"Sounds like life, Pal," James joked.

"You betcha!" Brian grinned, and concluded with, "We thought it might provide an *in-cen-tive*." He elongated it syllable by syllable to drive the idea home.

"So, when does this launch?"

"It'll be version 2.0, and it'll launch later in 2008. Great thing about this version is we can also change it any time one of your sociological 'dealies' changes."

"Dealies?" James pretended to be insulted, not even knowing if there was such a word.

"Yeah, man, you know. One of them things Andy and I told you our generation was being destroyed by."

"James," Andy said, deciding to translate, "he means one of the factors we worked into the equation before we flushed out the common denominator."

"Yeah, sure, I knew that," James said, pretending to understand. "But, what's the change?"

"We have a way of reprogramming the game to insert the actual incident—and let the game player figure a way around it, so he can continue trying to win."

"Andy, are you talking real time here?" James queried.

"Yeah, James, we are. Something bad happens in the US—if it's consistent with our analysis about the psych drugs—we'll insert it. Nothing like letting the player play in real time, huh?"

James liked this. He really liked this. He knew enough of the game to know this would empower the person playing it to test his own ideas in the actual situation, simulated in the game. He smiled. Then he laughed.

"What?" Andy asked.

"Well, Andy, it's all about judgment isn't it? Drugs impair it; your game restores it!"

There was silence between the three of them as each looked at that last remark. And for a moment, Andy looked off into the distance and smiled.

CHAPTER 40

"*B*lue skies, smiling on me..." someone was singing, slightly flat.

Andy looked over his shoulder, wondering where the voice was coming from. He heard it again. "Nothin' but blue skies, do I see . . . "

Spotting James coming out of the front hall washroom in the new digs Andy shared with Brian, he asked, "James, is that you making that annoying sound?"

"What sound?" James asked innocently.

"The singing, James, the singing," Andy teased.

"Oh that. Yeah, that was me. Sorry...didn't realize I was."

Andy had never heard James sing—ever. So, he just looked at him as if to decide whether the man was running a fever or not. Deciding not to make too big a deal of it, he asked, "Something special happen?"

"Nah...I'm heading over to a museum to confirm some of the research you guys used in that new section of your game. I found a place that's got quite a time line laid out on these so-called medicos. I'm going to run a check on us and them. You know, see if we're both accurate."

Andy nodded agreement, still wondering why that would prompt singing, let alone that particular song. Then, just as he slipped out the door, James tossed over his shoulder, "And I'm taking Kelly with me."

Brian came in just in time to hear the last. "What'd he say?"

Puzzled, Andy answered, "He's taking Mom to a museum."

"A museum!" Brian scoffed, pursing his lips as if he'd eaten something distasteful. "What is that, a date? Is he taking her on a *date?*"

———————————

"Hey, Kid." James sighed dejectedly as he came in and slumped onto the sofa in the great room that overlooked the city. An early-evening fog bank was shrouding the city's lights, dampening any view—almost as if in sympathy with James. "That didn't work out too well."

Andy said nothing. He really didn't know where James was going with this, or what he was doing. "I don't think she liked it much."

Andy paused for a moment, scrutinizing his friend, and then asked, "James, did you take my mom on a date?"

The question must have startled James because he responded like a teenage boy getting his date home late and having to answer to an angry dad. "Yeah, sure," he fumbled. "I mean, I didn't mean anything by it. It was just a date."

Before he could continue, Andy jumped in. "James, James, settle down. It's okay if you took her on a date. It's okay."

"Yeah?" James looked hopeful.

"Sure. I just didn't know. That's all. She didn't tell me."

"Well, I think that's because she didn't know it was a date…" James' voice trailed off, and he looked really embarrassed now.

Pulling up a chair, facing James, Andy couldn't wait to hear more. "James, how do you take a girl out, and she doesn't know it's a date?"

"Well . . . " James struggled with this a moment, squirming on the sofa. "You know, Kid, it's been a long time since I asked anyone out on a date." James looked at that statement for a moment, snorted, and added, "In fact, I don't think I've ever asked anyone on a date." There, he'd admitted it.

Thank God Brian isn't here, Andy thought. *He'd have a field day with this.* But Andy understood. James Mikolas had spent his youth on dangerous assignments in Eastern Europe. There had never been time to have a girlfriend, let alone a wife. His locations changed constantly, and his identities as well. Not exactly the stuff of a trusting relationship. So, at this moment, Andy might as well have been the older brother coaching his younger brother on the ins and outs of asking a girl out. He proceeded as such.

"All right...all right. We'll figure this out," he said, reassuring James. "Where did you go?"

"To the Industry of Betrayal Museum. I thought she'd find it interesting. I just asked her if she'd like to go to a museum, and she said yes."

Andy suppressed a smile. "And what upset her?"

"Zawahiri. We found Zawahiri there." James paused for a moment, then added, "I don't think it was him so much, by himself. I think it was that he was the last in a long line of guys who do what he does."

Andy nodded. "I can imagine."

"She didn't handle the George Washington part too well, either, come to think of it."

Andy had no idea what George Washington had to do with psychiatry, or Zawahiri, or anything else they had researched. He was so stunned, he just sat there. Finally, he asked, "James, what are you talking about?"

Deciding to put it behind him, go home, and lick his wounds, James stood up and somewhat defiantly concluded with, "You'll have to ask Kelly about that. You'll have to ask Kelly."

Following him to the door, Andy opened it and ended the conversation. "Well, good then. I'm glad we talked. Hope you feel better."

James smiled feebly and said quietly, "I do, Kid, really I do. Thanks for the advice."

What advice? Looking over the pieces of this bizarre conversation, Andy shook his head and thought, *I gotta call my mom!*

CHAPTER 41

*A*ndy's new BMW Z4 was parked on the street in front of his home. Just as he was driving away, he looked up in time to see James running toward him, waving his arms. Rolling down the window he asked, "What's up?" as James reached the car, out of breath.

"You headed over to Kelly's by any chance?" James asked, holding firmly onto a box he had secured under his right arm.

Andy nodded.

"Great!" James sighed. "I was hoping you could give her something for me."

Andy noticed the box and wondered if James was giving Kelly a gift as an amends for their disastrous date. He didn't ask, however. Instead, he just smiled and said, "Sure."

James was a little slow, a little awkward. But he found the words. "Thanks, Kid. I remember she wanted some better water, so I bought this best-in-its-class water system. It's supposed to be the best, anyway." He slid it through the window, as if passing it to Andy would somehow make it better with Kelly.

Seeing that James was uncomfortable about this whole thing, Andy decided to lighten it up a bit. "You're giving her a water treatment system?"

James nodded and grinned, obviously proud of himself.

"Geez, James, remind me to teach you about dating, and what kinds of gifts impress a woman."

"What?" James looked perturbed. Recovering quickly from the ribbing, he zinged Andy. "And great one you are to be teaching me about women and dating! What do you know on the subject?"

Shaking his head in amazement, Andy couldn't let it pass.

"James, my friend, I *used* to date a lot in high school." He paused and let that sink in before adding, "Before I met you, and before we went down this rabbit hole together."

James nodded his understanding.

"But, not to worry, it's like riding a bike. Once you get it, you have it for life."

"Really?" James asked sincerely.

"Yup. And I'll teach you, James, I promise."

James let out a huge sigh of relief, and the color returned to his face. "Thanks." He started to walk back towards his own car, which was parked a little farther down the street. Then he remembered something and turned back toward Andy. "But you will deliver the water filter, right?"

"Done deal," Andy assured him, and drove off.

"Andy," Kelly squealed, as she opened the door to her apartment. "What a surprise! I'm glad you stopped by." Then she sobered up. "I need to talk to you about something."

Thinking she was referring to the disastrous date James had described, he immediately went to James' defense. "Oh yeah, Mom, James feels terrible about that. He wanted me to give you this."

Though she looked puzzled, Andy noticed she took the box eagerly and went straight to the kitchen with it. Calling back over her shoulder she said, "This is exactly what I have been wanting. That is so dear of him to remember. Do you think you can install it for me?"

Andy grinned. He was always happy to be able to do something for his mother that his dad would have done. He'd been a good stand-in through the years for those seemingly insignificant things men do for women, but which women seem to be so appreciative of for some reason. It was a little thing. But he knew it meant a lot to his mom, so he was always happy to oblige. Now that she lived in an apartment, rather than their home in Arlington, there had not even been lawn-mowing he could do for her. So this was a nice chance to be with her, and serve her.

"There, that should do it," he said, climbing out from under the sink about an hour later. "I think that was a good amends, don't you think?"

"What are you talking about?" Kelly asked.

"You know, an amends for that disastrous date you and James had."

"That was a date? The museum was a date?"

Boy, these two are really not on the same page, Andy mused. *I better tread carefully here.* He chose his words, chewed on them a bit, and then answered, "Yeah, well James thought it was."

Suddenly Kelly giggled, then immediately suppressed it and tried to keep a straight face. Andy had caught it, however. Her eyes were smiling though, giving her away. "Really? I had no idea. I wish he'd told me."

Andy let that sit there for a moment. He was beginning to feel a bit awkward himself being in the middle between his mom and his friend. "Yeah, well, I'll speak to him about that." Then he abruptly added, "For the future of course."

"Thanks, dear, that would probably be helpful." She smiled again, and immediately squashed it again. "He is *something*, that man." That was all she said. Turning her attention to the water filter, she turned it on, let the water run, and looked out the window. Apparently she remembered something Andy had said, because she turned with a quizzical look and asked, "But what was so disastrous about it?"

Grabbing a glass from her cupboard, Andy filled it and responded directly. "Well, he realized taking you to the Industry of Betrayal Museum was probably a really poor choice—you know, upsetting and all. I agree it's not the best place to take someone you want to, you know, impress." Now Andy was stuck, too, so he just shut up, drank the water, and looked out the window as well.

It took her awhile, but then she got it. "Oh, I see. He thought it was Zawahiri, didn't he?"

"Yeah, absolutely."

Now she laughed without suppressing it, and explained. "No, Andy, it wasn't Zawahiri. I've gotten used to the reality that he is a truly brilliant and evil man. You two convinced me of that back in Arlington." She let that sink in for a moment and added, "Of course, being seized at gunpoint in my own home was a little hard to overlook."

Andy cringed. Their near miss with the deranged Al Qaeda operative who had been stalking him had never really lessened as an image. He had hoped a change of location would have dissipated the memory for her. Now he doubted it. "Mom, you know I would have spared you that if I could."

"I know, Andy. I've always known that." She continued to reassure him. "That's not why I mentioned it. I know Zawahiri's slime, and I know you are still looking for him, and, I would guess, for where he will attack. I don't ask questions much, because I know you two are on your own project, and determined to stop him. There's not really much for me to say to that."

He wondered if this ended the discussion, since she was so emphatic about it. It did not. She went on. "Given what I saw at that museum, I'm guessing you boys and James are honing in on the profession he will use for his attack."

Andy nodded affirmatively.

"That was shocking, frankly. I've had suspicions for a very long time, Andy. Your dad did, too. But to see the time-line laid out on the progression of eugenics, and the institutions used to dominate and control people, was shocking." She paused for a moment. "It was sickening actually. And I hope you two take down the whole lot of them. I really do."

It was said so vehemently that Andy now wanted to know just exactly what it was that had set Kelly off. Knowing his mom, he knew she would tell him. She did. "I was doing okay with it, Andy, until the Benjamin Rush stuff. The cockamamie theories about Negritude—that being black was a form of mental illness…" She spat it out, as if the very concept was distasteful to her. He killed George Washington, you know, and I never knew it."

History had never been Andy's strong suit, much less the history of psychiatry in the United States. Benjamin Rush was the father of American psychiatry. Andy, like most Americans, did not know this. He did know that Benjamin Rush was a doctor, and a signatory on the Declaration of Independence. And he'd paid no attention to anything else about the man.

"Mom, what are you referring to?"

"You've never been to this museum?" she asked.

"No, I haven't. James is always poking around in the research area, not me."

"Well, you should go. You'd learn something."

Overlooking the terseness with which she had responded, Andy wanted more. "Mom, how did he kill Washington?"

"He was his personal physician, Andy. Washington had a minor cold, and Rush bled him until he died."

"Why?" Andy was beginning to get the idea there were secrets buried in history.

"Because the idiot had a theory that all illnesses come from too much blood in the brain. And the way to handle that was to bleed the patient to drain the blood from the brain."

"Wow."

"Yes, wow. So, he drained nine pints of blood from his friend in one day. And Washington, who had nothing more than a sore throat, died after the treatment by his *brilliant* friend."

"And that is what upset you so?" Andy was a little mystified.

"Well, it's about betrayal, son, isn't it?" She had asked it rhetorically, and did not expect an answer. Continuing, she added, "You might say Benjamin Rush was just ignorant, with a stupid theory—that it was unwitting. Or you might say he knew it was dangerous and acted prematurely and devastatingly—that it was witting. Either way, Washington died. The father of our country died at the hands of the father of Psychiatry."

"Okay, Mom, spell it out for me. What upset you so much?"

It was simple actually, and she answered easily. "The fact that they started out ignorant and arrogant, and they still are. That's what upset me, Andy. That and the fact I couldn't help asking myself how many are dying today as a result of their stupid theories."

She waited a long moment, watching to see if Andy understood. He did. Suddenly, she hugged him. It was a passionate hug. He remembered her holding him just that way the day of his dad's burial at Arlington National Cemetery. Quietly she finished and let him go. "And for a moment I was overtaken with the searing question of how many does Zawahiri plan to kill? And how will he attack?"

Looking Andy straight in the eyes, she challenged the young man who was no longer her boy. He was a grown man now, deeply involved in defusing Zawahiri's plan. "Andy, I don't think

I really understood until now what you and James are up against."
She took a deep breath. "You're the brightest, kindest person I
have ever known. Your father would be so proud of you. But he
would be afraid for you, too, Andy."

"How so, Mom?"

"Because he would know that you are not going to back
down from this. You are a brave person, and you are going to
fight to the death. James, too. Zawahiri fails, or you do. There is
no in-between here. That is what your father would have known,
and it is what I now know."

The tension was palpable. Kelly was right. Andy knew it. He
smiled at her. Trying to lighten it up, he joked, "Well, we'll win you
know, because we've got you and your Irish temper on our side!"

"I believe in you, Andy, I always have. But, truth be told, I
haven't really been on your side."

"Aw, come on, Mom, you have; you know you have," he said,
contradicting her.

"No, Andy," she insisted. "I supported you. But I had so
many reservations, restrictions, doubts. Looking back, I can see I
was probably a well-intentioned obstacle you and James had to
overcome to continue your mission."

"Mom, please don't say that."

"Okay. But you asked what had upset me. That was it. I
wasn't really there with you. I was behind you, but not *with* you.
And I am changing that right now."

"What do you mean?"

"I mean, we all face this man—until he is stopped. You tell
James that all he has to do is tell me how I can *really* help you
two—" She corrected herself, "—you three, and I will do it. You
tell him to consider this a four-way deal, not three-way. I'm in—
all the way."

Andy understood now something his father had said to him
shortly before he died. Trying to brace the young ten-year-old for
the fact that he would be leaving and that Andy would need to take
care of his mother, Andy's dad had said, "We are all soldiers now."

What Andy understood today, that he had never understood
before, was that Kelly was part of that, too. She had always been.
He bit his lip to choke back the emotion, for he realized now that
Kelly had had his back for a long time. She knew very well how

high the stakes were. She knew the dangers. And she had just declared she was going to face them with him, and with Brian and James.

This was a fight they could not lose. And Kelly had just added one more member to the squad. Andy smiled and looked at her with deep admiration. "What?" she asked.

"Oh, nothing," he fibbed. "Nothing. No wonder James likes you so much."

"You will tell him?"

"I'll tell him."

Andy stopped by James' apartment on the way home. He felt lighter somehow. Truth be told, he had worried about his mother. She *had* always been a factor that he and James had had to take into account. They had, in the past, worked to find ways to make their mission palatable for her. All that had changed now.

Guessing that she had really been there all along—whether she knew it or not—he had matured today and realized that men don't always get it right. *No wonder James was in a tizzy! They're harder to figure out than I thought.*

Before he could get out the key he'd kept from when he'd lived there, James opened the door and blurted out, "Did she like the water system?"

"Yeah, definitely." Andy teased him a bit by almost dismissing it. But, relenting, he decided to give James a break and answer more enthusiastically, "Definitely."

"Well, come on, Kid, what did she say?" James was on pins and needles, like a teenage, 21st-century Cyrano.

Pausing for effect, Andy answered, "She says she's got your back."

Andy winked, turned, and abruptly left. James flinched slightly, as if he'd been struck. Then he recovered, looked at what Andy had said, displayed a relieved smile, and whispered to himself as he closed the door, "Son of a gun!"

CHAPTER 42

"*H*elp me."
      The Administrator stopped abruptly, certain he had heard a cry. Just as he was about to continue his walk around the mental hospital he owned, in a remote village in the Kerman section of Iran, he heard it again.

"Help me." The voice was weak and raspy, a stumbling plea. Looking up in the direction from which it appeared to be coming, the Administrator saw the open window. Then again, "Help me!"

Oh no, he thought, quite certain now that the sound was coming from that window. *Please let him be all right.* He prayed to Allah as he raced back toward the rear entrance nearest the window. *I should not have changed his medication. Oh me, I am in terrible trouble.* He was running now, leaping up the stairs two at a time to get to the man's room.

This man was his best patient. He remembered vividly the day the man was dropped off at the hospital by two aides, subdued into near catatonia by his Thorazine, in late December of 2001. In the ensuing years, the money he had received to care for this man had saved his mental facility, and himself.

Though the man had identification papers, the Administrator had long suspected they were forgeries. But he had never tried to probe the mystery, as the monthly stipend forwarded to their facility on behalf of the patient had paid for food and medication for all his patients. And it had afforded him and his wife a small home as well. Frankly, the Administrator had felt it was a blessing from Allah, and that he was entitled to keep some of the man's stipend, given the exceptional care he and his staff provided him. He was being paid to keep quiet. He knew the man must be important in some way. Why else would there be such secrecy about his location, and such determinedly excellent care provided for, in what was otherwise a truly wretched environment?

That's why he was so fearful now as he rapidly walked along the corridor, trying not to alarm anyone else. A few days earlier, he had reduced the amount of Thorazine prescribed by the man's absent doctor in order to handle a lung infection that had developed. Seeing no harm in weaning him off the medication for a few days, he didn't want to run the risk of negative side effects that might occur with the combination of the psychotropic medication and the antibiotic necessary to handle the infection.

Just last night the nurse had informed him that the patient was responding, and that the fever was down. He had been so relieved, because he could not imagine a greater catastrophe than losing this patient, and the money that came with him. The man had had only one visitor in the years he had been there with them—his personal physician had come to check up on him one time. *There was something odd about that,* he reflected.

Looking back on it now, he remembered that during the short visit, he had kept his distance from the doctor and his patient, not wanting to interfere or risk losing the patient. But he had stayed close enough to eavesdrop when the door was closed, for he was sure he'd heard voices in the room. The patient had been so drugged he was completely incapable of verbal communication. Only his lips contorted now and again, but that phenomenon was one of the side effects of a prolonged and strong dose of Thorazine. Yet that day, he was certain he had heard two men's voices.

Perhaps he's able to talk now, the Administrator concluded. *The cessation of the medication may have done something.*

His heart was pounding when he entered the patient's room. It was large, with an excellent view of the garden below. And the patient was the sole occupant. His doctor had insisted upon that when he left the treatment regimen with the hospital administrator. Usually, the patient sat in his chair near the window, looking, without seeing anything outside. But, he had seemed to be calmer at the window and that, then, had become his usual position.

Half expecting to see the man on the floor in some type of

convulsion, the Administrator was relieved to see the man still in his chair. He was leaning forward though, as if propping himself up using the window frame. Then again, the ghostly utterance from the man, "Help me."

Completely unaware of the Administrator's presence in the room, the patient seemed to be struggling to call out the window in the hopes of someone hearing. Cautiously the Administrator came up behind him, gently pulling him back into his chair by his shoulders.

At first, the patient flinched and tried to withdraw, but then he relaxed, and the fleeting look of fear in his eyes dissipated. He relaxed even further when the Administrator, in a calm voice, said, "It's all right. I am here. I will help you."

Despite the fact that the Administrator had been paid to keep quiet, not to nose around, he realized this was perhaps his opportunity to find out the man's identity. It would have been too dangerous to ask the man's benefactor and physician, but he sensed the possibility that he could ask the man himself now. Perhaps the drug was sufficiently removed from his system to permit him to talk. He decided to try.

Coming around to the front so that he could face the patient, he noticed the patient's eyes following him, and then he noticed the patient turned his body so that he, too, could face the Administrator. Despite how difficult and awkward it was for the man to use his motor controls and move his body, he somehow managed to do so.

The Administrator then bent over, so that the patient could easily see him. Quietly he asked the question he had been desperate to ask for so long. "Sir, who are you?"

The release of fear was immediate, and the patient's first response was a vocal expression of deep relief. It was barely audible. Next, the patient used heroic effort to raise himself up in his seat and meet the question, and the questioner, head-on. Mustering what little lung power remained after his illness, and his repeated attempts to call out for help, he nonetheless inhaled deeply enough to provide an answer befitting his rank. Slowly he answered, "Usama bin Laden."

CHAPTER 43

*H*e had just vomited his guts out in his patient's bedpan. It was the closest thing he could find, and the Administrator could not risk anyone seeing him in the hallway—especially not in this state. *What am I going to do?* he pleaded to no one. *What am I going to do?! He'll kill me for sure.*

Though there was a good possibility that this is *exactly* what Usama Bin Laden would do if he were allowed to return to normalcy physically, the Administrator was torn apart with indecision about what to do with his patient next. *The man's doctor has been so generous with us; surely I cannot betray him. He'll kill me for sure.* As soon as he thought it, he realized he was in a no-win situation. If he let Bin Laden live, Bin Laden would surely have him killed for participating in this involuntary incarceration and drugging. If he killed him, the man's doctor would surely kill him for killing his patient. The doctor seemed to need this man alive very badly. He had figured out by now that there had been some kind of catastrophic change in the leadership of Al Qaeda, and that he and his tiny hospital were now deeply involved in it.

Leaning out the window to get air, he tried to avoid looking at the man in the wheelchair. Until a few minutes ago, the man had been just a heavily drugged patient, whose benefactors paid handsomely to keep him secreted in this unknown place. But now everything had changed. *I have to be smart,* he coached himself, trying to gulp in air and swallow it. Then it came to him. There was a third choice. *Of course.* He exhaled as he relaxed a bit. *Of course, that is the way. Allah be praised, I am saved.*

It seemed simple enough. Chest infection or no chest infection, he would begin to re-establish the patient—he preferred to call him that—to the original medicine regimen. In a day or two, this man Bin Laden would be back in the state in which he had started. That way, Bin Laden could not harm him, and the man's doctor would never know the Administrator had tampered with the regimen. He was much calmer now, and was resolved to save himself.

The patient's medications were in a cabinet in his room. Vial after vial was stored there so whoever was administering his medications could easily get them, and administer them to the patient quickly and simply. Sliding past the patient's chair, the Administrator managed to avoid eye contact with the man. *Why did I have to ask him?* He backslid and chastised himself unmercifully. *Why did I just have to know?* Fear started to rise again, and he squashed it immediately. *I can do this. I can. No one will know.*

Just as he approached the patient with the syringe, the man turned and looked him directly in the eyes. There was no fear, but the man's eyes betrayed awareness that this was his last play—he would prevail here or not at all. Before the Administrator could accomplish the task of reinserting the IV, Usama Bin Laden, guessing that this man was motivated by money and the fear of losing it, and that the man would try to subdue him so as to go on safely collecting his funds, quietly said, "I have a great deal of money."

It hung there for a moment. Both men's eyes were locked, and neither was willing to flinch. In the end, it was the wretched Administrator's humanity that won out. For that long moment, he held his breath and calculated. Either man could kill him. Either man could pay him. But this man, the patient in front of him, was helpless. He was showing no signs of anger or hatred, or vengeance. He wanted to live and move, and think. The other man had treated the Administrator with condescension. Though he'd pretended to, he had cared nothing really for the Administrator's goals, or the needs of the other patients. Rather he had only used them as leverage to buy the Administrator's cooperation—and silence.

And not a single day in those five years had gone by without the Administrator knowing that truly there was nothing mentally wrong with this patient that warranted the brutality of this drugging. Every day he had known the violation he was committing against another man. He had paid a heavy price for that compromise of his own pathetic values.

Knowing now that the man was Usama Bin Laden, he could easily justify keeping him on drugs. After all, he *was* the most wanted man in the world. Turning him in for the reward was not an option, however, as he knew Bin Laden's doctor would hunt him down and kill him. The status quo was indeed tempting. But in the end, the Administrator—who ran a degraded facility in a God-forsaken area of Iran, and who had never had a truly righteous day in his life—decided that the hospital was still a hospital and that this patient deserved the same protection he provided the other miserable souls.

"I'm going to need it." Removing his hand from Bin Laden, he pulled back the IV tubing and started to return the stand to the back wall. Almost as an afterthought, not even daring to look at Bin Laden, he asked, "Will you take care of the people here?"

"Yes."

CHAPTER 44

"*I*'m so sorry," the Administrator wailed, weeping. "The money meant so much to me and my family." Then he added, to make the point, "And to all the patients here. I am so sorry."

Bin Laden was awake enough now, after an additional two days off from his psychiatric medication Thorazine, to think and formulate questions. His mind, keen before, was somewhat befuddled, and he was having particular problems with time lines. There seemed to be a terrible gap between his paltry recollections and his present circumstances. But, he did know who he was.

"Friend, you are forgiven. You did not know who I was; the people who brought me were not suspicious to you. I am sure it seemed like a well-deserved windfall. Believe me, I am grateful you are helping me now."

The Administrator was relieved to hear Bin Laden speak so forgivingly, and so coherently. Miraculously, there didn't appear to be permanent brain damage from the incessant chemical toxins. *Allah has protected him*, he thought. *All I have to do now is help orient him.*

Awkwardly he asked, "I do not know how you want me to address you."

"Usama will do. I have never stood on formality with friends."

The Administrator did not know whether Usama Bin Laden truly regarded him as a friend, or whether he was merely patronizing him in order to secure his own safety. It was an interesting game of cat and mouse they were playing. Whatever, it did seem they were linked now, and would use each other to their best advantage. *I guess that is the best I can hope for under the circumstances.*

Bin Laden broke the silence. "Can you tell me how I got here?"

"You were brought here, nearly comatose, by two men who seemed to care for you very much. They said you were very important to them and that they wanted the best of care for you. And they gave me your medical folder and the precise regimen we were to follow. That folder insisted I keep you in the condition you arrived in, and that I monitor your health closely."

Whoever these men were, Bin Laden apparently decided it did not matter. He knew they would have been trusted emissaries from Ayman Al-Zawahiri, and he guessed they were his own personal bodyguards. He had guessed right.

Wanting to unburden himself further, the Administrator hastily added, "We received a very generous stipend every month, which I used to provide medicines, food, clothing, and supplies for the people here."

"And did anyone else come?" Bin Laden asked. His memory was sketchy, but he seemed to remember Ayman himself visiting.

"Yes, once. Your personal physician came to check on you one time. He stayed a few days." Choosing to omit the fact that he had heard the two men talking, he added, "I have no idea what he did, except that he seemed to have taken you off your medications."

"And why do you suppose that, my friend?"

"Because he said the treatment here of your diabetes and other maladies had been excellent, and that the Thorazine was keeping you stable," he responded hastily. Then, wanting to be clear, he added, "And he instructed me to make certain we put you back on the exact same regimen."

"And did you?"

"Yes, sir, I had no reason to do otherwise." The tears overcame him again, and the Administrator choked out, "I am so sorry. I thought he was your friend."

"As did I, my friend, as did I." It was said ominously, and the Administrator knew that lines were now drawn in the sand. He had made his choice, and now he would have to abide by it. Whatever happened, he knew he was now aiding Usama Bin Laden, and that the man whose money he had so willingly taken must have been the Doctor himself, Ayman Al-Zawahiri.

The man's fear must have been palpable because Bin Laden seemed to be trying to reassure him. "My friend, we will have to move. It is no longer safe here. He could arrive at any time."

This did not comfort the Administrator. If Bin Laden moved, and Zawahiri came to visit and found him gone, surely that would mean his own death, and probably that of all his patients and staff. He hardly knew how to express it.

Fortunately, Bin Laden was indeed alert enough to sense the man's consideration. Or perhaps he could smell his fear. Regardless, he reassured him once again. "No, my friend, I mean the entire hospital. You and all your staff and patients will need to be moved."

"But..."

Bin Laden interrupted him. "Do not concern yourself with how we will do that. This is an area in which I have a great deal of experience." Then he laughed, wanting the Administrator to understand he had made a joke.

For a moment, the Administrator looked puzzled; then he got it. He was shocked Bin Laden could joke in such dire circumstances, but it gave him some hope. Bin Laden continued. "I have money and resources. All I have to do is tap into them. We will go into hiding some place else. But we are not safe here." Bin Laden assessed the man for a moment, and added firmly, "Do you understand that?"

The Administrator nodded. "What do you need from me and my people?" he queried.

"Only your assurance that you will tend to me medically and see that I continue to recover."

"You have that without exception."

Satisfied that the man was sincere, Bin Laden began to draw up plans for the disappearance of the entire hospital. If Zawahiri came for him, he would discover that all of them had simply vanished. He smiled, thinking, *All the times we have disappeared right before the eyes of our enemies! All the practice! I'll do it once again. And he'll have no idea where I am.*

Breaking his own reverie, Bin Laden asked, "Tell me one thing. And it is important." He paused to make certain this frightened weasel was fully attentive. "Does the world believe I am still alive?"

Without hesitation the Administrator responded, "Yes, sir, they do. I do not receive much news, but I think I can assure you that everyone is still looking for you. And that they believe you are alive."

"Excellent." Suddenly he laughed. "I guess it's time for me to communicate then, isn't it, my friend?"

This time the Administrator laughed nervously with him. He had no idea what Usama Bin Laden's real intentions were. If he had, he would not have been afraid. For Bin Laden did indeed need the Administrator. And he would happily pay for the relocation of all the paraphernalia that went with him—and the riff raff. What he needed to find out though, with absolute certainty, was whether or not his top leadership believed him dead or alive. Were they all in on this, or just Ayman? Had Ayman made them believe he was dead?

He accepted totally the validity of making the rank and file, as well as the rest of the world's intelligence communities believe that he was alive and hiding. What haunted him now, however, was the question of who stood to gain if the senior leaders of Al Qaeda assumed he was dead. They would certainly sustain the ruse with the rest of the world, since it was in their best interests for the intelligence community to believe Bin Laden was alive. If his own men thought he was dead, they would not let on, especially not to those who were being recruited. *But who stands to gain by making my senior leaders think I am dead?* He knew of only one man who would. *Ayman, why did you do this?*

He knew the answer of course. Perhaps he would have done the same himself. He had in the past. But today was different. Today it was Usama Bin Laden who was being jettisoned from the game. In his mind, that was an unacceptable scenario. *The worm is about to turn.* Again smiling, he gently cajoled the Administrator. "Come, friend, it is not safe here. We must make preparations."

CHAPTER 45

"Well done," the Italian-suited man said to Andy as he
breezed past him and hurried out to his car.

Frowning, Andy wondered who that guy was, and what he
was doing at their house. Dropping his keys onto the table in the
hallway, he called out, "Brian?"

"Yeah, here in the kitchen."

"Who was that guy who just left?"

Brian snorted in disbelief. Patiently he answered, as if
instructing a child, "Andy, he is the company's accountant." He
paused for effect. Andy was still frowning, shrugging his
shoulders. It was obvious he wasn't remembering. "You hired
him yourself, Andy."

"I did?" Andy was mystified. "Did he look the same way?"

That was too much for Brian, who tossed a donut at him.
"Andy, yes, he looked pretty much the same." Then Brian also
stopped talking, searching his memory truly for what the man had
looked like. Getting the image, he grinned sheepishly. "Son of a
gun," he said. "You're right. He didn't look the same."

"Yeah?" Andy said, as he looked for a place to toss the
donut.

"Yeah, man, he was wearing a JC Penney suit when you
interviewed him at the office. Today he was wearing a $2,500
Italian suit!" Brian couldn't suppress the grin, just thinking about
it. "I'm telling you, money changes a man. It surely does."

"Well, it changed his car for sure! Did you see the ride he's
got?"

Brian shook his head no, and despondently looked as if he'd
missed out. Remembering though why he was excited to see
Andy, he changed the subject. "Well, whatever he was driving, he

sure had some good news for us." The quarterly report for Carver and Weir, Inc. lay on the table, ensconced in a simple manila folder. Brian tapped it playfully. "We're up 45%!"

"Awesome!" Andy exclaimed.

"I'm talking profits, man, not revenue. It gets even better. Our man in the suit was filling me in on this extremely well-run business we've got and how our expenses are totally under control, while the income is growing exponentially."

Truth be told, Andy cared more about the game and its market penetration than he did about its profitability. Brian was the same way. They were just two kids trying to defeat an enemy, and they knew they were starting to make some headway now. Keeping track of how much money they made was why they had hired "the suit." For that reason, Brian had been taken aback when the man explained the bottom line of it all to him. He paused, waiting for Andy to react.

"You know, Brian, we're not playing a game here," Andy challenged. "If you plan to toss the ball, toss it."

"Okay, pal, you asked for it." Pushing the folder across the table, he quietly and emotionlessly said, "Turns out, we're rich."

"Really?" That got Andy's attention. He sat down to look at the figures more closely, wondering just what "rich" meant to Brian. The phone rang, and Brian jumped up to get it, leaving Andy to digest the financial results.

While Andy read, Brian at first listened quietly and then started bouncing in place, as he had in his football days before the ball was coming to him. Brian and Andy both loved games, and they also loved winning. Abruptly, Brian hung up the phone, saying goodbye. "You bet. That's off the chain, man, off the chain. Just let us know when." Barely able to contain himself, he started his hop around the kitchen table, dodging down and in toward Andy, and then away, as if to tease him.

"All right, Brian, what is it? Who was that?"

"That was Tate and Donovan. Did you ever notice, Andy, how those two look exactly alike?" Andy didn't answer, finding this too much to get involved in. He waited and Brian continued, after putting Tate and Donovan to rest with, "Yeah, funny really. They're not even related, and they're like twins!"

"Brian…" Andy's voice betrayed his impatience.

"Sure, sure. They wanted us to know they just got a call from *Inc.* magazine, and they want to do a story on us—front cover, featured story, the whole enchilada!"

"Are you kidding me?" Andy knew Brian wasn't. Now he was up, hugging his partner. "That is something, just something." Regaining his composure, he asked, "When?"

"Before the end of the year. They want it out next June."

"Wow, that's a long time from now."

"Yeah, who knew it takes that long?" Brian captured the papers that had slipped around the tabletop while they had been roughhousing. "Anyway, I guess these guys really do their research, from what our man Tate said."

"They do. They do. I know my mom said they are the real champions of entrepreneurs. The *cover* of *Inc....*" His thought trailed off. He was obviously enjoying this. The two of them sat down and just looked inward for a few moments. They had come so far. They were calm on the outside now, but each one knew this would be terrific public relations for their game, and would put it right smack dab in the middle of business news, with a spotlight on them. It was a huge victory. They had been winning below the radar, by innovatively using the new media lines, which had started developing in the Internet age. Now they were about to surface into mainstream business as well—and in a big way.

Neither knew at that moment what would find them, once the radar of international business found them. It was best that way. Neither could have borne it, had they known.

CHAPTER 46

*I*t was a quiet night on patrol in Fallujah, Iraq. Corporal Roger Whitehauser was expecting to make a round and say his usual goodnight to the three boys in the house around the corner from his barracks. He was eager to get back in tonight, as he was going to have Internet access—his first in a long time.

He was anticipating the opportunity to email his parents about the extraordinary turn of events in the city where he was posted. Sheik al-Hadyr, a rabid Sunni and collaborator with the Al Qaeda insurgents, had spoken to him directly a while back. He remembered well the day he'd received the attention of a man who controlled the switch on hatred of Americans, and attacks against them.

His unit was assigned to facilitate the neighboring Iraqi leaders in finishing and bringing online a local hospital, equipped with surgical supplies. He and the men in his squad did everything frankly. One day they were helping to construct the place, using whatever masonry skills they had. The next day they were guarding the local leaders as those newly-elected officials interviewed and hired staff. When the opening of the facility looked as if it would be delayed because they were short on materiel—gurneys, medicines, gauze, you name it—he had personally used some arm-twisting tricks he'd learned back home in Michigan, and some people skills he'd learned in the military, to *persuade* a couple of guys to mysteriously and immediately secure the needed supplies and get them to the hospital.

Everyone in the unit knew it was him, and the neighborhood workers must have known as well. And, it must have been one of them that told the Sheik. The man had lived his life in distrust of anything Western, and had spent the last four years doing what he could to aide Al Qaeda, whom he believed to be sincere in wanting to help the Sunnis in Iraq. But now he was torn with internal conflict, and found himself in a dilemma.

The insurgents' strikes over the last year, under the strategy of Abou Al-Zarqawi and his successors, had resulted in countless dead among his own community. He was failing to see exactly how Al Qaeda was helping the Sunnis when they were boldly and deliberately killing so many of them with improvised explosives devices and any other type of bomb they could create. True, a few Americans died, but as far as he could see, the main victims here were his own people.

Everyday he saw the young Americans, led by their Corporal, tirelessly working to provide health services and surgical capabilities to his people—who had never had it. Saddam had certainly never cared for his people, he reasoned. *And this place is for our people, not government soldiers,* he had debated in his mind. The hospital was entirely civilian, and was costing a great deal to build, under difficult circumstances. *Why are these Americans doing this?* he had asked himself. *Why are they risking their lives so my children will have a hospital?* The answer in the end was simple. They had been told to. And try as he might, day by day, his rancor was evaporating. He just could not seem to dismiss from his mind the lie he had been told. *Al Qaeda killed my people, and they provided nothing to them. The Americans tried to save them, and are building them hospitals.*

The Sheik had listened to propaganda, and he had spewed propaganda in his career. Nonetheless, he was responsible for his people. That was a deeply personal matter, and it played out, not in trite scenarios emphasized by the news media around the world, but in the day-to-day progress in his neighborhood, in the sound of laughter from children as they played in the streets— and in the speed with which they ran to that small squad of American soldiers every day.

Every morning the Corporal brought his men out, dozens of children would race past the Sheik as he stood outside his mosque, and crowd around the soldiers. *It can't be candy,* he had pondered. *If it were candy, they'd disperse. I don't see them with anything in their hands.*

One morning, when he could stand the mystery no longer, he had approached the Corporal just as the soldier sat down to rest and take in some water. The young man looked up without suspicion, though his hand was on his weapon as a matter of training and habit.

"Please, please," the Sheik had begun sincerely. "May I have a word with you?"

"Yes, sir."

There it is again, the respectful salutation, he observed. Motioning his desire to sit, the soldier had invited him to do just that. He did. At first, he hadn't known how to begin. He just sat there knowing how ridiculous this would appear to the people of his neighborhood—and how potentially dangerous as well. But the young man seemed a mere boy, like so many he knew, and he seemed smart, hard-working. He had to risk the personal danger to find out. Suddenly he blurted out, in what English he could muster, "Why do the children run to you?"

The young man smiled, chuckled, and looked away for a moment. Turning slightly toward the Sheik, he shrugged his shoulders and answered, "Truthfully, sir, I don't know. I guess they just like us."

It had been said without a hint of manipulation. There had been no point to prove, no axe to grind—just a simple answer. And for the first time in as long as he could remember, the Sheik felt a pervasive sense of calm come over him, and his body relaxed totally. His mind was still questioning, however, for he needed to know. Rephrasing the question, he asked, "They stay with you for hours. What do you *give* them, young man?"

"Work...we give them work." That was all he had said. Rising, he politely said he, too, had to get back to that very thing, and excused himself.

The Sheik had stood up quickly as well, dusting himself off. But he could not get that simple truth out of his mind. The Corporal and his men treated these young children as equals, and gave them something productive to do. And apparently, they taught them trade skills as well. The Americans were teaching his young people how to build something, how to create. And in that very moment of realization, the Sheik switched sides. His responsibility had been all along to his people. Al Qaeda could say what they wanted, but their actions spoke louder than words. The Sheik had concluded they were, in fact, destroyers.

That had started it. It was months before the Sheik's subsequent actions were especially noticed by Al Qaeda. All they knew, and all the media knew, was that where there once had been no "intel," now there was. Where Al Qaeda had been aided and even hidden, now they were not. Where they had felt safe, now they were hunted effectively by the Americans and Iraqis. They were losing ground in Anbar—the one province the entire world regarded as lost to Al Qaeda.

Every day the Sheik had begun to spend time with the children and the Americans—most specifically the Corporal. His wife had even brought food to them regularly. She seemed happy to be able to provide indigenous and fresh nourishment to the young boys in the Western garb. Over time, the Sheik had let down his guard when he was out with them, and he failed to notice that he was being watched. Neither, apparently, did the American squad.

Today, the Corporal was trying to finish his rounds so that he could tell his family the amazing news about his personal invitation to dinner with the Sheik and his family. That afternoon, as they were all securing final window treatments for a section of the building, the Sheik had come up to embrace him on both cheeks. That was a sign of intense respect, and the soldier accepted it graciously. The next words were, "My family and I would be honored if you were to join us this evening after prayers."

Cleared by his CO, the officer had told him to eat dinner with the Sheik, but to politely keep it as brief as he could. The plan was for him to then complete his nightly responsibilities, and report to base. As an extra bit of appreciation the CO had added, "Well done, son. I expect you'd like to tell your folks about that." With that, he added Internet privileges for the Corporal past the normal curfew time. All in all, it had been a magnificent day.

He was just rounding the corner when the round hit him. This time it was not a bomb. It was a sniper. The leadership of Al Qaeda in Anbar Province had concluded this young American was the reason their Sheik had turned his people against Al Qaeda. The decision was made locally. It had not been cleared with Makkawi. After all, it was nothing significant. It was just one annoying American who was unduly influencing the Sheik. This ought to get rid of the American, end his influence, and set the Sheik straight. That was the reasoning.

The sniper slipped away across a rooftop before the lifeless body of the Corporal sank to the ground. His death was instantaneous. It was over quickly. But the repercussions of that one choice would destroy Al Qaeda in Anbar Province before the end of 2007. The reason was simple. The death of his young friend did not "set the Sheik straight." Instead, it galvanized him and all of his Sheiks into a full revolt. The province, once regarded as lost, was now influenced by men and women allied with the US.

For Zawahiri, this setback—and the attention it was beginning to grab in some international press—was what is known in Public Relations as a PR flap. Though he agreed whole-heartedly with the strategy and tactics his team had deployed in Iraq, he was going to have to do something about this before the American media got a grasp of its significance.

It's the choice I would have made, the Doctor reassured himself. *But the outcome is not what I would have hoped for. Ah, well, if only Zarqawi had been there to do this himself.*

Ending his lament about the loss of their rogue superstar, he emailed Samir's Paris office an apparent magazine ad proof, asking if Samir's firm felt this approach would work for a small hotel chain operating in Europe. Using the technique of steganography, which he and his men had relied upon before, he had imbedded a question inside the email. "Can you handle this?"

Samir's answer was immediate. On the encrypted satellite phone the two used for live communication while the Doctor was in Panama, Samir's response was short. Not wanting to risk the possibility of interception, he merely said, "Consider it done."

Chapter 47

"*F*ive minutes and we're ready for you, Samir," the second assistant director barked, sticking his head into the Green Room where Samir was waiting for his appearance on WNG's Los Angeles based news show, anchored by Alicia Quixote.

In recent months, as Alicia's star continued to rise with the news giant, she had taken over more and more control of her show, introducing a feature segment into the news itself. Rather than go to an outside correspondent to reinforce a story, she used this segment as if she were a TV talk show host, whereby she relied on guest appearances of "experts" to help her and her viewers understand an issue—at least understand the issue according to Alicia Quixote.

Bud Walker didn't care. He cared that she was getting ratings. By 2008, he planned to move her to New York, and phase her into the elite circle of journalists and TV personalities who dominated cable news. Frankly, he was tired of the area being dominated by men. He bore no animosity to O'Reilly, Beck, Hannity, Matthews, Olbermann—none of them. He just felt it was time for the "boys club" to change. And he wanted to break new ground, keeping his network out in front, with everybody else looking up his rear, rather than the other way around.

Knowing and respecting Samir as he did, Bud was willing to have him added to the "TV-friendly experts" list that he kept. In fact, he was more than willing. Not only was the man extremely bright and articulate, but he was also young and extremely good-looking. Putting him on the air with Alicia would make the show even more attractive to the viewer who wanted a little sizzle, but also credible, intelligent discussion.

A few minutes earlier, he had stopped in the Green Room to

say hello, and encourage Samir, since this was his first appearance on the air. Many times, they had talked and Walker had bounced ideas and perceptions off this PR genius, but this was the first time they'd asked Samir to make an appearance. Then Bud had gone home to dress and attend a major charity concert at the Walt Disney Concert Hall in downtown Los Angeles.

Alicia's story tonight was on the apparent disowning of Al Qaeda by the Sunnis of Iraq—at the very least the Sunnis in Anbar Province. She wanted to know if this were something of true importance—and what it boded for the future of Iraq, and for the Bush Administration's policy, knowing that, whatever the reality was of the fighting and the politics, the issue would really be one of propaganda and how it would be used by the United States and Britain, and by Al Qaeda. Therefore, she felt that the best guest she could have would be a public relations expert. *Let those other guys do their military analysis,* she had told herself. *I'll launch in a different direction, really get everyone's imagination going.*

Without a doubt, the best PR man she knew was Samir. He not only knew Public Relations, but he also came to it with a distinctly European viewpoint. She felt that an analysis and evaluation by him would not only be fresh but would also likely be more accurate than any analysis emanating from the clichéd US news guys. *These guys are all sounding like parrots,* she mentally derided them. *I hope they're watching this tonight.*

In talking with him briefly when she booked Samir for the show, he had indicated to her his serious doubts that this situation in Anbar Province would significantly impact Iraq in total. Persuasively, he had assured her that Iraq's people would not turn decisively against the insurgents, or Al Qaeda. He was prepared to dismiss that idea altogether as just wishful thinking on the part of the US government, and he was prepared to explain from a public relations standpoint how the Administration would attempt to "spin" this insignificant setback into a major strategic victory for the US. "After all, my dear," he had carefully and patiently explained to her, "they need to find something that they can take to Europe, to Italy, and to Great Britain. They've got to make it appear there are some victories there, or they won't be able to sustain public willingness to stay involved, let alone garner the financial support they need globally." It had sounded good to her, and she was sure he would help the American people see it that way as well.

Then, to be sure he was being fair and balanced, Samir had added, "And, of course, you can expect Al Qaeda to downplay the apparent reversal altogether. It's not good for their *image* to be attacked by a group they regarded as an ally. They'll characterize it as some minor grievance blown way out of proportion by the Western media." Then he had continued in a condescension she did not even notice, "And, my dear, that is exactly what this is—a 'mountain out of a molehill' I believe you Americans call it." And he had laughed charmingly. She fell for it.

That was the message Samir intended to give tonight. He was confident, and thrilled actually, that now the United States media appeared to have him on their list of "experts" in the affairs of Al Qaeda. *If only they knew!* He relished the deception. *Fools!*

That euphoric moment didn't last, however, as his Ipod vibrated in his pocket. The vibration was a signal of an incoming encrypted text message. Guessing that he had time to look at it, he pulled it out and entered a code that vacated the encryption. He saw that it was a phone number followed by 911. He knew the number to be a secure satellite phone number used only by the senior Al Qaeda team. The suffix 911 number was their code for emergency, dial the number at once.

Looking at the clock, he decided he had time to dial and receive the communication, whatever it was, even if he would not have time just now to handle it. Expecting Zawahiri, or Makkawi, to be on the end of the line as it was picked up, he immediately started the conversation with an exuberant, "My friend, how are you?" It was said loudly and playfully enough that anyone listening would think he was merely catching up with a buddy.

If one had been observing him, however, they would have seen him pale as he listened. For the voice on the other end of the phone was soft, gentle—even mellifluous. It was unmistakable. "I am very well, my friend. Are you surprised?"

Samir slumped down onto the overstuffed sofa the network generously provided for guests. *Usama!*

"Sir, we thought you were dead," Samir explained sotto voce, despite the fact he was now safely inside his apartment. "I am sorry I could not talk to you before; I was about to go on the air on WNG. But I can talk freely now."

"Are we secure?"

"Most definitely. I…" Samir stopped, trying to find the words. His mind was racing trying to digest the import of this call, and the re-emergence of their leader Usama Bin Laden. Truthfully, he was elated to hear from Bin Laden, but his mind was already trying to configure the possible propaganda aspects of his re-appearance on the scene. A moment later, his mind called his attention to his own vulnerability here. *Be careful, Samir. After all, what do you know of what truly happened here? Protect yourself.* He knew it was important to proceed prudently. He stumbled a bit. "I…I…uh…I am overjoyed to hear your voice. But, I must confess, my friend, that I am confused."

"Why is that, Samir? Surely you knew I would resurface at some appropriate moment, did you not?"

Samir could not tell whether the question was a trap, or a sincere one. Through the years that he had worked with Bin Laden and Zawahiri, he had known them both to be soft-spoken men who were also stone-cold killers. The treacherous intrigues in which they had both engaged, in order to rise to the power they now wielded, had taught them to shroud their true intentions to even those closest to them. And he knew both of them were masters of deception.

In light of that, the public relations genius, who was now the propaganda chief of Al Qaeda, decided to take a different tack tonight. *No PR. Tell the absolute truth, Samir. It is the only thing that may save you now.* "I would have prayed for that, sir. But we were told by the Doctor that you were dead." Samir could still visualize Bin Laden's body lying in the cave back near Tora Bora. It was even cold. Surely, there was no way he could have known it was a ruse. The only question in his mind now was whether Bin Laden had been privy to the deception, or had been the victim of it.

"I saw your body, Usama. It was cold. We were certain you were dead."

"Yes, I'm sure you were, Samir. I do not doubt you," Bin Laden answered reassuringly.

Is he baiting me? Samir took a deep breath and held it. He slowly let out the air with, "Thank you, Usama. Thank you."

Usama Bin Laden seemed to have an agenda, and wanted this conversation to be brief. Succinctly he queried, "Who else believes me to be dead? I know the rest of the world, and seemingly the rank and file of Al Qaeda, believe me to have humiliated the Americans by hiding so long. But, I am most curious to discover who believes me to be dead."

"Yes, yes, I understand," Samir hastily answered. "The only ones still alive are Makkawi, myself, and the Doctor." As soon as he said it, he realized how absurd it was to include the Doctor amongst those who didn't know. As Bin Laden's personal physician, surely *he* was the one who had made Usama appear dead, who had apparently staged a mock cremation and burial, and who had taken command of Al Qaeda and all its operations.

"Samir, please tell me all of the names of those who thought me dead." His voice was very firm now, commanding.

"In addition to us, there was Atef, of course, and Nanda, and the Doctor's double—Nanda's father."

"And what became of them?"

Surely he knows this, Samir thought. Convinced that Bin Laden was testing him, he sustained the path of the truth and answered easily. "Atef was killed in an American air strike; Nanda disappeared in Iraq and is presumed dead, and the Doctor's double was confirmed killed in a strike intended for the Doctor."

"Well at least that worked!" Bin Laden laughed.

"Sir?"

"The deception...Ayman always felt that double would save his life." Again, he laughed. "He's good at deception, don't you think?"

Now Samir was certain Bin Laden was probing, testing him. His next answer would be very important. Knowing there was no point in trying to finesse anything, he answered candidly, but with sarcasm, "It appears so."

There was silence on the other end. For a moment, he thought the connection might have been interrupted, but then Bin Laden concluded with, "Well, as for you, I want to commend the brilliant work you have been doing. You've pretty well tied the Americans in knots. You've made every military defeat into a victory for us, and you've promoted every victory to stunning, worldwide awareness and agreement. Ayman said you were the best in your field. We are all thankful, Samir, that you are on our side."

"Thank you, Usama, I am honored to serve. And I will continue—if you will give me leave to do so—with my primary strategy of helping the Americans turn their strengths into weaknesses, thereby devouring themselves."

"Of course. With my blessing. And with the blessings of Allah," Bin Laden responded almost kindly. Then he added suddenly, "There is one more thing you can do for me, Samir, if you will."

"Absolutely."

"Do not speak to Ayman about our conversation tonight." He paused to let the silence on the line penetrate Samir's thought process.

It did. At that moment, Samir concluded that Bin Laden had most probably not known of his "death"—rather that he had been a victim of it. Whatever the reason, the disappearance of Usama Bin Laden from the world scene had apparently been without his agreement. He was back, and the game was changed. Samir knew that. And he knew, somehow, that he once again had to pass muster.

CHAPTER 48

J ames was standing at the kitchen window lamenting the fact that autumn didn't really happen in Los Angeles. He missed the blaze of color, leaf smells, and cooler air that accompanied the change of seasons in Virginia and North Carolina. It was October, his favorite month back East, and, when the call came in, he was stoically trying to avoid thinking about it too much.

Happy to be aroused from his reverie, he answered, "Mikolas here."

"You might want to log onto Al-Jazeera."

James recognized Ari Ben-Gurian's accent and voice immediately.

He had no idea why Ari would call him, and he was long past wondering how Israel's Mossad knew his personal phone number in an apartment far from his home. Frankly, it was comforting to James Mikolas to know that someone in the intelligence community was keeping tabs on him. "Why?" he asked, with genuine curiosity.

"He's back. Thought you should know." And then his counterpart in the intelligence world hung up, just as suddenly as he had called.

Cussing at the computer for taking so long to bring up the Al-Jazeera site, James' curiosity was at a peak level. And there it was—a newly released audio tape by Usama Bin Laden. *This isn't the first tape by this guy,* James thought. *What's got Ari spooked enough to call me?*

Whether Usama Bin Laden still lived was the big debate in the intelligence communities—whether told to the public or not. About half the world's intelligence people felt the various videos and audio tapes that had been released since 2001 did not absolutely confirm that he was still alive.

The other half felt the voice authentications were accurate and that indeed, he was still breathing. Though they had no idea where he was, or had been, the hunt for Bin Laden justified their activities, and those of their governments, and they were going to need absolute proof of death to be willing to give up that search. *So, what's different about this one?* James reflected, as he downloaded the file.

Five minutes later, he concluded it was in fact Bin Laden, and that the rat was still alive. It was the content of the audiotape that convinced him. Bin Laden seemed to be apologizing for the actions of Al Qaeda over the last two years in Iraq, especially in Anbar Province, where they had killed and maimed thousands of Sunnis. The killing of Muslim by Muslim in the name of Islam was backfiring and had caused the Sunnis to turn and support the United States in the area, for the purpose of rooting out the insurgents they now viewed as unwelcome killers.

The Sunnis no longer viewed themselves as brothers in arms with this bunch—quite the contrary. Their leaders had come to view Al Qaeda as worse for their people than the Americans, and they had been cooperating with the Americans to oust the group. Bin Laden appeared to realize that he was losing ground in Iraq through extremism, and was giving an eloquent apology and argument for Muslims to stick together in order to achieve victory over the Americans, and any Iraqis who had abandoned their faith and brotherhood.

"Odd," James said to no one. Then, he smiled and let out a long, slow sigh of relief. "Son of a gun, they're losing." He knew the "Military" game was nowhere near as important as media and governments appraised it, but he was pleased nonetheless. *What was that delicious phrase my mother used to use?* he asked himself. His mind offered it up easily. *Ah, yes, "hoisted by their own petard!"*

The moment didn't last, however. For it was but a second later that another question emerged and pressed out the victory. *So, he's alive! Then where the hell is he?!*

The Doctor pushed his chair back from the computer, as if to gain some distance from the screen, but he could move no further. His eyes were riveted on the computer monitor as he listened again to the plea by Bin Laden for all Muslims to avoid extremism, and to remember who their true enemy was.

Though there were no neighbors on the top floor where ST & Associates had secret offices, old habit forced him to keep the volume low, and the low volume demanded he remain close to the monitor. He was certain the voice was authentic, and he could barely suppress the rising panic. Before he could get his breathing or his sphincter muscle under control, the quiet of his room was interrupted by the satellite phone. He knew by the signal it emitted that the call was coming from Samir. And he knew, further, that he had to answer it.

Stay calm, he admonished himself. *Just listen, and stay calm.*

"Yes?" he answered with a question.

"Did we do this?" Samir's question was insistent in its tone. What the Doctor could not see was the lone bead of sweat trickling down Samir's right temple, as he sat erect and tense at the mahogany desk in his apartment. For Samir was heroically attempting to ascertain to the best certainty he could just who *was* in control of Al Qaeda. The reappearance of a ghost in a phone call to him had left him knowing one thing for sure—someone had been betrayed.

Not knowing whether it had been the Doctor betraying *all* of them, or just Bin Laden, it was clear to him that Bin Laden had been betrayed. What he did not know was whether the betrayal was warranted. Frankly, Samir felt no hesitation whatsoever in the game of betrayal. He was not the least bit squeamish about such intrigue. If it was a necessary play to achieve an end, he was ruthless enough to do it. In addition, he had no real dog in this religious fight, or the contorted crusade to restore the caliphate— quite the contrary. He was paid, and paid well, to create confusion and confound Bin Laden's and Zawahiri's enemies. He was good at it. And whether or not these two were at war with each other now mattered very little to Samir.

What he did care about deeply was figuring out who, in fact, was on top, and making sure he held his own position of favor with them. Samir was not a stupid man, and he knew he was now in the middle, and that he was in danger. So, he had admonished himself thoroughly to *be alert* before he picked up the phone and called his superior.

"Yes, we did," the Doctor lied, hoping to divert attention away from the implicit criticism of their strategy and tactics, which Bin Laden's speech offered. If there was going to be hell to pay, he would prefer to take a stand on *why* he had told senior Al Qaeda leaders that Bin Laden was dead. If he was very clever now, he reasoned, he just might pull this out. What was important was to convince them that he and Bin Laden were in agreement on this six-year ruse, and that it had been necessary in order for the healthier leaders to carry on and prevail.

Samir said nothing, so the Doctor continued quickly. "Usama and I authorized the release of this tape, but did not expect it to air so quickly." Again he lied. "It was my plan to reach all of you and advise you of the fact that our leader lives."

Samir was in a dilemma now—to tell the Doctor about Bin Laden's call to Samir and Bin Laden's request that he keep silent, or not? His gut told him Bin Laden himself had been playing it pretty close to the chest—not totally sure of the Doctor's motives—and that Usama was hoping to discern whether the takeover of Al Qaeda by the Doctor had indeed been necessary, or whether there was a much more sinister motive.

Being a master propagandist, Samir suddenly smiled, appreciating the irony of this propaganda mess. It was the goal to have the rest of the world confused about whereabouts and allegiances, not to have Al Qaeda itself conflicted and torn apart. *It's delicious actually,* he concluded. *Who's hunting whom?*

At that moment, he decided not to tell the Doctor—to let the Doctor squirm a bit and perhaps slip up and reveal his presumed treachery. The pragmatist in him realized that, whatever the motive had been, they had accomplished great feats without Bin Laden. His "disappearance" had in fact confounded their enemies and furthered their own cause. What concerned him now, as the Public Relations chief, was how to prevent the world's intelligence communities from putting two and two together, concluding that there was a schism in Al Qaeda at the highest levels, and a probable usurpation of power by the "second-in-command."

The truth was, the same concern weighed on the mind of Ayman Al-Zawahiri. He would handle Bin Laden—one way or another. But Al Qaeda had to appear to be intact, and capable of functioning dangerously.

"It would have been better, Ayman, if I *had* been apprised," Samir said unthreateningly.

"No doubt. And I apologize for that. Al-Jazeera jumped the gun, most decidedly, but it won't happen again."

"I meant, Ayman, I should have been told of the deception. I should have been 'in the know' that he was still alive."

His use of my familiar name is disrespectful, the Doctor thought. *What does he really know?* Without hesitating noticeably, however, the Doctor took control once again. "I understand that, from your perspective, but Usama and I had concluded differently. We felt for this escape and preservation to work that all senior Al Qaeda who might have been captured would, unequivocally, need to believe he was gone. And that would be what they would confirm to our enemies under interrogation."

There, he'd said it. The next move was Samir's.

Some static came through on the line, but otherwise, just silence.

Samir had to be careful here. He could not reveal he had been contacted by Bin Laden. This had to be between him and Ayman, or Ayman would guess he was in doubt. And he had seen what happened to anyone who doubted or crossed Ayman Al-Zawahiri. Rather submissively, he asked, "So, this was the best way you two could hide him?"

"*And* secure his health, my friend, don't forget that." The Doctor paused for a second before continuing. "Remember, Usama was very ill at the time, and he was experiencing extreme anxiety. To save him, he and I agreed that I would secure a calm, safe place where he could recuperate mentally and physically."

"Oh…" Samir feigned interest.

"Yes, my friend. And blessedly, he has recovered. He has decided to emerge onto the stage again. My apologies for being so far away that I failed to communicate properly with you. You know how valuable you are to us both?"

"Yes, yes I do!" This time Samir was not lying. He was smirking. *What a delicious position I find myself in. Dangerous, but delicious!*

Samir decided to press his advantage a little bit and asked, "So, you know he is still safely hidden?"

"Yes, of course. Why do you ask?" The Doctor sounded perturbed.

"No reason, really," he lied. "It's just a bit reckless for him to suddenly make a tape and get it released without using his own propaganda chief—especially one which implicitly criticizes our own strategies over the last few years."

"I agree with you on that, my friend. It would have been far better if the three of us had worked out what the message was to be." He paused a moment. "But Usama concluded, quite correctly I think, that we need to win the Sunnis over, that we had lost their allegiance, and that a message from him personally would be more powerful and would serve as a reminder of his vision and leadership in our struggle against the great Satan."

"Yes, well, be that as it may, I hope he did not jeopardize his security by coming out of hiding and using a team I clearly had no awareness of." It was said somewhat defiantly, but did not alarm the Doctor. Zawahiri regarded Samir's attitudes and statements to be consistent with his responsibilities, and did not feel any sense of alarm.

Attempting to reassure him, the Doctor quietly added, "I assure you he is safe. And I assure you we will coordinate better with you, if Usama feels the need to personally speak out again in a way that deviates from our pre-recorded tapes."

"Fine, Ayman," Samir concluded. "Thank you for your time. I have just one more thing to add."

"What is that?"

"May Allah be praised that our leader in fact lives, and that he is healed!"

"Yes indeed. We are blessed!" Zawahiri purred, all the while cringing.

The instant he hung up the phone, the Doctor dialed another number. It rang once and then he hung up. Knowing the signal would be recognized by his former bodyguard, and knowing it would be six hours before the man would make contact with him, he concluded things had gone as well as they could with Samir, that he could contain this yet, and that there would be no repeat of this fiasco.

By the Doctor's estimation, his conversation with Makkawi went somewhat better than the one with Samir. He felt less anxious now, for he could see that even if the Al Qaeda leaders didn't fully believe his story about this all having been in everyone's best interest, they were stuck with it. There was no way they could reveal to the United States that there was a rift inside the command level of Al Qaeda. That would be like throwing red meat to a lion, and it would embolden the United States at a time when their propaganda efforts were in fact weakening the Americans' resolve. He knew Makkawi would keep the status quo, if for no other reason than to keep the pressure on in the United States to withdraw from the area.

Meanwhile, he had dispatched his two bodyguards to the hospital in Iran. In December of 2001, they had deposited Bin Laden there, heavily medicated. They were to do some surveillance, and advise the Doctor about Bin Laden's condition. He knew full well the men would be happy to see Bin Laden again, so he had given them the assignment to make certain Bin Laden was being properly medicated, and to deliver to the Administrator of the hospital an additional prescription for Bin Laden.

Knowing that Bin Laden was allergic to this medication, and knowing the combination of Thorazine and this medicine would be especially potent, the Doctor was very sure this would handle his "Bin Laden problem" once and for all.

Frankly, he had given no more thought to it. When the Americans concluded and announced they could not confirm whether the Bin Laden tape was authentic, he felt he'd been given a reprieve. *Ah, the world of lies versus lies,* he reflected. *No one can tell who is telling the truth!*

Therefore, he was completely unprepared when he received the encrypted message via the Internet. It was the report coming in from the two men he had sent into Iran to locate Bin Laden, and he opened it eagerly. Reading it, he swallowed as if choking on something stuck in his throat. Rubbing his eyes, he put on his better glasses, as if that might change the content. The message said simply, "Hospital empty. No one there. Target missing."

303

CHAPTER 49

*A*s American presidential politics turned into theater of the absurd, the political parties, the media, and the candidates closed out their primaries in a way that could only be described as shocking. While the candidates prepared for their Conventions and the final months of what was becoming an historic election—albeit a vitriolic one—a change was happening in the country. No one interested in politics had the vaguest idea of it, however, and perhaps none even had any interest.

Such is often the case with sociological change. It begins where no one is looking, and rises over time into a shift so obvious that even the obtuse get it. And by then they wander around and debate on television the question, "Where did this come from?"

The interview of Carver and Weir was complete and ready for press. With the media's attention understandably on the twisting and turning US presidential election, very little time was devoted to coverage of business news unless it was relevant to the election and the fate of candidates, or conveyed news of a souring economy.

And throughout the summer of 2008, there was plenty of that. With the bailout of Freddie Mac and Fannie Mae, on the heals of an earlier bailout and restructuring of the entire real estate lending market, the news media in the business sector had its hands full.

So, the cover article about two young men whose game company was a shimmering star in the world of entrepreneurism escaped the notice of Samir. He was distracted with fomenting as much division within the US as he could before the election in November.

The article had produced tremendous awareness of Carver and Weir, however, in business circles. More importantly, though, was a growing awareness amongst ministers and community affairs people of the effects of their game. Invitations were pouring in from almost every inner city in America to recognize these two young men for their contribution to what had been drug-infested, crime-ridden, gang-controlled neighborhoods. A change had been taking place. And, at first, only the ministers had noticed.

Brian, Andy, James, and Kelly were all in formal attire, seated as the guests of honor at a community event sponsored by an alliance of churches in South Central Los Angeles. The heads of these churches—of all denominations—were seated at the . adjacent tables, beaming with enthusiasm and pride. Brian and Andy were somewhat stunned and subdued by the number of people in attendance. Every seat in this two thousand-seat ballroom was taken. It was especially gratifying for Kelly to see the boys honored in such a way. Periodically, she'd sneak a glance at James, and smile with pride if he returned her look.

An astonishing thing had been developing over the last year in particular. The game "White King Rising," nicknamed on the street as "02 Hero," had been tested with gang members from some of their churches, with athletes at the famous Los Angeles Western University, and with youth in general. But, it was what had taken place in their communities subsequent to the game becoming a national best-seller, which inspired. One year later, these ministers, who labored diligently to fight against the ravages of the drug culture upon their young parishioners, were discovering a "miracle" taking place. Drug usage was down, shootings were down, robberies were down, and murders were down. Suicide rates had tumbled, and police were reporting a dramatic reduction in the number of domestic violence calls. And best of all, the young men and women who had been targeted by the drug dealers, and by an almost-criminal pharmaceutical industry, were helping each other.

There was an upswing in attendance at the most effective literacy projects in the areas. And beyond even the poorer areas, this resurgence in literacy, and the resultant cessation of drug dependency, was spreading into wealthy areas as well. Drug prescriptions were being refused regularly by patients of all ages—especially in the anti-depressant class. Nutritionists, chiropractors, and various related specialties were experiencing a coincidental surge.

And tonight, the Reverend Doctor Isaac Williams was proud to honor the two men he had concluded were responsible for this resurgence of hope, and the elimination of generational blight in this section of Los Angeles.

"Hope's a funny thing," he told the grateful teens, parents, community leaders, and law enforcement that were in attendance. "Naysayers will deny that any of this is caused by something as simple as a game. They will holler to the rafters that none of the miraculous changes we are experiencing with our precious young can be laid at the feet of some computer game."

He paused for effect, raising his eyes toward God, and the audience laughed with him. For they knew this colorful, spirit-filled man was truly a man of God, and that he called things exactly as he saw them. A Baptist, with the pugnacity of an old-style Catholic priest, he never minced words. And he held people accountable.

He smiled. "But the Man upstairs has always, always had a sense of humor!"

"Amen," the audience punctuated.

"And he has always delivered miracles through the grace of the Child—the little Child."

Softly, at most tables, people were nodding, almost rocking back and forth in agreement.

"My friends, these are tortured times, but God has seen to it that his message was delivered in the exact right vehicle to reach and rescue your struggling families and communities. Using the very vehicle that has wasted so many of our lambs' precious hours, he has delivered through the game "White King Rising" the salvation of the children of this great city of ours. He delivered the end of drugs as the recreation of choice. He delivered control of one's own mind as the highest goal, not the

number of mind-altering drugs one can take and still survive..."
He stopped deliberately to let that sink in, and to gather his own
breath. "My friends, we are here tonight to honor two young
men of valor. Their own lives have not been easy ones. They
have borne a mighty burden themselves, but out of their own
loss, they have created our victory—and a victory for every
child in this country. And, dear friends, listen to me now. For as
the children go, so goes the country. We are on the verge of
victory now. We have hope. You know me, and you know
thanks belong to Almighty God, but tonight all of us," he
paused and turned to address Andy and Brian directly before
continuing, "all of us owe the creators of this magnificent game
our gratitude and support. And we are proud to honor them
with our city's highest citizen award. Andrew Weir and Brian
Washington Carver, would you please come up here and accept
the thanks of a grateful city?"

An hour later, Kelly was wiping tears from her eyes and
James was assisting the Reverend, Andy, and Brian with the final
goodbyes. It had been a humbling evening for all of them. They
had begun a journey together to reach and rescue the White
King. They had doubted along the way, and they had sacrificed.
Though money had come to them in abundance, nothing
matched for them the transcendent experience of actually seeing
the results of their work.

Each had seen the game's players having fun, getting
realizations, and making decisions. But tonight, for the first time,
Carver and Weir had seen the end result of their game—a
changed society.

In destroying the top two layers of the Doctor's game—
"Medical" and "Money"—they had created something better. A
society of hope was emerging. *And hope is a funny thing,* James
reflected silently. *The Reverend was right.* He laughed. *It's contagious.*

As they climbed into the limo, Brian was the last to enter. He
had been silent the longest, seeming to be chewing on something.
Andy knew him. He knew to wait until Brian chose to speak.
James and Kelly had a tacit understanding of that as well. So,
gingerly, they sat there, staring at him kindly.

"My mama would have been proud of me tonight," he said
finally, "and Pappy." His voice broke, and he cleared his throat.

The others remained silent, as the limo glided easily through the streets of Los Angeles.

The limo dropped Kelly off first, then Brian, James, and Andy. Before heading back to his own apartment, James decided to turn on the big screen TV down in the boys' entertainment center. Over the years, he'd developed a habit of checking cable news just to see what, if anything, he could glean from it. *Old habits die hard,* he chided himself, clicking off the remote. *Guess I'll grab a soda before I hit the road.*

Just as he exited the kitchen with a bottle of old-fashioned root beer in his hand, his eye caught a glimpse of Brian sitting on the edge of a chaise out on the patio. The patio looked out over the city, with its resplendent lights, but Brian didn't appear to be looking at anything in particular. Rather, he seemed lost in thought, shoulders slumped, as if something were weighing on him.

Andy must have observed it as well, for he was standing in the sliding glass pocket-doorway that led to the large Italian stone patio, just watching his friend. The frown on his face told James that Andy was deliberating about something. He'd seen that look many times since they'd met and had begun to try to untangle some of the world's best-kept terror secrets.

Without saying a word, James slid over next to Andy. The stealth move didn't go unnoticed. Andy tipped his head toward Brian as if to say, "Look at him."

"Yeah?" James responded to the unspoken question.

Leaning over to Andy, James whispered, "Do you think he's all right? He's awfully contemplative."

"Sure. He's all right. What I'm debating is whether or not to interrupt, that's all."

"Ah." James turned his gaze back out to Brian. "I get it."

Andy must have decided to engage in conversation and find out what his friend was thinking, because he strode out onto the patio boldly, pulled up a somewhat uncomfortable-looking steel arm chair, and sat down. "So, great night, huh?"

Brian nodded first, then spoke. "Yeah, most definitely…" His voice trailed off. He looked up to the sky for a brief moment. "It got me thinking 'bout Grandpa, though."

"How so?" Andy asked, motioning for James to pull up one of the matching chairs. James did so, and Brian was now flanked, left and right.

"Well, you know, Andy, that's the thing. It appears your analysis, yours and James'," he added deferentially, "was right." He hesitated a moment and then added, "Not that I doubted the analysis; it's just I don't think I ever really understood that the game would work. I hoped it would, but I didn't really believe. Tonight, though, seeing those people, hearing their stories, it's clear it did work. Whew!" He let out a huge, long, whistling sigh. "That's heady stuff, brother."

"Yeah, I know. Makes it kind of all worthwhile, I felt."

Andy had said it simply. All three now sat contemplating the evening, gazing off into nothingness. The only sound was that of an ambulance siren below on Sunset Blvd. Brian apparently reminded himself he had been talking about his grandpa. "I understand him now, Andy. I never did before."

"I know. None of us did."

"I didn't know how to help him really, and I sure as hell didn't pay any attention when they started him on those drugs. He's no mass murderer, though; I know that now!" he stated defiantly. "He was just a poor son-of-a-bitch who had a terrible reaction to the drugs, and did a terrible thing. That's all."

Suddenly Brian sniffed, as if trying to clear his nostrils. He was a tough guy after all, and didn't want these two to see him tearing up. But his voice betrayed the emotion. "I just…I just regret we found this all out too late to help him, that's all."

Andy didn't know how long the three of them sat there, thinking about that. It was awhile. "Well, bro, we're saving some now, aren't we? Your game's done it. You did it, Brian. An awful lot of people are going to live better because of you. So, I say, put the game behind you, and just go forward."

Geez, I love these boys, James thought. *I wonder if they really know what's happening here?* He decided to weigh in. "You know, Brian, I'd like to tell you guys something, if you'll allow me."

"Sure, James, anything. I didn't mean to be so morose. Just got me thinking is all."

"Right. Well let me give you some *real* food for thought." There was a gentle, satisfied smile on James' face as he started. "Either of you guys know how the Soviets nearly beat us?"

It was such a non-sequitur that both young men snapped back into present time, and out of their reverie. Seeing that he had their attention now, James became the coach. "Yep, darn near beat us. Frankly, I felt they had, until I hooked up with you two characters."

Seeing the question marks on both their faces, and noticing they were checking to see what kind of bottle he was actually holding, he went forward. "It wasn't military. They knew ultimately that wouldn't work. The United States will always win in a stand-up fight. No, they used another strategy, and it's that strategy that led me to Zawahiri. What's delicious now is that you're using the same strategy to defeat him. It'll defeat any residual Soviet crap as well. Now there's a serendipity!"

"Let me handle this," Andy joked, playfully egging James on. "I've had to deal with this since 2001." Turning to face James, he challenged, "Okay, James, you have my full attention." Seeing that James doubted that somehow, he stressed, "No, no, you really do. You too, right, Brian?" He turned to his cohort for support.

"Absolutely. For real."

"Something Stalin understood. You fight ideas with ideas. They didn't like the idea of freedom, capitalism, free enterprise, democracies, you name it. So, they brought in the mind guys, relics from Hitler, and even their home-grown Pavlov, and they figured out to fight our idea with their own idea of Communism. Everywhere in the world their propaganda machine triumphed as it got more and more people to accept the *idea*." He paused for emphasis, then added, "Damned near worked, too."

James took a final swig from his root beer. "Zawahiri, he's their successor, see. He's taken an old line they laid in to bring us down from within, using brainwashing—ideas. Only he's upgraded it into the 21st century with chemical ways of delivering the *idea*, and he's targeting your generation, that's all." Checking to see if they were following, and they were, he finished with, "He's fighting us with an idea—and your game is fighting his *idea* with an idea."

"What I want you two to remember—especially you, Brian— is that your game is the delivery mechanism for that new idea. It delivers the idea of a better life to a generation desperately in search of good ideas. And do either of you know why I feel good right now?"

"We're winning?" Andy offered tentatively.

"Well, that, too," James conceded. "But what I realized along this journey with you two is that you're the only ones who *can* deliver it. The media can't. Washington can't. No one group can. But a *big game* can. It can deliver the idea powerfully, and it can duplicate fast enough. We've got a fighting chance now."

"Just because we created a game, James?" Brian seemed a little questioning. He continued thinking out loud though. "No, not just by creating the game. I get it. There are a gazillion games out there." He was grinning now.

"I get it. It's not the game by itself; it's the marketing. The marketing is getting the idea across."

"Bingo, my young friend, bingo. Propaganda is marketing. The enemy is attacking the White King with an idea of depression, failure, weakness, capitulation—basically your long and winding road to slavery. Your game reverses that."

"I'm with you, man, I'm with you." Brian jumped up in his characteristic left to right dance. Andy grinned. "I just got it! It's not enough to just have the idea; you have to have a way of getting it across. And that's Marketing!"

Without knowing it, Brian had just arrived at the top of the game board Andy and James had been working on for years. The delivery mechanism to take the game they believed Zawahiri was playing, of drugging a population to make them more compliant and suggestible, was direct-to-consumer marketing. James and Andy had found it, and induced where they would find Zawahiri. They had almost gotten him four years earlier.

Their next line of attack had been to defuse the line along which he would attack. Brian had brought not only his computer game ability to that project but also his marketing genius. For the first time, he saw that now. Until tonight, he had felt more like a tag-along on the project—just the guy making the game. But, tonight, he *knew* why he was aboard. In a life of triumphs and setbacks, but not one driven by any real purpose, Brian Washington Carver had discovered his purpose. Deep inside he knew he would be a man to deliver the message of hope. And for the first time in his life that he could remember, he felt calm. There was a peace settling over him, and, whether he spotted it or not, his physical demeanor changed. The left to right dance slowed, and centered serenely. *Son of a gun, no wonder I picked Marketing!*

He spoke softly to James. "So what's next?"

Smiling, James tossed the answer over his shoulder as he picked up his tuxedo jacket and headed for the front door. "Well, I don't know about you, but now that we got those top level games neutralized, I'm planning on looking for *who* is handling marketing for Al Qaeda in the United States. He's the delivery mechanism. We neutralize him, and it's 'game over' for these guys."

He stopped at the door, turning. "One last thing…"

"What?" they both asked simultaneously.

"I'm proud of you."

CHAPTER 50

*T*he days seemed more purposeful for James, too. Truth be told, he hadn't really known why *he* was along on this project of Brian and Andy's. It had started way back with his obsession with finding Zawahiri, but the business arena in which he currently found himself operating was completely foreign to James, and he'd been feeling left out recently. It wasn't the first time in his career as a shadow warrior that, when the job was done, he'd been left dangling with no idea of what would be next. But he'd passed through that now, and had found a new mission. Confident that someone was deliberately delivering Zawahiri's message inside the United States, he decided to be the "Analyst" one more time, and begin the hunt for what he believed to be a vital part of the Fifth Column.

And there was something else on his mind as well. He'd been alone for years, with no family to be with or celebrate with. These last seven years, however, had altered all that. To be sure, the relationship he had with Kelly, Andy, and Brian would certainly not fall under the heading of conventional, but they were family to him nonetheless. He was comfortable and happy with that—except for one thing.

He'd been thinking about this for weeks, debating it over and over again in his mind. Finally, he decided to just talk to Andy about it. Andy was the man of the house now. Pulling up in front of Andy and Brian's place, he hesitated in front of the door. Deciding not to use his own key and let himself in, he chose the more formal approach. He rang the bell.

"James!" Andy exclaimed, opening the door. "Geez, man, what'd you do, lose your key?"

"Nah, just thought I'd knock, for once," James fibbed.

"Well, come on in. You're just in time."

"For what?" James asked.

"We're just going over to Mom's—and do I have a surprise for her!" Andy was exuberant, and a little distracted. Apparently, he was on unfamiliar ground here. James waited, knowing he'd get the scoop sooner or later. Suddenly Brian ran up the stairs, too, gingerly holding a small Tiffany box.

"Almost forgot this," he apologized.

"Well, that would have spoiled it." Andy was amused, more than annoyed, but still a bit jumpy. Before James could ask, however, he said, "James, you coming with us?"

"Sure." He'd answered before he even knew where they were going. When that dawned on him, he asked rather shyly, as they all approached Brian's Mercedes, "But, where are we going?"

"Over to Mrs. Weir's, bro," Brian responded, opening up the rear door for James. Jokingly, he added, "After you, sir!"

"Andy, what the heck is going on here? You two are acting just a tad strange today."

Andy laughed and turned around in his seat to fill James in. "I know. I know. It's just we've got this amazing surprise for Mom for her birthday, and we're taking it over to her now." Then, he added sincerely, "So glad you got here, too. She'll be glad to see you."

Guessing the present had something to do with that box, James was happy to be included. He'd concluded the boys had bought Kelly some very expensive piece of jewelry from one of Beverly Hills' iconic stores, and he too couldn't wait to see her face.

Just then, Andy remembered that James had come over to them unannounced, and he didn't know why. Concluding James must have had a reason, Andy politely turned around again and asked, "Sorry, James, what was it you came over for?"

James was at a loss. Somehow, his prepared speech had just vanished, leaving him like a fish out of water. He didn't know quite how to regain his footing, what with the boys' excitement over their surprise for Kelly. He looked out the window for just a second, then back to Andy, and said, "Uh…uh…nothing, really. It can wait."

Kelly was just closing the salon when the three of them walked in. She was startled, as apparently they hadn't made plans or let her know they were coming. *These three are a riot,* she told herself. *I never know when they are going to show up with some scheme or other.*

She decided to take the bull by the horns. "All right, guys, what's up?"

"Well, nothing too much," Andy lied. "We wanted to take you for a ride, for your birthday."

"That's nice, Andy, but my birthday's tomorrow."

"We know. I know. Right." All three of them spoke at once. That, at least, was true.

"Well, Mrs. Weir, Andy's got a surprise for you. And we, James and I, just decided we had to see your face, too."

Laughing now, Kelly said, "Okay. Okay. You three are something! I'm ready. So?"

Andy walked up to Kelly, putting his arm out to invite her to take it. As she did so, he said, "Come with me, my dear; we are going for a short ride."

Brian drove. Andy remained up front, and Kelly and James were in the back seat. A little hesitantly, Brian turned up one of the quiet hillside streets that wind their way up into the affluent residential area of Glendale. Though just a few blocks from the dense apartment buildings that crammed all the streets in the level section of the city, once the car started up the hill and into the tree-lined areas, it was another world—much like the prestigious Beverly Hills Trousdale Estates.

Kelly was looking out the window, smiling. She loved this area of town, and walked up into these hills as often as she could. She told herself it was to get some exercise, but she really liked how the area made her feel. The views were awesome, even if she did have to peek between the houses. Nonetheless, she could imagine what the interiors must be like, and how striking the vistas must be from inside.

Her walks had also allowed her to indulge in the fragrance of orange blossoms and jasmine, and to relish the astonishing variety of colors displayed in the gardens and hillside ground cover. *Only in a city like Los Angeles would the ground cover be as breathtaking as most lawns and gardens back east,* she reflected, as the car came to a stop.

Turning her attention back toward Andy, she noticed he was holding out a small box. "Happy birthday, Mom!"

She recognized the box. Any woman would, as it was perhaps the most famous jewelry box in the world. In her whole life, the only nice piece of jewelry Kelly had owned was her wedding set from Greg. They hadn't had much money, so the stone was small. But he had secured a very high quality diamond, and she had cherished it. Though he'd been dead now longer than she had known him, she still wore it.

Quickly opening it, she pulled out the inner leather box and popped the lid. Something in there surprised her and her head jerked back a bit. Pulling out a gold key, she held it up for James to see.

He was as confused as she was, so she turned to her son. "Andy?"

Grinning from ear to ear, with his mate Brian doing the same, Andy proudly explained. "Mom, I wanted you to have your own place—with a garden and a view. Once, when you and I were taking a walk up here, you commented that you liked this house, and guessed it must have a spectacular view. Well, it does. And I bought it for you." He proudly pointed to the house set into the hill just to the right of their car.

At first, Kelly didn't seem to quite get it. She shook her head, as if to wake herself up. No one said anything. They were waiting for her. Then she fixated on the key, studying it and turning it over and over. Still no one said anything. James looked to Andy, who was still grinning.

"Is this..." She didn't even finish the question.

"Yup, the key to the house. Want a tour?"

Kelly pursed her lips now, as if that could keep her eyes from welling up. It didn't work, however, and tears overflowed. But she was smiling when she nodded and softly said, "Yes."

As all four got out of the car, Kelly did indeed recognize the home. The garage was at street level, and there was a set of stairs leading to the main entrance one floor up. She remembered the house because it always seemed to have the blinds closed, and that seemed odd to her given the fact that the entire house faced out over, and had an unobstructed view of, Glendale and Los Angeles.

"Oh my, oh my. I always liked this place, Andy!"

"And wait 'til you see the inside. It's cool!" Brian was beaming now, too. Jokingly, he added, "And it's just like you, Mrs. Weir—*conservative*, and *cool.*" Kelly accepted the compliment graciously.

"The owner's expecting us. He's going to give you a personal tour, you know, show you where all the light switches are, all that." Andy led the way, followed by Brian and Kelly. James was lagging behind, desperately asking himself, *What do I do now?*

Dismissing it until he could address it later, he was just reaching the top of the stairs when the front door opened and Andy greeted the owner with, "Mr. Roos, good to see you. May I introduce you to my mother, Kelly Weir?" Kelly extended her hand politely as Andy finished, "Mom, meet Ali Roos."

CHAPTER 51

*T*o the Doctor, the ceiling fan's reverberation, as it rotated rhythmically over his head, sounded like an approaching helicopter. He lay, sweating and in pain, trying futilely to rest. The heat was oppressive, and he was so sensitive to the sound and motion of the fan that it produced an almost hypnotic effect upon him.

Anxiety was an almost constant companion now. There were so many arenas he was monitoring that he was feeling more and more overwhelmed by the sheer motion of it all. His best results seemed to be in the hysteria mounting in the United States Presidential election. Once again, the country was evenly divided, and becoming more vitriolic in its rhetoric and hysterical in its political tactics.

Yes, we've achieved a great victory there! the Doctor thought, congratulating himself. *My student learned so well how to use the concept that when there is a stalemate there is no decision; and with no decision there is no action, and then there's a subsequent loss of self-confidence.* To be sure, every time the Doctor turned on news from the United States, he saw ever-growing signs of the complete accomplishment of their goal to neutralize America's normal strength and reason. That plan had bought them time, and it was festering now in the United States in such a way as to leave the country weakened for generations.

But the Doctor knew he did not have generations of time. Soon he would have to meet Usama face to face. That would be a day of reckoning—for one or the other. Each day that passed from the moment he knew Bin Laden had escaped and was back in the game had emboldened the Doctor. *He must not know where I am,* he reassured himself daily. *Otherwise, he would have sent someone.*

His comfort was fleeting, however, as he was in a mystery as to the loyalties of Makkawi and Samir. Their business-as-usual approach to his missives and communications over the last eight months could be subterfuge, he knew. Yet, their steadfast follow-through on their battle plans made him think they were still with him. *Where is Usama in all this?* That question kept him awake at night, and in a fear so steady it had solidified in his stomach area and never left.

No matter what happens, he thought, *I still have Ali Roos. No one knows. They will carry through whether all of us have returned to Allah or not. I still have Ali Roos.*

That thought settled him down enough to re-engage his mind with two issues. First, there was Mexico. For some unfathomable reason, the US Administration still refused to close the border, despite the extraordinary work Samir had done in turning nearly all of the President's allies against him on this issue. Though the Doctor had no real interest in any of the men and women of American politics, he was secretly relieved to know that Bush would soon be gone. Surely, the Americans wouldn't field a second one that stubborn. He had long ago concluded that Americans were truly plebian chess players—their moves being limited and predictable, and shortsighted. *They'll most likely change directions. They've developed a habit of planning no further than eight years, and I doubt they can contemplate twenty-five years of moves,* he reassured himself.

Then, doubt crept in. The Doctor suffered from paranoia and a cynical mistrust of everyone. He repeated to himself often the old joke that "just because I'm paranoid doesn't mean someone isn't after me." It had served him well through the years since his imprisonment. *Maybe Samir deliberately failed to deliver the full plan regarding the Mexico border. Maybe he has turned. Maybe he held back his best propaganda effort.*

Catching himself sliding down this slippery mental slope, the Doctor brought himself around by asserting, *No, Ayman, get a hold of yourself here. The border issue is still there, and it is still hot. The man did his job.* Wisely, he decided to postpone the final analysis of it, and put his mind on something he could actually review.

And that produced a huge smile. Though he could still smell the foul body odors of La Hyena in the jungle, he knew that the FARC was performing brilliantly in Mexico. He had no idea really if

Venezuela and Cuba had followed through. In his mind, they both were wannabes—talking big, certainly having the capability, but more likely to wait to see who was still standing when the dust settled. In the end, they were just as bureaucratic as any other country, and just like any other country, they would predictably expose themselves only if their cause seemed victorious. Otherwise, they would sit back in the shadows, waiting.

Happily for the worldwide terror movement, the Doctor and Bin Laden were both men of action. Striking out with their own goals, and own resources, they had forever defined who could and who should play in this game of domination. Spitting into his sink, the Doctor barely noticed the pinkish cast to his phlegm. *No matter. We're close now. I may just make it yet!* He laughed out loud.

Assessing the accomplishments in Mexico, he took heart in the fact that, although the Marxist/Socialist candidate had been defeated, Calderon was hanging on by a mere thread. In fact, he seemed to be losing control of the country. The FARC's masterful implementation of violence and kidnappings had nearly paralyzed Mexico by the summer of '08. The completely random, stunningly frequent, and violently unpredictable nature of these acts was signature of the FARC, and the Doctor admired that group's special brand of terror.

He could clearly see how disruptive it was, and how destabilizing. *Yes, they'll fall yet. The Mexican people will do this. I am confident. They are reacting like sheep now. And they are afraid. Good.*

This certainly provided *one* ace he could hold in reserve, in the event he had to prove to Usama that all of his choices had been motivated by one thing only—the good of their mission. Whether Venezuela and Cuba were involved or not, he was quite certain now that the next Al Qaeda staging ground was being created day by day as the people of Mexico lived in fear of being kidnapped. Fear was palpable; their distrust of their government, rampant.

Once change occurred, the new regime would "miraculously" put an end to the brutality. That would be easy. The new regime would *be* the ones who had done it, or *had* it done. The FARC would quietly disengage, and return again later. And Al Qaeda would expand and slide into territories well suited to training and hiding. La Hyena himself had promised to guide them to impenetrable areas, as safe as the hiding places of the Hindu Kush.

Satisfied of success there, providing that Calderon did tumble—and providing the people of the United States kept pressure on closing the border and shutting off the money flow from illegal aliens to their families back in Mexico—the Doctor turned now to speculate on the size of the Ali Roos attack upon the United States.

It had been months since he had reviewed his own stock values, and it had been almost a year since he had monitored drug sales in general. Samir's firm was representing most of the pharmaceutical companies, driving their sales through the roof by means of his ingenious use of direct-to-consumer marketing. Nearly all television programs were sponsored now by drug companies, with their magnificently filmed and appealing commercials. At least, that *had* been the case.

But even brilliant people can miss something. They can fail to account for that one thing which may cause a plan to collapse. There is always the possibility of error. And Ayman Al-Zawahiri had made one. Perhaps it was his unique arrogance. Perhaps it was his hatred for the very generation he was using to carry out Al Qaeda's goals in suicide missions around the world. Perhaps it was his hatred for American youth. Whatever the reason, the Doctor had underestimated the power of a game, and in fact was at that moment oblivious to the existence of the world's latest game sensation.

Desiring to calm his nerves and relax his stomach, the Doctor opened up the computer to the cube-shaped game he kept stored there. He felt doing an assessment of the eight different game areas would assuage this ever-rising and relentless fear. The very bottom-most game was "Religion." Though the world viewed Islam as the key issue in the threats countries were facing, in reality the "Religion" game was merely a fabulous recruiting tool for Al Qaeda. *You can always get someone to die for God,* he thought, smirking.

As he studied the reports, however, which had just been transmitted by Makkawi regarding recruiting, he saw that recruiting was down—worldwide. Had it been only that, the Doctor would have been less intimidated. But, he sought good news in the second game tier, labeled "Military." And there, as well, he found shocking statistics of Al Qaeda experiencing heavy and devastating losses. With losses high, and recruiting down, this entire game was endangered.

The only bright spot there was the rise in suicides amongst US soldiers, and reports of increasingly violent behavior, coupled with the fact that 15% of US combat soldiers in Afghanistan alone were taking anti-depressants, anti-anxiety medications, or sleeping pills. The Doctor smiled, thinking, *Psychological warfare they understand. But the imbeciles have tunnel vision. They know what using psychiatric drugs does to an enemy, but they never thought to look at what would happen when they give those drugs to their own men. A blessing— small—but a blessing nonetheless.*

The "Intelligence" game afforded no solace either, as it was apparent to him that in Iraq and Pakistan, they were playing defense. No longer were their intelligence sources on the offense; rather, they were being ferreted out on an almost-daily basis by United States and Pakistani intelligence.

Had it not been for the stunningly effective "Public Relations" game, where Samir was winning unquestionably in the United States, France, and the UK with his strategy of "a lie told often enough becomes the truth," the bottom four games would clearly show a devastating and losing score for Al Qaeda.

Moving up the cube with his cursor, he highlighted the next game—"Weapons." His breathing normalized somewhat as he examined the data relevant to this level, and most specifically, the data relevant to their fear campaign. Following the guidance of Lenin, Ayman Al-Zawahiri had long believed one of the most effective weapons ever brought to bear throughout history was the debilitating tool of "fear." And, to his relief, he felt Al Qaeda could claim a major victory in this area, since the United States, and indeed the rest of the world, were in the grips of fear pertaining to the economic crises that were emerging. His Public Relations machine, through the amazing skill sets of Samir, was hammering away on that arena, and the American people seemed unable to take a breath without inhaling the incessant ranting of economic woes.

And that led to their greatest and strongest areas. They were winning, no question—at least by the Doctor's reasoning—in the complete sociological disruption of the United States. The Fifth Column was proving to be their main attack column, and he felt confident US leadership was witless to the possibility of this, let alone in possession of the capability to reverse it.

Feeling better now, and having reassured himself that victory ultimately would be theirs, he washed his face, changed his underwear, and settled down at the computer again to relish the sales stats he expected to see in the game tier labeled "Medical."

Sheer panic, however, attacked him when he saw the dropping sales statistics in the pharmaceutical industry, most specifically in the area of psychotropic drugs. *This can't be! It can't be! The Fifth Column is a complete success. How can the sales be down?*

A pervasive sense of dread overwhelmed him at that moment. He could not shake it, and it rocked him to the point where he had to open the window for some air. Feebly gasping, all he took in was the putrid stench from the alleyway below. And that caused Ayman Al-Zawahiri to vomit uncontrollably, until there was nothing but acidic bile coming up. *Face it, Ayman, face it whatever it is,* he coached himself.

His first reaction, when he saw the shocking drop in stock value of the shares he secretly held in DECU-HEHIZ, was to curse that company's president for incompetence. The value had fallen nearly 50%, and was still on a declining graph. His body reacted immediately to those numbers with knife-like pain in the abdomen, and acid once again in his throat.

Is this a blowback from the economic crises that are developing? Is the demand for the drugs down? Why? Who? He had more questions than his mind could process at one time. Immediately he turned on his satellite television and began channel surfing, looking for advertisements. Shockingly, much of cable news was now being sponsored by cereal, shampoo, toilet paper, and weight-loss products. These were interspersed with the pharmaceutical ads. But the Doctor was stunned at the shrinking penetration of the drug ads. Samir's work had led to almost complete saturation of the major advertising markets by the pharmaceutical companies, with his firm, ST & Associates, representing the largest ones.

Why, now, were the advertising dollars drying up? *There should have been more money to sponsor TV and news, not less.* His mind was racing. First, he asked himself out loud, "Is this Samir? Has he turned? Is he reversing our gains deliberately?"

Getting a hold of himself quickly, he realized this would not be the work of Samir. "It would lead right to his doorstep," the Doctor reasoned, pacing the floor of his puny accommodations. "He would know I would discover this." *Besides, he knows nothing of my plan. He's not part of this cell. And he knows nothing of my personal fortune, made by drugging the poor, depressed Americans. He just knows that the advice I have given him to concentrate in that area has created his own personal gain and fortune.*

The Doctor was sweating profusely now. His mind was racing, thoughts tumbling over one another. Valiantly slowing his thoughts down in an attempt to examine them, he could feel his pulse settle down, and his breathing return to normal. *No, this is not his doing.*

The Doctor had reasoned correctly. Instinctively he recognized the game had changed somehow. Someone had made a move he had not anticipated, in a game to which he was not even paying attention. The oversight was indeed his. It would cost him.

For now, however, he was on top of it. Needing to know why the drug advertising was down, he engaged the maximum encryption, and called his man in Los Angeles.

Samir answered the call immediately. "Yes?"

"Samir, my friend, how are you doing financially?" The Doctor preferred the non-sequitur question. He had learned long ago that a question asked out of the blue surprised the recipient enough to reveal their true colors. It was a technique the Doctor used often when he wanted to take the measure of an individual.

"Are you speaking of me personally, or of my company?" The response was immediate, and nonchalant.

"Today I have interest in your company. After all, my friend, I set you on this path. And I'm curious." The Doctor's voice was quiet and somewhat menacing.

"To be honest with you, the revenues are down. Our clients are doing less advertising, and that means less for us."

This was not what the Doctor had hoped for. His doubts about Samir, if he had any remaining on this issue, abated however. He had heard disappointment in Samir's voice. He continued in the tone of a financial advisor, or senior executive seeking answers from a competent junior. "Why is the advertising less, do you think?"

"Regrettably, Ayman—" He caught and corrected himself almost immediately. "Excuse me, sir, that was a lapse." Stopping for the Doctor's reaction to this egregious error, which was both a security breach and a disrespectful familiarity, he sighed.

"And not to be repeated," the Doctor asserted. "Continue your thought."

"Regrettably, sir, their sales revenues are down."

Changing the subject for the moment, the Doctor asked if Samir's personal finances were in jeopardy. Samir reassured him they were not, as he had wisely taken the Doctor's advice and diversified the types of clients he represented. Having spread into other industries—even into the entertainment industry—and having wisely invested, upon the insights and recommendations of Bud Walker, he was personally fine. He concluded with the report that only that one division of his advertising agency was in flux.

Swinging back around, the Doctor asked, "Why are the revenues down?"

"Frankly, sir, I do not know."

"Well find out." And the line was disconnected.

"Hey, Andy, there he is again!" Brian called downstairs to get Andy's attention.

"Who?"

"James! What the heck is he doing just standing outside the house for? Doesn't the fool know he has a key?" Brian joked.

"Well, let him in then," Andy hollered, as he bounded up the circular stair into the terrazzo-tiled entryway, two steps at a time. He reached the top just as Brian was opening the door. In a mock gesture of chivalry, Brian bowed from the waist and, with a sweeping motion of his right arm, invited James in.

Shaking his head, James just looked at the pair and said, "You guys!" Then he fell awkwardly silent. Brian spotted it right away. That instinct of a wide receiver just never let him down. He always knew when a ball was coming to him, and when it was not. Tonight he knew James had something to say to Andy. He had no idea what that was, but he just knew it was between the two of them.

"Say, James, I was just heading to our favorite Szechuan place to pick up some take-out. You want anything?"

"No, no thank you." James smiled. "I'll probably be gone when you get back."

"Fair enough. See you later then." Brian picked up his car keys, patted his sweatpants pocket to verify he had cash, and darted out the door.

Closing it, Andy got right to the point. "So, James, what's on your mind?"

He didn't know whether to laugh, cry, or just sit there. The reversal of roles was truly ironic. But here he was, listening to his friend and mentor. He had to admit, James had really surprised him here.

"So, what do you think, Andy? Do you think she would marry me?"

Andy looked into the distance briefly and smiled. Turning back to James, he said, as kindly and as honestly as he could, "To be honest, James, I have no idea!"

James dropped his head, looking dejected. Wanting to pep him up, Andy added, "But, James, how in the heck would I know that? She's my mom, for Pete's sake. You're going to have to ask her yourself."

Nodding agreement, James said what he had really come here to ask. "Right. Of course. But, is it all right with you? I wanted your approval first."

Andy's sudden grin told James what he needed to know. His laughter cinched it. "Heck yes, man. You've been part of the family a long time, in case you hadn't noticed." Now they both laughed.

James got up, and just as he reached the door, he turned. "I feel better, knowing you approve. It just seemed necessary somehow, and I didn't know what to do when you went and bought her a house. It just seemed you were the one I needed to get approval from."

Slapping him on the back, and hugging his neck, Andy added, "Well, I'm glad you did. But, actually, the one whose approval you need is Mom."

"Right. Right. Well, I guess I'll go see her now."

With that, he was gone. A minute later, Brian reentered with two huge white paper bags, smacking his lips. "James gone?"

"Oh yeah."

"What'd he want?"

Deciding he'd better keep this to himself for a while, he laughed and said, "You wouldn't believe me if I told you!"

Andy could never tell whether Brian was truly obtuse sometimes, or just pretended to be. Either way, it gave him a certain grace in human relations. Brian could just glide by certain things sometimes. And he did that right then with, "Okay. Let's eat. I got extra shrimp this time."

CHAPTER 52

"*H*ey, James, come on in. You can help me hang this picture," Kelly exclaimed, as she walked back over to the sofa along the wall.

"Sure, no problem." It was the first time James had been in the house since Kelly had moved in. Her belongings were meager, since most of her household was still in Arlington. Nonetheless, it appeared she still had boxes to unpack. And then, there were always pictures.

Less than thirty minutes later, the James Coleman picture "Mystic Night" was mounted above what appeared to be a new bamboo-colored sofa. Taking time to look around, he recognized quite a few new things. It seems Andy had showered her with more than just a house. He smiled.

"Nice stuff."

"Yes, isn't it? I had a lot of fun shopping at Bombay. And look . . . " She handed him a catalog that had been lying open on the sofa. "The Box Unlimited. Never heard of them before, but they have some awesome furniture." She stopped, turned a page or two, dog-earing something that caught her eye, and closed the catalog. "I've had a lot of fun. First time really."

"What, having fun?" James asked incredulously.

"No, silly! Buying new things. Everything I had before was given to me by parents or grandparents to help me and Greg get started."

"Oh, I see." The conversation came to a halt.

Kelly was peering at him a little quizzically now, wondering why her friend was uncharacteristically awkward. She hadn't seen that demeanor since the days back in Arlington when he would sheepishly try to explain some new danger he and Andy were getting themselves into. Always, he said it was perfectly safe, but she knew by his stance that he wasn't telling the whole story. She sensed that now.

Taking the bull by the horns, Kelly almost commanded, "All right, you, let's adjourn to the kitchen, and, if I can find two cups, I'll make us some tea, and you can tell me what you're scheming up now."

Obediently James followed, happy for the extra two minutes or so to get his act together. As they passed through the rectangular dining room and on into the kitchen, James was struck by the extraordinary view. The previous owner was noted for keeping the blinds closed, but not Kelly. She had all of them open all the time. And it gave one the feeling of floating out over the city. Yet, the place was homey already. James admired Kelly for that. She seemed to imbue a place with a degree of comfort and simplicity.

All right, James, you came here on a mission, he scolded himself, *so, carry on.*

He waited for her to sit down, and then he just blurted it out. "Kelly, I've grown accustomed to our family…well, your family. Since I met you and Andy, for the first time in a very long time I felt like I belonged somewhere, and that someone was watching out for me, too."

She nodded. He took that as a good sign, and forged ahead. "But I realized recently, it wasn't just Andy and that eccentric, brilliant 'boy from the hood' he hangs out with." She smiled now. "It's you. I've come to feel you and I are a team. And I was wondering, and hoping, that you might consider making it a permanent thing." There, he'd said it. He looked over to see how she was taking it. Her jaw was dropped slightly, as if she were looking at something surprising. He didn't know quite what to make of that, so he said nothing.

Then, she closed her own jaw, smiled slightly, and said, "James, was that a proposal? 'Cause it sounded like a proposal."

"Yeah, sure. I wanted to know if you would marry me?"

"You know, I think I'm beginning to figure you out, James. You have a really unique way of asking a girl on a date, and…" She paused for effect. " . . . and an especially unusual way of proposing."

James knew by now that if Andy were here he'd be wincing,

shaking his head at the hopelessness of his student. Suddenly he got just how ludicrous this was. He was sixty years old, for heavens sake, and he knew what he wanted. He'd never been an uncertain type, and he wasn't now. Whatever doubts, or insecurities, or lack of experience he had in the area, which had caused him to doubt his ability to communicate his feelings, vanished. Squaring up, he very calmly and sincerely said, "Kelly, I want to start again."

She gestured to go ahead, and seemed to square up as well. "I'm not one to say a lot, you know that. But, along this amazing journey you and I and Andy have taken, my respect for you grew into an abiding friendship for you, and into a deep love. Frankly, Kelly, I cannot imagine life without you. And I know you have Andy to provide for your needs and take care of you. But there are *some* needs I would like to take care of. And I would be honored and humbled if you would marry me."

Kelly's hands were folded in her lap, and she looked down at them for just a moment. Then, softly she responded, "James, I'm honored, truly honored with what you just said, and what you asked."

"But?"

"No *but*. It's just taken me completely off-guard is all. And, you know, I'd never thought about getting married again. I had Andy to raise, and then I had your project to support. I hadn't really looked ahead. But, clearly Andy is a man now, and totally on his own. Just recently I've had thoughts about my future, and what I want, and who I want in it."

James looked at her hopefully.

Almost timidly, she asked, "James, would I be blowing it if I said I wanted a few weeks to think about it? My feelings are pretty much the same as yours. I just need to be sure I'm ready to meet your needs. You're the most special man I've ever met. And I have learned so much from you. Could I have just a little time, without hurting you in any way?"

"Yes, you can," James responded immediately and sincerely. "I'm relieved to just have the topic up on the table where it belongs. Makes me feel like we've actually been dating," he joked. "And now, we're thinking about taking the relationship to the next level. It's fine, Kelly. You don't ever have to worry about hurting me. You tell me when you want to tell me. Okay?"

She was grinning now, her eyes glistening. "Okay!" Like a gentleman, he got up and showed himself to the door.

James was whistling as he skipped down the steps to his parked car. "Oh what a night, oh what a lady, what a night!" he sang under his breath.

———————————

The Doctor didn't know what to make of the manila envelope he found in the center of the rickety table at the fifth floor walk-up offices of ST & Associates. He recognized Samir's handwriting on the outside, and knew it must have been important enough for Samir to have delivered it in person.

As he opened it, there were just two things in the envelope— a note and a copy of the June issue of *Inc.* magazine. He read the note first. "You asked why sales in a particular drug class were down. Here's why...Meet me at the Canal, first lock overlook, 6PM. S."

Examining the magazine, his attention went first to the cover. The issue apparently featured these two young men and their meteoric rise in the business world. Standing back to back, arms folded like two Wall Street-types, one was holding a football, and the other what appeared to be an iPod. The subtitle said, "Winning pair win nationally this time with the game sensation, 'White King Rising.'"

He read the article from first word to the last, and studied the pictures of the two men, one white and one black. It was clear from the article that these two had created some kind of game, formed a company, and had taken the computer gaming world by storm. Further, although the journalist kept the content and end result of the game secret, the Doctor deduced that it had to do with drugs and choices. And that apparently it was producing a profound sociological effect in communities across the United States.

This game is why sales revenues have imploded? the Doctor asked himself. *Is this really what Samir found?* He knew it was. Something was nagging here, some memory from the past. It had something to do with one of the pages in the article. These two had apparently played football together in Arlington, Va. before going their separate ways to college. Both were bright. One was a Grandmaster chess champion, and star quarterback; the other, one of the country's most gifted wide receivers, headed for professional football.

His eye kept going back over and over that paragraph. Each time he stopped at the Grandmaster chess champion, wondering what was trying to surface. Suddenly, it did. About five years ago, his friend, Professor George Nasser, had been sending some mysterious messages through Al Qaeda's Internet chess games. The message had ultimately reached Zawahiri, but he had given no credence to it. The only reason he was connecting the dots now was that he had heard nothing further from Nasser since right around the time these two young men seemed to have paired up. Nasser had been given the assignment to monitor all chess tournaments for possible CIA plants. He himself was quite a player, an avid fan, and easily kept track of all chess stars and their accomplishments.

Could it be? He couldn't shake it now. *Was Nasser trying to contact Al Qaeda about this boy, Weir? Did he consider him a threat? What did Nasser have to say?* Knowing that he could not go to Manhattan University himself and look the man up, he resolved to have Samir ferret out the information. *Is there some kind of link between Weir and Al Qaeda? Could it actually be Weir's game that is undermining the very thing I am using to subvert the reasoning capability of the American people? Is this game preventing me from turning them into a stimulus-response hysteria that would have made Pavlov's dog pale in comparison? And who is this dark-skinned Carver?*

He could hardly wait for 6PM to arrive. Reaching the overlook of the magnificent first lock of the Panama Canal, he saw the benches were quite full—tourists, families, lovers. Selecting one where he could observe the surrounding benches, and the canal as well, he sat down, the manila envelope prominently situated on his lap.

Shortly after, Samir sat down beside him. Each looked at the other briefly, more to size one another up than to exchange a greeting. There was no time for either to assess just how much the other knew about Bin Laden and his whereabouts and intentions. Now, they had a more pressing problem.

The mercenary motivation of Samir dominated today. He was very interested in ascertaining whether this game was actually causing his bread and butter to dry up. Though a wealthy man now, he was not willing to see such a passive income as he had developed disappear because two punks made up a game.

"Interesting reading, huh?" Samir began.

"Very." The Doctor paused for a moment, still clearing his head of questions about Samir's loyalty and involvement with Bin Laden. Resuming, he asked politely, "Are you sure this is the cause?"

"Yes, regrettably. I researched all the companies, and their own investigations have revealed a reduction in demand for their anti-depressant class of drugs coincident with the release and escalation of this game's notoriety."

"Has anyone played the game?" the Doctor asked impatiently, still smiling to keep up appearances for the nearby crowd.

"Yes. Apparently, the drug companies have *now*. And that is why they are quite certain the game is the cause."

"The article says nothing about that."

"Correct." Samir examined that a moment, and then theorized, "I expect their purpose was just to shine a spotlight on this new success story in American Entrepreneurism. I doubt they cared what the game did—only that it was popular."

"I see."

Angling his body toward Samir, the Doctor addressed him very personally and very pointedly. "Samir, can you reverse this?"

Samir inhaled deeply, and exhaled. "Perhaps. I expected you to ask that. And I have a few options." He stopped abruptly, deciding whether to tell Ayman this next bit or not. He concluded it would ingratiate the Doctor to him, and provide for himself some leverage, so he added, "I met these two once, about two years ago."

"In what capacity?"

"Bud Walker referred me to an investor who thought I might want to handle their PR campaign. We took a lunch, and mutually agreed to take a pass."

"I see." The way the Doctor said that confirmed for Samir that he had struck his mark. He would exploit that leverage and make himself absolutely necessary to both Bin Laden and the Doctor, if either was to accomplish their goals. Each needed his public relations genius, and now more than ever, they needed *him* to further their ends inside the United States.

"One thing more, Ayman."

"Yes?"

"It appears this has affected the demand on the street as well. You might want to talk to your people. We need that income for our operations."

The Doctor tried to camouflage his surprise at this news. The idea that street drugs and psychiatric drugs, both, were diminishing, was stunning. On his way to the meeting, he had feared the possibility of a covert op here. Sure of it now, he gave one additional assignment to Samir. "Friend, I know you will submit to me your plans on how to reverse the effects of the game. I need you to do one additional thing for me."

"Of course."

"I need you to find Professor George Nasser for me. The last contact we had from him was in 2004, some time late in the year. He was at Manhattan University at that time, but I do not know his whereabouts now. We went to university together in Cairo, and I believe he has some information for me regarding this man." He slid the magazine out of the folder and pointed to Andrew Weir.

"The chess player?"

"Yes, the chess player. Find out what Nasser was trying to communicate to me. And thank him for his efforts. He will understand why I cannot do that in person."

Both laughed at the idea of that. Samir rose, followed by the Doctor. The two embraced, and departed in opposite directions. The instant they left, a young boy and his two sisters happily grabbed their bench, waiting for the blood-red Panamanian sun to set.

CHAPTER 53

*T*he next days were anxious ones for the Doctor. It had never occurred to him that someone might actually be opposing him in a game. To be sure, he and Bin Laden knew their enemies were looking for them, as they had for almost two decades now. They knew also the United States government would be trying to foil every plan they were developing militarily, and financially.

But this went beyond that. For the first time he realized his nightmares and feelings of being chased and opposed were not some unwanted neurotic residual from his days of torture in Egypt. That gave him little comfort, however. For, along with his realization that someone was indeed making opposing moves, came the unanswered questions of who, and why, and worst of all, how much did they know?

Until then he thought he only had to outsmart the western political leaders, and any disgruntled or greedy comrades in his, or other, terror groups. That had been enough intrigue for him. But now, he was overtaken with this sense of foreboding—that there was in fact another player in his elaborate set of chess games. Only Nasser could answer that, and he was growing impatient and more aggravated waiting to hear from Samir.

Then it arrived. The message, which was encrypted inside an attachment from Samir, almost stopped his heart. It read simply, "The educator you desire left his university for a family emergency in 2004. Apartment closed and re-leased. Contract with university cancelled one year later when he did not return from his sabbatical. Confirmed no family in Egypt. Whereabouts unknown."

Presumed dead, the Doctor concluded. "The United States government is involved in this somehow," he spat out. "No one vanishes like that without some help." What he needed to know, and now never would, was what Weir—if indeed it was Weir—was doing that had caused Nasser to try repeatedly to reach him, and which had ultimately led to his death. *What did he stumble on?*

Ayman Al-Zawahiri was a very bright man, and he never mourned the loss of colleagues. Knowing that men die in his line of work, he turned his cunning to the real problem at hand—how to destroy "White King Rising" and get those drugs moving again. He was convinced now that Weir was in fact an adversary, and not an accidental one. More importantly, his master plan required high drug demand in order to reap the devastation he intended.

Though he responded to Samir to seek out Carver and Weir again, see if he could win the account, and somehow insidiously destroy the company from within through misdirected advertising strategies, he became even more agitated at Samir's next communiqué.

It seemed the problem had spread beyond just the game's market. According to Samir, some Los Angeles based human rights group had seized upon the game's popularity to fuel its attack upon Big Pharma and the Psychiatric profession. Having regularly testified before Congress on related issues for more than twenty years, they were known, and trusted by a growing number of US Congressmen and women. Once it was proven to them that the demand for drugs was drying up, and being reversed by the patients themselves, Congress started to reduce its funding to public institutions for drugs.

"Oh, they are covering their asses now," he hissed. "With no money to buy drugs, and the willingness to take them declining like this, how am I to succeed?"

That question tormented and preoccupied him daily now. He could not address it with Samir, though, as his public relations officer had no idea of the existence of that cell or its instructions, let alone the diabolical importance the Doctor placed on the attack. Samir would simply conclude the Doctor's agitation had to do with his investments. Perhaps, if Samir were very smart, he would link it to their overall strategy of mind control. "Yes," he told himself. "Yes. That will work. If the Americans are not 'off their game' due to the influence of drugs, they are less vulnerable to our propaganda. We can't have that!" There, he felt better now. At least he had a plausible reason for giving Samir the marching orders he had.

The Doctor decided to wait for a report from Samir on his progress with Carver and Weir before reconnecting with La Hyena and the FARC. That meeting was overdue now, given that the Americans, with the help of the Sunnis, had in fact recovered Anbar Province in Iraq. Though the US media was thankfully not reporting that decisive US victory in Iraq—probably due to their own elections in a few months—the Doctor knew it meant failure in Iraq.

What they had hoped to gain in the form of a training and staging ground, coupled with a public relations humiliation of the Americans, had been lost. Not only was this a victory for the Americans but it would also demand that Samir exert any influence he could to either keep it from the American people, or to carp at it and reduce its significance in their minds. He knew his man would be on top of that already. Samir knew his field.

Where to go next, however, was the most pressing dilemma. Until he met with La Hyena, he could not confirm that the FARC were ready—truly ready—to harbor Al Qaeda. Knowing Makkawi, he surmised his military commander would pull their people—what remained of them—back into Afghanistan.

In fact, that is just what Makkawi had been doing. The choice of routes back, however, was treacherous. What seemed to work the best were escape routes through Iran, using the cover of the Iranian insurgents. Once inside Afghanistan, however, a regrouping was proving almost futile. Most sections of the country seemed to have embraced this foolish democracy idea, and the military presence of the United States and its surrogates was daunting.

Makkawi's challenge was to get his men through Afghanistan and back into a sanctuary inside Pakistan. Things were heating up all throughout that region. And what with the successful assassination of Benezir Bhutto at the peak of her campaign, Musharraf was under increasing fire from the Americans as well as his own people. Political instability always aided Al Qaeda, and the last months had indeed provided the chance for many of their warriors to get back to a safe haven. From there, they had commenced attacks inside Afghanistan.

But Makkawi had a dreadful sense of foreboding about all this. As a military commander, he knew that the necessary regrouping of his forces was placing them all in one area. He could not get the words of the former Secretary of Defense out of his mind: "We'll drain the swamp."

Knowing that to be a very valid strategy, and suspecting that even with Rumsfeld ousted the Americans would still be pursuing that strategy, he had concluded two things. He must get Zawahiri to authorize the move of Al Qaeda to South America. And he must find Bin Laden. Like the other top-level Al Qaeda commanders, he had believed Bin Laden to be dead. Now, after the release in October of the Bin Laden tape, he was convinced he lived.

Fear gripped him as well, for he did not know why neither the Doctor nor Bin Laden had taken him into their confidence. He had more unanswered questions than he could clear from his mind. Were they in on it together, and deliberately abandoning him and his men in Pakistan? Or was there a deep rift between them, leaving him in the middle? Was Samir part of this as well?

The good and loyal soldier in him had warned the Doctor not to come back to Pakistan, that it was too dangerous here. Now, however, he wished both Bin Laden and the Doctor would return. Dread was growing in his mind. Clearly, the senior command level—if it still existed—needed to reconvene. Makkawi knew he was in over his head now. He could feel a trap. He was certain the Americans had set one.

Just as the Doctor waited for confirmation from Samir that he had been successful in securing the Carver and Weir account before the Doctor would meet with the FARC, Makkawi waited in his safe house for word from the Doctor that their operations could shift to a new continent before he dared move any of his men. At prayers, he carefully placed his mat and secretly prayed for deliverance from the burdens of his command. He would not have to wait long.

———————————

At first, all he heard was a scuffle outside the modest home where he was headquartered and hunkered-down. It was brief. Trying to rouse himself from a much-needed deep sleep, Makkawi was not even standing when the rough, wooden door opened and sunlight from the setting sun penetrated the darkness. The silhouette of a tall man entering was the only thing he could see.

Believing this to be the Pakistan Army hunting them down finally, he tried to reach for his rifle. Before his hand grabbed the weapon, however, he recognized a familiar voice. "Be still, Makkawi, it is I."

"Usama? Is it really you?" Makkawi asked hopefully, forcing his eyes to adjust.

"Yes, my friend. Please lower your voice. I do not want to arouse a great many."

The degree of the embrace between the two men must have been satisfying to Bin Laden. It was spontaneous, and sincere. Of one thing he was now sure—Makkawi was not part of the deception. He was instead a victim of it. And in that, they had much in common.

What Makkawi didn't know was that Bin Laden had not known for sure either. His careful escape from the southeastern region of Iran through the predominantly stable lower regions of Pakistan, and up into the safety of this tribal area, had placed him in mortal jeopardy for weeks. Thankfully, the hospital Administrator who had become his accomplice had camouflaged Bin Laden well amongst the feeble and insane he was ostensibly transporting to a hospital near Islamabad. That had been their cover, and it had worked.

It was ingenious actually, for no one likes to be around the insane. Every time they were stopped their papers were checked, but guards or police inspecting the Red Crescent van found the smells, appearances, and behaviors of the dozen or so passengers to be repulsive. Therefore, they had let them pass.

But, according to plan, it had enabled Bin Laden to get very close to Makkawi. Once he was inside familiar tribal areas, the people recognized him, and aided him. Believing him to have been alive the whole time, they found his presence invigorating. He was the hero who had defied the Americans, and they directed him easily to the town, and eventually the meager house, in which his commander was headquartered.

"I am most relieved to see you, Usama. I am in need of your guidance."

"Of course, my friend. I am here now. And I am in command. But first, will you feed these unfortunate souls whose infirmity has helped me escape?" Usama gestured to the Administrator and his patients, who had crowded into the small room and were trying to remain as unobtrusive as possible in this awkward situation.

The presence of any unauthorized personnel within his cramped headquarters would have been disturbing enough to Makkawi. But seeing the obvious mental infirmities of these men and women was truly unnerving. Nonetheless, Bin Laden appeared to owe them a debt of gratitude, and Makkawi responded with as much hospitality as he could muster in his own meager circumstances. "We have nothing lavish," Makkawi offered, "but of course we will share."

"Good. After that, see that they are given shelter—in our compound."

Though that prospect horrified Makkawi considerably, he recognized quickly that too many new additions to the community at large would invite questions that could not be answered. And he knew too that informants were now even in this area. *I will wait until our commander is fed and rested before I brief him on that,* he told himself.

His response was quick. "To be sure, Usama. Our *compound* is but one building, but it is done."

"Good. Then, we must talk. I wish to recall all senior commanders from the locations where they have been hiding following our attacks on 9/11."

"All, sir?"

"All."

"That may take some time, Usama," he offered earnestly, deciding not to inform the man that he had no idea where the Doctor was, and that he could only reach him through Samir. He further felt it best not to discuss those who had perished. He presumed Bin Laden knew of those losses, especially since Bin Laden seemed to be treating him as the senior military

340

commander who had replaced Mohamed Atef after the Americans killed Atef. He assumed also that Bin Laden knew of the death of their bomb-maker at the hands of the Pakistanis, and of the killing of their chemical weapons chief.

But, he most likely does not know about Nanda, he guessed, since not even Al-Jazeera knew who their media chief had been. *I'll wait for a better time. Perhaps I should even let Samir break that news to him.*

Bin Laden interrupted Makkawi's thoughts. "I will be patient. And I will enjoy some rest."

CHAPTER 54

*B*rian and Andy both noticed that James was in an uncharacteristically good mood these days. Since Kelly had said nothing to Andy, and James even less, he was biding his time, and keeping his mouth shut. *After all, it's their business,* he reminded himself. But today's entrance by James into their offices on Olympic Blvd. was over the top. He was whistling, actually whistling.

"Is he whistling?" Brian asked Andy in mock concern.

"I do believe he is, brother."

"He's whistling," Brian repeated, as if to convince himself. "Strange dude!"

Andy pretended not to notice that last comment and came up to James just as James was settling down at his desk. "James, any news?" He guessed that was sufficiently vague enough to maintain some discretion.

At first, James was inclined to ask, "About what?" But he remembered quickly that Brian wasn't in on any of this intrigue regarding Kelly. So, he changed the intent of the question to one he was prepared to answer.

Reaching into the small refrigerator he had installed in the lower right hand drawer of his desk, he pulled out a sugar-free energy drink, popped the top, and cryptically responded, "I have a renewed interest in history, my boy, a renewed interest in history." Seeing the expression of complete confusion on both boys' faces, he ratcheted it up with, "The enslaver always traps himself and becomes enslaved."

"Okay, James," Andy started, as both boys pulled their chairs around and sat down facing James, leaning in. "You have our attention. Now what the heck are you talking about?"

James was enjoying this now, for the game seemed to be coming back around to his area of expertise after all. "That's a truth, my young friends—a truth born out by all history. Take Marat and Robespierre even in the French Revolution. Those two enslaved a lot of people, beheading them by the thousands. And in the end, those they had freed enslaved and beheaded them."

Andy appreciated the history lesson, Brian less so, but neither saw what this had to do with anything. *Well, I guess this didn't have to do with Mom,* Andy mused. Turning to Brian, he reminded him that this was James, "the Analyst," in front of them, and that this was the kind of talk he'd had to put up with for years. James would get a bright idea, and then end up explaining it to Andy.

Brian nodded his agreement. "Yeah, I've seen this with him before, too."

"Here's the deal, guys," James said, launching into it. "Remember we spotted that it was your marketing gift, Brian, that got the message of your game across? You know, you had the game, but without the marketing no one would have bought it."

They did. "Well, that got me thinking that the same would have been true for the enemy. Andy and I had figured out that the Doctor was most likely involved in the pharmaceutical industry somehow, effecting some type of sociological change through the use of medicine and drugs—most likely for money."

"And that idea nearly got us shot, James. Don't tell me we're going back there again."

"Not exactly, Andy, but we are going to do a reverse vector on the issue."

Before either could protest about this being too ambiguous, James elaborated. "Here's my thinking. He had the drugs. But he, like you, needed the marketing strategy to get the sales he needs. This asshole accomplished all this by direct-to-consumer marketing. He got his idea across, very well as it turned out, and created a huge increase in the sales of drugs. My friend, who works with the Mossad in Israel, informed me some time back that they had, in fact, traced him to a pharmaceutical company in Geneva, Switzerland."

This confirmation of his earlier theory was new news to Andy, and most certainly to Brian. Their tone became more serious now. "Go on."

"It appears he was a major investor, and camouflaged as a model citizen of that city. The company was cleared under investigation—nothing unusual other than their rise to dominance in the anti-depressant market under the advice of this *investor*." James paused for effect now. "Seems he dreamed up this marketing concept, and got it implemented."

"How did he do that?" Andy was really getting into this now.

"Don't know yet, boys. But that is what I am about to find out. How *did* he implement it?" Noticing they were still sitting there, riveted, he asked, "Do you have work to do, or are you planning on listening in?"

"Listening is good." "We're planning on listening in." Andy and Brian overlapped each other.

Looking at his watch, he concluded it wasn't too late to reach Ari Ben-Gurion, whether he was in Europe somewhere, or back in Jerusalem, and hit the speed dial on his phone. Ari picked up immediately and James greeted him with, "Hi, it's me. I need you to check something for me."

Ari must have agreed, because the next thing the boys heard was, "Okay. I need you to tell me what advertising agencies or PR firms handle DECU-HEHIZ—especially their international marketing campaigns. It's important."

"I'll get into the file and get back to you." Ari then added, "Are you on to something?"

"I may be, so 'as fast as you can' would be appreciated."

Ending the call, he started whistling again. "We find the marketing team; we find another piece of the Al Qaeda puzzle." James had a Cheshire grin plastered all over his face, and added playfully, "Well, boys, this isn't going to happen in the next five minutes, so I think I'll take a little break."

Before Brian could even add that James had just gotten there, James dialed another number on his phone, smiled, and said, "Hi, it's me. Don't suppose you'd have a lunch break in that schedule book of yours?"

Apparently the person did, because the next words James said were, "Great, see you in about a half hour." Ending the call, he said, "I'll be back in a couple of hours. Hopefully he'll have something for us by then."

As it turned out, Kelly had an unexpected walk-in and was in the midst of a cut when James arrived. He saw immediately that their lunch date was off. Excusing herself for just a moment, she followed him outside. "I'm so sorry, James. She just came in. And she's someone I promoted myself to at the grocery store, so I didn't…"

He interrupted her with, "Not a problem. I understand. But tell me, what was the question you wanted to ask me?"

Remembering her message on his cell, she smiled a little abashedly and asked only, "Where would we live, do you think?" That was all she said before she excused herself and dashed back into her client.

Whoa, now we're getting somewhere, James concluded, and headed back to the office. Passing Bob's Big Boy, he decided to grab lunch.

"Of course I'll see Samir," the Investor said politely to her assistant. "Show him in."

"Samir, she's available and is happy to see you."

"Great!"

As Samir entered the pristine and elegant office of the Investor, he was struck as everyone always was at the absolutely astonishing view it offered of the Southland. He stopped just inside the door, riveted on the panorama. She was used to this of course, and broke the freeze-frame by coming around her glass desk, extending her hand to him. "Samir, it's a pleasure. Did Bud send you?"

"No, actually, I'm here on my own."

Smiling and wanting to take good care of any friend of Bud Walker's, she helpfully said, "What can I do for you?"

Not wanting to seem to hesitate, or be needy, he came right to the point. "Actually, I feel I made a misjudgment a couple of years back regarding a referral you sent my way, and I was hoping you could provide some influence to allow me to revisit the issue."

The Investor knew exactly what account he was referring to. Frankly, she had been surprised then that he had turned down Carver & Weir. After all, she had been doing Bud a favor, and she was the principal investor, so she had expected he would recognize that the young firm held great potential. She wasn't known for having anything except a golden touch.

"I presume you are referring to Carver & Weir?"

"Yes," he answered simply, looking directly at her.

"Well, Bud has been a friend a very long time. And he believes very strongly in your extraordinary capabilities..." She didn't finish her sentence. "Let me see if I still have any influence over there." This one she dialed personally.

"Andy, it's your Investor calling," she joked. "Do I still have any influence with you boys?" Samir strained to hear through the receiver. He was unable to, however, and just had to sit back and wait. "Well, that's good to hear. Because I'd appreciate it if you would allow ST & Associates to present some ideas to you." Quickly she added, to forestall any possible disagreement, "I know you two are very happy with Tate & Donovan, but I think you should hear him out." She smiled. "Excellent. I thank you."

"All right, Samir, they are at least willing to listen. Good luck. I hope it works out well for you."

"Thank you very much, Madame, it is greatly appreciated. I'll keep you apprised."

CHAPTER 55

"You're back early," Andy commented, leaning into James' glass office cubicle. "Were you having lunch with Mom?"

"Well, I thought so, Kid, but turns out I joined Bob instead." Andy had no idea who Bob was, and his expression must have given that away, because James grinned and added, "Bob's Big Boy. Kelly had to take a walk-in, so we'll have to talk later."

Andy decided not to press the issue any more. James' demeanor was playful, so he had to assume something was in the works, and that he'd just have to wait out the suspense on this one. Changing the subject he said, "Great, because we have a walk-in coming over as well."

"What do you mean?"

"While you were out we got a call from the Investor. She wants us to revisit the ST & Associates PR firm again; says he's got some good ideas for us."

This puzzled James—not so much that a PR firm would be pitching one of the most successful start-up companies in America, but rather that Andy and Brian would even consider it. He didn't want to meddle, but he decided to anyway. "Why would you want to make a change? Tate & Donovan have been stellar."

"We don't," Andy offered reassuringly, "but we don't want to offend her either. She's been great. So we figured, what the hell, we can hear him out, and tell him we'll get back to him."

"Makes sense." James could see through the glass cubicle to the front entrance, and noticed Samir entering into the open waiting area. Pointing to him, James informed Andy that Samir was already here.

"Geez, that was fast!" Andy remarked. He quickly exited the

office, waved to Samir that he would be right there, and knocked on the glass of Brian's cubicle. The two then ceremoniously escorted Samir into the conference room—which was also clear glass on all four sides.

I wonder why? James pondered.

———————————

He didn't get much time to think about it, as his cell phone pulsed, vibrating sufficiently to almost jump off his desk. Capturing it just before it could drop off the edge and onto his chair, he looked at the caller ID and recognized it was Ari Ben-Gurion calling.

"Yeah, Ari, what do you have for me?"

James was staring straight ahead, through the transparent offices, directly into the conference room where Samir was animatedly discussing something with Andy and Brian. They were listening politely. Samir was standing at the conference table, on the opposite side, facing James.

"James, the records indicate that DECU-HEHIZ has only one public relations firm. That firm does all the advertising and PR for the company." James was making notes as Ari gave him the details. "They're based in Paris, however, not Geneva. And they checked out clean when we did our review of the whole DECU-HEHIZ operation."

That wasn't exactly what James had hoped for, but he politely acknowledged, "Okay, got it." Then, almost as an afterthought, he asked, "What's their name?"

"ST & Associates," Ari responded simply.

James' heart was racing fast now, and he could almost taste the adrenalin pumping into his system. *Jesus Christ, that can't be a coincidence!* Collecting his thoughts—knowing that if he could see Samir, Samir could see him—he decided to reveal a bit of this to Ari. "Well, it may not be as simple as it seems, Ari, because Samir, the owner of ST & Associates, is about forty feet away from me in my conference room trying to get my boys as a client."

Oddly, there was silence on the line. "Ari, are you there?"

"Yes, my friend, I am. Quite a coincidence."

"I think so," James joked. "I don't suppose you can tell me Samir's last name, can you?"

"That, I can do. It's Taghavi, a nice Persian name…" His voice trailed away. Before James could inquire, Ari somewhat abruptly added, "James, I see something here I do not like. I'm going to have to get back to you." And he hung up.

At that moment, Samir looked up and saw James staring at him. James had been in similar positions before, staring right at a "mark." *Well, if he is a mark, better be cool here,* he admonished himself. Then he smiled slightly and nodded to Samir.

Samir hesitated for just a split second and then decided to take James' nod as a salutation. He returned the nod, and sat down facing Andy and Brian.

———————

The meeting in the conference room broke up cordially, with Brian adhering to the script with, "Samir, thank you for coming in. We will give this some consideration, and we will get back to you."

"Thank you, gentlemen. I do appreciate your seeing me on such short notice. And I look forward to hearing from you."

James came out of his office and joined them just as Samir was turning toward the exit. Deciding to face him, Samir turned around, extended his hand in greeting, and said, somewhat obsequiously, "Forgive me. It's nice to see you again. It's James, isn't it?"

"That's right," James responded succinctly, returning the handshake.

"Please forgive me. I do not believe I got your surname that day we were introduced."

"It's Mikolas. James Mikolas."

"Yes, of course. Well, I'll be on my way."

Once he was safely out the door, Brian exhaled slowly. "Well, that was awkward."

Believing him to mean interviewing someone you have no intention of hiring, Andy seconded it with, "Yeah, for sure."

James' phone pulsed again. This time he had it on him, and he pounced on it. "Ari? What do you have?"

The three just stood there in the hallway as James listened. Then, when James quickly returned to his cubicle to make some notes, Andy and Brian followed, curious about this unexpected phone call from a man they knew only as James' contact with the Mossad. James was listening and writing.

"I was concerned about the file, James. The name Taghavi...something made me check. There are two things you should know. Your Samir Taghavi—according to the background check I just ran—has expanded his operations. ST & Associates is no longer based only in Paris. It seems he's got offices in New York, Los Angeles, and Panama City."

"Did you say Panama City?" James was struck by this.

"Affirmative, my friend."

"What the hell would he be doing in Panama City?"

Ari was quick to respond. "Exactly. He could just be trying to branch out into the PR of international banking, or it could be something worse." Wondering if James was still on top of his game, he asked, "You *are* aware we are getting intel that Al Qaeda is setting up money operations in Panama?"

"Yup, figures." James looked at the page and then asked, "You said a second thing. What is that?"

"The reason we didn't red-flag anything when we looked into him before was that he was educated at Princeton in Public Relations—a real superstar at your university, and all of his background checked out. But...and I'm sorry to say we missed this, James...his name. I assumed it was Persian, and that he was Iranian."

"He's not?"

"Regrettably, no."

"All right, Ari, break the suspense here will you?" James was almost pleading. "Where is he from?"

"Egypt—the small town of El Minya, not far from Cairo."

James simply exhaled. Brian and Andy waited, having no idea what was transpiring here. Each, however, had a nervous stomach developing. Ari concluded with, "Clearly, we have more to examine with this ST & Associates. We'll start with the Paris office."

"Thank you."

Brian was the first to break the silence. "So, I gather from your dumb-founded look, and complete silence, brother, that Samir is a candidate we should take a pass on?"

It was said with such flippancy that Andy snorted. *Man, he's irreverent! Hope James has a sense of humor here.*

To their surprise, when James looked up, he was smiling. "Yes, but keep him on the string for awhile. I want to be able to find this guy easily. After all, it is the second time you've seen him."

"Third actually," Brian corrected. Neither James nor Andy seemed to be following, so he amplified, "Second time pitching. First time we pitched him. This time he pitched us. I kept thinking this guy was familiar to me. Today I got it. Andy and I have seen him before."

"We have?" Andy seemed clueless.

"Sure. One time."

"Where? I don't remember," Andy asked sincerely.

"It wasn't business, bro, relax. It was way back, when you and I used to go to Ugo's." Brian paused to see if Andy was catching up. He wasn't. "Come on, Andy, don't you remember?" Still, Andy didn't seem to remember, so Brian jogged it a bit. "James, Andy, we were at Ugo's eyeing that hottie, Alicia Quixote—you know, the anchor woman at WNG. And she was with this guy."

Andy recollected the event now and said, "Oh, yeah...yeah. I remember, I told you she was taken." He paused for a moment, revisiting the memory. Though dim, he did remember. "Well, son of a gun. That *was* him, wasn't it? You've got a terrific eye, Brian. I didn't put it together."

James was stuttering a bit now. "Wait. Wait. You guys telling me this Samir *Taghavi* was with Alicia Quixote? The one we see on WNG-LA? Bud Walker's protégé?"

"Yeah." They both nodded.

"What was she doing with him? Was she interviewing him?"

Suddenly Brian and Andy laughed, and told James gingerly, "No, James, she was *with* him." They paused for him to get it. He did.

"Oh, this is just great!" James spat it out sarcastically at first. "We have, possibly, Zawahiri's Public Relations chief, inside the media." He stopped. And, for the first time in a long time, he was gripped by fear. *How far inside? How far has this gone?*

351

———————————————

"James, can you talk?" Kelly had called back a few minutes later.

Though it was a distraction from the shocking and potentially horrifying discoveries of the last hour, James was eager to hear from her. "Sure. Let me close the door." As he did so, he added eagerly, "Now, what did you mean, where would we live?"

CHAPTER 56

J ames and Kelly had to postpone that conversation until the evening, as it was obviously going to be more than a minute's discussion. Moreover, since he was waiting for Ari to get back to him, he was a little reluctant to get too far from his own computer and notes.

Kelly, as usual, was very accommodating. She'd really just wanted to talk about Arlington, had confided in James that, although she loved her new home in Glendale, she preferred the East Coast. "Do you think Andy would be able to handle it, if I kept this house, but went back East?"

"The Kid could handle anything," James had responded sincerely. He hesitated for a moment, wondering if this would work over the phone. Deciding it was his best option, he asked, "You asked where would *we* live? Were you asking if I would want to go back East, too, or whether I was going to suggest you live in my apartment?"

Abruptly she laughed that delightful laugh, and joked, "James, don't be silly. Of course we couldn't live in your apartment. That is obvious."

Kelly didn't even give a thought as to whether or not he'd be offended, for she knew he wouldn't be. James had no illusions that any of his living quarters were suitable for a couple, so he took it in stride. Enjoying her humor, he playfully teased, "Actually, I was thinking Cape Fear." Now that did stop her. There was absolute silence for more than a moment, and he wondered if she had taken that seriously. Although, he did have to admit, he missed the place. At least, he missed the tranquility of the place.

She seemed to really be looking at that option, and then

concluded, "No, that's a good place to keep for a get-away place. But, I don't think the bathroom situation would work, do you?"

She had taken it seriously. He was shocked. *She really is looking at where we would live.* It hadn't escaped him that this must mean her answer was yes. But, if she felt his proposals were odd, this "answer" took the cake. Deciding to just wait it out, he knew she'd answer the way she wanted, when she wanted. For now, he was overjoyed to be talking about living quarters. He decided to play along. "You're right. It's not. What's your idea?"

He was hoping she wasn't thinking of the home in Arlington. That was another man's home, and it was full of another man's life. And it also held memories of terror and near-death from their encounter with Professor George Nasser. *I truly hope she's not expecting it to be Arlington.*

Any fears he had were allayed in her next sentence. "Well, anyway, I'm thinking of selling the Arlington house. It's time. Maybe find something nearby. I always liked Alexandria."

That was it. And for James, it was enough to make him euphoric. He felt he was riding high now—getting the woman he wanted, and getting the man he had hunted for so long. His confidence was never higher than at that moment.

It would not last.

ST & Associates in Paris had forwarded a large advertising package for approval to Samir's office in Los Angeles. Imbedded in one of the attachments was the message coming through from Makkawi. Since the Paris office was the only one that was actually an Al Qaeda cell, the office manager in Paris immediately recognized its importance. Elated that Bin Laden was back, and that he was calling for a meeting of all senior Al Qaeda, he breathed a sigh of relief and pride when his computer signaled the successful transmission of the file.

Later that day, Samir opened the file in question. His response was less than enthusiastic, however. The idea of Bin Laden and Zawahiri coming together presented perplexing issues for Samir. For he was confident the Doctor did not know Bin Laden had contacted him directly. This smelled like a loyalty check to him, and the possibilities were explosive.

Though the United States never spoke of this much, terror networks were rampant with intrigue and power-struggles. And he was sure he was walking into the mother of them all now. What was at stake was the control of Al Qaeda. And he didn't think either would relinquish it easily.

Perhaps they'll work it out for mutual benefit, he prayed. *One thing's for sure, though. I have to pass this summons on.* Though he would have preferred to use any excuse on earth to miss this summit, he knew he had to be there. It was the only chance he had of surviving, let alone of coming out on top. Staring at the document once again to commit its instructions to memory, he couldn't help but reflect on how much of a problem getting to the forsaken and squalid rendezvous place would pose. *Less for me, though, than him.*

And, with that thought, he transported the file to Ayman Al-Zawahiri, having no idea when the Doctor would actually receive it, nor even where he was at that exact moment.

Samir had no way of knowing, but the Doctor received the document almost immediately. He had been up for days, sleepless and in pain from his stomach ulcers, and he had kept an eager eye on his computer. Not only was he expecting communication from men inside Cuba and Colombia, regarding the meeting he had asked for, but he also knew the showdown with Bin Laden was imminent.

From the moment he had heard Bin Laden's tape almost a year earlier, he knew it was only a matter of time. The other shoe would have to drop. And frankly, he welcomed it now. *No more deception; no worrying about where he is. Now I know.* He succeeded in bolstering himself. Supremely confident that this would play out the way he wanted it to, the Doctor was relieved to make preparations for the meeting. In order to prevail, he had to be face to face with all the players. It was the only way he could take a true measure of their intentions, and their loyalty. And it was the only way his argument, which would be stunningly persuasive, would reach all the department heads at once.

He'd performed brilliantly before, when he had assumed command of Al Qaeda, and he relished the idea now of ending it once and for all—never having to look over his shoulder again to see if the specter of Usama Bin Laden was following him.

But he did have his attention on something. It wasn't so much what was in the communication from Samir as it was what was *not*. Samir had not confirmed his being hired by Carver & Weir, and that, realistically, was more important to the Doctor than any drama that would play out impromptu in the tribal villages of Pakistan.

Samir had not made such a confirmation to the Doctor because he had not yet heard from Carver & Weir. And he had no way of knowing that day that he never would.

CHAPTER 57

*T*he raid was swift and stunning. Israel would record it as a Mossad operation. It surely had their speed and stealth. With no warning whatsoever, the Paris offices of ST & Associates were raided while the staff was working. All computers were seized and ferried to the awaiting unmarked vans. And the staff vanished. The interrogations would not occur on French soil.

But, one of the last communications transmitted, before the raiding party reached the office manager, went straight to Samir. It simply said, "Fire in the hole."

Samir knew there was likely no coordination between the Israel and the United States on this, and that the oversight requirements in the US would allow him hours, if not days, to vanish. Nonetheless, he had no intention of risking capture. *Well, I guess I'll have to put on those damned robes again after all.*

"I'll be in our Paris office for a few weeks," he emailed to the office managers in Los Angeles, New York City, and for appearances, Panama City. He did not want anything unusual to cross their desks until the raids he knew would come. For now, he wanted the two offices that were unwitting accomplices to continue to perform their PR functions. None was Al Qaeda, and none would have anything to offer the FBI except vociferous protestations, and the acquisition of some of the finest lawyers their cities had to offer.

But, like his cool-headed office manager in Paris, he, too, got off one communiqué before fleeing. It read, "Paris burning. Abandoning ship."

There, I've done my duty, he congratulated himself. *We'll just have to see who arrives at the rendezvous now.* Using his office computer one last time, he logged on to his travel agency and booked a flight to Paris. *That'll buy me a little time; put a little flack on the line for them to sort through.*

Five minutes later, he was at his bank at Sunset and Doheny. They were cordial as usual and escorted him to a private room, where he could open his safety deposit box. The contents of this particular bank's vault were all for emergency measures, if a sudden escape became necessary. There was cash, a sidearm, and several passports. Taking the cash, he left the sidearm, and, after some deliberation, decided to take all three passports.

The one he would use was the Moroccan passport. The other two would be sewn inside the lining of his carry-on. Guessing that he would blend easily into the landscape there, and wanting the nervousness in his stomach to settle down, he booked a flight to Tangier while still inside the vault—concluding it would be safer to do so inside the vault, and that hiding there for even a short time would leave him less time out in the open.

Well, Ayman, I have a price on my head now, he lamented to himself. Knowing that the life he had created, which allowed him to travel freely about the world, implementing Al Qaeda's propaganda strategies without being on the radar screens of any intelligence agencies, was over, Samir Taghavi took a deep breath and made his break for it, planning to slip away unnoticed.

Unfortunately, he ran into Alicia coming into the bank, just as he was leaving. Despite his being in a hurry, she insisted upon their kiss, and wanted to chat a bit. Neither knew that this exchange was also being recorded on film. Among the many things rarely discussed in the media was the growing degree of surveillance done by business establishments on their perimeters. Necessitated by the escalating crime statistics, most businesses justified the expense as a form of corporate self-defense. Either way, almost everyone and every transaction was being monitored.

Samir feigned interest in Alicia's quick recitation of her daily planner. Frankly, he had none whatsoever, and hadn't even planned a cover exit for her. For all he cared, she could just think he'd dumped her, and returned to his beloved France. Finally, needing to catch a cab so as not to flag any attention at LAX, he convincingly said, "Alicia, my dear, I would love to hear all about it, but unfortunately, I am racing to catch a flight to Paris. There is a problem that requires my attention, and I must leave tonight. I will call you from the airport, either here, or when I land."

Though that disappointed her, it didn't even raise the least bit of a red flag. After all, Samir was one of the most in-demand PR men in the world. Her beau was quite a catch she felt, and she couldn't wait to introduce him to those same high school friends from El Paso who rejoiced regularly through Facebook about the success of "one of their own."

Just as he was turning to wave a cab, she called after him, "Samir, don't I get my goodbye kiss?"

"Don't I get my kiss?"

"What did you just say?" Kelly asked.

James and Kelly had been talking it over, at her kitchen table, for more than an hour. Truthfully, each felt more comfortable back East, and had concluded that Brian and Andy would be on their own course now anyway. The time when all of them needed to occupy the same space was over.

It was time for all of them to move on with their lives. Mysteriously enough, Kelly still hadn't said yes, but she was clearly testing the water with regard to their moving to a different location. They were in agreement on this. And, it wasn't a matter of compromise for either of them. *Truth be told,* James reasoned, *she and I actually do agree on almost everything.*

He was roused out of his reverie by Kelly interrupting, "Oh, James, I almost forgot. I have something to show you."

She went into her bedroom for a moment and emerged holding what looked like a travel folder. Placing it on the table in front of him, she said, "Look what Andy gave me as a pre-Christmas present!"

It was an all-expense paid trip to Venice and Rome, commencing Oct. 30, 2008. At that time, the United States embassy in Yemen had not yet been bombed, in what would be Usama Bin Laden's first true executive order in years. Lehman Brothers had not yet collapsed, leading to criminal investigations all up and down Wall Street. And Sarah Palin had not yet burst onto the American political landscape.

Andy knew that his mother had always dreamed of a trip to Venice, and that she, moreover, thirsted for an opportunity to see the Vatican, to take communion in St. Peter's Basilica, and to see the early decorations for the holiday she loved so much. In an unconscious, but prophetic gesture, he had scheduled her for a two-month vacation in Italy—making it the first time they would be separated during the Christmas holidays in their entire history together.

"Wow," was all James could say. "This is an amazing trip. You will love it!"

"Well, there's a problem now, James."

"What's that? How to vote?" he joked.

"No, James," she admonished. "I've got my absentee ballot for that! First, it's a long trip. That part I'd love, but it is Christmas time. I've never been gone at Christmas."

James simply acknowledged that with, "Mmm."

Immediately, she interjected, "I can handle that—you know; we're all on our own now. I can handle that."

"You said, 'first,'" James reminded her. "What's second?"

Instantly, she blushed. "Well, it's just for one. Andy wouldn't have known to make it for two. And I don't want to leave you here by yourself, not with, well you know, things as they are between us."

James suppressed a smile. *Honestly, women really are different!* James thought. He decided to encourage her. "Kelly, do not worry about this. This is a wonderful trip; you will love it. You should do it."

"You think so?" she asked, as if she didn't want to risk losing something.

"Absolutely!" Guessing what she was afraid of, he instinctively reassured her, "I am not going anywhere, Kelly. I'll stay here and 'mind the boys' while you experience an amazing city at a truly splendid time of year."

She sighed deeply and loudly, and meticulously folded the brochure back up. "That's settled then. I'll go." Then, as an afterthought, she added, "And what would you like?"

His answer was simple. "What about my kiss?"

Kelly was speechless. Realizing that they had never even kissed, she playfully responded with, "Well, that is an oversight, isn't it?" He nodded that it was. "And it should be corrected right now," she concluded, as she first embraced him, and then kissed him. Had anyone been looking through the always-open blinds, they would have observed that it all seemed right, and natural.

"Are you sure?" Ayman Al-Zawahiri struggled to camouflage any anxiety in his voice.

"Yes, sir," Samir responded via encrypted satellite phone. "Have you secured yourself?"

Frankly, that was the first thing the Doctor had done when he opened the document summoning him to a meeting with Bin Laden. Now, knowing the sequence of raid and seizure the enemy was likely to use, and knowing the lack of civil rights protection one had in Panama, he knew the raid on their offices in Panama City would be only minutes behind. Having packed his gear and belongings earlier, fortunately he had already escaped when this call came in from Samir. By the time the Panamanian officials stormed the office, there would be absolutely nothing linking him to that now-empty space—quite the contrary. The lease papers led straight back to ST & Associates.

They can raid all they want, he had concluded. *They won't find me. And Samir has never known where I am. He might speculate, but he doesn't know for sure.* It seemed that the Doctor's genius in creating the cell structure of Al Qaeda extended even to himself. Though he was a common denominator to more than one cell, no one in any cell had any idea of his whereabouts. He was untraceable.

So, though he knew now the imperative of wrapping up a deal with the FARC, he still had time to probe Samir, and perhaps strike a blow against Carver & Weir—perhaps. "Samir, tell me, were you successful in securing the Carver & Weir account?" He knew the answer to that was immaterial now, given Samir's necessary escape. Nonetheless, he was surprised and angered when Samir responded.

"No. And, my friend, even if they decide to hire me, it is a moot point. My help to you in that area is obviously compromised." As far as Samir was concerned, this was a minor matter. Frankly, he was somewhat surprised that the master-mind of Al Qaeda would be so preoccupied with something that could be doing nothing more than filling his pockets with gold. *Surely there are things more important than Ayman's personal finances to be considered at a time like this*, he criticized internally.

But truly, he did not know the importance of drug demand to the Doctor's plans, and to Al Qaeda's ultimate victory. No one did. And the one man who did understand was certainly not going to bring anyone else into what appeared to be a narrowing circle—a tightening noose.

"All right, all right," the Doctor demurred. "That opportunity is lost." He paused to let that settle in a bit with Samir. Sensing a relaxation of tension, he added, "How much do you know about these two, Samir? I mean, what intel did you gather in order to play them?"

Realizing Samir might wonder why it even mattered, he immediately added, "You know, Samir, I am very angry with Andrew Weir and Brian Washington Carver—very angry."

"Yes, I am aware of that, with good reason."

"And I will hurt them, Samir. They have interfered with an operational strategy, and are hindering our ability to take the United States out of the game permanently. For that they will pay."

"I understand." He didn't really, but Samir decided to forestall any confrontation with Ayman Al-Zawahiri until he and everyone else were in the presence of Usama Bin Laden.

"What I need from you are the addresses of these two men, if you have them—and anyone else who is close to them. I would need names and addresses of any close family, or friends. Do you still have access to such information?"

"Most definitely. I have my personal computer with me. All sensitive business has always been transacted on my laptop. They will find nothing incriminating in my office computer." Looking it over in his mind, he felt he could offer the Doctor some consolation. "I can tell you it will not be a long list, however. One lost almost all his family to one of those sordid, and uniquely American, murder-suicide events. He's a near-orphan, as far as I can tell. The other has only his mother, and a very mysterious friend."

"Male or female?" Zawahiri asked, regarding the friend.

"Male. I do not have time to produce the data right now, as I need to board my plane. But, I will get it to you once I land at the first leg."

"Safe journey, my friend. I will see you at the rendezvous point. And I eagerly await this information I have asked for." Ayman Al-Zawahiri ended the conversation first, on his own terms, determined to seek his revenge.

CHAPTER 58

"**A** pasado algo de tiempo desde la ultima vez que hablamos, Señor," La Hyena said, as he stepped out of the shadows, intercepting the Doctor on a densely covered path. Zawahiri's Spanish had improved over the months, and he was not startled to pick up the mildly critical tone in La Hyena's voice, given the amount of time that had lapsed since their first meeting.

The Doctor decided to ignore any disrespect from the man and pursue what he came for. Despite the fact that he had been here once before, his recollection of the area was vague. Every vista in the tropical forests appeared the same as all the others. The forest enshrouded a man so completely that there were no landmarks on the horizon for Zawahiri to use to get his bearings. It was unnerving. But in fact, he had selected this area of the world, to augment their operations in the Philippines, for precisely this reason.

Not only did it accomplish their objective of being close to Mexico, and thereby the United States, but the landscape was almost impenetrable. The Colombian government, aided by the United States and others, had been trying to locate and destroy the FARC for years. And, although there was an occasional success, the beast only seemed to get stronger.

"That is true. And I have good news." The Doctor was proud of his command of the Spanish language, but thought he heard La Hyena laugh quietly under his breath nonetheless.

Once again, the Doctor's head was covered by a hood, and, once again, he was led deeper and higher into the protective cover. Just about the time he was feeling weak, and in need of water, La Hyena stopped and removed the hood. Looking around, reminding himself to maintain the appearance of perfect control and confidence, the Doctor sat and took a long drink. He was thinking. And, it had not escaped his notice that today there were just the two of them, accompanied by the lone interpreter he had used before.

This confirms my estimation that La Hyena is actually the man in charge, the Doctor thought, applauding himself. Easing into the conversation, but wanting to maintain the upper hand, the Doctor said, "I presume we are not waiting for the men from Venezuela or Cuba."

La Hyena smiled. Because his face was dirty, and his complexion dark, his teeth looked abnormally prominent as he did so. Most assuredly, the man did not smile often, and the Doctor could not help but reflect how truly terrifying it would be for La Hyena's victims to witness that smile, just as they were dying. He looked like an emissary from Satan for sure. This pleased the Doctor.

"Are you ready for us?" he asked, without ceremony of any kind.

"Nosotros estamos," the man confirmed immediately; then he continued through the interpreter who shadowed him. "We feel you should continue your activities in the Philippines as well. But, we are most definitely ready for you all to receive safe-harbor from us. And you will also find it a very desirable training ground."

Knowing that he would have time to view this, the Doctor was eager to conclude this negotiation step. "And your demands in return, or, should I say, your expectations?"

"A percentage of your heroin and opium trade—worldwide."

Before he could play the game of pretending to yield to great demands, the Doctor first needed to know what percentage. "And the percentage, my friend?"

At that point, La Hyena suddenly snapped a limb from the tree they were resting under, and drew a number in the moist soil at their feet. It was high, very high. But the Doctor knew the options were limited now. Not wanting to give that away, he frowned for a moment, carefully making certain La Hyena observed this. "And what of the Venezuelan and Cuban portion?"

La Hyena laughed characteristically. "This is between you and me, señor. They're backed off in a holding pattern, awaiting the larger political aspects of our game. Their gain comes in the more international scope of this, per your original—and I might add—brilliant plan."

"So, this is strictly our billet for accommodations, then?"

"Very well put."

Two hours later, the Doctor completed his inspection of the housing and training areas that Al Qaeda would be using for operations in this part of the world. During that time, he had seen many well-armed and well-trained men. And, he felt comfortable.

"What is our best direction of approach?"

"Bring your men in through Peru, or Ecuador; avoid Panama. When we know your men are coming, we will send people to bring them to us here."

"Fair enough. And you have the authority to conclude this today?"

"Yo lo hago," he confirmed. However, La Hyena seemed to be holding something back, something unspoken.

"I also have authority from UBL to conclude this."

Now La Hyena laughed abruptly, disarming the Doctor momentarily. Quickly he added, "Of course you do!" Seeing that the Doctor was not following, he grinned, winked, and added, "You look very different from your pictures."

Not knowing how much the man knew, or if he was just bluffing, the Doctor decided not to tip his hand. "Yes, well you know what they say about television cameras—they make you look pounds heavier." He turned to face La Hyena squarely when he completed his response, ready for anything.

Fortunately, La Hyena laughed robustly and loudly, smacked the Doctor on the back very familiarly, and said, "Me gustas tu! We will be good friends, Señor."

The Doctor nodded his agreement. Feeling he had something concrete to take to Usama, something which might further the justification he would provide for having taken control of Al Qaeda and having drugged its commander, he started to relax. *I gambled, and I have won, again,* he silently congratulated himself. *I am the link. Usama has no deal, and no new staging ground, without me— alive. Only I know who this new friend of mine is, and how to find him.*

He took a deep breath and reminded himself, *He demands a great deal, this new friend of mine. He must need money. And I must keep an eye on him. Treachery is his love.* Then, apparently satisfied that he could handle it, he concluded, *And that will make him mine to control.*

Though this was clearly a victory for Al Qaeda, or at the very least a respite for them, the other events and losses still weighed on Zawahiri's mind. With a heavy heart, he knew he would have to keep the rendezvous appointment in Pakistan. It was set for November 4, 2008—and it was a meeting at which he would have to appear in person. If he survived it, he would return to *this* forbidding place to begin again.

He would have to, for they had lost Iraq. They would lose Pakistan, and Afghanistan a second time. He knew his military games too well, and his intelligence games. The longer a military engagement with the United States goes on, history had shown, the more determined the military becomes, and the more adaptive they become.

With Samir out of the game temporarily, there were no offsetting public relations campaigns that could be guaranteed to engender fear and create enough havoc with the neurotic American public. Short of the mind-control he had come so close to perfecting, whereby he could control the American people remotely, by increasing their demand for drugs that impaired their judgment, he saw no way for this to end well for Al Qaeda.

His one small hope was that they would at least escape to this new place, select and train new commanders, and survive to fight again. For him, though, the delicious victory he had hoped to live long enough to witness seemed to be evaporating in front of him. Carver & Weir had done this.

What infuriated him the most was the idea that he was facing checkmate moves on multiple games, and he doubted these two had any idea they were even interfering with his master plan, let alone playing the most elaborate set of interconnected chess games ever conceived. There was not a war college on the planet that could have imagined this. Of that, he was sure. *How could these two have guessed?* the Doctor lamented. *No one could have guessed what I planned, let alone how I planned to do it—no one.*

The loss of the one thing he needed to accomplish his masterpiece, however, was the most galling of all. It had wormed its way into Ayman Al-Zawahiri's psyche, and he could not shake it. For Ali Roos's cell to prevail, and create the devastation he salivated over, the market for drugs of all kinds had to remain at the high he had so skillfully engineered for the last twenty years. It was not. Carver & Weir's game "White King Rising" had changed all that. And, without Samir in place, he saw no realistic way of counteracting the game's effects—not with literacy groups, ministers, and a whole bunch of what the Doctor called "do-gooders" jumping on the bandwagon. No, this game was lost—at least for now.

Trying to regain some mental footing, as he and La Hyena carefully navigated physically down the path to their origin point, he took some small comfort in the fact that Roos's attack would launch nonetheless. The pharmacist was on a timer. *Even if it is 10 million, not 50 million, it will still be the greatest single attack in history. Even if 1 million....* He sustained the dwindling spiral of expectation.

At the foot of the path, rage returned. Folklore says that when a dragon is mortally wounded, the dragon is still capable of inflicting some of its greatest damage, in its death throes. As it flails, and rages, its tail alone can sweep and destroy anything in its path. And that is exactly what would happen now, as this dragon died.

"My friend, one last request, before I return to Usama."

"Sí?" La Hyena straightened up.

"There is some unfinished business in the States." Reaching into his pocket, the Doctor pulled out the folded email Samir had sent him with two names and addresses on it. Looking at it briefly, he deliberated over which would cause the greatest pain. *Revenge demands pain, more than damage.* And he intended the revenge of a terrorist to be silent, cunning, and shattering.

Hopefully, he looked to La Hyena and asked, "Do you have someone who can 'take care' of this person for me?" Without taking his eyes off his accomplice, he pointed to one name.

La Hyena's left brow raised slightly. He asked simply, "Tiene usted una fotografia?"

"I do not," the Doctor responded, trying to conceal his chagrin at not providing a picture of the target.

"No matter," La Hyena concluded. "We do have someone. He is known as El Viper."

"Fine."

"Cuando le gustaria esto teminado, señor?"

"Before the end of the year."

"Of course, I do not know the man's schedule," La Hyena spoke somewhat deferentially, "but I would expect that to be doable." He spat on the ground, the silence interrupted by what sounded like cicadas in the trees overhead. Then he whispered, "El es muy caro."

Is he testing me? Is this fool testing me to see if Al Qaeda can pay? Ayman seethed beneath his apparent smile of gratitude. *He has no idea who he is dealing with!* "I expect he would be. Thank you. I will personally compensate him."

La Hyena nodded, and pointed the Doctor to the last stretch of the road, which would return him to sunlight, and the city. As La Hyena vanished into the forest, the Doctor smiled, and said out loud, "Well, Mr. Andrew Weir, the tail of the dragon is sweeping!"

The Doctor was clearing the last lock of the Panama Canal, on a ship heading west to ports in Jakarta, Indonesia; Mumbai, India; and Karachi, Pakistan, when his computer signaled the successful transfer of funds from his personal account in Panama to an account in the Grand Caymans. He did not know the name of the recipient. He only knew the nickname, "the Viper."

There, that's done! He congratulated himself, enjoying the view of the city behind him. *Now, on to more important things.*

One week later, a handsome, well-dressed man of apparent Mediterranean descent boarded a non-stop flight from Caracas, Venezuela to Los Angeles. His credentials said he worked for the government of Venezuela, and, when he arrived at Los Angeles

369

International Airport, he stated the purpose for his visit to the United States as "business." His name was Rodrigo Ramirez. And no one in the Venezuelan government had ever heard of him. His visa was valid, however. Whether or not Customs and Immigration liked the idea of admitting visitors from an avowed enemy of the United States, the visa issued by the Department of State superseded their personal opinions.

No one stopped "the Viper." He had not expected them to.

CHAPTER 59

"*H*e's gone to ground."

"Shit!" James shouted to no one in particular inside the Air Italia concourse at LAX. The vehemence and volume of it, however, caused Kelly to turn, as well as Andy and Brian.

"What?" she asked, startled by the outburst, since foul language was extremely uncharacteristic of James. Andy rolled his eyes as well, for he had never even heard James swear. Not one of the three could fathom what had gotten him so agitated.

Feebly, he spoke into the phone, "My apologies, Ari." At the same time, he gestured an apology to strangers in the corridor who'd had their conversations interrupted by his explosion. Motioning to the others to go on ahead to the gate, he stayed back. "This is not good news."

"Well, in a way it is."

"What the hell do you mean by that?" James' voice was low, but the intensity of the question reached its mark.

"That fact proves his complicity." Ari's answer was succinct, almost curt. Then, somewhat more moderately, he added, "James, I know you are out of the game now. But you must understand, this enemy is a patient one—and we are equally patient. Your theory about the investor in the Swiss pharmaceutical company is now validated. You have identified his public relations team, and the head of that team has fled. And my experience has been that innocent men generally do not run."

"I would have preferred to hear you had him in custody."

"As would I, my friend," Ari responded sincerely, "but we have his men, and we have, more importantly, their computers. Our encryption teams, and our steganography experts, are working with the content even as we speak."

Assuaged now, and regaining his normal composure, James thanked his friend. "You know I appreciate the briefing, Ari. Frankly, without you, I would not be in the loop at all."

"Quite the contrary, James. It is Israeli Intelligence that owes you. Without your tip, we would not have thought to look there."

"Right. I see." James said, almost passively.

"My friend, let us, you and me, pray this proves to be a gold mine."

Now James was smiling, and nodding. "You bet. I'm with you 100 percent on that!"

As they were ending the call, Kelly walked back. Her confused look said, "What's going on?"

James pocketed his cell phone and rejoined the three just in time to hear the airline call initial boarding for the non-stop flight to Milan. Andy had purchased a first class ticket for her, and had supplied her with separate envelopes, full of cash, which were to be spent at special locations.

Knowing how frugally Kelly had had to live since the death of his father, he knew she would visit some of these places, but would not spend money. So, the night before, as she was packing for her lengthy trip, he had placed ten separate envelopes on the top of her suitcase. Each place he wanted her to visit and spend money was labeled on the outside, and inside was cash sufficient for her to really experience that location. The places ranged from famous cafes and patisseries to the Pauli Glass Works—one of the most prestigious glass artisans in Venice.

Everyone who visits Venice is told to visit the Murano Glass Works. Few know of Pauli. Kelly did, however, as she had always wanted fine glassware. Whether it was Waterford crystal from Ireland or something exquisite from Venice, she had harbored that desire.

When she opened that particular envelope, Kelly at first had protested that $5,000 was way beyond what he should have expended. "Mom, I am a pretty wealthy guy. And, in case you hadn't noticed, you're my girl!" It was all he had said.

Once they cleared the first hurdle, she was gleeful and almost giddy about each of the remaining envelopes. She looked forward to the whole experience—including the indulgence of the money—for Kelly Weir had never had the luxury of spending any money on herself. Married to a young military man, the little money they did make was spent on the family. Upon the early death of her husband due to cancer, she had nothing left. And anything she earned went to her gifted son.

Her sacrifices had not gone unnoticed over the years. And, long before he had any true way of providing some luxuries for his mother, Andrew Weir had dreamed of it, and made a list. Today, at the airport, he was fulfilling one of his dreams, as much as Kelly was fulfilling one of hers.

"So, you got the envelopes where you can find them?"

"You bet!" She exuded enthusiasm. "First one is in Venice. I guess I'll convert it to Euros there."

Then, she noticed James standing nearby, grinning. "What are you grinning about?" she asked playfully.

"Oh, nothing. I'm just excited for you." James just gazed at her, then, leaning in to her for some privacy, he added softly, "You look beautiful."

Hearing the call now for First Class, Kelly grabbed her purse and overnight carry-on and said, "Well, I think I'll board now."

"So early? You got an hour still!" "Give us a call when you land." "I'll miss you." They all overlapped to the point she couldn't tell who had said what. So, she simply hugged each man, separately and distinctly, and started toward the gate door. Just as she was about to walk down the gangway, she stopped, turned, and called to James, "James, the answer is *yes*." She winked, and then she was gone.

Brian and Andy turned to James, as if to inquire what that was all about, but James beat them to it. "Did she just say, 'the answer is yes'?" They nodded. "She said, 'yes.'"

"Yes," Andy responded, nudging Brian with his right elbow. "She said yes."

Pretending he was still clueless on this, Brian said, "I...I...don't get it. Yes to what?"

"Kid, Pal, let me buy you a drink." Pausing for effect, James couldn't contain it any longer, and added, "I am an engaged man!"

A quick round of beer later, James set down his glass and announced, "I have to talk to the FBI." Then he left. Andy jokingly called after him, to no avail, "Hey, I thought you said you were buying!"

Brian was laughing. Turning to his friend, Andy challenged him. "What? What you laughin' at?"

"Oh, nothin'. Not a thing!" Cuffing Andy slightly on the back of the head, he added, "This has been a *really* good day!"

As Brian signaled for the tab, the bartender handed another patron, who was sitting to Brian's right, his credit card and receipt. "Thank you, Mr. Ramirez. I appreciate it." The bartender fawned over the man, pleased with the generous tip.

"You are most welcome," Rodrigo Ramirez responded, as he gracefully rose and exited the bar.

CHAPTER 60

*B*yron Johnson was a thirty-year veteran of the Federal Bureau of Investigation, and the man in charge of the Bureau's Los Angeles office. He'd seen a lot of things in his career, and he'd had his fair share of shocking revelations.

But, what he read in the copy of James Mikolas's original report to the CIA regarding a game theory he and this chess wizard, Andrew Weir, developed, was the epitome of revelations.

The idea that the mastermind of Al Qaeda was only vaguely interested in religion and war, and truly hell-bent on using propaganda, fear, media, and pharmaceuticals to render Americans irrational and incompetent, all the while getting rich, was stunning.

Almost four years earlier, officials at Langley had concluded Mikolas had lost it at best, and was possibly complicit at worst. Had Byron not spent his career in a city noted for its imagination, he might have dismissed it with the same derision the CIA bosses had. But, he had a somewhat different take today.

Part of it stemmed from the fact that James, whom he'd had dealings with over the years, was sitting calmly, though intently, at his desk, waiting while Johnson read the report. The other was that in the FBI files on James Mikolas, and in their files on counterterrorism, there was a report from Israel's intelligence agency. It seems the Israelis gave more credence to James' theories than his own government did.

Doesn't surprise me one bit, Byron thought critically. *That agency of ours was behind in the game, and still is.* He decided to run with his own instinct. Closing the file, he sat down opposite James and asked, "Okay, James, so, what's the sequel?"

James couldn't help but smile at that reference, and was relieved to be taken seriously.

It took him only a few minutes to lay out their current conclusions that, not only was Zawahiri the Swiss pharmaceutical investor the Israelis had identified who had miraculously escaped just as Mossad was closing in, but that Samir Taghavi was more than just a gifted and highly paid owner of an advertising and marketing firm—much more. They believed him to be Al Qaeda's public relations chief, and worse than that, they believed him to be operating inside the United States.

"James, you sure your man Ari will confirm they tracked this guy Samir, and took down his Paris operation, and have confirmed an Al Qaeda public relations cell?"

Without even a second's hesitation, James confirmed. "He will." Wanting to get moving, James pushed Byron a bit. "That's why time is imperative here, Byron. The man's other operations are inside the US, at least two of them, and we have a chance of getting him."

The prospect of capturing a high-level Al Qaeda operative inside the US almost made Johnson salivate. To be sure, it would be one of the biggest busts of his already-illustrious career. But failure would be a bust of a whole other nature. And like his predecessors at the CIA before him, he had to decide just how much of his pension and career he was willing to risk on a man the insiders regarded to be a quack.

"Okay, help me here, James." Byron tried to settle James down. "Let's say this guy is who you and the Israelis think he is." Before James could protest about his apparent speculation, he quickly raised a hand and said, "Now hold on there. Let me just talk this through a bit." James relaxed, nodded his submission, and Byron continued. "All right. We have Al Qaeda's PR chief inside the US, and God knows where else. He's here. What is he here for?"

"Spreading disinformation, and redirecting some of our watchdogs."

When Byron looked up at James, he saw a bulldog look, and a real determination. He just knew this next answer was not going to be pleasant. *Shit, and I had dinner plans tonight!* But he asked the question, knowing full well the answer would be shattering. Fortifying himself with a gigantic intake of air, Byron Johnson asked, "All right, who?"

James didn't want the man to have to hold his breath too long, so he answered only with what he knew, not what he and Andy might still be speculating on. "We know he is hooked up with the WNG-LA anchorwoman, Alicia Quixote. He has been interviewed on major network news as an expert on the public relations aspects of our activities in Iraq and Afghanistan, and the probable negative consequences of those actions."

Byron now looked as sick as he felt. And he knew the other shoe was about to drop, because he could see James wasn't done. Feebly, he reached for his water glass and took a sip. James couldn't help but notice that Byron's hand was shaking. Wanting to get this over with, he concluded, "And we know he is often a personal guest of Bud Walker's at private media and industry get-togethers."

"Which means he's wormed his way into the media."

"Precisely," James confirmed laconically.

"Can you prove his connection to this Quixote woman and Walker, and Al Qaeda?"

"Not without your help," James answered, and then qualified it a bit. "At least the woman and Walker part."

Byron Johnson got up slowly from his desk and walked to one of the picture windows, which afforded him a view up into the hills above Beverly Hills. His heart was pounding. He knew what he wanted to do. And he knew what he couldn't do. Now, he had to explain this to an obviously dedicated and passionate hunter of vermin.

"James, it's not that I don't believe you. I do." He noticed Mikolas' jaw was setting, thrusting forward, and a vein in his temple was pulsing, so Byron spat it out as quickly as he could. "I do. But you and I both know I cannot take this upstairs, given that it involves an internationally known businessman—and philanthropist I might add—and one of the largest news agencies in the world."

"Why the hell not?" James asked belligerently. "No one is above the law. Besides, we don't know if they've done anything wrong. They may just lead us to him, and save themselves in the process."

"Don't look at me like I don't have a pair," Byron retorted. "I've got as good a set as you. But, you don't get it. The election's next week. What, five days away?"

"I know when the damned election is!" James shouted.

"What the hell does that have to do with anything?"

Byron snorted and laughed. "It has everything to do with it." Seeing that James truly was not following this, he explained. "Do you have any idea what would happen if the FBI starts looking for, questioning, interviewing—or any other damned thing—a close friend of one of the candidates?"

This truly did take James' breath away, for he had given no consideration whatsoever to the political ramifications of the FBI investigating a major network for its relationships to Al Qaeda, five days before the election. Even he could see it would be viewed as sandbagging or ambushing a political campaign in order to sway the election outcome by besmirching known associates of candidates—and, worse yet, done by an agency of the United States. *God damn,* he cursed to himself, *the son of a bitch is going to get away. And he may get away with it.*

Seeing that James was as subdued as any handcuffed individual they'd had in these interrogation rooms, Byron offered him one bit of hope. "James, you see what I'm up against here?" James silently nodded that he did. "Well, the election will be over in five days. My investigation, however, will just be beginning. And, I promise you, James Mikolas, that I will conduct a good one—and there won't be any damned leaks to compromise it, and there won't be any accusations that can't be proved, and I do not go to the prosecutors until I am ready." He stopped to let that sink in, and then added, "And if Mr. Walker is involved, well too bad for him. If he's not, we may at least rescue the poor stupid, what was it you called him?"

"Watchdog."

"Right. Watchdog. Let's hope he *is* one, and not a traitor—for all our sakes."

James knew that was the right viewpoint. It was hard to see as clearly as he wanted through his disappointment, but he knew they still had a shot here. Maybe they couldn't get Samir this time, but they would get some result. He asked with a hint of irony, "Isn't there anything we can do *today?* The man would possess so much intel. You guys need that."

Byron was ahead of James. He was back at his desk, making entries on a form. Looking up, he smiled. "Yup. There's one thing."

"Yeah, what's that?"

On the basis of your report, James, and this recent intel from Israel, I'm authorizing a stakeout on your man, Samir. He's probably switched identities by now—if Mossad is right. But maybe he'll turn up at one of his haunts. We'll pull video on him right now to get a good photo. We'll spot him."

"If he's still here."

"If he's still here," Byron repeated. "We'll be looking at all international flights."

As he was leaving, James turned to Byron Johnson and cordially advised, "You'd better hurry. These people are very smart."

"Would you like an extra pillow, Mr. Ramirez?" the flight attendant asked dutifully. "We're flying light tonight, and we have extra."

"No, thank you. I am most comfortable already."

"Andy, you would not believe how beautiful this city is!" Kelly exclaimed into the cell phone Andy had provided. It would receive calls anywhere in Europe. "I'm on the Lido, and I can't believe it. It's November already, but it is still warm here, and is just so colorful and clear."

Happy that she was enjoying this first leg of her trip, he reminded her, "That's great, Mom, I thought you'd enjoy staying outside of Venice and get a thrill out of taking the launches into the city. One thing, though, don't forget the envelope I gave you for Venice."

"Oh no, I haven't. In fact, tomorrow I'm going to San Marco square. And, after lunch, I'm spending the afternoon at the glass works."

"Mom," Andy added, not knowing why, "If you need more

money, just call. You know, in case you want something special for the, you know, wedding." He couldn't believe he'd said that. He'd never thought his mother would remarry. But, he was truly joyful that she was, and especially that she and James had finally realized what Andy had seen for some time.

She giggled, almost squealed, and for a moment, mother and son enjoyed a silent appreciation of things that do turn out right in life. Then, putting her mom hat back on, she said, "Thank you. I may take you up on that."

Then, before signing off, she remembered why she'd called in the first place. The next day, Andy and Brian were the featured speakers at a college forum in San Francisco. Given their planned remarks, and that the questions they wanted to address pertained to the responsibilities of the young, and the forces that inhibit those young, Carver & Weir were entering into a new level of advocacy. Their message was clear, and they intended to use the idea of games to invigorate and mobilize a generation to play a game that led to sanity, peace, and awareness. Money had brought them the wherewithal; the game had provided them the platform; their life experiences had inspired their cause.

"Andy, you have your first forum tomorrow." It was a statement, not a question, and Andy knew that meant some advice was to follow. "I want you to know that I am so proud of you. I'm sorry I won't be there to hear you in person, but I know you and Brian are embarking on something that will influence so many, in such a great way. And I wish you luck."

"Thanks, Mom. We're videoing, so you can watch it later."

"You bet. My last event is Christmas Mass at the Vatican, and then I'll be headed back. So, I'll watch all your videos before New Years. Love you, son."

"Love you, too, Mom."

CHAPTER 61

"*G*razi," Kelly said, with true appreciation as the waiter placed her cup of cappuccino in front of her. She didn't really need a hot drink today, as Venice was enjoying a splendid fall afternoon, but it was an indulgence she could afford.

Sitting alongside San Marco Square at a sidewalk café, she was watching the crowd in the piazza, and observing the many types of people who were coming and going from the Cathedral. Though she'd seen pictures many times of this famous square, with all its pigeons, she didn't really know how much a part of the landscape they were. There were thousands of them. Some walked on the ground, seeking any scrap that might be left from the myriad cafes that framed the square. Others perched, then swept upward with a truly noisy flutter of wings. Many roosted in the crevices of buildings centuries old, and cooed. But, they provided an unmistakable mystique to this mysterious city of canals and alleys.

Beaming, Kelly felt she should pinch herself. *What a change a year makes,* she reflected. *Andy, Brian—now James and me—we are all living different lives.* Making a joke, she said out loud, "Wonder if this is what Obama had in mind?" Then reproaching herself just a little, she paid her bill, draped around her shoulder the new grey and mauve silk shawl she'd purchased in a charming cubby-hole shop, and stepped out into the square.

Debating whether to see the Cathedral first, or go to the Pauli Glass Works, which were behind the edifice and down a short alley, she decided to use the envelope first; relish the shopping; and then go and say her rosary and light a candle.

Judging by the density of the crowd now in the mid-afternoon sun, she concluded that this was a smart choice. *Too many people right now. I'd like a little quiet in the church.* And she wove her way through the crowd, trying not to disrupt too many of the picture-takers. She had not noticed the man at the table next to her, who likewise rose and strode into the crowd. To an observer, it would have looked as though he was letting her clear the way, and that he was merely slipping in behind her to avoid the jostling crowd.

Stopping for just a second to verify the street name, she continued into a much narrower street, eager to get to the factory. Though narrower, the small via was crowded as well. *There is something I would like for James and me,* she thought, making a mental note. *I hope they have it, and I hope they have it in blue.*

James would never know what gift Kelly had in mind for him. For, just as the idea of it brought an uninhibited, broad smile to her face, the man known as the Viper slid up behind her. And, with the thrust of his dagger, he penetrated and stopped Kelly Weir's heart.

His skill was legendary. She was gone before her body slipped to the pavement, and before he had vanished.

James was just listening to a heartbreaking but inevitable message from Byron Johnson. As he had feared, Samir was gone. Seems he'd booked a flight to Paris, and never boarded. Their look into his bank accounts—now that he was officially "suspicious"—revealed he had left most of his money there. But, that "look" also revealed he had entered his safety deposit box. All that remained in the box was a weapon. Knowing now that James' theory about the man was likely true, Johnson had more to take upstairs. It had been only a matter of minutes before the FBI had secured the surveillance cameras inside and outside the bank.

"And, that has revealed something—I should say *someone*—very interesting. Call me." That was the end of the voicemail. Just as he was putting the phone back into his pocket, hoping to catch the last of the boys' talk, Andy's cell phone went off. James had been put in charge of it, so there wouldn't be any distractions during their presentation. James answered it.

Brian and Andy were both on stage, facing some fairly hostile questions, frankly, when James took the unexpected call on Andy's cell phone. Brian had finished his remarks and happened to look out to the audience just at that moment.

He saw it first—the shock on James' face, followed by an immediate draining of blood. Pale and wobbly, James struggled to maintain his balance, nearly knocking over a student as he tried to brace himself against the back of a chair.

"Hey, man," Brian whispered to himself, wishing he could lip read.

James looked at Brian and seemed to murmur some kind of apology. He was clearly stricken. Lip reading or no, Brian Carver had made a career of knowing when a ball was coming to him. And today was no exception.

Andy had some very important concluding remarks, and some truly salient points, for these young students. If Andy's argument penetrated, by the end of the day, several hundred young men and women would be taking a hard look at the choices they had made, and the ones they could make. It was important for Andy to finish.

Leaning in to Andy, Brian whispered, "Hey, I'm done here. You take 'em on home, brother. You're the man!" Then he smiled, and left the stage.

Andy didn't see the exchange between James and Brian. He was totally into the final moments of a truly remarkable presentation on the ravages of drugs, and the responsibilities of their generation, and was revving up for the conclusion. It was just as well.

Brian took James outside the auditorium, sat him down, and then got him a paper cup of water from the hall dispenser. Waiting, he knew there was some truly bad news. Once James had recovered, and relayed the message he had just received from the American Consulate in Venice, Brian had nothing to say for the first moment. He struggled to repress the terrible images coming into his mind of his own family's tragedy.

Brian Washington Carver was a disciplined young man. He controlled his mind that day, coaching himself. *Do not fail me now!*

The tragic memories responded, as if on command, and receded.

Squatting down in front of James, he firmly said, "James." He repeated it, "James, I am going to tell Andy in a few minutes." Both could hear the loud applause inside, and they knew it would be only a few minutes before Andy would extricate himself from the group and come looking for them.

James started to protest, rousing himself to do what needed to be done. But, Brian placed a hand on his shoulder, and held him firmly in his chair. "James, listen to me, brother. I am the one to do it." Seeing James' questioning expression, he explained, "Mrs. Weir was the messenger who came to me that day." His voice faltered momentarily. "I have to do this for her now. You have to trust me here, James. Some messages have to be delivered by a 'brother.'"

CHAPTER 62

*T*he dangers of getting here outweighed, frankly, the danger of being here, the Doctor concluded, as he struggled against the almost unimaginable cold and wind he'd endured during the last quarter-mile trek to the rendezvous point.

He had had some weeks to prepare his strategy—look over the chess board, if you will—and identify what move Bin Laden would likely make next. It was in that process that he had seen it. It was simple really. Bin Laden was not much of a chess player, actually, but he was a practical man. And the more the Doctor thought about it, the more he realized Bin Laden's choices were limited. Smiling, he congratulated himself on having maneuvered the game in such a way as to give Bin Laden only one move.

"Amazing," he had said to himself. "Usama is bright. He'll see this."

They were all there. The four of them stood in the crude but well-heated shelter inside the Waziristan section of Pakistan. They were all that remained of the original cadre of commanders of Al Qaeda. All others had been killed or captured. Though the realization of that was a somber moment for each of them, they at least were safe, for now, amongst tribes who supported them, and who hated the free Pakistan that was developing. Solemnly, the rendezvous commenced.

Makkawi was the least "in the know," and would prove to be the most compliant. He should be. He was, after all, a subordinate, nothing more.

Samir, in his somewhat less strenuous journey to the rendezvous, had concluded his necessary next move as well. His only ambition today was to *stay alive*, and *needed*, by whoever emerged on top. The political infighting of his superiors had never held interest or intrigue for him in the past, and did not today. It was just a showdown to survive, as far as he was concerned.

And Usama Bin Laden *had* chosen exactly as the Doctor had foreseen. After all, he reasoned, what choice did he have? In a showdown between him and the Doctor, he had no real proof of treachery or betrayal by Zawahiri. He had the word of the Administrator who had rescued him from drugs, but the reality was he had been cared for and kept alive for years. And that was the nagging question Bin Laden played over and over in his own mind: *Why did he keep me alive? If he wanted control of Al Qaeda, why didn't he kill me? The others thought me dead. The mythical proportions are indeed greater if I were dead, and never found.* For weeks, this inconsistency of motive had hounded Bin Laden.

Finally, he had seen what the Doctor knew he would. Bin Laden could not risk a division and rift within Al Qaeda. For recruiting, fund-raising, negotiating—everything—this group, though diminished in numbers by the American military, had to appear to be as united and as threatening as ever. *Divided, they fall.* It was true for the Americans, and it was true for Al Qaeda.

And the Doctor, knowing Bin Laden and the others truly needed him to relocate them to their new sanctuary and training grounds, had concluded there would be no killing here today— and none in the foreseeable future. He knew he could handle Bin Laden when he wanted to. He had adeptly handled their Atef problem, and their Zarqawi problem. He could handle their Bin Laden problem as well. *After all, I am still the man's physician, and he is still sick.*

So, an unspoken agreement cemented immediately between Ayman Al-Zawahiri and Usama Bin Laden. They had been conspirators long enough to decide that what they knew about each other would remain a secret to the others. One day, one would emerge on top. But, for now, their surviving warriors deserved a modicum of peace of mind, and their cause deserved some resurgence.

The tension in the room was palpable though, as no one dared be the first to speak. Like experienced card players concealing their hands, bluffing in their posturing, no one wanted to be the first to "call." Finally exhaling, with his breath condensing due to the coldness of the room, Usama took the lead. "Ayman, my friend, I am so very glad to see you once again, and I commend your efforts on our behalf."

He opened his arms for the customary embrace. While the others dared to exhale in relief, the Doctor took Bin Laden's cue and convincingly said, "And I am most grateful to be returned to your presence as well, and honored to have served." They embraced—each man thinking, *Keep your enemies close.*

Then, as if they had rehearsed it all, Usama joked as only he could, "So, Ayman, what do you make of our little charade? Did we fool them all?"

Observing the barely-camouflaged looks of confusion on the faces of Makkawi and Samir, who had yet to even take a seat, the Doctor responded, "It would seem so, my friend, it would seem so."

Beckoning for his three primary players to remove their outer garments, to be seated near the fire where their spirits as well as their bodies could thaw, and to take some repast, Bin Laden's direct question opened Al Qaeda's new chapter. "So, now that I have returned, what do we have in store for the Americans next?"

Unbeknownst to Ayman Al-Zawahiri, he faced an additional enemy now—one he had helped to create but whose development threatened his plan at its most sinister core. As the senior members of Al Qaeda gloated in their accomplishments and in the international economic spirals and free-falls they had created, they had overlooked one thing.

Andrew Weir had stated years earlier that Zawahiri would make a mistake, and that it would be his undoing. Weir was right, though he, too, would not have guessed the area of the oversight, or its magnitude.

Despising the United States as they did, and despising everything about its Free Enterprise and Capitalistic system, the Doctor had overlooked a particular trait of American businesses— particularly Big Business. Never having espoused the socialist tendency to take care of everybody, even if it meant the corporation and everyone in it went down, American corporations could be counted on to lay people off in hard economic times. It was one of their most dreaded traits. No one could have guessed that this often-criticized mindset was about to subvert Ayman Al-Zawahiri's doomsday plan—least of all the Doctor.

While he plotted his continued control of Al Qaeda, and anticipated June 30, 2011, he had failed also to consider the second-most-dreaded trait of America's corporations—their propensity for laying off their most senior, most experienced people, especially if doing so saved them a pension payout. The older executives would be booted, and the responsibilities turned over to younger, lesser-experienced people who cost less. Such a viewpoint would never have occurred to Bin Laden or Zawahiri. In their minds, your best men are your best men; you keep them; you don't get rid of them for inexperienced personnel. That, through all the years, was their operational philosophy.

Yet, five giant pharmaceutical manufacturers in the United States, who were facing catastrophic sales losses in their previous year, had drawn up the list of names of managers who could be pared from their rosters as lay-offs became necessary. Ironically, each senior vice president of operations had independently concluded that his production manager, who supervised the final stages of drug production, was dispensable. Especially since these production managers had been climbing the corporate ladder for almost twenty years now, it was determined they would have to go, and their responsibilities be turned over to the newer, less costly generation of managers.

Each of the men affected by his termination notice knew the significance to the attack scheduled for June 30, 2011 of his being fired, but none knew the fate of the others, and none knew how to reach the Doctor. Without his even knowing it, the foolproof security the Doctor had so brilliantly implemented to preserve the autonomy of each cell became a boomerang, taking out his insidious plan.

Of the cell the Doctor had so painstakingly put together, and nourished secretly for fifteen years, only Ali Roos still had a job. And, on election morning, after returning from casting his ballot, Ali Roos was called to the office of the hospital administrator for a "talk."

EPILOGUE

*J*ames recognized him immediately. Ari's demeanor never changed, nor did his appetite. James approached him deferentially, as he couldn't help but think that if he had only understood Ari the first time they had met here in the 1990s, Ayman Al-Zawahiri would never have lived to commit his heinous crimes—and Kelly would never have died.

Silently, he slipped into a chair at Ari's table and waited for Ari to swallow the last of his pastry. Ari took a deep breath, gently wiped his mouth with the checkered napkin, and finally looked at his colleague. "Was she someone special to you?"

James looked up and answered deliberately, "Yes. Very." That was all he said, but Ari knew how much James was withholding. He also knew not to ask. It was an unspoken rule among men in their profession never to ask the personal question. In their world of secrets, each man deserved respect.

Instead, he pulled out a small manila folder from his briefcase, placed it on the table directly in front of James, and said, "Then you will want to see this."

Eagerly James opened the folder and stared at the face of the man who had taken so much from Andy and from him. He knew this must be the man, since Ari had called requesting the meeting. "Is this him?"

"Yes."

"Are you certain?"

"Yes. He showed up on the Venice police report in an addendum they did to Interpol. The Italians are sure he is the one who killed the American woman. It matches his signature of kills." As soon as he said it, Ari wished he had been more circumspect. After all, they weren't just talking about *any* victim.

389

This woman meant something to James. Ari scolded himself for never having any tact.

James, however, did not seem to care. Mercifully, he seemed to be detached from the emotion of it, holding his professional demeanor with the grit Ari remembered. "His name is Rodrigo Ramirez, or at least that's the last alias Interpol has on him. He is from Venezuela. His code name is 'the Viper,' in deference to how close and personal he gets to his victims." Apologetically he added, "I'm sorry, James."

"Don't be. It helps to know who."

Ari nodded, but said nothing further. Both men sat for a minute, as if enjoying the sun splash on their table. The clouds were breaking up. James broke the silence. "What's next?"

Quietly, Ari reached across the table, closed the folder, and slipped it into his briefcase once again. Rising, he stood straight as a soldier and said, "This one I will handle myself."

James stood to pull a couple of bills from his pocket for the waitress. He almost couldn't ask, but he had to. "Do you know where he is?"

"No. But I will soon." It was said with such certainty. James admired this trait in the Israeli's—this absolute confidence that they were ahead in the game. Given that Interpol had no idea where Ramirez was, and that he was as illusive as a viper, James decided to ask.

"How do you know that?"

Ari was glad he'd asked. He was proud of his game, and especially proud of the trap he had created for Rodrigo Ramirez. Uncharacteristically, he smiled and slapped James on the back. "Because I'm about to hire him to do a job for *us*. He's negotiating via email as we speak. That should bring me up close and personal to this 'viper,' don't you think?" Then, as if to sober the conversation appropriately, he added, "Be well, my friend."

There was sadness around James now. Kelly was gone; he was on his way to Arlington. The man who killed her would be taken out, but not the man who sent him—at least not by Ari, or the Israelis, or the Pakistanis. It would be the White King who would take him down now. Brian and Andy would stay with the White King until the job was done. Ayman Al-Zawahiri would lose his game to drug Americans and exercise the mass brainwashing and sedation he had planned. Whatever apocalypse he planned after that would be a moot point.

Though James could barely contain the grief, there was the definite bittersweet sense of victory he had felt before. James Mikolas was a disciplined man. He would face this. He had to. And now, he had to get to Arlington.

Brian arrived first. Not wanting to get to the grave early, he was hanging out at the entrance when Andy arrived holding the ivory chess box Kelly had given him under his right arm.

Both men walked briskly down the familiar path to the grave. Though wives were rarely allowed to be buried with their men at Arlington, Andy had decided that Kelly would be with his father. James had tried all his connections within the government, but no one had any more interest in helping them with *this* than they had in the first few years after 9/11. But Andy was never one to be deterred, and he had figured a way.

James joined them just as they reached the Tomb of the Unknown Soldier. The guard detail knew them, and the Captain of the Guard guessed why they were there, and what they were about to do.

My job is to guard the Tomb, he told himself. *I can't be babysitting the rest of this cemetery.* And with that, he brought himself and the two guards to attention as James, Brian, and Andy passed. It was the least he could do for the courageous woman who had been so kind to him and his men through the years. It was the least he could do for his dead buddy, and he was not going to interfere with this son, and his final plans.

As they approached Greg Weir's grave, James asked, pointing to the ivory box, "Is that…?"

"Yes. She told me once she wanted to be cremated." And then, as an afterthought, he added, "She probably expected me to do something more creative with this chess box she gave me on my twenty-first birthday, but it was the most fitting thing I could think of."

James nodded. Brian said nothing, chewing on his lower lip.

The afternoon was turning into a perfect Thanksgiving Day. It was early yet, and the damp cold that plagued Washington in the winter months was not even a threat today. Today *was* perfect.

Andy could not bury his mother at Arlington. But he could scatter her ashes over the grave of his father. And he intended to do so. There were rules about this, but frankly, he didn't care. No one would know. By nightfall, her ashes would have kissed his father's grave, and then blown on to grace the area around. That is how he would remember her grave—not as a stone monument or cross—but as the light, faithful spirit he loved.

"Thank you, Mom," he said softly, as he took the lid off the chess box and gingerly dropped the ashes it contained onto the area around the grave. James could barely breathe, and looked away to his friend, Abe. Sunlight reflected off the famous monument, making it appear almost golden at that moment. Brian placed his arm gently around his partner's shoulder. "I will miss you. And I want you to keep the faith, Mom. We will come through this. Brian and I—and James—will bring the White King through this. I promise."

That was all he said before he closed the lid and returned the box to its position under his arm. The three turned to leave, intending to take a different pathway back to the exit. It was then that he saw her.

He didn't know if she was there tending a grave, or just pensively exploring the cemetery that was ironically a tourist attraction. All he saw was her red hair. It was the color Kelly's hair had been when Andy was a boy. In the afternoon sun, it shimmered like a precious metal. She paused on the path in front of them, as if she wanted to say something to him. But she hesitated to speak.

Years earlier, Andy would have walked by. But Andy had changed. He didn't know why, but he felt he should address her. Motioning to Brian and James to go on ahead, he stopped.

"Do I know you?"

She waited a moment and then answered. "No. Why?"

"You reminded me of someone, that's all—and you looked as if you wanted to say something to me." He smiled.

She looked at him for a moment, just long enough for him to notice her magnificent green eyes, and their genuine sparkle. Then she spoke. "I did. You're Andrew Weir of Carver and Weir, aren't you? The game guy?"

Andy didn't know what to make of this. The conversation had taken a turn he was unprepared for. "Yes, that's me."

She smiled and extended her hand. "I thought so. My name is Reagan, Reagan Lynch."

He took her hand and shook it politely. "It's nice to meet you Reagan Lynch. I'm Andy Weir." Then he added, "Do you work in the District?"

"No, I'm here testifying for a congressional hearing on Monday, and decided to take a walk across the bridge. It's such a beautiful day. I thought I would see the Kennedy grave site and the Tomb of the Unknown Soldier."

"And what do you do, Reagan?"

"I'm a Human Rights Activist, and I'm here to get Americans off drugs."

She had said it so emphatically, so confidently. He looked away for a moment, into the distance, and smiled. Knowing that Kelly would approve, he turned back to this brilliant young woman and asked, "Would you like to join me for a coffee?"

ACKNOWLEDGMENTS

*A*long the way, friends and professional colleagues provided invaluable help with promoting the first book, *White King and the Doctor*, thereby creating a demand for the sequel. Their encouragement and support are profoundly appreciated. Thank you to Steve & Jeannie Luckey, Paul & Muffin Vallely, Rex & Judy Nichols, Theresa Hafen, Ann Good, Kyle Baughan, Ivan & Anne Passer, Jeff Hodgson, Rich DeVos, Marcy Sanders, Juanda Marshall, Marcia Powell, Linda Lombardo, Charles & Tanii Carr, Liam & Shannon Leahy, Suzette Howe, James Krepsbach, Margarete Gowart, Marti Baer, Cat Tebar, Randy Stith, Mary Lou McFate, London Garcia, Ariella Kapelner, "Sam" Warner, Michael Fairman, Verna Sabelle, Chris Hendrie, Millicent Crisp, Todd Smith, Bruce Gridley, Louise & Richard Cole, John & Martha Stevens, Keith & Miriam Schumacher, and to Dana Crisp, who extended her hand to a stranger.

To my dear friend, Jack Potter of www.jbpotter.com, I am much indebted for your swift and spot-on creation of the publishing logo. Thank you for being the artist you are.

I am especially appreciative of the magnificent cover design by Linda Gipson of www.gipsonstudio.com, and of the brilliant editing assistance and internal book design and layout by Stephanee of www.integrativeink.com. You wonderful ladies made this whole process fun and rewarding.

To Eileen Batson of www.BatsonGroupMarketingandPR.blogspot.com – not only a creative publicist, but also an extraordinary friend who has picked up the baton from our dear Jeff—thank you. You are appreciated more than you know.

And last, a heartfelt thank you to my publicist, Laurie

Jessup, whose faith and "no quit" attitude opened doors and put a spotlight on this project. You truly are helping the White King rise.

About The Author

*L*ee Kessler is a television actress, screenwriter, playwright, and stage director. Her career in Hollywood and New York spans thirty-five years, and includes dozens of guest starring roles in episodic TV, mini-series, and movies-of-the-week. She had reoccurring roles in the series *Hill Street Blues* and *Matlock*, and was submitted for Emmy nominations twice for her starring roles in the movie *Collision Course*, and the ABC special, *Which Mother Is Mine?* She co-starred with Peter O'Toole in the movie *Creator*.

Lee became the first actress in the world authorized to portray the legendary diarist Anais Nin when her play, "Anais Nin—the Paris Years," was produced in New York and Los Angeles, with a subsequent tour on the West Coast. She also directed the West Coast premiere of A.R. Gurney's "Who Killed Richard Cory?"

Since the publication of her suspense novel entitled *White King and the Doctor*, Lee has made numerous radio and TV appearances discussing the book's relevance to the outcome of the War on Terror, and has spoken often at book signings and private readings in New York and Los Angeles.

In addition, during the development of her entertainment industry career, Lee became a successful entrepreneur, a pioneer in Internet commerce, and today owns an international Internet business, which operates throughout the United States. She currently resides in Montana.